Praise for Stephen Leather

The Double Tap

'A damn good thriller writer'

Campbell Armstrong

'Masterful plotting . . . rapid-fire prose'

Sunday Express

'One of the most breathlessly exciting thrillers around . . . puts [Leather] in the frame to take over Jack Higgins's mantle'

The Evening Telegraph, Peterborough

'A fine tale, brilliantly told – excitement which is brilliantly orchestrated'

The Oxford Times

The Birthday Girl

'Action and scalpel-sharp suspense'

Daily Telegraph

'Terrifying, fast-moving and exciting thriller'

Independent, Ireland

'A whirlwind of action, suspense and vivid excitement'

Irish Times

About the author

A journalist for more than ten years, working for a number of newspapers including *The Times*, the *Daily Mail*, the *Glasgow Herald* and the *South China Morning Post* in Hong Kong, Stephen Leather joined the front rank of British thriller writers with his bestselling novel *The Chinaman*. His other highly acclaimed bestsellers include *The Vets*, *The Long Shot*, *The Birthday Girl* and *The Double Tap*. The author lives in Dublin.

Also by Stephen Leather and published by Coronet

The Solitary Man

Stephen Leather

CORONET BOOKS
Hodder and Stoughton

A CIP catalogue record for this title
is available from the British Library.

ISBN 0 340 62837 5

Typeset by Hewer Text Composition Services, Edinburgh
Printed and bound in Great Britain by
Mackays of Chatham PLC

Hodder and Stoughton
A division of Hodder Headline PLC
338 Euston Road
London NW1 3BH

For Toy

THE PRISONER LAY IN the damp grass and watched the building. It was in complete darkness. To his left was a line of small planes, standing like soldiers on parade, their noses pointing towards the distant runway. Two of the planes were four-seater Cessnas and he memorised their numbers. A police car sped down the road that ran parallel to the airfield, its siren on and lights flashing. The prisoner flattened himself into the grass, spread-eagled like a skydiver. He closed his eyes and breathed in the fragrance of the wet grass. Dew had coated his beard and he wiped his face with his sleeve. The siren sounded closer and closer and then began to recede. The prisoner lifted his head. It wouldn't be long before they searched the airfield.

He got to his feet and ran towards the single-storey building. There was a main entrance and a fire exit, and a window that overlooked the parked planes. Two locks secured the main door: a Yale and a deadbolt. The Yale he could pick but he'd need a drill for the deadbolt. He scuttled around the side of the building and checked the emergency exit. There was no lock to pick, but the wooden door didn't look too strong. A couple of hard kicks would probably do it. The moon emerged from behind a cloud,

1

making the thick yellow stripes that ran down both sides of his blue denim uniform glow.

A truck rattled down the road. The prisoner took a step back from the door, then waited until the truck was close to the entrance to the airfield. When the truck's engine noise was at its loudest, he kicked the door hard, putting all of his weight behind the blow. The wood splintered, and it gave way on the second kick. He pushed the door open and ducked inside. The keys were in a cabinet mounted on the far wall of the office.

He dashed over to the planes. The fuel tanks of the first Cessna he tried were almost empty. He said a silent prayer and went over to the second four-seater, a blue and white Cessna 172. He fumbled for the keys, then unlocked the door on the pilot's side and switched on the electronics. Both tanks were half-full. The prisoner smiled to himself. More than enough to get him well away from the island. He untied the chains that kept the plane tethered to the metal rings embedded in the concrete parking area.

In the distance a dog barked. The prisoner stopped dead and listened intently. There was another bark, closer to the airfield. A big dog, a German Shepherd maybe, the sort of dog that the police would use. He walked quickly to the front of the plane and climbed into the pilot's seat. He let his hands play over the control wheel for a few seconds. There was so much to remember. He closed his eyes and took several deep breaths. Carburettor heat in, throttle in a quarter of an inch, just enough to get the engine turning over. He turned the key. The engine burst into life. He pushed the throttle further in and the engine roared.

The noise was deafening. He hadn't realised how loud it would be. It was the first time the prisoner had ever been in a small plane. He shook his head. He was wasting time, and the dogs were getting closer. He put his feet on the rudder pedals and released the handbrake. The plane lurched forward.

He wrenched the control wheel to the right but the plane kept going straight ahead. Only then did he remember what Ronnie had told him: on the ground, you steered with your feet. The control wheel was only effective in the air. The prisoner took a hand off the wheel and wiped his forehead. He had to stay calm; he had to remember everything that Ronnie had taught him.

He pushed his right foot forward and immediately the plane veered to the right. He overcompensated and tried to use the control wheel to get the plane back on course. 'Rudder,' he muttered to himself.

He jiggled the pedals and manoeuvred the plane to the end of the runway. The windsock down the runway was blowing towards him, so he'd be flying straight into the wind. He pushed the top of both pedals forward to operate the brakes, and held the plane steady. The gyroscopic compass was about twenty degrees adrift, according to the magnetic compass, so he reset it. A heading of 340 Ronnie had said. North-north-west. He pushed in the throttle as far as it would go and let his feet slide off the pedals. The plane rolled forward, accelerating quickly. He used the pedals to keep the nose heading down the middle of the runway, resisting the urge to turn the control wheel.

His eyes flicked from the windscreen to the airspeed indicator. Thirty, thirty-five, forty. The runway slid by, faster and faster until it was a grey blur. He waited until the airspeed hit sixty-five and then pulled back on the control wheel. The plane leaped into the air. His stomach lurched and he eased back on the wheel, levelling the plane off. A gust of wind made the plane veer to the left and he pulled back on the wheel again and started to climb.

Below, houses and gardens flashed by, then a road. He began to laugh. He was doing it. He was actually doing it. He was flying.

He looked at the altimeter. Five hundred feet and climbing. Wisps of cloud hit the windscreen and then were gone. Ahead of him were grey clouds, but he could see large areas of clear sky between them.

The control wheel kicked in his hands as he hit an air pocket and he gripped it tightly. He scanned the instruments. Everything seemed to be okay. He looked down at his feet and realised he'd left the fuel selector switch in the 'off' position. He reached down and turned it to 'both', freeing up the fuel in both tanks. That had been a stupid mistake. Running out of fuel wouldn't have been smart.

He took the plane up to a thousand feet and levelled it off, pulling back on the throttle as Ronnie had told him. He looked out of the window to his right. There was a beach below, and then he was flying over the Solent, towards the town of Lymington. The muscles in his neck were locked tight with the tension and he rolled his neck. Taking off was the easy part, Ronnie had warned. Getting the plane back on the ground would be a lot harder.

He flew through a patch of cloud and for a moment he began to panic as everything went white, then just as quickly he was back in clear sky. Ahead of him were more clouds. They were grey and forbidding, and the prisoner was suddenly scared. He pushed the control wheel forward and took the plane down a few hundred feet but all he could see ahead of him were the slate-grey clouds. Far off to his right was a flash of lightning. The clouds seemed to rush towards him and he turned the control wheel to the left, figuring he'd try to fly around the storm, but he was too late.

Before he could react, he was inside the storm, the plane buffeted by the turbulent air. He could see nothing but impenetrable cloud. It was totally white, as if he were surrounded by a thick, cloying mist. There was no way of telling whether his wings were level or not, no sense of which was up and which was down.

The engine began to roar and he pulled back on the throttle. It didn't make any difference. He scanned the instrument panel and saw that his airspeed was rising rapidly. He was diving. Diving towards the sea. He yanked the control wheel back and his stomach went into freefall. His compass was whirling around but nothing he did stopped the spin.

He began to panic. He'd been crazy even to think that he could fly. Crazy. The engine was screaming now, screaming like a tortured animal, and the plane was shaking and juddering like a car being driven over rough ground.

He yelled as the plane dropped out of the clouds and he saw that he was only fifty feet above the waves. His left wing had dipped so far down that he was almost inverted. He wrenched the control wheel to the right and kicked his right rudder pedal, his cries merging with the roar of the engine.

WRECKAGE FROM THE SMALL plane was found floating in the Solent two days later. After a week police divers discovered the bulk of the plane scattered over the sea bed. There was blood on the windshield where the prisoner's head had slammed into the Plexiglas. Of the body there was no sign, but one of the doors had sprung open on impact and the tides in the area were strong, and the Hampshire police knew that it wasn't true that the sea always gave up its dead. The file on prisoner E563228 was closed and his belongings sent to his ex-wife, who was listed on his files as his next of kin.

THE FARMER KNELT DOWN, took a handful of reddish soil, and held it up to his lips. He sniffed, inhaling its fragrance like a wine connoisseur sampling the bouquet of an expensive claret. He took a mouthful and chewed slowly, then he nodded, satisfied. He had worked the land for more than three decades, and could taste the quality of the soil, could tell from its sweetness whether it was rich enough in alkaline limestone to produce a good crop of opium poppies.

It was important to choose the right land to grow the poppies, because if the crop was bad, the farmer would be blamed, and with blame came punishment. So the farmer chewed carefully, mixing the soil with his saliva and allowing it to roll around his mouth. It was good. It was very good. He nodded.

'Yes?' said the man on the white horse.

'Yes,' said the farmer. He stood up and surveyed the hillside. 'This will be a good place.'

The man on the horse wore a shirt of green and brown camouflage material, with matching pants. Black boots that stopped just below his knees were thrust deep into the stirrups and he had a riding crop tucked under his left arm. The horse stood up straight, its ears pricked as it too looked at the hillside. They were more than three thousand feet above sea level, in a mountain hollow which would protect the crop against high winds, but high enough that the plants would be nurtured by the night fogs. The ground sloped away gently, providing good drainage,

7

but not so steeply as to make planting and harvesting difficult.

'How long will it take to clear the land?' asked the man on the horse. He watched the farmer through impenetrable sunglasses.

The farmer ran a hand through his hair. If he over-estimated, Zhou Yuanyi would think he was being slothful. If he under-estimated, he might not be able to finish the work in time. He thought it would take eight days, if all the men and women in the village helped. 'Nine days to cut,' he said.

Zhou Yuanyi nodded. 'I think eight,' he said.

The farmer shrugged. 'Maybe eight,' he agreed.

'Start tomorrow.'

The trees and bushes would have to be slashed down with machetes. It would be hard work, back breaking, and they'd have to toil from first light until dark, but the farmer knew he would be well rewarded. Zhou Yuanyi was a hard taskmaster, brutal at times, but he paid well for the opium the farmer grew. He paid well, and he offered protection: protection from the other opium kings in the Golden Triangle, and protection from the Burmese troops who wanted to smash the poppy-growers of the region.

Once the area had been cleared, the cut vegetation would be left to dry on the ground for four weeks, then it would be burned, the ashes providing essential calcium, potassium and phosphate, a natural fertiliser. The land would be ruined, of course, good for only three years, maybe four, but by then the farmer would have cleared new fields and be ready to move on.

'How many rais?' asked Zhou Yuanyi. A rai was just over a third of an acre.

'Twenty. Maybe twenty-one.'

Zhou Yuanyi sniffed. He cleared his throat and spat at the ground. 'Not enough,' he said. 'Find me another field as well. Soon.'

THE IRISHMAN SHADED HIS eyes with the flat of his hand and peered down the crowded street. Both sides were lined with stalls selling dried fish, counterfeit cassette tapes and cheap clothes. The smell of spices, fried food and sewage was overpowering. 'Bloody hell, Park, how much further?' he asked.

His Thai companion flashed a broad smile. 'There,' he nodded. 'The big building.'

The Irishman squinted at a four-storey concrete block with iron bars over its windows. There were several signs affixed to the side of the building, all of them in Thai, but he recognised a red and white Coca-Cola symbol and a sign advertising Kodak film.

He shuddered. He didn't like being among crowds, and the street was packed with sweating bodies: old women huddled over trays of cigarettes; men sleeping on sunloungers while their wives stood guard over their stalls; bare-chested and shoeless children running between the shoppers, giggling and pointing at the sweating foreigner. A three-wheeled tuk-tuk sped down the narrow street, narrowly missing a teenage boy, its two-stroke engine belching out black fumes.

'Come on,' said Park. 'We said three o'clock.'

The Irishman looked at his watch. 'Shit, if we're late

we're late,' he said. 'This is Thailand, right? No one's ever on time here.' Rivulets of sweat trickled down his back and his shirt was practically glued to his skin. According to Park, it would get even hotter in the weeks to come, but by then the Irishman would be back in Dublin, drinking Guinness and chatting up the local talent. The Thai girls were pretty enough with their soft brown skin and glossy black hair, but the Irishman preferred blue-eyed blondes.

Park walked down the street with an easy, relaxed stride, covering the maximum amount of distance with the minimum of effort. He scratched his right cheek as he walked. The skin there was rough and ridged with scar tissue. Park had told the Irishman that he used to be a kickboxer, but this wasn't the sort of scarring that a man would get from fighting with fists or feet. The Irishman hurried after Park, sweat pouring down his face.

They were followed by two Thai men, friends of Park with virtually unpronounceable names who'd met them at Chiang Mai airport. They smiled a lot but the Irishman didn't trust them. But then he didn't trust anybody in Thailand, not since he'd given money to a beggar with no arms as he'd left his hotel in Bangkok. The beggar had been sitting cross-legged at the bottom of a footbridge over one of the city's perpetually congested roads. He had been in his early twenties, dirty and dishevelled and holding a polystyrene cup in his teeth, the empty sleeves of his T-shirt dangling at his sides. The Irishman had dropped two ten-baht coins into the cup and Park had roared with laughter. It was only then that the Irishman had noticed the bulges and realised that the beggar had his arms folded behind his back. He had reached towards the cup to take back his money, but Park had restrained him, laughing and explaining that the beggar was simply like everyone else in the city, trying to make a living. Since then, he had taken nothing at face value.

He stepped aside to allow three saffron-robed monks to walk by. The monk bringing up the rear was a young boy who smiled up at the Irishman. It was a guileless smile and the boy's eyes were bright and friendly. The Irishman grinned back. It seemed as though everyone he met in Thailand smiled, no matter what their circumstances.

Park took them around the side of the building to a loading ramp. The four men walked up the ramp to a steel shutter which Park banged on with the flat of his hand, three short raps followed by two more in quick succession. A door set into the shutter opened a couple of inches and someone inside muttered a few words in Thai. Park replied and the door opened wide. He motioned for the Irishman to go in first.

It was dark inside and the Irishman blinked as his eyes became accustomed to the gloom. The warehouse was hot and airless. The area around the door was bare except for a small steel table and two wooden stools, but the rest of the building was packed with wooden crates and cardboard boxes which reached almost to the ceiling. A line of bare lightbulbs provided the only illumination in the warehouse, but there were so many crates and boxes that much of the interior was in shadow, adding to the Irishman's feeling of claustrophobia. He wiped his damp forehead with his sleeve.

Park smiled sympathetically. 'We check, then we go,' he said.

The Irishman nodded. 'Let's get on with it, then.'

The man who'd opened the door was short and squat

with a tattoo of a tiger on his left forearm and a handgun stuck into the belt of his pants. He had a frog-like face with bulging eyes, and around his neck was a thick gold chain from which dangled a small circular piece of jade. He grinned at Park and nodded towards the far end of the warehouse. Three more Thais in T-shirts and jeans with guns in their belts materialised from the shadows. The Irishman looked at Park, and the Thai gave him a reassuring smile. Together they walked down an aisle between the towering boxes, following the man with the tiger tattoo. They turned to the left down another aisle where a large space had been cleared. A cardboard box had been opened and half a dozen Panasonic video recorders taken out. The man with the tattoo spoke to Park in rapid Thai.

'He wants you to choose one,' Park explained.

The Irishman shrugged carelessly. 'You choose,' he said.

Park squatted down and tapped one of the machines with his finger. The man with the tiger tattoo picked up a screwdriver and quickly removed a panel from the bottom of the video recorder. He pulled out three polythene-covered packages containing white powder and handed one to the Irishman.

The Irishman walked over to a stack of boxes. He indicated the cardboard box at the bottom of the stack. 'That one,' he said.

The man with the tiger tattoo began to talk quickly but Park silenced him with a wave of his hand. Park said something in Thai but the man continued to protest. 'He says it's too much work,' Park translated. 'He says they're all the same.'

The Irishman's eyes hardened. 'Tell him I want to see one from that box.'

Park turned to the man with the tattoo and spoke to him again. There was something pleading about Park's voice, as if he didn't want to cause offence. Eventually the man with the tattoo shrugged and smiled at the Irishman. He waved his two colleagues over and they helped him take down the upper boxes until they had uncovered the one on the bottom. They dragged it into the centre of the space. The man with the tattoo handed a crowbar to the Irishman and pointed at the box.

'He wants you to—'

'I know what he wants,' said the Irishman, weighing the crowbar in his hand. The metal was warm and his palms were damp with sweat. He stared at the man with the tattoo as if daring him to argue, but the Thai just smiled good-naturedly as if his earlier protests had never occurred. The Irishman inserted the end of the crowbar into the top of the box and pushed down. There was a crashing sound from the far end of the warehouse followed by shouts. He looked across at Park.

The man with the tiger tattoo pulled his gun from his belt and ran towards the entrance to the warehouse. His two companions followed. Park yelled at his own two men to go with them.

'What's happening?' shouted the Irishman.

'Maybe nothing,' said Park.

'Maybe nothing, my arse,' the Irishman shouted. 'This is a fucking set-up.' He jumped as a gun went off, the sound deafening in the confines of the building. There were more shots, louder than the first. The Irishman glared at Park. 'Maybe nothing?' he yelled.

Park looked left and right, then grabbed the Irishman by the arm. 'This way,' he said, pulling him down the aisle. They ran between the stacks of boxes.

'Is it the cops?' asked the Irishman, gasping for breath.

'Maybe,' said Park. 'I don't know.'

A bullet thwacked into a cardboard box above the Irishman's head and he ducked down. 'The cops wouldn't just shoot, would they?' he asked.

'This is Thailand,' said Park. 'The police can do anything they want.' He kicked an emergency door and it crashed open. Sunlight streamed in, so bright that the Irishman flinched. Park seized him by the belt of his jeans and pulled him across the threshold, then stopped dead.

It took the Irishman a second or two to realise that the once noisy street was now totally silent. He blinked and shielded his eyes from the blinding sun. The stall-owners had gone, and so had the crowds. Khaki Land-Rovers had been arranged haphazardly around the building and red and white barriers had been erected across the alley. Behind the vehicles and the barriers crouched men with rifles, in dark brown uniforms and sunglasses. The Irishman whirled around but immediately knew that there was no escape. They were surrounded. Three rugged Thais with assault rifles stood at the emergency exit, their fingers on the triggers of their weapons.

A megaphone-amplified Thai voice echoed off the walls of the alley.

'Drop the crowbar,' said Park calmly. 'Drop the crowbar and put your hands above your head. Very slowly.'

The Irishman did as he was told.

THE SOLITARY MAN

THE PANELS PROTECTING THE CD player swished open as the young man brought his hand close to the controls. He slotted in the CD and pressed the select button until he got the track he wanted. A few seconds later the mournful tones of Leonard Cohen filled the apartment: 'Hey, That's No Way To Say Goodbye'. The smoked glass panels whispered shut again. He stood with his eyes closed and let the music flow over him, swaying backwards and forwards like a sailor trying to maintain his equilibrium on a gently rocking boat, breathing softly through his nose.

He didn't open his eyes until the track had finished, and then he went over to a low coffee table and picked up the remote control unit. He aimed it at the stereo as if it were a loaded gun and selected the same track again.

The sliding glass door leading to the balcony was open and the night breeze blew in, chilled by the East River. The young man was wearing only a white T-shirt and blue jeans but he showed no sign of noticing the cold. He stood looking over the water, its glistening black surface speckled by moonlight. He stretched his arms out in front of himself and breathed deeply, like a high diver preparing to leave his board. He closed his eyes, then after a few seconds opened them again.

'Damn you, Charlie,' he whispered. 'Get the hell out of my mind.'

He went back into the lounge and grabbed the telephone off the sideboard. He tapped out her number and paced up and down in front of the stereo as he waited for her to answer. Her machine kicked in. The young man didn't wait for the beeps. He cut the connection. She was there, he was sure she was there. It was three o'clock in the morning, where else would she be? He pressed the redial button again and got the engaged tone. For a second his heart leaped as he thought that maybe she was calling him, but then he realised that it was probably her answering machine resetting itself.

The stereo went quiet but before the CD player could move on to the next track, he pressed the replay button. There was only one song on the album that he wanted to hear. He hit the phone's redial button again. 'Hi, this is Charlotte . . .' He clicked the phone off. The answer machine was by her bed and he knew that Charlie was a light sleeper. How dare she ignore him like this? It wasn't fair, he thought angrily. She had no right to do this to him.

He took the phone out on to the balcony. He wondered if there was somebody with her, somebody else lying under the thick feather-filled duvet. He stabbed savagely at the redial button. 'Hi, this is Charlotte . . .'

He glared at the phone and for a moment considered throwing it away. He pictured it arcing over the river, twisting in the night air like the bone thrown by the ape in *2001* just before it turned into the spaceship. He smiled at the image. It was a great movie, he thought. Maybe he'd put Charlotte in a screenplay, have her be the victim of a knife-wielding maniac, stalked and terrified and eventually butchered. That was the great thing about being a writer: nothing was wasted. Every experience, every emotion, it could all be put to use. Even being dumped.

His word processor sat on a desk by the kitchen door, stuck in the corner so that he wouldn't be distracted by the view from his window. He switched it on, but immediately realised that he wouldn't be able to write. He'd barely written anything since Charlie had told him that she needed time alone. Space, she said. She needed space. That had been two weeks ago, and now he was behind on two assignments and his tutor was breathing down his neck wanting to see his work in progress. It was all Charlie's fault, he thought. She'd given him writer's block.

He opened the bottom drawer of his desk and took out a small leather bag that had once contained a shoeshine kit. He weighed the bag in his hand, then tapped it against his cheek. The leather was soft and supple and he could still smell shoe polish. He thought about ringing her one last time, but he couldn't face listening to her perky message again. He dropped down on to the sofa, unzipped the bag and laid out the contents on the coffee table, then took a small polythene bag of white powder from the back pocket of his jeans. He'd bought the drug the previous day from his regular supplier, a small, weasely thirty-something man who lived on 77th Street and who delivered as promptly as a pizza company, promising a twenty per cent discount if he didn't arrive within an hour.

The young man hummed along with the CD as he prepared the heroin. It was one of the reasons that Charlie had said she wanted some time on her own. She'd said that he was crazy using the stuff and that only addicts injected. He'd told her that it was safe, that he never, ever shared his needles or syringes, and that it was more cost-effective to inject. And when he'd said that she didn't appear to have any reservations about smoking pot or sniffing cocaine she'd lost

17

her temper and accused him of being obtuse. He smiled to himself as he drew the heroin up into the syringe. Obtuse, he thought. She didn't get it and she thought he was obtuse.

He took the leather belt from around his waist, deftly wound it around his left upper arm and tightened it. He'd only been injecting for two weeks or so but he had no trouble in raising a vein and injecting the contents of the syringe. His supplier had shown him how to do it, had even thrown in the first few hits free of charge. Not that he couldn't afford to buy his own; the drug was cheaper than it had ever been. As he'd told Charlie, it was almost cheaper getting high on heroin than it was getting a buzz from beer. And without the calories. He put the empty syringe down on the coffee table and loosened the belt, then settled back on the sofa, his eyes closed, a lazy smile on his face as he waited for the rush. The telephone began to ring, but to the young man it sounded as if it was a million miles away. He tried to open his eyes but the effort was too much for him; it was as if his eyelids had been sewn shut. Something felt wrong, but he couldn't work out what it was, then the feeling passed and his jaw dropped open and a thin dribble of frothy spittle oozed from between his lips. His breathing grew slower and slower and then stopped altogether.

The telephone continued to ring out, then it too stopped and the only sound in the apartment was the humming of the word processor.

THE YOUNG GIRL KNELT down and pulled a spinach plant out of the ground. She shook the reddish soil from its roots and put it in the large wicker basket with the ones she'd already picked. She hated gathering vegetables from among the poppy plants. It was back-breaking work, made all the harder because she had to take care not to damage any of the poppy plants as she moved across the field. Her father had explained to her how important the vegetables were, how the beans and spinach helped keep the field clear of weeds, and how they added nutrients to the soil, nutrients that would enhance the poppy crop. The better the crop, the more opium the poppies produced, the more money her father would make. The girl stood up and arched her back. Something clicked, like a small twig snapping. She wiped her hands on her black trousers then rubbed the base of her spine with her knuckles.

It would be almost two months yet before the opium plants would be ready. The red and white flowers had yet to appear, though the girl could see already that it was going to be a good crop. The plants were over a foot tall, strong and healthy, and the majority had five stems per plant. Her father had said that was a good sign. In a bad year, there would be only three stems on a plant. Four was good, five was reason for celebration. She picked up the basket and carried it a few steps forward. Her mother wanted a full basket of spinach, enough to feed the men in the compound. The men paid well for fresh vegetables. They were soldiers, not farmers, and didn't like getting their hands dirty. She bent down and pulled up another plant.

She jumped as she heard a loud snort from behind her. She dropped the plant in surprise and whirled around. A large white horse stood at the edge of the field, its rider wearing a camouflage uniform and dark sunglasses watching her. He had a peaked cap on his head, also of camouflage material, and strapped to his back was a rifle. The man kicked the horse with his heels and the animal moved forward.

The girl opened her mouth to tell the man to be careful, that his horse was trampling the poppies, but something about his demeanour warned her that he would not take kindly to being told what to do. She put her hand over her mouth. The horse snorted again. It was a huge animal, the top of the girl's head barely reaching its shoulder. She had to bend her neck back to look up at the man's face. He was middle aged, smooth shaven with a round face that might have been pleasant if it weren't for the sunglasses. They were so black that she couldn't see his eyes.

The man smiled for the first time showing white, even teeth. '*Ga-la had-you dumnya,*' he said.

The girl was suddenly embarrassed at the unexpected greeting and she averted her eyes.

'*Chum ya-ah you con-tee?*' he asked.

The girl blushed furiously. Why did he want to know her name?

'Can't speak?' said the man, amused by her silence.

'No, sir. I mean, yes, sir.'

'How old are you, child?'

'Fourteen, sir.'

She glanced up, saw that he was still smiling at her, and bowed her head again and clasped her hands. The man walked the horse slowly around her. She could smell its warm, sweet breath and she could hear the clink of its bridle and the thud of its hoofs on the soft earth, but she steadfastly refused to look up.

'What is your name, child?'

'Amiyo, sir.'

'Do you know who I am?'

'No, sir.'

'Are you sure? Have you never heard of Zhou Yuanyi?' She caught her breath. Everyone knew of Zhou. Zhou the warlord. Zhou the opium king. 'Well?'

'Yes, sir.'

'Look at me, child.' The girl looked up. The horse snorted as she did and she flinched. 'There's no need to be afraid,' Zhou said. He looked enormous, sitting astride the animal. His riding boots shone, and there wasn't a fleck of dirt on his uniform. In his right hand was a leather crop. The horse stamped its feet impatiently. Amiyo looked up at the man's face. She could see her reflection in the sunglasses. 'Have you been up to the compound?' he asked.

She nodded. Her mother took her with her when she delivered vegetables to the kitchens there. It was where the soldiers were based, and where the opium was processed.

'I want you to come along to see me tonight.'

'But, sir, my father—'

'Your father won't mind,' he interrupted. 'Tell him you've spoken to me.'

'Sir, I . . .'

Zhou slammed his riding crop against the horse's neck. The horse jerked away but Zhou kept a tight grip on the reins and swiftly brought it under control. 'Do not argue, child.'

Amiyo lowered her eyes and said nothing.

Zhou ran the tip of his crop along her left arm, down to her elbow. 'That's better,' he soothed. 'Tell your mother you are to wear something pretty.' He kicked the horse and it broke into a trot.

Amiyo didn't look up until the sound of the horse's hoofs had faded away. There were tears in her eyes.

THE TWO MEN SAT together in the corner of the bar, their heads so close that they were almost touching, as if one was a priest hearing the other's confession. The older and more priestly of the two had thick greying hair and he peered over the top of a pair of hornrimmed spectacles as he listened.

The confessor, at fifty-two years old a full decade younger than his companion, had florid cheeks as if he'd spent much of his life outdoors and had the stocky build of a labourer. His hair was grey but thinning and from time to time he ran a veined hand over the top of his head as if to reassure himself that his comb-over was still in place. 'He's just a boy, Mr McCormack,' he said, his voice a low growl. 'We can't let him rot in that hellhole.'

Thomas McCormack nodded. 'I know, Paddy.'

'He did as he was told. He kept his mouth shut, he told them nothing.'

'I know, Paddy, and we respect that.' McCormack lifted his glass to his mouth and sipped his whiskey.

'My own sister's boy, Mr McCormack. Can you imagine what she's been like these past few weeks? Fifty years. Fifty years without parole. Jesus, even the British don't hand out sentences like that.'

McCormack put his glass down on the small circular wooden table. 'Paddy, it'll be taken care of.'

'When?' Paddy Dunne glared at McCormack with cold, hard eyes as if daring him to look away.

McCormack met the man's stare. For several seconds

their eyes remained locked, a mental trial of strength that neither man was prepared to lose. McCormack reached across and laid his hand on Dunne's sleeve. 'You've got to trust me. It's going to take time.'

For a moment it looked as if Dunne was going to argue but then he slowly nodded. 'Okay, Mr McCormack. I'm sorry. Okay.' He pulled his arm away from the older man's touch and cupped his large nail-bitten hands around his pint of Guinness. 'Ray's not taking it well, you know? It's a hellhole, a cockroach-infested, AIDS-ridden hellhole. I'm not sure how long he can stand it.'

'Soon,' said McCormack. 'You have my word.'

Dunne drank his Guinness, then wiped his upper lip with his jacket sleeve. 'Is there anything I can do?'

McCormack shook his head. 'Best you leave it with me, Paddy.' Dunne drank again, draining his glass. McCormack caught a young barman's eye and nodded at the two empty glasses.

'Fifty years,' muttered Dunne. 'Fifty bloody years. That's almost as long as I've lived. What sort of people are they, Mr McCormack?'

McCormack shrugged.

The barman came over, placed a glass of foaming Guinness and a double measure of whiskey on the table. 'Compliments of Mr Delaney,' he said, picking up their empty glasses. McCormack raised his glass in salute to a small, neat man in a tweed suit who was standing at the end of the bar. Jimmy Delaney was the owner of the establishment and an old friend of McCormack's. Delaney lifted his own glass and nodded at McCormack but made no move to come over, realising that the two men didn't want to be disturbed.

Dunne took a long pull at his Guinness. 'What makes it worse is that we can't even go and visit him.'

'It has to be that way, Paddy. You can see that, surely.'

'Aye, but that doesn't make it any easier.' Dunne slammed his glass down on the table. Several heads turned to look at the source of the noise, but they quickly looked away. Thomas McCormack was well known around Dublin and there weren't many people prepared to openly stare at a member of the IRA Army Executive.

'Easy, Paddy. He'll be back here before you know it.'

Dunne slumped down in his chair. 'I'm sorry, Mr McCormack. I'm sorry. But you don't know what it's been like. It's all that Brit bastard's fault.'

'That's going to be taken care of, too, Paddy.'

'It's all his fault and yet he's still swanning around the city in his flash cars as if he owns the place. Something should be done about him.'

'Something will be done, Paddy, but we have to get Ray out first.' McCormack took off his spectacles and polished them with a large, red handkerchief. 'Tell your sister not to worry. We're sending money in so that he can buy himself a few luxuries. But tell her one thing more, Paddy.' McCormack waited until Dunne looked up before continuing. 'She's starting to talk, Paddy, and we can't have that. It's local at the moment and I can keep a lid on it, so far. But if the Press gets to hear of it, if anyone makes the connection, the Organisation will have to embark on a damage limitation exercise. And that could get messy, Paddy. Very messy. Best we don't let it get to that stage.' McCormack looked at Dunne steadily.

He looked a lot less like a man of the cloth without his hornrimmed spectacles.

'Aye, Mr McCormack. I'll talk to her,' said Dunne.

McCormack held his look for several seconds, then replaced his glasses. The hardness slipped away from his eyes and he smiled avuncularly. 'And don't worry about the Brit. You'll have your revenge, Paddy. We all will. But first things first.'

CABBAGES AND KINGS. THE phrase rattled around in Tim Carver's head as he watched the photographers click away at the Thai farmer and his field of poppies. It came from a poem or something, something he'd studied at school, but for the life of him he couldn't remember anything else, just the one phrase. One of the photographers, a balding Australian with a huge beer gut, growled at the female interpreter to tell the farmer to hold out his hands and to smile. The interpreter translated and the farmer did as he was asked, standing as if crucified among the flowers, grinning like a demented scarecrow. The cameras clicked like crickets on a hot night.

A lanky young man with a notebook appeared at Carver's shoulder. 'What do you think, Tim? Think this'll make a difference?' The accent was British, the tone sarcastic. His name was Richard Kay, a reporter from London, and he'd sat next to Carver on the helicopter that had taken them from Chiang Rai.

Carver smiled wearily. 'Cabbages and kings,' he said.

'What?'

'Just thinking out loud, Richard. Of course it'll make a difference. These people just want to make a living, they don't care what happens to the poppies. They don't even know that the opium harvested here ends up on the streets of American cities. All they want to do is to earn enough to feed their families.'

Another journalist walked up and stood listening to them. 'Lester Middlehurst, *New York Times*,' he said, holding up a small tape recorder. 'How many acres are we talking about here, Tim?'

'Just over fifty.'

'And the DEA is buying the land, is that how it works?'

'Not exactly, no. For a start, this is a United Nations programme, not a DEA initiative. And secondly, the UN is paying the farmer not to grow poppies, and we teach him how to grow alternative crops.'

'Cabbages, right?'

Carver nodded. 'Cabbages. And potatoes.'

'But effectively you're buying the poppies, aren't you?' Middlehurst asked.

Carver looked across at a battered army truck where two Thai soldiers were being fitted with cumbersome flamethrowers. Carver's sandy fringe fell over his eyes and he flicked it away with a jerk of his neck. 'I'm with the DEA guys; you should be talking to the UN people,' he said. 'They're the ones persuading them to change crops. It's just a form of farming subsidy, but one that keeps drugs from getting to the United States.'

'Yeah, but at the end of the day, the United States is buying opium, isn't it? They're putting up the bulk of the cash for this programme, right?'

Carver held up his hands in surrender. 'Come on, Lester, stop putting words into my mouth. And remember, everything you get from me is totally off the record. If you want a quote, talk to Janis over there.' He nodded at the pretty blonde Press officer from the United Nations office in Bangkok who was fielding questions from a trio of Australian journalists.

Kay slapped a mosquito on his neck and examined the splattered remains of the insect on his palm. 'Okay, Tim, but off the record, we all know this is a complete and utter waste of time, don't we?'

Middlehurst put his tape recorder close to Carver's face to better record his answer to the British journalist's question.

The flamethrowers burst into life and the two soldiers tested them gingerly. The photographers turned their attention away from the Thai farmer and concentrated on the soldiers and their equipment.

'I'm not sure what you mean,' said Carver.

'For a start, most of the heroin comes from over the border, from the Golden Triangle,' Kay pressed. 'And how much heroin does fifty acres produce? A few kilos?'

'More.'

'Yeah? I was told it takes a third of an acre to produce a kilo of raw opium. Does that sound right to you?'

'Ballpark, I guess.'

'So fifty acres is a drop in the ocean.'

Carver grinned ruefully. 'You know damn well that I'm not going to say that. On the record or off.'

Kay grinned back. 'Wouldn't expect you to, Tim.' He nodded towards the field and its mass of red and white poppies. 'The farmer says he's been growing poppies here

27

for three years. But the land is only good for four years, total. After that all the nutrients have been sucked out of the soil and it's useless.'

Carver raised an eyebrow, impressed by the British journalist's knowledge. 'Fertiliser,' he said.

Kay's grin widened. 'Is that another way of saying bullshit, Tim? Come on, you know I'm right. These farmers don't know the first thing about land management. They slash and burn, grow what they can and then move on. That's why this country's jungle is disappearing at such an alarming rate. This guy was probably going to give up this land next year anyway. He can't believe his luck.'

'We're making a start, Richard. We're giving them a chance to grow other cash crops. Tea, coffee, cabbages, potatoes. We're showing them how to use the land in other ways, to stop them being reliant on opium.'

The British journalist nodded sympathetically. 'I'm sure you are, but that's not what's going on here. This is a public relations exercise, a photo opportunity. And that's all it is.'

Carver nodded over at the pack of photographers who were clicking away at the soldiers and their flamethrowers. 'Got you guys out here, didn't it?'

'Sure, we'll play the game, the Press always does. They'll use the picture and they'll use a few sentences from me as a caption, but this is all shit, Tim. The bulk of the stuff is coming from across the border, and the heroin kingpins there aren't going to stop growing poppies just because you throw a few hundred dollars at them. The market's worth billions and they're not going to give it up to grow cabbages.'

The two soldiers began to walk across the poppy field, away from the photographers. Janis shouted for the journalists to keep back. Middlehurst's recorder clicked off as it came to the end of his tape. He took it away from Carver's face and went over to join the photographers.

Carver and Kay watched the pack jostle for position to get the best shot. A sheet of fire exploded from the barrel of one of the flamethrowers. The soldier raked the flame across the field and the poppy plants burst into flames. The motor drives went crazy, whirring like angry bees. The second flamethrower burst into life.

'What's the drugs problem like back in Britain?' asked Carver.

'It's getting pretty bad,' said Kay. 'It's like cable TV, fast food, and American humour: eventually we get everything you get.'

Carver nodded. 'Yeah, well, I hope this time it's different,' he said. He took a packet of Marlboro from his shirt pocket and offered one to the journalist. Kay took one and Carver lit it for him.

The two men stood in silence and watched the poppies crackle and burn under the onslaught of the flamethrowers. Kay exhaled deeply, blowing plumes of smoke through his nostrils. ' "The Walrus and the Carpenter," ' he said.

'Huh?' said Carver, confused.

'Cabbages and kings. That's where the phrase comes from. Lewis Carroll, I think. It's time to talk of many things, of something, something, something something, and cabbages and kings. It's a bit of nonsense.'

Carver stared out across the burning field. 'Yeah,' he said. 'You're right. It is.'

THE SMALL HELICOPTER BUZZED overhead, then hovered like a hawk preparing to sweep on its prey. The mourners standing around the grave tried to ignore the intrusion and to concentrate on the elderly priest and his words of comfort for a family stricken with grief. There were two dozen men and women and a scattering of children, all dressed in black, all with their heads bowed. Some distance away, parked on a ribbon of tarmac, was a line of black limousines, their engines running.

One of the mourners, a tall, thin man in a cashmere overcoat, lifted his head and glared at the helicopter. 'Vultures,' John Mallen muttered under his breath. Under normal circumstances Mallen was good looking, handsome even, with a squarish face and blond hair that was greying only slightly over his temples, but there were deep lines etched around his eyes and either side of his mouth, and the whites of his eyes were bloodshot as if it had been some time since he'd had a good night's sleep.

His wife, her blonde hair tucked under a wide-brimmed black hat and her face hidden by a veil, squeezed his arm gently and he grimaced.

'Sorry,' he whispered. She smiled and slipped her hand into his.

Between the parked limousines and the funeral party stood two men, broad shouldered, with impassive faces. They wore dark suits but despite the cold they had no overcoats or gloves. One of the men put his hand up to his ear and lightly fingered an earpiece. He nodded as he listened and looked up at the helicopter. A few seconds later the helicopter banked and flew away, a man with a television camera on his shoulder leaning out of its open doorway, his feet on the skids.

The funeral service came to an end and the mourners began to drift over to the limousines. A pretty young brunette with tear-stained eyes walked hesitantly over to Mallen. She carried a small black handbag which she clutched to her stomach like a field dressing. He saw her coming and put his arm around his wife's shoulders, steering her away from the brunette and towards the limousine parked on the road that wound through the cemetery. The driver already had the door open.

'You should have spoken to her, John,' Mallen's wife said, her voice little more than a whisper.

'Not yet,' said Mallen, putting a hand on her shoulder. 'I can't. Not yet.'

'It wasn't her fault.'

'I know that. I don't blame her.'

The woman nodded slowly. 'Yes, you do, John. You think you don't, but you do.' She stood up on tiptoe, raised her veil and kissed him softly on the cheek, close to his lips. 'She loved him, too, you know.'

'She had a strange way of showing it,' said Mallen bitterly.

'They'd have worked things out, if . . .' She left the sentence unfinished.

'Yes,' said her husband. 'If.'

The two men in dark suits came up behind Mallen, their eyes watchful. One got into the front passenger seat, the other stood slightly behind the couple.

'Aren't you coming?' she asked.

Mallen shook his head. 'Duty calls.'

'Today of all days?'

Mallen shrugged. His wife shook her head sadly and climbed into the back of the limousine. Mallen turned and walked away as the limousine drove off.

Further down the road a short, stocky man in an overcoat a size too small for his massive shoulders stood waiting by another limousine.

'Thanks for coming, Jake,' said Mallen. They shook hands. Both men had firm grips but the handshake was no trial of strength; they knew each other too well to play games.

'He was a good boy. He'll be missed.'

'There's no need to patronise me, Jake. He was an arsehole,' said Mallen, as he slid into the back of the limousine.

Jake Gregory followed him into the car and pulled the door shut. The soundproofed panel separating the passengers from the driver was closed and they were cocooned in silence. The car pulled smoothly away from the kerb. A dark blue saloon with three men in suits followed them.

Mallen looked around. 'How come you don't have babysitters?' he asked. 'I'd have thought the number two man in the Drug Enforcement Administration would be guarded like Fort Knox.'

Gregory shrugged his wrestler's shoulders. 'Low profile. When was the last time you saw me on the cover of *Time* magazine?'

Mallen smiled tightly as he settled back in his seat and unbuttoned his overcoat. 'So, I'm listening.'

'The heroin that killed Mark was part of a batch that

came from an area of the Golden Triangle close to the border between Burma and Thailand under the control of a Chinese warlord called Zhou Yuanyi. He's relatively new, up and coming you might say. He's moved into the areas that Khun Sa used to control, and he's trying to grab a bigger share of the market. He's brought in a team of chemists from Russia and has started purifying his own opium before shipping it across the border into Thailand. As a result there's been something of a price war, both out in the Far East and here at home. We've been aware of this for some time; on the streets heroin is now almost sixty-six per cent pure compared with six per cent in 1979. But as the quality has improved, the price has dropped, to about a third of its cost in the late seventies. In real terms, heroin is now about one-thirtieth of the cost it used to be, which is why it's starting to become the drug of choice again.'

Mallen folded his arms across his chest and studied Gregory with unblinking eyes.

'Your son isn't the only one to have died,' Gregory continued. 'The stuff's getting so pure now that it's practically lethal. The pusher has to really know what he's doing. If he doesn't tell his customers what the purity is . . .'

'I get the point, Jake,' said Mallen. 'Tell me about Zhou.'

'Zhou was one of the warlords in the Golden Triangle we targeted in Operation Tiger Trap, but so far we've had no notable success,' Gregory continued. 'In fact we lost two Hong Kong Chinese agents just last month.'

'Lost?' Mallen repeated disdainfully. 'Lost in what way, Jake?'

'They were tortured and killed. Impaled on stakes at

the entrance to Zhou's camp as a warning to others. It's a jungle out there. Literally and figuratively.'

Mallen tutted impatiently. 'We spend fifteen billion dollars a year on the war against drugs and the best we can do is to send in two Chinese?' he said.

'The undercover operations are a small part of Operation Tiger Trap. The bulk goes on satellite and plane surveillance, intelligence gathering, Customs inspections, border controls.'

'Maybe it's about time we tried something else.'

'These things take time,' said Gregory. 'We need the co-operation of the Thai and Burmese authorities, and they're not the easiest people to deal with. It's not just the politics involved, either. The big problem is that we have no way of knowing who we can trust and who's on the take. For instance, it's practically impossible for Zhou to be getting his stuff across the border without the assistance of the Thai army, so we know he has contacts there. That means mounting any sort of military operation is next to impossible. Sure, they've raided a few of his camps, closed down a refinery or two, but Zhou has always been long gone. He invariably knows exactly when and where we're going to strike.'

'So ignore the Thais.'

'Difficult,' said Gregory. 'We pretty much do that already as regards intelligence gathering. We share with the Brits and the Australians, and a dozen or so other agencies through the Foreign Anti-Narcotic Community, meetings which take place in Bangkok every month, and the Thais are excluded from that, but we don't have the authority to make arrests. For that we have to go through the Thai police.'

Mallen took a quick look at his slim gold wristwatch. He leaned forward, his eyes suddenly intense. 'I'm not talking about arrests, Jake.' Mallen's voice dropped to a whisper. 'I want him dead. I want the head of the man who killed my son. It doesn't have to be on a plate, I don't have to see the body, I just have to know that the bastard's dead.'

Gregory swallowed. He wiped the palms of his hands on his trousers. 'You know I can't—'

Mallen didn't even give him time to finish the sentence. 'Look, I can't very well ask the CIA, can I? They're trying to be whiter than white after the Guatemala fiasco and they'll just throw Executive Order 11905 in my face. Thou shalt not kill.'

'That applies to my agency, too,' said Gregory. 'We're not in the business of executing—'

'You do as I tell you, Jake,' interrupted Mallen. 'You owe me, remember. You owe me big time.'

Gregory's cheeks reddened as if he'd been slapped. 'I'm just pointing out the jurisdictional—'

Mallen held up a hand to silence him. 'Fuck jurisdiction. We didn't worry about jurisdiction when we wanted Noriega. We just sent twenty-four thousand troops into Panama and brought him out. And Grenada wasn't actually our turf, was it? This monster's poisoning our streets, he's crippling our economy, he's killing our children, for God's sake. He's a cancer, and I want you to operate, Jake. I've made the diagnosis, now I want you to be the surgeon.'

'But you can't . . .'

Mallen snorted angrily. 'I'm the Vice President of the United States. I can do pretty much anything I want. Within reason.'

Gregory wiped his hands again. 'But that's the point, isn't it? What constitutes reasonable?'

'I'm not asking for a discussion about morality, Jake. I don't give a shit about the rights and wrongs of this, I just want the fucker dead. Do I have to spell it out for you? D-E-A-D. Don't make me call in my markers, we go back too far for that.'

Gregory held up his hands in surrender. 'I'm not arguing, I'm not saying no. I'm just pointing out the downside, that's all.'

Mallen sighed impatiently. 'There is no downside. You'll be doing the world a favour.'

The two men rode in silence for a while. A small vein pulsed in Gregory's temple. He massaged the bridge of his nose and closed his eyes.

Mallen's voice became softer and he patted Gregory gently on the knee. 'Look, Jake, I didn't mean to snap at you. You know how rough it's been, the last few days. Keeping the real cause of his death under wraps, dealing with the media. With Angela. Look, don't think of this as taking out the man, think of it as hitting his operation, his headquarters. And if he happens to get caught in the crossfire, well, that'll just be a bonus.'

Gregory's eyes remained closed. He could feel the Vice President's will enveloping him like a cloud, seeping through his pores, into his very soul. It was persistent. Insidious. Gregory could feel sweat beading on his forehead. The hand tightened on his knee.

'I have the President's approval on this, Jake,' Mallen continued. 'Nothing in writing, no medals for those involved, but he's given me a green light. Whatever resources you need, whatever you feel is necessary. He wants this as much as I do. He wants to show the world that we're doing something. A retaliatory strike. A lesson for the others.'

Gregory nodded. He opened his eyes. All resistance had gone. There was no point in protesting any more. 'Financing?' he asked.

'Lose it in your budget. It's big enough.'

'And I have *carte blanche*?'

'You and Frank Sinatra, Jake. Do it your way. Just get it done.' The Vice President took his hand off Gregory's knee. 'I won't forget this, Jake.' He smiled at the DEA executive, a gleaming white smile that had no warmth in it. His eyes sparkled like ice freezing on the surface of a lake.

THE ONE THOUGHT THAT Billy Winter clung to as he rattled around in the boot of the big car was that they'd been wearing ski masks. If they'd felt it necessary to conceal their identities then they probably didn't mean to kill him. Probably. Winter wasn't sure just how much store he could put by his theory, but he clung to it nevertheless. Just then it was all he had.

He'd been sitting in his white bathrobe, drawing on a big cigar and watching two highly paid hookers do their stuff, when they'd come for him. Three men – not particularly big, but then size wasn't important when sawn-off shotguns and semi-automatic pistols were involved – wearing leather bomber jackets, blue jeans and training shoes. And black ski masks. They hadn't said anything, the men. They hadn't needed to.

The two hookers, one blonde, one brunette, hadn't been to Ireland before – Winter had flown them in from London on the recommendation of an old pal – but they knew what men in ski masks meant and they hadn't said a word as Winter had been hustled out of the house. The girls were probably already at the airport. Money for old rope. They'd barely started on their lesbian show – guaranteed to get an erection from the dead, Winter's pal had promised – before the men had burst in.

Winter had asked the men if they'd give him time to get dressed, and one of them had pistol-whipped him, hard enough to stun but not hard enough to knock him out. Winter could feel blood trickling down his cheek as he lay in the car boot, his knees up tight against his chin, his hands tied behind his back. If they were going to kill him, he thought, they'd have done it back at the house. His nearest neighbour lived half a mile away and it was farming country; no one would think twice about a shotgun blast, even late at night.

The car bucked and lurched and Winter's head banged against the floor. They'd been driving for thirty minutes or so but Winter was finding it difficult to keep track of time. Besides, it made no difference where they were taking him, the only thing that mattered was what they planned to do with him.

The car braked and they came to a sudden halt. Winter heard the car doors open and close and then the boot was thrown open and hands dragged him roughly out. A bag was pulled down over his head and he was frogmarched away from the car. He stumbled and his bare feet scraped across rough concrete. They still hadn't said a word, but the bag reassured him; it was another sign that they didn't want to be recognised, which suggested that they were probably going to let him live. Probably.

The bathrobe flapped open but despite the cold night air Winter was sweating. He splashed through a puddle then he heard a metal door rattle. As he stumbled over a step the hands holding his arms gripped even tighter. They forced him to his knees and he felt the barrel of a gun press against the back of his neck. He took a deep breath and fought to stop himself shaking. It wasn't the first time that Billy Winter had been at the wrong end of a loaded gun, but that didn't make the experience any easier to handle.

'Whatever they're paying you, I'll treble it,' he said. There was no reply and Winter wondered if they'd heard him through the bag. 'Whatever they're paying . . .' he began but the gun barrel clipped the side of his head and he realised it was pointless to continue. He heard muffled voices, and footsteps, and then the metal door clanged shut. The gun barrel was taken away and the hood was pulled off his head. A single light shone into his eyes and he squinted. There was a strong acrid smell that he realised was pig manure, and something sweeter. Straw, maybe. He was in a barn, or a shed, somewhere pigs were kept.

Tears pricked his eyes and he blinked them away. He didn't want his captors to think that he was crying; it was the bright light that was making his eyes water. It had been a long, long time since Billy Winter had cried.

'Who are you?' he asked. 'What do you want?'

He could just about make out a figure holding the torch. Blue jeans and white trainers, now flecked with mud. A second figure walked from behind Winter and stood next to the man with the torch. He was holding a sawn-off shotgun, a gloved finger hooked around the trigger. It was a pump-action Remington, Winter realised, five shells. Winter stared at the finger on the trigger.

'If it's money, I can give you all the money you want,' said Winter quietly.

The finger tightened.

'What is it, then? Political? Is this political? I've got friends . . .'

Winter flinched as the finger pulled back the trigger. He screamed with rage and turned his head away. There was no explosion, no hail of shot, just a hammer clicking down on an empty chamber. Winter's bowels turned liquid and he felt urine stream down his leg. He began to gag and he retched but nothing came up, just a bitter taste at the back of his mouth. 'You bastards,' he mumbled.

Gloved hands grabbed his hair and forced him to look straight ahead, into the torch beam. A third figure appeared, a man wearing a long coat. Winter squinted up at the new arrival. He wasn't wearing a ski mask and Winter recognised him.

'Thomas?' he said.

'Hello, Billy,' said Thomas McCormack. His hands were thrust deep into the pockets of his coat and he wore a red woollen scarf wrapped tightly around his neck as if he feared catching a chill.

'What's this about, Thomas?'

'Ray Harrigan,' said McCormack.

'Harrigan? What about him?'

'We want him back.'

Winter cleared his throat and swallowed. 'So why didn't you use the blower? Why the heavies?'

McCormack peered over the top of his spectacles. 'I wanted you to know how serious this was, Billy. I wanted you to be in no doubt what will happen if you don't bring the Harrigan boy home.'

'I thought we were friends, Thomas. I thought we had an understanding.'

McCormack shrugged. 'An understanding, perhaps, but not a friendship, Billy.'

'It's not my fault Harrigan got caught.'

'So whose fault would it be? They were your contacts, you put the meeting together.'

'Maybe someone talked.'

'Not Ray Harrigan,' insisted McCormack. 'The boy went through the trial without saying a word. If anyone talked it was one of your people. That makes it your responsibility.'

Winter nodded slowly. 'Okay. I'll do what I can, Thomas.'

McCormack shook his head. 'That's not good enough, Billy. You bring him back, or next time the shotgun won't be empty.'

As if to emphasise McCormack's words, the man with the shotgun waved it menacingly in front of Winter's face. McCormack turned and walked away. The bag was pulled down over Winter's head and he was dragged to his feet.

Winter felt his confidence return. 'Any chance of me riding in the front this time, lads?' he said, and he laughed dryly. He was still chuckling when something hard slammed against his left temple and everything went red, then black.

THE CANADIAN HELD THE metal spoon over the candle flame and watched the colourless liquid sizzle on the hot metal. He coughed, a dry hacking sound that echoed around the cell. Ray Harrigan watched as the Canadian put the spoon on to the concrete floor and wiped the syringe needle on his sleeve. He dipped the end of the needle into the liquid and drew it up into the barrel of the syringe, holding his breath as it filled. He looked up and saw Harrigan watching him.

'You want some?' the Canadian asked.

Harrigan shook his head.

'Fifty baht and you can have a hit.' The Canadian used a shoelace as a tourniquet around his upper arm to raise a vein.

'No,' said Harrigan.

'Suit yourself,' he said, carefully inserting the needle into the vein. He withdrew blood into the syringe and allowed it to mix with the heroin. Harrigan watched, fascinated, as the Canadian injected the blood and heroin mixture back into the vein, then loosened the tourniquet and slumped back against the wall, a look of rapture on his face. 'You've never taken drugs?' he asked Harrigan.

'No. I can't stand needles.'

The Canadian smiled lazily. A dribble of blood ran down his arm like a tear. 'It's the only way out of this place,' he said, and tapped the side of his forehead. 'They can't imprison your mind, man. They can fuck with your body, but they can't keep my mind in here.'

Harrigan looked at the syringe lying on the floor. 'Do you share your needle?' he asked.

The Canadian's eyes went wide. 'Fuck, no. No one even touches my works. Do you think I'm stupid?'

A large cockroach scuttled past Harrigan's feet. He pulled them back involuntarily. He'd never get used to the size of the insects, or the speed with which they moved. They didn't bite or sting but he couldn't bear being near them. Harrigan closed his eyes and ran his hands through his hair. It was greasy and he could feel that his scalp was covered in small scabs. His mattress was infected with fleas and mites and his whole body itched.

Harrigan fought to contain the panic that kept threatening to overwhelm him. Fifty years. Fifty godforsaken years. He could barely imagine that length of time. Fifty years ago there'd been no colour televisions, no portable telephones, no digital watches. Fifty years ago his parents were still at school. The war was only just over. The Second World War, for God's sake. The panic grew like a living thing, making his heart beat faster and his breathing come in rapid gasps. He took deep breaths of the rancid air, forcing himself to stay calm. It was going to be all right, he kept repeating to himself. They'd get him out. They wouldn't leave him to rot. He'd done as they'd asked, he'd kept his mouth shut, he'd followed orders. He'd done everything the Organisation had asked. So why was it taking them so long?

'Hey, chill, man,' said the Canadian. 'You're breathing like a train.'

Harrigan opened his eyes. 'I'm okay,' he said.

'You're burning up,' said the Canadian.

'Of course I'm burning up. It's almost ninety in here.'

The Canadian started to giggle. He stretched out on his bed and rolled over, resting his head in the crook of his right arm, the one he hadn't injected into. His eyes seemed to stare right through Harrigan, as if he wasn't there. Harrigan envied the Canadian the fact that he could look forward to being released at some point. He was hoping to be repatriated to Canada to serve the remainder of his sentence, but even if that fell through he'd still be out in six years. He had something to aim for, he knew he had a life ahead of him, a life outside. But fifty years wasn't a life sentence, it was a death sentence. Unless the Organisation got him out, he'd die within the walls of the prison. He banged the back of his head against the tiled wall. They had to get him out. He wouldn't grow old and die in prison, he'd rather kill himself first. He banged his head again, harder this time. There was something cleansing about the pain, it helped him focus his thoughts, his anger. He did it again, so hard that the dull thud echoed around the cell. Harrigan began to cry. He bit down on his lower lip so that he didn't sob out loud, but his body trembled and shook.

THE PORTABLE TELEPHONE BLEEPED and the Chinese teenager unclipped it from his belt and spoke into it. Down on the pitch the South Africans were warming up.

'What a wanker,' said Tim Metcalfe, pouring himself a tumbler of lager from a green and white Carlsberg jug. 'Fancy bringing his phone to the rugby sevens. No class, no class at all.'

Warren Hastings grinned at Metcalfe. With his ripped and stained fake Lacoste polo shirt and baggy shorts, Metcalfe was hardly the epitome of good taste himself.

'What? What are you grinning at?' Metcalfe asked, wiping foam from his upper lip with the back of his arm.

'Nothing, Tim.'

'Well, come on, you've got to agree with me, right? We're here to watch the rugby, not to talk on the phone. Well, am I right or am I right?'

'You're right,' agreed Hastings. It paid not to argue with Metcalfe, who had the tenaciousness of a bulldog and would continue pressing his point home until he'd beaten down all opposition. It was a skill honed from years of selling life insurance.

Chris Davies, a burly bearded photographer, put a large hand into a McDonald's bag and pulled out a cheeseburger.

Metcalfe reached over and plucked the burger from Davies' hands. 'Thanks, Digger,' he said.

'You've the manners of a pig, Tim,' said Davies.

'That's an insult to pigs everywhere,' said Hastings, pouring the last of the lager into his tumbler. He tossed the empty jug into Metcalfe's lap. Metcalfe didn't notice – his eyes were fixed on the far side of the pitch. Hastings turned to see what he was staring at. A female streaker had climbed on to the field and was running across the grass, chased by Gurkha security guards dressed in red tracksuits. The girl was in her twenties with long blonde hair and large pendulous breasts that swung to and fro as she ran.

'Bloody hell,' wailed Metcalfe. 'Would you look at them buggers move.'

Hastings wasn't sure whether his friend was referring to the girl's breasts or the diminutive Gurkhas in pursuit. The stadium was filled with roars and catcalls and someone let off an airhorn high up in the stands. The referee blew his whistle and the players stopped to watch the girl run to the centre of the pitch, her hands raised above her head, waving to the crowd. The spectators in front of Hastings got to their feet to get a better look.

'Come on, get her off the pitch!' shouted Davies. 'Get on with the game!'

'Hey, give the girl a chance,' said Metcalfe. He had a pair of binoculars around his neck and he raised them to his eyes. 'Bloody hell,' he repeated.

Hastings arched his back and rotated his neck. He'd been sitting for more than two hours, and although he was enjoying the rugby, the stadium seats were far from comfortable. He took off his steel-framed spectacles and polished them with the bottom of his shirt.

One of the Gurkhas lunged at the girl but she swerved and the man fell at her feet. The crowd roared with delight and the girl stopped and took a bow.

'Shit, we could use her on our team,' said Davies in admiration.

Hastings put his glasses back on. Suddenly the hairs on the back of his neck stood up as if someone had touched his spine with a piece of ice. He had a feeling of dread, as if something terrible was about to happen, but for the life of him he couldn't imagine what it was. The streaker had started running again, but the Gurkhas had surrounded her and Hastings could see that it would only be a matter of time before they brought her down. He massaged the back of his neck, wondering if the feeling of unease was nothing more than the onset of flu. Around him spectators were cheering the girl and whistling at the security guards. Hastings shivered. He looked over to his left. All eyes were on the streaker, with one exception.

A grey-haired man in his late fifties was looking away from the pitch, towards where Hastings was sitting. He was about two hundred feet away, in the top tier of the stadium, five rows from the front, high up beyond the corporate boxes. He was wearing an off-white jacket and a dark shirt and smoking a large cigar. Hastings frowned. The man was too far away for Hastings to make out his features, but he was sure that the man was staring right at him, staring at him and grinning. It was an eerie sensation, as if something physical linked the two men, something that cut through the crowds and set them apart from everybody else.

The noise of the crowd swelled to a deafening roar. Metcalfe grabbed Hastings by the shoulder and shook him. Hastings looked at the pitch. Three Gurkhas had wrestled the naked girl to the ground but she was covered in perspiration and they were having difficulty holding on to her as she wriggled and shook like a stranded fish.

Hastings twisted around to look at the upper tier again but he couldn't see the man with the cigar. The spectators at the front of the tier were waving a large South African flag and cheering. Hastings craned his neck but the flag blocked his view.

Down below, the Gurkhas carried the naked girl off the pitch and the spectators sat down, eager for the game to restart. On the upper tier, the South African supporters dropped back down into their seats. Hastings cupped his hands around his eyes to shield them from the sun. The seat where the man with the cigar had been sitting was empty. Hastings wracked his brains, trying to remember where he'd seen the man before.

'What's up, Warren?' asked Davies.

'Nothing,' said Hastings, sitting down.

'You look like somebody just walked over your grave.'

Hastings shivered again. Davies was right. That was exactly what it had felt like.

PADDY DUNNE USED HIS key to open the front door of his sister's house. On previous visits he'd rung the doorbell, but she'd paid it no attention as if unwilling to allow anything to intrude on her grief. 'Tess,' he called. 'It's me, Tess.'

There were three letters on the carpet, an electricity bill and two circulars, and Dunne put them on the hall table. He went through to the kitchen where his sister was sitting at a wooden table, a cup of tea in front of her. The tea had long since gone cold and a brown scum had settled on to its surface. Tess was staring at the cup as if it were a crystal ball into which she was looking for some sign of what the future held for her.

'How about a smile for your brother, then?' said Dunne as cheerfully as possible.

Tess didn't look up. Dunne was carrying a plastic bag of provisions which he took over to the refrigerator. He opened the door and put the carton of milk and the packets of cheese and butter on to the top shelf, then put a loaf of brown bread into the pine bread bin by the stove. He looked in the sink. There were no dirty dishes there, no sign that his sister had eaten breakfast.

'Are you hungry, Tess, love?' he asked. She didn't even bother to shake her head. 'How about a nice piece of toast? With some lemon curd, like we used to have when we were kids? How about that, Tess? Does that sound nice?'

Dunne sat down opposite her and took her hands in his. Her skin was cold and dry, the nails bitten to the quick. He held her hands gently as if afraid they might break. 'It's going to be all right,' he said. 'Mr McCormack phoned me this morning.' He hunched forward over the table. He was twelve years older than his sister, but since her son had been arrested she'd aged dramatically, and the life seemed to be ebbing out of her. There were dark circles under her eyes and her hair was dull and lifeless, hanging in uncombed strands around her sunken cheeks. Her son's arrest seemed to have hit her even harder than the death of her husband, five years earlier.

'It won't be long now, Tess. Mr McCormack said it's being taken care of, they're going to get Ray out.'

For the first time she looked at him. 'I want my boy back,' she said, her voice a cracked whisper.

'He's coming, Tess,' promised Dunne.

'I want my boy back,' she repeated, as if she hadn't heard him.

THE OLD WOMAN HELD the egg-shaped poppy pod between the first finger and thumb of her left hand and collected the congealed sap with her metal scraper. The scraper was the size of a small saucer with a crescent cut out of it, blackened from years of use. The old woman had been given the scraper when she was a child, when she'd worked the poppy fields of northern Thailand, long before she'd crossed the border into Burma with her family, chased out by the Thai army.

It was the second time the poppy field had been harvested. It was a good crop, one of the best she'd ever seen. It had rained only twice during the cold season and the plants were healthy and tall, with many of them producing five flowers. She scraped carefully and methodically, but quickly, her fingers nimble despite her years. There were three parallel lines of brown sap, and close by them were three scars where the pod had been cut the previous week. Each poppy pod could be cut three, maybe four times over a period of six weeks. Then she and the rest of the workers would collect the biggest and best of the pods to get seeds for next year's crop.

The work was repetitive, but the old woman was lucky: she was small and the poppy pods came up to her chest so she could harvest the pea-sized balls of sticky latex without bending. She and the six other women working the field had to be finished before midday. In the morning the sap was moist and easily scraped. By early afternoon it would set and the work would be that much harder, so the opium collectors had gone into the field at first light and would be finished before the sun was high overhead.

The old woman wiped her resinous scrapings into the small brass cup hanging around her neck. The cup was old, too, older than the woman herself. It had belonged to her mother and she'd been given it on her twelfth birthday, the year she'd married.

She moved on to the next plant. The old woman preferred collecting sap to making the incisions on the poppy pods. The pods had to be cut from midday onwards, when the sun was at its hottest, so that the heat would force out the milky white sap. It was unbearably hot in the fields in the afternoon, even with a wide-brimmed straw hat, and the sun was merciless on any uncovered skin. The old woman's skin had long ago turned to the colour and texture of leather, but she still burned if she didn't take care.

The cutting was done with a three-bladed knife, and the making of the parallel incisions was the most skilful of the jobs involved in the opium harvest. Too deep and the sap would drip to the ground and be wasted; too shallow and not enough would trickle out. The cutting required more concentration than the collecting of the sap, and any lapse could result in sliced fingers. The old woman's fingers were crisscrossed with thin white scars.

Another reason the old woman preferred collecting the opium to making the incisions was that workers had to walk backwards when they were cutting so that they didn't smear the opium on their clothes as they moved through the field. It was slow, hard work, but it had to be done. She'd been working in opium fields for almost sixty years and had never complained. The opium paid for her food, her clothes, and had allowed her to raise a family.

She looked across at her grand-daughter who was using a small oblong scraper to collect sap from the plant next to hers. The old woman smiled down at the little girl in her white cotton dress, amused at the way her tongue was stuck between her teeth as she concentrated on her task. The girl knelt down and scraped the resin into a bowl which she kept on the soil by her feet, then grinned up as she realised that her grandmother was looking at her.

'Not tired?' the old woman asked.

The little girl shook her head. She wiped her forehead with her arm and sighed theatrically. 'No. I'm fine.'

'We'll have a break soon. You can drink some water.' A break would also give the old woman a chance to smoke some opium. Not the fresh sap that she'd just harvested but opium from the previous year's crop which she kept in a horn box in the pocket of the black apron that she wore over her red embroidered jacket. Her opium lamp and spirit pipe were in a bag at the edge of the field.

'Who's that, Grandmother?' the little girl asked, pointing up the hill.

The old woman narrowed her eyes and looked in the direction the girl was pointing. At the crest of a hill was a man on a horse. The horse was big, much bigger than the packhorses and mules that carried the opium through the jungle and which brought supplies to the village, and it was white, gleaming in the early morning sun. It stood proudly, as if aware of the attention it was attracting. One by one the women in the fields stopped what they were doing to look up the hill. The man in the saddle sat ramrod straight, as proudly as his horse. He scanned the fields with a pair of binoculars.

'That's Zhou Yuanyi,' said the old woman. 'Get back to work.' She seized another oval pod.

'Who's Zhou Yuanyi?' asked the little girl.

'It's his fields we're working in,' said the old woman. 'These are his poppies.'

'Wah!' said the little girl. She looked around the field in amazement. 'He owns all these flowers? All of them?'

The old woman grinned, showing the gap where her two top front teeth had once been. 'Child, he owns the whole mountain. And those beyond.'

The little girl stared back at the man on the horse. 'He must be very rich.'

The old woman scraped the opium sap from a large pod. 'The richest man in the world,' she said. 'Now get back to work. Don't let him see you staring at him. Zhou Yuanyi doesn't like being stared at.'

The old woman took a quick look over her shoulder, up the hill. Zhou Yuanyi took the binoculars away from his eyes. He was wearing sunglasses, but from a distance it looked as if he had no eyes, just black, empty sockets. He kicked the white horse hard in the ribs, jerked on the reins and turned it around, riding down the far side of the hill, out of sight. The old woman watched him go, then turned back to her poppy plants. There was still much work to do.

WARREN HASTINGS PRESSED A yellow button on the dashboard of his Range Rover and the wrought-iron gates glided open. He nudged the car forward into the compound, its tyres crunching on the gravel drive. His two-storey house with its white walls and red-tiled Spanish-style roof was illuminated by his headlights, and long black shadows were thrown up against the tree-lined hillside behind the building.

He'd stayed on Hong Kong Island until late, knowing that both cross-harbour tunnels would be blocked solid by spectators returning to Kowloon and the New Territories. Two large Dobermanns came running around the side of the house, their stubby tails wagging and their long pink tongues lolling out of their mouths.

Hastings cut the engine and climbed out of the Range Rover. 'Hiya Mickey, hiya Minnie,' he said, greeting the dogs with pats on their heads.

Behind him the wrought-iron gates began to close, but as they did two headlight beams swept across the compound and a Mercedes saloon accelerated through the gap. It braked hard and skidded several yards across the gravelled drive. The dogs stared at the car, their ears up.

The engine of the Mercedes was switched off, but the headlights stayed on, blinding Hastings. He was as tense as the two dogs, aware of every sound in the night air: the metallic creaking of the two engines as they cooled, the Geiger-counter clicks of the crickets on the hillside and the far-off rumble of a minibus heading towards Sai Kung. Mickey looked up at Hastings, his eyes bright and inquisitive.

'Trousers,' said Hastings, squinting into the lights.

He heard the driver's door open and first one foot then another step on to the gravel. The door clunked shut, the sound echoing off the hillside.

'Who is it?' Hastings called. 'What do you want?'

Mickey took two paces forward, his hackles up. Whoever it was remained silent. Hastings put up a hand, trying to block out the blinding headlights.

'That's no way to greet an old friend, is it now, Hutch?' The voice was gruff, almost hoarse, the accent pure Geordie.

Hutch stiffened at the use of his real name. It had been

a long time since anyone had used it. He screwed up his eyes, but he still couldn't see who it was.

The visitor walked to stand in front of the car, between the headlights. 'You don't look bad for a man who's been dead for seven years,' he said.

The man chuckled and it was the sound of rustling leaves, an ironic, bitter laugh devoid of amusement. He walked forward. As he got closer, Hutch could just about make out the man's features: he had grey hair, slicked back from his forehead and curly at the ends, thin lips, a nose that was slightly crooked. It was the man who'd been staring at him in the stadium. Billy Winter.

'What do you want, Billy?' he asked.

'Brandy and Coke would be nice.' Winter extended his hand, but Hutch ignored it.

Mickey and Minnie both took a step forward, their teeth bared in silent snarls. Hutch stroked the back of Mickey's neck. 'Trousers,' he said, his eyes fixed on Winter. 'How did you find me?'

'It wasn't hard.' Winter kept his hand out and eventually Hutch shook it. 'That's better,' said Winter. 'Can we go inside? It's like a sauna here.' He took a large white handkerchief from the top pocket of his jacket and wiped his forehead. 'And what's this business about trousers?'

'They're trained to obey key words,' said Hutch. 'That way no one else can give them instructions.'

'Yeah?' said Winter. He looked at the dogs. 'Sit,' he said. The dogs stared at him. 'What makes them sit?' Winter asked. He spoke out of the corner of his mouth as if he feared being overheard.

'Blue,' said Hutch. Both animals sat obediently.

Winter raised an eyebrow, impressed. 'Trained to kill, are they?'

'Do you want me to say the word?'

Winter grinned but didn't reply. He started walking towards the house.

'How did you find me, Billy?' Hutch asked.

'All in good time, old lad.'

Hutch hesitated for a moment, then he followed Winter. The front door had two security locks and Winter stood to the side while Hutch opened them.

'Takes you back, doesn't it?' said Winter. 'All the locks. There's something about the rattle of keys, still gives me the willies, even now.'

'Yeah? I never give it much thought.' He pushed open the door and let Winter walk in first.

Winter frowned as he heard a rapid beeping noise. 'What's that?' he asked.

'Security system,' said Hutch. He walked over to a console on the wall by the kitchen door and tapped in a four-digit code. The beeping stopped. Mickey and Minnie stood at the threshold waiting for permission to enter. Hutch waved them through and they trotted obediently into the hallway. 'Through there,' Hutch told Winter and indicated the door to the sitting-room.

As Winter sat down on a long brown leather sofa, Hutch went over to a rattan drinks cabinet. 'No Coke,' he said.

'Brandy and ice'll be just fine,' said Winter, adjusting the creases on his slacks. He looked around the room. 'Nice place,' he said amicably. 'You wouldn't know you were in Hong Kong, would you? It's a little piece of England, isn't it?' He patted the arms of the chair with the palms of his hand. 'I must admit I was surprised to discover that a man who spent so much of his time in solitary confinement had decided to hide in the most crowded city in the world.' Mickey and Minnie stood by the french windows, watching the visitor. Winter stared back at them. 'Sit,' he said. The dogs didn't move. 'Blue,' said Winter, louder this time. The dogs remained standing, their ears pricked, their mouths slightly open. 'What's wrong with them?' Winter asked Hutch.

'They're trained not to obey strangers,' said Hutch, heading towards the kitchen with an empty ice bucket.

Winter glared at the Dobermanns. 'Stay!' he said authoritatively. The dogs stood stock still. 'Gotcha!' said Winter.

When Hutch returned with the bucket filled with ice, Winter and the dogs were still staring at each other.

'You look better without the beard,' said Winter. 'Made you look like a bit of a wild man, you know. The glasses suit you, too. They make you look almost intellectual. I nearly didn't recognise you.'

'Thanks for the character analysis,' said Hutch, without warmth. 'How did you know where I was?' He poured a large measure of brandy into a glass and dropped in three cubes of ice.

'Looked you up in the phone book,' said Winter. Hutch gave him his drink. 'Aren't you having anything?' Winter asked.

Hutch shook his head. 'How did you . . . ?' Realisation dawned. 'Eddie Archer.'

'Best paperwork in the business,' said Winter. He sipped his brandy and smacked his lips in appreciation. 'Oh, yeah, your passport runs out in two years. Eddie asked me to tell you not to apply through official channels. It's genuine,

57

but the birth certificate isn't. He'll fix you up with a new one, but you ought to know that his prices have gone up substantially.'

'So much for honour among thieves.'

Winter grinned. 'You always said you were innocent, Hutch.'

'You know what I mean.'

'I've known Eddie a lot longer than you. We grew up together in Newcastle . . .'

'Spare me the deprived childhood story, Billy. I know it by heart.' Hutch went over to a wood-framed armchair and sat down. Mickey padded over to stand next to him but Minnie remained with her eyes fixed on Winter. 'So you heard that my body wasn't in the plane, and you paid Eddie a visit. Who else knows?'

'Just Eddie. And me.'

'What do you want, Billy?'

Winter studied Hutch as if wondering how to phrase his reply. He swirled the brandy around his glass. 'I need you to do a job for me.'

'What sort of a job?'

'The sort only you are qualified to do, Hutch. I need you to help me get a guy out of prison.'

Hutch shook his head. 'I'm not going back to the UK.'

'He's out here. In Bangkok.'

Hutch sighed deeply. 'Billy, I run a kennels. I train dogs. I breed Dobermanns. I don't break people out of prisons.'

'You're the best. You escaped from Parkhurst, you got clean away.' He paused, then smiled slyly. 'Almost clean away.' He put his brandy glass down on a hardwood side table, then took a large cigar from his jacket pocket and lit it.

'I can't help you. I've too much to lose.'

'Exactly,' said Winter. The two men locked eyes. Minnie growled, sensing the hostility in the room. 'Don't make me force you, Hutch.'

'I can't help you.'

'You don't have any choice.'

'We were friends, Billy.'

Winter shook his head. 'This is nothing to do with friendship. You're coming with me to Bangkok tomorrow.'

'And if I refuse?'

'You can't refuse. I make one phone call to Plod and you go back to finish your life sentence, plus whatever they add on top for your escape.'

'You'd grass on me?'

'I don't think I'll have to. But a threat isn't a threat unless I have the balls to go through with it. And believe me, Hutch, I've got the balls.'

Hutch glared at Winter. 'You bastard,' he said.

Winter shrugged. 'Sticks and stones, old lad. Sticks and stones.' He took a long drag on the cigar and stood up. The two Dobermanns watched him intently. Winter stared back at them. He took the cigar out of his mouth and snarled at the dogs.

'Don't tease them,' warned Hutch.

'I killed a dog once. When I was a kid. Did I ever tell you about that?'

'No. No, you didn't.'

'With a cricket bat. Thwack. Never forgotten the sound.' Minnie bared her teeth and growled.

'You'd better go,' said Hutch.

Winter got to his feet. Ash from his cigar spilled on to the floor. 'I'll pick you up at noon tomorrow. We'll only be away for a couple of days.' He turned and walked out of the room without a backward look.

The two Dobermanns stood looking at Hutch, sensing his anxiety. Mickey growled softly and Hutch stroked his head. 'It's okay,' he said. 'Just an old friend, that's all.' He went over to the console, pressing the button that opened the main gates. He watched Winter drive out of the compound on a black and white monitor set into the wall. Winter waved out of the window of his Mercedes as if he knew he was being watched.

TIM CARVER LOOKED AT his wristwatch for the hundredth time. His driver was tapping his fingers on the steering wheel and the noise was driving Carver crazy, but if he told him to stop the man would probably sulk for a week. If there was one thing that Carver had learned since he had been assigned to Thailand, it was that Thais did not react well to criticism.

The traffic ahead appeared to be locked solid, par for the course on the roads leading out of Bangkok at rush hour. In fact, the city's streets were jammed pretty much around the clock, and Carver had long become accustomed to sitting in his car waiting for interminable periods before crawling forward a few yards and stopping again. Carver usually played through his Thai language tapes during traffic jams, brushing up on his vocabulary, but today he decided to use the time to get his thoughts in order.

The regular monthly meeting of the Foreign Anti-Narcotic Community had gone on longer than usual: two Thai undercover agents had been found floating in a canal close to the city's Chinatown, their bodies mutilated, and the overseas agents were worried about the ramifications for the safety of their own people.

It had been Carver's turn to host the lunch, and over beer and sandwiches at the DEA's offices the FANC members had pored over the police report on the deaths. It was a foregone conclusion that the Thai agents had been betrayed by one of their own; what worried Carver and his colleagues was at what level the betrayal had occurred. The primary reason for the formation of the FANC had been the rampant corruption within the Thai police force which had led to countless undercover operations being blown long before arrests could be made. The members of the FANC, primarily representing American, European and Australian drug agencies, shared information and consolidated their efforts to fight the drug trade, and only contacted Thai police and intelligence officials at the end-phase of any operation. Carver and his counterparts would have preferred to have excluded the Thais completely, but they didn't have the power to make arrests, or even to carry weapons in the country. The trick was to call in the Thais at the last minute, minimising the opportunity for the targets to be tipped off.

The British Customs official at the FANC meeting had announced that his bosses had decided to pull out one of their agents, a Taiwanese who'd been trying to infiltrate a team responsible for smuggling heroin into Manila. He'd been working in a Chinese restaurant near where the bodies were discovered and the Brits were worried that it might have been a warning. Carver had pointed out that generally the drug gangs didn't bother with warnings, but the Brits were getting jumpy. Hell, everyone was jumpy, thought Carver, and with good cause.

The traffic began to move again. Ahead Carver could see a brown uniformed motorcycle cop standing at the roadside wearing a cotton mask strapped across the bottom of his face. He'd flagged down a green Mercedes and was talking to the driver. Carver smiled wryly as they drove slowly by. Whatever the infraction, it clearly wasn't speeding. A motorcycle taxi scraped by the car, the rider nodding to Carver's driver, the driver nodding back. Simple everyday Thai politeness, thought Carver, even at rush hour. The rider's skin was dark and leathery and he had his helmet tipped back as far as it would go on his head. His passenger was a middle-aged woman in a bright pink suit, sitting side saddle with her legs pressed together, a handbag in her lap. She held her bag with one hand and her long hair with the other, preventing it from blowing in the wind. She smiled at Carver and he smiled back.

Carver wondered why Jake Gregory was making an unplanned visit to Thailand and why the DEA executive had insisted that Carver meet him at the airport. Gregory had visited the organisation's Bangkok offices at least half a dozen times during Carver's stint in Thailand and he'd always made his own way in from the airport, usually spurning an office car in favour of a taxi. Gregory had worked his way from a front-line agent to the number two man in the agency but had never forgotten his roots, and was the last person Carver would have expected to use an agent as a porter. Not that Carver minded, it never paid to turn down an offer to earn Brownie points from a superior.

Carver got to the airport about fifteen minutes after Gregory's flight was scheduled to touch down, but he didn't rush to the arrivals area. It took an average of thirty minutes to clear immigration, with an hour-long wait not uncommon.

Carver bought a cup of black coffee and sipped it as he waited. A group of European tourists streamed out of the immigration hall, pasty faced and sweating, and lined up at the taxi counter with their suitcases. Carver wondered if they realised they faced a two-hour wait in the heavy traffic. So much time was now spent in traffic jams, the city's filling stations all now stocked small portable urinals which drivers could use while stuck behind the wheel. Carver had one under his seat, though thankfully he'd never had to use it. He could imagine the amused looks he'd get: a farang taking a piss in his car.

Two stunning Thai girls with waist-length hair walked hand in hand, each pulling a wheeled suitcase behind her. They had bright gold chains around their necks, glittering bracelets on their wrists, and lipstick as red as fresh blood. They were almost certainly exotic dancers back from working in Hong Kong or Japan, Carver decided. Or high-class hookers. One of them smiled at him as she went by and he smiled back. Everyone smiled in Thailand, it was practically a national pastime, but Carver got the impression that the girl meant it. He turned to watch her go, but she didn't look back and as she reached the exit a large Thai with bulging forearms emphasised by a too-tight short-sleeved shirt, stepped forward and took her suitcase.

'Hell of a butt, huh?' said a gruff voice behind Carver. He whirled around and found himself looking into the amused eyes of Jake Gregory. He was wearing a green polo shirt and grey slacks and was carrying a black leather holdall.

'Sorry,' said Carver, momentarily flustered. He recovered quickly and stuck out his hand. Gregory gripped it and they shook hands firmly. Carver looked at the holdall. 'Is that all the luggage you've got?'

'Flying visit, son,' said Gregory, running his hand through his crew cut. 'Hit and run.'

Carver reached for Gregory's bag, but Gregory swung it out of his reach. 'That's all right, son. I can carry my own bag.'

Carver nodded and turned towards the exit. Gregory put a restraining hand on his shoulder. 'Not so fast,' said Gregory, good naturedly.

'The car's outside . . .' Carver began, but Gregory shook his head.

'I'm just passing through,' said Gregory. Gregory glanced at his watch, a scratched driving model that looked as if it had been on his wrist for decades. 'My flight's in two hours. Is there somewhere we can talk?'

'There's a restaurant upstairs.' Carver led the DEA executive to the stairs, dropping his cup of coffee into a rubbish bin on the way.

Gregory looked surprisingly refreshed for a man who'd just spent almost twenty hours in the air, and he took the stairs two at a time so that Carver had to hurry after him. Gregory was thickset, almost heavy, but it was clearly all muscle, and he had the build of a Marine drill sergeant.

The restaurant was self-service. Gregory helped himself to a salad, a wholemeal bread roll and a Diet Coke while Carver chose a plate of pad thai – thin rice noddles fried with bean curd, egg, vegetables and peanuts. Gregory wrinkled his nose at Carver's choice but didn't say anything. He went over to an empty corner table and left Carver to pay. When Carver joined him, Gregory was breaking the bread roll apart with his hands.

'Rabbit food,' said Gregory, nodding at his salad. 'Had a bit of a heart scare a few months back. Doc told me to cut out red meat, Southern Comfort and cigars. I compromised and kept the cigars.' He popped a piece of bread between his thin lips and chewed without relish.

'You should try Thai food,' said Carver, digging his fork into the noodles. 'It's almost zero fat. The Thais have got the lowest incidence of heart disease in the world.'

'Yeah, maybe you're right,' said the DEA executive unenthusiastically. 'But as soon as my cholesterol drops to normal I'm having a fucking huge steak.' He grinned wolfishly and took a gulp of cola. 'Okay, let's get down to business,' he said. 'What do you know about Zhou Yuanyi?' He studied Carver with unblinking blue eyes.

Carver's fork stopped on the way to his mouth, suspended in mid-air. 'Zhou Yuanyi?' he repeated. Carver put his fork down. 'He's a Chinese warlord, based in the Golden Triangle. Strictly speaking he's in Burma, but the region is constantly being fought over by private armies who control the opium fields. They're unreachable. Unreachable and untouchable. And Zhou Yuanyi is the toughest of them all. The last time Zhou's people caught someone trying to infiltrate his network, they impaled the intruder alive at the entrance to their compound.'

Gregory nodded slowly. He popped another chunk of bread roll into his mouth. 'Not one of ours?' he said.

Carver shook his head. 'A Thai. Working for the Australians.'

'Impaled, huh?'

'A stake up the arse. Took him two days to die.'

Gregory frowned. 'How do you know that?' he asked.

'The Australians received a video. Just to ram home the point.' He smiled grimly at the unintended pun.

Gregory took another look at his wristwatch. 'You know we've no pictures of Zhou on file?'

'He's never been photographed. He's not political like some of the warlords, he doesn't give interviews. He's in it solely for the money.'

'What are the chances of getting a picture?'

'Zero. We can't get near the guy. He has a private army of more than five hundred soldiers, he moves from camp to camp within the area he controls and he's got an intelligence network that puts the CIA to shame. He's better protected than the President.'

Gregory nodded slowly. He speared a slice of cucumber and waved it in front of Carver's face. 'That might be so, son, but we're going to change all that.' Carver sat back in his plastic chair, intrigued, and Gregory leaned forward as if reluctant to allow the agent to put more distance between them. 'We're gonna get this Zhou. His chickens are coming home to roost.'

Carver raised his eyebrows. 'Great,' he said. 'It's about time we did something.'

'Yeah, I've read your reports,' said Gregory. 'You're getting pretty frustrated with the way things are going here.'

'We're just not making any progress,' Carver said. 'Sure, the Thais make arrests, but it's usually mules at the airports. They don't go near the really big guys, the ones that run the drug-smuggling operations. And the guys like Zhou – hell, in the Golden Triangle they reckon Zhou's a hero. Half the border guards, Thai and Burmese, are on his payroll and every undercover operation we've ever put together has been blown.'

Gregory put down his fork and clasped his hands together. 'This time it's gonna be different. I'm putting together an operation that positively, absolutely is not going to be blown. And I'm going to need your help.'

Carver's eyes widened. 'Whatever it takes,' he said.

THE TWO THAI TECHNICIANS grunted as they man-handled the metal drum off the fire, using pieces of wet sacking to protect their hands. They eased it on to the soil and stood back to allow it to cool.

The boiling mixture contained raw opium, water and lime fertiliser. The fertiliser had been brought across the border from Thailand, driven across in trucks and then loaded on the backs of donkeys for the thirty-mile treck through the jungle to Zhou's camp.

The Thais worked outside, downwind from the main part of the camp because the fumes were unpleasant. Not as dangerous as the later stages of the process, but the technicians weren't trusted to do that. The technicians were paid to turn Zhou Yuanyi's raw opium into morphine, nothing more. He used an industrial chemist to transform the morphine into heroin. It was a loss of face for the technicians, but secretly they were glad not to have to be involved. They'd heard stories of technicians being blown up when the process went wrong. Blown up or burned alive. Better to work with the drum and the open fire, better to be outdoors so that if anything happened they could run like the wind.

One of the technicians, a twenty-three-year-old former soldier in the Burmese army called Em, nodded at two boys who were sitting in the shade of a spreading tree and fanning themselves with banana leaves. They scampered to their feet and ran over to help. The four of them carried the drum over to a nearby stream. The boys picked up the filter, a metre wide strip of flannel cloth which had been stretched across a wooden frame, and held it a foot above the flowing stream while Em and the other technician lifted the drum of opium suspension and carefully drained off the water.

The technicians took the container over to another drum, one the boys had scrubbed clean earlier, and emptied the opium solution into it. The technicians left the dirty drum by the side of the stream for the boys to clean later.

When the solution was boiling again the technicians took half a dozen plastic bottles of concentrated ammonia from a hut and poured them in one by one after tying strips of cloth across the lower half of their faces to protect themselves from the fumes.

The morphine began to settle out, sinking to the bottom like a snowfall. Em nodded at his older colleague Ah-Jan and they lifted the drum off the fire. He shouted over at the boys to get the filter ready again.

Em and Ah-Jan took the drum over to the stream and as the boys held out the flannel filter, they drained off the water. Left behind were globules of morphine, glistening wetly on the filter. Em would leave the boys to press the morphine into blocks and then wrap them with banana leaves. He and Ah-Jan had more opium and fertiliser to prepare. They would face Zhou's wrath if they didn't meet their daily quota. And Zhou's anger was a fearful thing to behold; the body of an informer was still decomposing on a stake at the entrance to the camp, his flesh eaten by ants, his eyes pecked out by birds.

MICKEY AND MINNIE MADE soft growling noises as if they realised that it was the last time they'd see Hutch. He knelt down and the two Dobermanns licked his face eagerly.

'How long will you be gone?' asked Chau-ling, his head kennel maid. She'd worked with him for almost five years and had been invaluable in building up the business. Her father was a shipping tycoon and he'd wanted her to join the family firm, but Chau-ling loved dogs and she'd pouted and sulked until he'd let her have her way. Despite having a multi-million-dollar trust fund and the sort of looks that had suitors queuing up to take her out, she worked long and hard and was one of Hutch's most loyal employees. He hated having to lie to her, but there was no way he could tell her what was wrong.

'A week. Maybe longer. You don't mind holding the fort?'

Chau-ling smiled broadly. Hutch knew she relished being left in charge and she'd regularly demonstrated how capable she was. As well as having killer cheekbones and the longest, straightest hair he'd seen outside of a shampoo advertisement, Chau-ling had a business studies degree from

Exeter University in the UK and an MBA from Harvard. Hutch had already decided that once he'd left Hong Kong, he'd write and let her know that the kennels were hers.

'And I can't reach you?'

'I'll call you.' He put his hands on her shoulders and looked deep into her oval brown eyes, as trusting as any of his dogs. He felt a sudden rush of guilt, so overwhelming that he caught his breath. 'I'm sorry,' he said.

'What? Sorry for what, Warren?'

Hutch forced a smile. 'For leaving you in the lurch like this.' He faked a slow punch to her chin and she grinned 'I'm going to have to give you a raise.' He picked up his black nylon holdall and patted his jacket pocket to check that his passport and ticket were there.

'Got everything?' Chau-ling asked.

Hutch looked around the room. His books, his CDs, the statues and trinkets he'd collected on his travels around the region, all the things that he owned, he was going to have to leave them all behind. 'Yes,' he said, almost to himself. 'I've got everything.' A change of clothes, his washbag, his electric razor, and his Filofax. Not much to show for six years, but he'd left with less before.

A red and grey taxi was waiting for him outside his front door. Chau-ling waved goodbye as he got into the back of the cab. Hutch closed his eyes and rested his head on the back of his seat. He was surprised at how guilty he'd felt when he'd lied to Chau-ling, surprised because ever since he'd arrived in Hong Kong he'd been living a lie. Even the name she knew him by wasn't real: Warren Hastings just happened to be the name that Eddie Archer had chosen for the paperwork he'd put together in his Tower Hamlets workshop.

He was going to miss Chau-ling, and the dogs, and his friends. He would have liked to have been able to have said a proper goodbye to Davies and Metcalfe but there would have been too many questions. Hutch couldn't afford to let anyone know what his plans were.

'Shit.'

'Huh?' grunted the taxi driver.

Hutch opened his eyes. He hadn't realised that he'd spoken out loud. *'M ganyu,'* he said. Nothing important, in Cantonese. He'd gone to a lot of time and trouble to learn the language, and now it would all be wasted. He'd have to run far away from Hong Kong, he'd have to cut all the connections with his old life, just as he'd done seven years earlier. It would be like a rebirth, but first he'd have to kill off Warren Hastings, kill him off so unequivocally that no one would go looking for him. He'd have to find a new occupation, too, and that was a shame because he'd loved training dogs. Chris Hutchison had been a locksmith, Warren Hastings had been a dog trainer; God alone knew what he'd end up doing in his next life. He was thirty-two years old and he was running out of options.

He patted the holdall. The Filofax in the bag contained details of the half-dozen bank accounts he'd set up in various offshore locations: Jersey, Guernsey, the Cayman Islands and Gibraltar. He wouldn't risk touching his two bank accounts with the Hong Kong and Shanghai Bank but he'd be able to transfer his money out of the offshore accounts as soon as he was out of the territory. It wasn't a fortune, most of his assets were tied up in the kennels and the house, but it would be enough to buy him a new identity.

The taxi dropped him in front of the airport terminal and Hutch strode into the departures hall. He went up to the Cathay Pacific sales desk and asked for a ticket on the next flight to Singapore. He planned to fly from there to the United States, and then he'd drive across the border into Mexico where he would kill off Warren Hastings. He'd be able to buy a new passport there and head south into Central America. It wasn't much of a plan, but bearing in mind it had only been eight hours since he'd been confronted by Billy Winter, Hutch reckoned he wasn't doing too badly. He pulled his wallet out of his back pocket and took out a credit card. He wouldn't need to start covering his tracks until he got to Singapore; Winter had said that he'd be at Hutch's house at noon. Even if he carried out his threat, Winter would have to call London. Hong Kong was seven hours ahead of the UK, so Winter would have to wait until three p.m. Hong Kong time, maybe four, and the police would have to check out his story before contacting the airlines. That was assuming that Winter went straight to the police, and Hutch doubted that he'd do that. Winter needed his help, so it was more likely that he'd try to track him down first.

'You won't be needing that, old lad,' said a voice behind Hutch. It was a gruff Geordie whisper.

Hutch's stomach lurched. He nodded at the Cathay Pacific salesgirl and slid the credit card back into his wallet. Only then did he turn around.

Billy Winter stood behind him, a big smile on his face. It was a predatory grin, like a shark preparing to strike. Winter picked up Hutch's holdall. 'The motor's outside,' he said.

Hutch put the wallet back into his pocket and followed Winter out of the terminal.

A green Rolls-Royce was waiting and the two men climbed into the back. Winter nodded at the liveried chauffeur and the Rolls-Royce pulled away from the kerb.

Hutch sat back, his hands clasped together in his lap. 'I didn't realise I was so predictable,' he said quietly.

Winter flipped open a drinks cabinet and poured himself a brandy. 'You want a snifter?' he asked Hutch.

'Bit early for me,' said Hutch.

Winter sipped his brandy, all the time watching Hutch with amused eyes. He warmed the glass between his hands. 'You're a runner, Hutch. That's what you do. When you're faced with a crisis, you run.' Hutch shrugged but didn't say anything. 'The only time you stand and fight is when you're in a corner. Like the guy you killed. You couldn't run then, could you?'

Hutch sighed. 'Where are we going, Billy?'

Winter's eyes hardened. 'I'm going to paint you into a corner, Hutch, old lad. I'm going to show you that there's no point in running.' He raised his brandy glass in salute. 'Cheers.'

The Rolls-Royce drove smoothly through the streets of Tsim Sha Tsui, past luxury hotels and expensive shops. The pavements were so densely packed that there appeared to be no space between the people: men in dark suits carrying portable phones rubbed shoulders with bare-chested labourers; sunburned tourists in shorts stared into shop windows while schoolchildren hurried by in neatly pressed uniforms, weighed down with stacks of schoolbooks in small rucksacks.

'They're going to rule the world one day, Hutch,' said Winter. 'Take my word for it.'

Hutch stared out of the window with unseeing eyes. He

felt sick and took deep breaths to try to steady his stomach. He wondered what Winter had planned for him.

'There's a billion of them,' Winter continued, lighting a cigar. 'A billion. And they work together, Hutch, that's what makes them unbeatable. Not like us and the Krauts and the Frogs, always fighting wars, always trying to fuck each other over. There's no one big enough to stand up to the Chinese – not the Americans, not the Japanese, not even a united Europe, even if there was such a thing. We're fucked, Hutch. Fucked and we don't even know it.'

The Rolls-Royce pulled up in front of the Peninsula Hotel. Winter took his cigar out of his mouth and jabbed it at the building. 'Look at that, old lad. That's class. They use Rollers for their punters, nothing but green Rollers. Costs an arm and a leg.'

Hutch didn't reply. He wasn't even listening. He was looking for a way out. He still had his passport, he could still run. There was no point in trying the airport again but he could get the hydrofoil to Macau and fly from there. But first he had to find out what it was that Winter thought he could use against him. Hutch wracked his brains. What could be worse than turning him in? What could be worse than going back to Parkhurst and spending the rest of his life behind bars?

A white-uniformed bellboy with a pillbox hat pulled open the door and Winter strode into the foyer. He surveyed the luxurious interior as if he owned the building, and put his arm around Hutch's shoulders. 'It don't get much better than this, do it? A chauffeur-driven Roller to one of the world's top hotels. I bet you never thought when we were banged up on the Isle of Wight, that we'd end up here, huh?'

He ushered Hutch over to the elevators, and stabbed at the button for the fifth floor. They rode up together in silence and walked along the plush carpet to Winter's room.

The view was spectacular but Hutch barely noticed it. He stood in the centre of the room and glared at Winter. 'Well?' he said defiantly.

'Sit down, Hutch,' said Winter, indicating a chair by the window. 'Sit down and shut up.' He stubbed his cigar out in a large crystal ashtray. Hutch stayed where he was, his hands on his hips, while Winter went over to his suitcase and took out a video cassette, then opened a cabinet to reveal a large television and a video recorder. 'Sit down,' he repeated. This time Hutch did as he was told.

Winter tapped the video cassette on his leg. For a moment he looked as if he wanted to say something, but then he shrugged and slotted the cassette into the recorder. He sat on the bed as the screen flickered. 'Don't look at me, Hutch. Look at the TV.'

Hutch stared at the flickering screen. It had obviously been filmed on a small camcorder; the picture wobbled and shook as if the person filming wasn't used to handling the equipment. It was a football match, boys eight or nine years old running after a bouncing ball, shrieking and yelling. The camcorder focused clumsily on a blond-haired boy with red cheeks wearing shorts several sizes too big for him.

'He's nine next month,' said Winter. 'He wants to play for Manchester United. He doesn't live in Manchester, in case you were thinking of looking for him. She's changed her name, of course. And his. New names, new life. She's seeing a man. A doctor. He's divorced, too. With two daughters, but his wife's got custody.'

The camcorder followed the boy as he kicked the ball

high into the air and ran after it, arms flailing. The goalkeeper, a gangly red-haired boy, rushed out of the goalmouth but he was too late and Hutch's son kicked the ball past him.

'Bit of a fluke, I thought, but a goal's a goal, right?' said Winter. Both teams of schoolboys ran back to their places to restart the game while a balding teacher in a baggy tracksuit picked the ball out of the net. 'It's a private school. Expensive. The doctor pays, of course. You should be proud of your boy, Hutch. Very proud.'

The screen went blank. Winter stood up and ejected the cassette. He pretended to throw it to Hutch, but at the last minute kept hold of it. 'No, I think not,' said Winter. 'You won't need it where we're going.'

Hutch stared at Winter, his stomach churning. 'You've changed,' he said quietly.

'Yeah? Well, we're all getting older.' He took a cigar case from his inside pocket.

'That's not what I mean and you know it. This isn't your style. You were never the sort to threaten a man's family.'

Winter smiled tightly, a grimace that was devoid of any humour. 'You never knew me on the outside.' He extracted a large cigar from the cigar case. 'Let's say I want someone to do something for me. Something dangerous. Something illegal. And say I tell whoever it is that if they do that dangerous thing for me, then I'll give him a house. Do you think he'll do it?' Winter didn't wait for Hutch to answer. 'Of course he won't,' he said. He bit the end of the cigar off and spat it towards a wastepaper basket in the corner of the room, missing by several feet. 'He's not going to trust me, he won't believe that I'll actually give him a house, right?' He reached into his jacket pocket and took out a book of matches.

'But if I go into his house late at night with a couple of heavies and a can of petrol, and if I pour the petrol over him and his wife in bed, and if I take out a box of matches . . .' Winter pulled a match out of the book and lit it. He used the match to get his cigar burning, then held it between his thumb and first finger as it burned. 'You see, Hutch, then he's going to believe that I'm going to do what I say. He's going to believe that I'll burn him and his wife and his house.' Winter tossed the match on to the carpeted floor. It spluttered and died out. 'The bad stuff he'll believe, the good stuff he won't.'

Hutch nodded. 'What time's our flight?'

JAKE GREGORY STOOD ON the veranda and stared out across Kandawgyi Lake. The rain came down in sheets, an endless torrent that beat down on the roof of the bungalow in a deafening roar. The sky above was gunmetal grey, the lake so dark it was almost black. The monsoon rain had washed the colour out of the landscape but there was no hiding the beauty of the jungle-covered hills. Gregory sipped his Diet Coke, lukewarm because he didn't trust the ice. He was only going to be in the country for twenty-four hours and if the price of avoiding diarrhoea was a warm Coke or two, he'd put up with it.

He saw the umbrella first, fluorescent orange and white stripes, moving from side to side in an almost random motion. As it came closer he saw there were two figures sheltering underneath it, stepping carefully to avoid the deeper puddles as they walked along the path to the bungalow. The taller of the two men was wearing a khaki uniform and holding the umbrella. The other man was broader and wearing a safari suit. Both had military haircuts, almost as short as Gregory's own crew cut. Gregory drained his can and put it down on a rattan table. He went to the front of the veranda and waited for his visitors to arrive. He smiled as he saw that the man in the safari suit had rolled up his trouser legs to keep them from getting wet in the downpour. It was a sensible move, but it made him look as if he was paddling in the sea.

'Mr Gregory,' said the man in the safari suit. He stepped on to the veranda, his arm extended. 'Welcome to Myanmar.' He was shorter than Gregory by several inches but kept his head tilted slightly up as if to compensate for his lack of stature.

Gregory shook the man's hand. 'General, it's good of you to come,' said Gregory. 'Shall we go inside?'

The General nodded and walked past him into the bungalow. The man with the umbrella remained resolutely in the rain. The air-conditioner was on, rumbling unobtrusively in the background.

'Can I get you a drink?' Gregory asked.

'Whisky, if you have it.'

Gregory suppressed a smile. He knew exactly what the General drank, and had bought a bottle of Johnnie Walker Black Label from the duty-free shop at the airport in Bangkok. He poured a large measure into a crystal tumbler and handed it to the General. The man with the umbrella had still made no move to come in out of the rain. Gregory closed the sliding glass door that led to the veranda and stood with his back to it as the General dropped down into a cane chair.

'So how do you find our country, Mr Gregory?' the General asked as he carefully unrolled the bottoms of his trousers. His English was flawless, the enunciation that of the British upper classes.

'Breathtaking scenery,' said Gregory.

The General smiled and savoured the bouquet of the whisky. 'Yes, our scenery is beautiful. Our temples are beautiful, too. Have you seen any of our temples?'

'I'm afraid not, no,' said Gregory.

'A pity. Scenery and temples, we have both in abundance.' He raised the whisky-filled glass. 'Other things are in short supply.' He smiled, showing white even teeth. 'So tell me, Mr Gregory, how can I help you?'

Gregory went over to a long sofa and sat down facing the General. 'Zhou Yuanyi,' he said.

'Ah yes. A thorn in my side.' The General drank his whisky slowly, savouring each swallow.

'And ours. He is swamping the east coast of America with heroin – heroin of a very high quality at a very low cost.'

The General nodded. 'A fact of which the government here is well aware, I can assure you.'

'Aware, yes. But to date you have been unable to resolve the problem.'

'There are . . . difficulties. He has a considerable number of men, highly trained, well equipped. And he has connections in Thailand.'

'Connections?'

The General drained his tumbler. Gregory picked up the bottle of Black Label and poured him another drink.

The General nodded his thanks. 'Much of Zhou's heroin is refined on our side of the border before being smuggled into Thailand. I say smuggled, but it actually goes over with the connivance of the Thai army. Zhou is not ungenerous with his associates. Several very high-ranking members of the Thai military have grown very rich thanks to Zhou. Very rich indeed.' He raised an eyebrow. 'Moral standards in Thailand are not quite as, how shall I put it, inflexible as they are here in Myanmar.'

Gregory resisted the urge to smile. Both men knew that corruption was equally rife on either side of the border. It was a way of life in South-east Asia, and it permeated from the upper echelons of government all the way down to the man on the street. 'You've tried several times to apprehend him, without success.'

The General shrugged. 'We have come close, but as you Americans say, no cigar.'

'Do you think he was tipped off?'

'Almost certainly. We've closed down several of his refineries, burned some of his poppy fields, imprisoned some of his men, but we've made no real progress. He moves too quickly. Have you been to the Golden Triangle?' Gregory nodded. 'Then you know what the terrain is like. We can't send in tanks or even jeeps, and helicopters aren't much use because his bases are too well camouflaged. Unless we know where to look, they can fly around for weeks and not see anything. But I'm not telling you anything you don't already know, Mr Gregory.'

'We in the United States appreciate the problems you have, General,' said Gregory. 'Which is why we have formulated a proposal which might interest you.'

The General gave Gregory a half-wave, indicating that he should continue. The rain beat heavily on the roof of the bungalow, abated for a few seconds, and then returned, even louder than before.

'We intend to locate Zhou's headquarters. More specifically, the man himself. I can't tell you how, but within the next few weeks we hope to have a clear indication of where he is.'

'And then?' asked the General.

'That depends on whether we can count on your co-operation or not.'

The General crossed his legs at the ankles and rested his tumbler of whisky on his knee. 'What form would my co-operation take?' he asked.

'The use of an airfield, as close to the Golden Triangle as possible. And facilities for a small contingent of American troops.'

'How small?'

'We don't envisage requiring more than twelve.'

The General raised his eyebrows in surprise. 'You intend to take on one of the most powerful warlords in Asia with a dozen men?'

'Not take on, General. Take out.'

The General leaned forward, intrigued. 'I think you should tell me exactly what you have in mind, Mr Gregory.'

The DEA executive went over to his holdall and took out another can of Diet Coke. He popped the tab, swallowed several mouthfuls of the lukewarm cola, and began to talk. The General sat and listened with rapt attention as Gregory told him what he had planned. Gregory spoke for a full ten minutes, pausing only to drink.

When he had finished, the General leaned back in his chair and stared up at the ceiling. 'You are here on a tourist visa, Mr Gregory,' he said eventually. 'And you made it quite clear that you wanted this meeting to be unofficial. Am I to assume from the secrecy that what you are proposing is not sanctioned by your government?'

'I have the full approval of the White House. If that wasn't the case, we wouldn't have access to either the manpower or the equipment.'

'And yet you are determined to keep a low profile?'

'We are quite happy for you to take the credit, General. It will demonstrate to the world that you are serious about dealing with your country's drug problem. You are free to suggest that the plan is yours and that you requested that the United States supply the necessary equipment. It will be a shining example of what co-operation between our two countries can achieve.'

The General nodded to himself, his eyes still on the ceiling. 'I don't understand why it is Zhou Yuanyi who is being targeted. There are many other drug kingpins who have much higher profiles.' He lowered his gaze so that he could watch Gregory's reaction.

'True,' admitted Gregory. 'But our assessment is that we have a higher probability of success if we go for Zhou.'

The General looked as if he were going to press the point, but instead he tapped a forefinger on the rim of his whisky tumbler. 'Of course, there will be substantial expenses incurred. On both sides.'

Gregory smiled thinly. He had been to South-east Asia enough times to know that nothing came without a price. 'We were thinking that expenses of two million dollars would be in order.'

The General pursed his lips. 'The US government offered that much in 1996 for information leading to the arrest of Khun Sa. You are asking a great deal more than information from me. I had a figure of five million in mind.'

Gregory looked pained, as if the money would be coming out of his own pocket. 'I suppose we could be persuaded to increase our fee to three million. Payable anywhere in the world, of course. In total confidence.'

'My dear Mr Gregory, I had assumed that that would be the case in any event. I hardly think either of us would want to issue receipts, now would we?' He grinned impishly, but the smile disappeared quickly as if he regretted the show of emotion. He steepled his fingers under his square chin and watched the DEA executive with unblinking brown eyes. 'Your country has earmarked almost fifteen billion dollars to fund its war against narcotics, and more than half of that will be spent trying to stop drugs coming into the country. I don't think four million dollars is an unreasonable request.' Gregory nodded agreement.

The General got to his feet and took a small white card from the top pocket of his safari suit. 'This is the number of my bank account in Geneva,' he said. 'Once the fee has been deposited, the airfield will be at your disposal.' He stood up and extended his right hand. The two men shook hands, then Gregory escorted him out on to the veranda. The soldier with the umbrella was still standing in the rain, a look of detached boredom on his face.

'One more thing,' said Gregory.

The General waited, his head on one side. Far off in the distance there was a flash of lightning.

'We would appreciate it if there was a request from your government for military aid to help quell the activities of the warlords on your border. Not a public request, of course, just so long as it is official.' There was a roll of thunder that went on for several seconds.

'So that America cannot be accused of sticking its nose in where it is not wanted?' said the General, his face breaking into an amused smile. 'Consider it done, Mr Gregory.'

Gregory watched the two men walk back along the path until they were swallowed up by the torrential rain.

HUTCH AND WINTER FLEW to Bangkok on the same plane but Winter insisted that they sit apart. Winter flew first class on the Thai Airways flight; Hutch was at the back in economy. Winter didn't explain why he wanted to travel separately, but Hutch figured that Winter was concerned about their names appearing together on the passenger list. Whatever the reason, Hutch was grateful for the separation; it gave him time to think, to look for a way out. If it hadn't been for the video that Winter had shown him, Hutch would have been tempted to run at the first opportunity. But the video had killed stone dead any thoughts of running, at least until Hutch was convinced that his son wasn't in danger.

Hutch had spent three years in Parkhurst prison with Billy Winter, and though Winter was in for armed robbery, he'd never actually shot anybody. Hutch remembered an argument he'd overheard between Winter and a young

Liverpudlian who was doing a life sentence for shooting a security guard on a wages snatch. Winter had claimed that only amateurs actually used violence; the professionals only had to threaten. A sawn-off shotgun was a prop, nothing more, he argued; a successful robbery was more often than not the result of mental intimidation rather than physical force. The Liverpudlian had taken the criticism personally and had tried to break a chair over Billy's head. Despite his small size Billy could handle himself, and Hutch could still remember the Liverpudlian's scream as Billy's foot embedded itself in the man's groin. At the time, Hutch had wondered how the kick to the groin reconciled itself with Winter's theory of non-violence, but as he sat on the Thai Airways 747 the event took on a greater significance. If necessary, if he had to protect himself, Billy Winter could be as vicious as any hardened criminal, and Hutch was certain that if he didn't do what Winter wanted, his son's life would truly be at risk.

The stewardesses rattled a trolley down the aisles, handing out trays and pouring drinks. Hutch always hated eating on planes. The prearranged trays, the casual service, the steel jugs of coffee all reminded him of prison meals.

He closed his eyes and rested his head on the back of his seat. In his mind he replayed the video that Winter had shown him. His son, the boy he hadn't seen for more than seven years. The last time Hutch had seen him he'd been a babe in arms. If Winter hadn't pointed the boy out, Hutch doubted that he'd have recognised him as his son. Kathy had refused to send him photographs of the boy, hadn't even replied to his letters. For a wild moment Hutch wondered if Winter was lying, if the boy in the video wasn't his son, but just as quickly he realised he was grasping at straws. There was no need for Winter to bluff. It wouldn't have been hard for him to have tracked down Kathy.

The flight to Bangkok took a little over two hours. Winter and the rest of the first and business class passengers were allowed off the plane first, and Hutch didn't see Winter again until they were in the Customs hall. Neither had suitcases, only hand luggage, so they walked out into the arrivals area together. There was a long queue in front of the desk where passengers booked taxis to the city, but Winter ignored it.

A broad-shouldered Thai with a thick gold chain tight around his bull neck stepped out of the crowd, grinning at Winter. They shook hands. The Thai was wearing a solid gold Rolex, studded with diamonds, and several large gold rings. He had a thin scar that ran from the top of his left ear to the side of his nose.

'This is Bird,' said Winter, patting the Thai on the shoulder. 'Bird's on the firm.'

Hutch forced a smile but made no move to shake the Thai's hand.

'Bird's going to look after you,' said Winter. 'He'll take you for a look-see at the prison.'

'Where are you going?' Hutch asked.

'The Oriental,' Winter answered. Hutch had never stayed at the Oriental, but he knew of the hotel. On the banks of the Chao Phraya River, it was consistently voted as the best in the world, with prices to match its exclusive reputation. Whatever Winter was doing these days, he was clearly not short of money.

'What's going on?'

'All in good time, old lad. All in good time.'

THE SOLITARY MAN

Winter walked away. He stopped in front of a white-uniformed driver who was holding a cardboard sign and said something to him. The man smiled and nodded and took Winter's bag from him, leading him to the exit.

Hutch looked at Bird, who grinned and asked, 'First time in Bangkok?'

Hutch shook his head. 'I've been here a few times.'

'Pat Pong, huh? You come for the girls? Thai girls are very pretty.'

'Where is the prison?'

'On the way to the city. About five miles. The car's this way.'

Bird took Hutch to the multi-storey car park close to the terminal and unlocked the door of a bright orange Ford Capri with a black vinyl roof. Bird saw the look on Hutch's face and mistook it for admiration. 'It's a 1968 two-litre Capri.'

'So I can see. I bet there aren't too many of these around.'

Bird nodded proudly. 'It's a classic.'

Hutch tried to suppress a grin. 'Oh yes, Bird. One of a kind.' He expected to see a pair of fluffy white dice hanging from the rear-view mirror but was only mildly relieved to find a garland of white and purple flowers. The dashboard had been lined with fake brown fur and a gold Buddha in a clear plastic case had been glued to the ashtray.

Hutch sat in silence until they were driving along the expressway. 'You work for Billy?' he asked.

'We're partners,' said Bird.

'In crime?'

Bird laughed, a deep-throated roar that almost deafened

Hutch. 'Partners in crime,' Bird repeated. 'That's English humour, huh?'

'Yeah. Sort of.' Hutch settled back in his seat. The air-conditioning was on full and cold air blew across his face. Hutch had been hoping that Winter was working alone, but if Bird and Winter really were partners, then maybe Bird, too, knew where a football-loving nine-year-old went to school. Hutch was running out of options.

Bird switched on the radio and flicked through the channels until he found one playing a Thai pop song. 'You like?' he asked Hutch, nodding at the speaker.

Hutch shrugged uninterestedly and looked out of the window. He knew nothing about the prisons in Thailand, other than that they were hellish places and that drug smugglers were given as long as fifty years. He wondered why Winter thought that Hutch would be able to get his friend out. It would have made more sense to use someone local. Someone like Bird.

'What's the name of the prison this guy's in?' Hutch asked.

'Klong Prem.'

'Have you been inside?'

Bird grinned. 'Not yet,' he said.

'How many prisoners?'

'Fifteen thousand or so.'

Hutch raised his eyebrows in surprise. 'What sort of security is there?'

Bird pursed his lips as he stared at the road ahead. 'I'm not sure,' he said eventually.

Hutch had expected Winter's partner to be a bit more forthcoming. 'You don't know?'

Bird shrugged noncommittally. 'That's why you're here,' he said.

'Bloody great,' sighed Hutch. 'Haven't you tried bribing one of the guards for a plan of the place?' Another shrug. Hutch shook his head in disbelief.

The Capri hit a traffic jam which seemed to stretch as far as the horizon. Bird resigned himself to a long wait.

Hutch closed his eyes. He was starting to get a headache and he massaged his temples, trying to rub away the pain.

Bird misunderstood the gesture and switched off the radio. 'You want to sleep?' he asked.

Hutch shook his head, his eyes still closed. Sleep was the last thing on his mind. He felt as if he'd boarded a roller coaster and was slowly being dragged up to the first peak, with no way of getting off, no choice other than to hang on and see what the ride held in store for him.

The traffic began to move again. Bird drove off the expressway and then made a right turn, heading west, cutting across the railway line that connected the airport to the city. The Capri rattled over the crossing and down a reddish dirt road lined with trees.

'The prison's over there,' said Bird, nodding to their left.

Hutch peered through the window. Through the trees, less than a hundred yards away, was a white-painted wall, and in the distance he could make out an observation turret, four-sided with large windows, topped by a radio mast. There were piles of dirt and stones at the edge of the road as if there was construction work in progress, but there were no labourers around. A driveway led from the dirt road to the main entrance of the prison, marked by a red, gold and blue insignia and four flags atop white poles. Inscribed in gold on a block of granite, underneath some Thai script, was written, in English, 'Klong Prem Central Prison'. Bird pulled hard on the steering wheel and headed towards the prison.

'Whoa!' shouted Hutch. 'What the hell are you doing?'

'It's okay, it's okay,' said Bird. 'Many visitors go to the prison.'

Hutch sank down into his seat. Ahead of them was a guardhouse, but its red and white barrier was raised and the brown-uniformed guard didn't even give them a second look. To the left of the driveway was a white structure that looked like an outside lavatory. Written on the side in large blue letters was 'ATM'.

'Is that a bank machine?' Hutch asked.

Bird nodded. 'Yes, so that visitors can send in money.'

Hutch's jaw dropped. This appeared to be like no other prison he'd ever seen, and he'd been in half a dozen in England. Behind the ATM stood a single-storey modern building with huge glass windows that revealed displays of gleaming furniture. The driveway curved either side of a well-tended circular garden, in the centre of which fluttered a red, white and blue Thai flag from a towering flagpole. There was a car park to the left and Bird brought the Capri to a halt next to a brand new minibus.

Hutch climbed out and wiped his forehead with the sleeve of his shirt. 'That looks like a furniture shop,' he said, nodding at the building.

'It is,' said Bird, locking the car doors. 'They make it in the prison factory.'

Hutch went over to the showroom and peered in through the window. There were tables, chairs and cabinets, all of a quality he'd expect to see in a Hong Kong department store. A middle-aged woman appeared out of the shadows inside the store, smiling broadly in anticipation of a potential sale. 'Does everyone work in the prison?' he asked Bird.

Bird shrugged his massive shoulders. 'I think so, but . . .'

'You don't know for sure.'

Bird avoided Hutch's look. Hutch shook his head and went after Bird, who was walking towards the main prison entrance. Two guards were lounging either side of an archway wide enough to admit a double-decker bus. They watched Bird and Hutch uninterestedly, and didn't appear to be carrying weapons. Hutch had the feeling that he could walk straight into the prison, right up to the huge white-painted metal gates that led into the secure area, but he stayed where he was and waited for Bird to join him.

'Visitors go there,' said Bird, pointing ahead. It was the first factual information that he'd supplied, and Hutch pointedly ignored him. This wasn't a briefing, it was a farce.

Hutch looked up at the observation tower. From a distance it had appeared to be glass-sided, but now that he was closer he could see that the windows were also barred, though they were open in places to allow in fresh air. He shielded his eyes with his hands but couldn't see anyone inside. They walked away from the archway, along a dirt road that followed the perimeter wall, though it was separated from it by a line of trees, a strip of ground-hugging vegetation and an area of bare earth.

On the right-hand side of the road a group of young men in T-shirts, jeans and baseball caps were sitting astride motorcycles, talking and smoking cigarettes. They paid Hutch and Bird as little attention as the guards had. Beyond them was a line of modern houses, painted the same white as the perimeter wall and with grey roofs. Ageing cars were parked outside several of the houses and washing blew on lines. Homes for the prison guards, Hutch guessed.

On the perimeter side of the road, in front of the line of trees that shielded the prison wall, an area had been cordoned off with white railings and inside was a large ornate shrine, bedecked with offerings of fruit and flowers. Two men in tattered white shirts tended bushes around the base of the shrine.

Hutch pretended to watch them, but his eyes roamed over the perimeter wall. It couldn't have been much more than twenty-five feet tall, with suspended wires running a foot or so above the top of it. The wire didn't appear to be electrified, nor was it barbed. Probably an alarm system, nothing more. Midway along the wall was a watchtower, open to the elements but with a circular metal roof held up by three legs. It was unoccupied. Nor did there appear to be any surveillance cameras. If it hadn't been for the sign at the entrance to the compound, Hutch would never have known it was a prison.

The base of the watchtower protruded from the wall and at the bottom of it there was a barred doorway. Hutch couldn't see whether the bars formed a gateway or a permanent barrier. He wished he could have a closer look at the barred doorway, but he doubted that he'd be allowed to walk unhindered across the bare ground to the base of the wall. Hutch shaded his eyes and examined the vegetation.

Something glittered in the sunlight. It wasn't earth, he realised. The wall was surrounded by a moat. 'That's water,' he said to Bird.

Bird nodded. 'It goes around three sides of the prison.'

'How deep is it?'

Bird shrugged carelessly. 'I don't know.'

'Hell, Bird. That's important. Can we wade across or would be have to swim?' Bird shrugged again and looked away. Hutch made a clicking sound with his tongue as he scrutinised the moat. He doubted that it was to stop prisoners escaping. It was far more likely intended to be a barrier to prevent vehicles getting too close to the walls.

Inside the wall was a building, possibly three hundred feet long and at least two storeys high, possibly three. Hutch could see the grey-tiled roof and just over half a floor. All the windows were open and he couldn't see any bars on them. It could have been an administration building, but it appeared to be unoccupied. Next to it was an equally long building, but it was lower, and all he could make out was the top of the roof. What Hutch really needed to make any sense of what he was looking at was an aerial plan of the compound, but he knew that there was no point in asking Bird if he had one. From where Hutch was standing, it looked as if the road ran the full length of the wall, and then branched off to the left, following the wall around.

It was too hot to walk, and Hutch's cotton shirt was already drenched with sweat. They went back to the car, past the same two bored guards. Two camera-bedecked tourists, Germans judging by their accents, arrived in a taxi and went over to the furniture store. Hutch guessed that the store, if not the prison itself, was on the tourist trail, which might account for the guards' lack of interest in visitors.

Bird drove slowly down the dirt road. At the far corner of the perimeter wall was a larger watchtower, with a searchlight. It had a similar barred doorway at the bottom. A hatless guard was smoking a cigarette, looking back into the prison. Hutch squinted, trying to see if the guard was armed. Bird groped under his seat and pulled out a pair of green rubber-covered binoculars and handed them to Hutch. Hutch took them gratefully and focused them on the watchtower. The guard wasn't holding a weapon, though that didn't mean he didn't have one close by. Hutch examined the doorway at the base of the watchtower through the binoculars. He could just about make out a lock, though he couldn't see what type it was.

Bird turned left, dropping down into first gear and slowing the Capri to a crawl. The perimeter wall was a different colour, beige rather than white. Ahead of them was a large shed, little more than a metal roof held up by white-painted steel beams which sheltered a line of grey and white coaches. The side windows were covered with thick wire mesh and Hutch realised they must be used for transporting prisoners. There were eight in all, and several other vehicles, mainly jeeps. There appeared to be no one around so Hutch told Bird to stop the car.

Hutch got out and went over to the nearest coach. On the side was a line of Thai writing and the prison insignia. Hutch tried the door to the driver's cab and wasn't surprised to find it locked. Next to the driver's seat were two other seats, presumably for guards. The main door was at the rear of the coach. It was also locked, but Hutch knew he wouldn't have trouble opening either door. And with security as lax it was, he doubted that he'd be stopped if he climbed in and drove one away. Hutch walked to the rear of the coach and looked in through the window, which had no bars or mesh. The seats in which the prisoners were transported were in a cage that ran almost the full length of the bus. At the back of it was a seating area, presumably for more guards.

If Winter's friend was taken out of the prison, and if he knew which coach would be used, then it wouldn't be difficult to hide a gun on board. He went back to the Capri and climbed in next to Bird. The sweat dried on his skin almost instantly. He pointed for Bird to drive on.

As far as Hutch could tell, there were no surveillance cameras and the watchtower halfway along the wall was empty. Beyond the wall was another two-storey building with a white sloping roof. A rope stretched from the windows of the top floor to the Capri would pass clear over the wall and the wire. Hutch checked out the upper windows through the binoculars. The rooms appeared to be empty. Maybe they were sleeping quarters and all the prisoners were in the prison workshops. If the rooms were where the prisoners spent the night, and if Winter's friend was on the top floor, and if they could get a rope to him, and if he could slide along it without being seen . . . Hutch smiled. There were so many 'ifs' that it was ridiculous. He wasn't drawing up a plan of action, he was clutching at straws.

Further along the road stood a terrace of two-storey houses, many with awnings in front to shield the lower rooms from the sun, and facing them was a new four-storey block of what looked like apartments for guards and other prison personnel. Some of the houses had been converted into small food shops selling noodles, soup and soft drinks, and several women looked up expectantly as the Capri drove by. The road ahead seemed to be a dead end. Bird did a three-point turn and drove back to the main road. Hutch took a last look at the perimeter wall. Unless he was missing something, it certainly wasn't a high-security institution. He hoped that Winter would have more information for him.

'Where do we go now?' he asked Bird.

'Your hotel,' Bird replied as he accelerated down the outside lane of the expressway to the city.

'The Oriental?'

Bird grinned. 'No. Not the Oriental.'

It wasn't until they drove down a narrow alleyway in the south of Bangkok that Hutch realised why Bird had smiled. At first he'd thought that they were taking a short cut but Bird brought the car to a halt in front of a shabby building. The entrance was open to the street, and a folding metal grille had been pulled back against a wall of peeling paint. A wrinkled old man wearing only knee-length shorts sat on a three-legged stool and worked a sodden toothpick in and out of his front teeth.

'You're joking,' said Hutch.

Bird gestured with his hand for Hutch to get out of the car.

Hutch opened the car door. The sounds of the street poured in, along with the heat and humidity. He took his holdall off the back seat as Bird got out of the car. Bird spoke to the old man in rapid Thai and the old man grinned and nodded. He continued to chew on his toothpick as he led the two men up a narrow staircase.

Cockroaches scattered underfoot and a small white lizard watched them from the ceiling where it hung upside down, its blinking eyes the only sign that it was a living thing. Hutch pulled a face at the smell of old sweat and rotting fruit. He looked through an open door into what was clearly a communal bathroom. There was a hole in the floor rimmed with dried faeces and a hosepipe connected to a tap on the wall. Hutch instinctively put his hand up to cover his mouth. The old man looked back over his shoulder and cackled.

Hutch's room was on the top floor. It was barely eight feet square with a single bed and a teak veneer wardrobe. There was no window and the lightbulb was of such a low wattage that murky shadows lurked in the corners. A cardboard cockroach trap lay half under the bed. He dropped his holdall on the floor. There were two sheets on the bed and no blankets, but it was so hot that Hutch doubted he'd need them. He bent down and examined the top sheet. There were tiny flecks of blood down one side. He straightened up, a look of disgust on his face.

'Why is Winter at the Oriental and I'm stuck away in this fleapit?'

'Fleapit?'

Hutch waved his arm around the room. 'This . . . this place. Why does he want me to stay here?'

'He didn't say.' He looked at his wristwatch. 'We must go.'

'Go where?'

Bird had already walked out of the room into the hallway. As the old man stepped aside to let Hutch follow him, Hutch saw that the jamb was splintered as if the door had once been kicked open. He suddenly realised that he'd left his holdall on the floor so he went back for it, then chased after Bird.

He caught up with him getting into the Capri. 'Where are we going?'

Bird waited until they were both sitting in the car before answering. The smile had vanished from Bird's face and his eyes had a hardness that hadn't been there before. 'It wasn't smart to talk about Billy in front of the old man,' he said, then started the car and drove on down the street.

It was a thirty minute drive to the Oriental Hotel, most of it through heavy traffic. The roads were hazy with exhaust fumes and motorcycles buzzed past both sides of the Capri.

Winter was waiting for them in the foyer of the hotel and when he saw the Capri pull up he walked out through the glass doors held open by two teenagers in white uniforms. He slid into the back of the car and Bird drove off.

Winter patted Hutch on the back. 'How did it go, old lad?'

Hutch twisted around in his seat and glared at him. 'What are you playing at, Billy?'

Winter raised his eyebrows in mock innocence. 'What do you mean?'

'Why am I in the Cockroach Motel and you're in a five-star hotel?'

Winter took a large cigar from his jacket pocket, bit off the end and lit it with a match. 'Best we're not seen together too much, Hutch. Best we keep our distance. You won't be there long.' The car was filling with cigar smoke, making Hutch's eyes water, so he wound down the window, but the exhaust fumes were just as bad. 'How did it go at the prison?' Winter asked.

'We drove around it. It doesn't look too secure.'

'Yeah, well, they execute the really tough criminals in Thailand,' said Winter with a grin.

'The wall doesn't look too difficult. A decent pole-vaulter wouldn't have any trouble.'

'I doubt that our man is up to pole-vaulting his way out,' said Winter.

'I was joking, Billy.'

Winter took his cigar out of his mouth and jabbed it at Hutch. 'Yeah, so was I.'

'I meant the wall is relatively easy to get over. The watchtowers look like the weak links; there seemed to be gates leading to the outside and certainly some of the towers were unoccupied.'

Winter drew deeply on his cigar. He held the smoke, then exhaled through his nostrils. 'The gates'll be locked, right?'

'I would have thought so.'

'Can you open them?'

Hutch rubbed his chin. 'Probably. They looked old, nothing too difficult. Assuming they're used, that is. They could be rusted, for all I know, or even welded shut. But I don't think I'd bother trying to pick them. We could use a Land-Rover with a winch. There's a moat but we could run a wire over it, attach a winch and rip the bloody thing out. If your man was waiting on the inside, he'd be able to walk out. Assuming he can get to the watchtower.' Winter pulled a face as if he had a bad taste in his mouth. 'What's wrong?' asked Hutch.

'Nothing,' said Winter. 'What would you need?'

Hutch shrugged. The Capri turned on to a main road and joined a line of unmoving traffic. 'That would depend on how easy it is for your man to move around inside the prison. Have you got a floor plan? Something that would give me an idea of the layout inside?'

Winter shook his head. 'Afraid not.'

'Can you get one?'

Winter took another long puff at his cigar, his pale eyes fixed on Hutch. He exhaled. 'That might not be necessary, old lad.'

Hutch frowned and twisted around in his seat. 'What do you mean?'

'I mean we're going to put you inside.'

'Inside? What, as a visitor?'

Winter's eyes narrowed. He was smiling but Hutch could see that there was no warmth in the expression. 'Not exactly,' he said.

TIM CARVER STOOD IN front of the large-scale map of the Golden Triangle which had been pinned up on the wall of his office since long before he'd been given his Bangkok posting. The map, predominantly dark and light greens, didn't do justice to the area. There was something primordial about the region, as if it belonged to a time long ago, before helicopters and automatic weapons and syringes, a time when men were hunter-gatherers, living off the land, struggling to survive because survival was a fulltime job. Carver wondered how long he'd have lasted out in such a wilderness, armed with nothing more threatening than a sharp stick. He smiled to himself. About a New York minute, he thought.

Myanmar was still shown under its old name, Burma, given to it by the British, and its capital marked as Rangoon instead of its new name of Yangon. Carver had been into Myanmar several times, as a guest of the government, to see how their armed forces were trying to deal with the opium warlords in the country's north-eastern Shan state. The four million Shan people had been fighting for independence since 1958, ten years after the British had pulled out, and for most of that time the opium trade had funded their military activities. The Burmese government wasn't just taking on a criminal organisation, it was facing armed guerrillas who were fighting for independence, and everything that Carver had seen suggested that the fight would continue for years.

Zhou Yuanyi was a different animal, though. He had no political ambitions, he was interested solely in the profits he was making from his drugs activities, and as such he was probably a softer target. Carver ran his finger along the blue strip that represented the Mekong River, then edged it upwards into the Golden Triangle. He circled the area with his finger, only a few square inches on the map but in the real world hundreds of square miles of jungle, more than enough space for an army to hide. Zhou had his poppy fields there, his heroin refineries, his supply dumps, his training grounds and his bases.

Carver went back to the desk and opened the file on Zhou Yuanyi. It was depressingly thin. Zhou was Chinese, probably from Yunnan. He'd been an officer in the Myanmar National Democratic Alliance Army, one of a number of resistance armies fighting the Burmese leadership. He'd quit the army when he was in his late twenties, taking with him a hundred or so soldiers. They set up their own camp and began levying taxes on opium traders operating in their area. More and more disenchanted guerrillas joined Zhou. He began to pay hilltribes to grow opium for him, and in the early nineties he'd started to set up his own refineries. The DEA estimated that Zhou's organisation was now responsible for up to ten per cent of the opium grown in the Golden Triangle. But whereas most of the drug warlords shipped raw opium out of the area, Zhou shipped high-grade heroin, vastly increasing his profits. Estimates of his wealth ranged from US$150 million to US$300 million, the bulk of it invested in property in Thailand and Hong Kong.

Much of what was in the file was second hand, intelligence gathered from the periphery of Zhou's operations. As Carver had told his boss, there were no photographs of the man, or his lieutenants, not even descriptions. Even the name on the file might not be genuine. The agents who had tried to get closer to the centre had all ended up dead.

Carver ran his hand through his hair and massaged the back of his neck. His first thought had been that Jake Gregory had set him an impossible task. How was he expected to do what the Burmese army had tried to do and failed? How was he supposed to get a man who had never been photographed and who was surrounded by hundreds of armed men? A man who was prepared to brutally torture and murder anyone he suspected of planning to betray him? Gregory hadn't even given Carver time to voice his reservations. Sitting in the airport restaurant he'd outlined his scheme, and Carver's role in it. There had been no discussion; Gregory hadn't even asked Carver for his opinion on the operation.

Carver flicked through the file. The last page was a list of names, members of Zhou's organisation who'd been imprisoned. Most of them were nothing more than mules, couriers who'd been caught trying to smuggle heroin out of the country, but a few were Thai middlemen, the equivalent of wholesalers, holding stocks of the drug before passing it on to the couriers. The arrests had been so low grade that Carver doubted that Zhou was even aware of them. In all, just two hundred kilos of Zhou's heroin had been seized in the past twelve months. He probably spilled as much in his refineries.

Carver took out the list and ran his eyes down it. He needed a man on the inside. Someone he could use. Someone he could send into the Golden Triangle. Someone expendable.

'YOU'VE GOT TO BE joking,' said Hutch, his drink halfway to his lips. He put the glass of beer down on the bar. 'No way.'

Winter raised his eyebrows in mock surprise. 'I thought you'd jump at the chance,' he said.

Hutch glared at the older man. Bird sat a few feet away, saying nothing. 'I'm not going inside. You can't make me.'

Winter sipped his brandy and Coke. 'Look, you're making a big thing out of nothing,' he said. 'You'll be inside for a week, no more. One week. Seven days. You did four years. You can do seven days standing on your head.'

'You don't know what you're talking about.'

Winter put his head close to Hutch's, so close that Hutch could smell the brandy on his breath. 'I did twelve years, old lad, don't forget that. I did a twelve stretch, so don't let me hear you crying about seven fucking days.'

'Why can't you speak to someone who's already done time there? They'll be able to tell you about the layout. Or bribe one of the guards.'

Winter swivelled around in his seat. Facing the bar was a large window, ten feet high and almost twenty feet wide. Through it he could see six rows of benches, filled with young Thai girls wearing white toga-like dresses. Each had a number on a small blue badge pinned to her chest. Some of the girls watched a television set, several were painting their nails, and one sat knitting, her mouth moving silently as she counted stitches. Most sat with sublimely bored expressions on their faces. When Hutch and Winter had first walked into the room the girls had all perked up and given them beaming smiles, but when it became clear that the men weren't in a rush to make their selection, they had settled back into inactivity.

'Because we have to make contact with our man inside,' said Winter. 'We have to tell him what we're planning to do. You're going to have to show him where to go, what he's got to do. You're going to have to hold his hand.'

Hutch looked at Winter sharply. 'Is he okay? There's something you're not telling me, isn't there?'

Winter studied Hutch for a few seconds. 'He's gone a bit stir-crazy, that's all. That's why you have to go in. He needs calming down.'

'Bloody terrific,' said Hutch. He put his head in his hands and closed his eyes. 'You're a bastard, Winter.'

'I'm no happier about this than you are. Believe me. I'm

not here by choice, either.' He looked at the girls, a slight smile on his face. 'See anything you fancy, Bird?' he said, speaking out of the corner of his mouth as always.

Bird shrugged uninterestedly. 'Thirty-eight.'

Winter peered at the girl wearing badge number thirty-eight. 'Good choice,' he said.

'And twenty-two,' added Bird.

Winter nodded. 'Another cracker. I had her a couple of weeks ago. Great mouth. She's got these razor scars all over her left wrist, long cuts but not deep. She did the first three when her mother died when she was a kid. The second group of three was after her brother crashed her motorcycle and the third lot was when she caught her farang boyfriend in bed with her sister. Now her wrist looks like a cheese-grater. What do you reckon to that, Hutch?' Hutch said nothing. 'Self-mutilation brought on by low self-esteem,' said Winter. 'Who said that Open University course was a waste of time?' He laughed and beat on the bar with the flat of his hands. 'Bloody playing at it, she was. I saw a guy slit his wrists for real in Durham. Red stuff all over the place. Dead in a minute. What about you, Hutch? See anything you want? Any last requests?'

Hutch didn't look around. The last thing he wanted was a massage. What he wanted was to be back home in Hong Kong with his dogs. 'How are you going to do it? How are you going to get me inside?'

Winter moved his bar stool closer to Hutch's. He put his arm around his shoulder. 'Piece of cake, old lad. Bird and I've got it all worked out.' He waved Bird over, who joined them in the huddle. 'We're gonna fix it so that you get arrested on a drugs charge. They'll throw you in with—'

'What!' said Hutch.

Winter patted him on the back. 'Hear me out, will you? We set you up. We put a small package of drugs in your luggage, then grass you to the cops. They pull you in, you say it's not down to you, but they'll throw you in the clink until they get the stuff tested.'

'Billy, they put you away for life for drugs here. Life and some.'

Winter wagged a finger at Hutch. 'That's the kicker: it won't be drugs.'

'So they find out I'm carrying talcum powder? They're not going to put me into prison for talc, are they?'

'They'll send the stuff away to be tested, Hutch. That'll take time.'

'What if they test it there and then? It's not going to taste like heroin, is it?'

Winter smiled thinly. 'You've been watching too many movies,' he said. 'The cops don't stick in a finger and suck it. It's evidence, right, and evidence has to be uncontaminated. It's sealed and sent off to a lab. And it'll take them at least five days to get the tests back.'

Hutch looked across at Bird. Bird nodded reassuringly. 'There's a backlog,' he said. 'Five days, maybe six. Seven at most.'

'Then what?' asked Hutch. 'They find out that it's talc or chalk dust, then what? They're going to wonder what the hell I'm playing at.'

'We've taken care of that,' said Bird. 'A man will come forward and claim that he did it, that you two had had a row and he was trying to get revenge. He'll get six months, a year at most.'

'That's the worst possible scenario,' interrupted Winter.

'We'll spread some money about and he'll get away with a fine. There'll be apologies all round, the chief of police'll probably shake you by the hand. But it'll be too late, you'll have cased the joint from the inside and briefed our man. Then you can fuck off back to Hong Kong, no hard feelings.'

'No hard feelings!' repeated Hutch in disbelief.

'It'll be a breeze,' said Winter. 'I'll even throw in a few grand for expenses.' He patted Hutch on the back. 'Seven days, Hutch. Maximum. You can do a seven-day stretch.'

Hutch shuddered. 'I don't know, Billy. It's the door clanging shut. The bars on the windows. The walls. It's . . .'

'It's seven days, Hutch. I know what you mean, I know what it's like inside, but last time you were facing life, with no parole date set. This time you're going to know that you'll be out in a week.'

'Do you know how many people are in that prison?'

'Fifteen thousand. Give or take.'

'So how do you expect me to find him? A needle in a haystack doesn't come close.'

Winter finished his drink and waved the barman over and ordered another before speaking. 'They put all the foreigners in the same place. Zone two. You'll be able to find him.'

'You haven't thought this through,' said Hutch. 'Even if you get him out, he's going to be trapped in Bangkok. They'll watch the airports, the ports . . .'

'I've got that in hand,' said Winter. 'We'll go up north and across the border into Burma. I've got contacts there. Good contacts. I can get us new passports there and get a ship to anywhere in the world. We'll be home free.'

'It isn't as easy as that,' said Hutch.

'This is Thailand. It's exactly as easy as that. There's a town up near the border called Fang. We'll pick up a guide there and he'll take us across. It happens all the time, every day. It's one of the most active smuggling routes in the world.'

Hutch shook his head. 'I can't do it,' he said.

Winter took his hand off Hutch's back. He looked across at Bird and raised an eyebrow. Bird went over to stand in front of the window and peered at the girls.

Winter and Hutch sat in silence. 'You don't have any say in the matter,' Winter said eventually. 'You'll do as you're fucking told.'

Hutch leaned forward, his hands clasped together either side of his glass. 'Billy, I wouldn't be able to take it. I'd crack up.'

'You're exaggerating.'

Hutch shook his head. 'You don't know me, you don't know what's inside my head.'

'I shared a cell with you, Hutch,' said Winter, his voice a menacing whisper. 'You know what we went through in choky. I know you better than you know yourself. All you need is the motivation, and I'm giving you that. If you don't do it, I'll slap you harder than you've ever been slapped in your life. And then I'll slap your kid.' He paused and stared at Hutch with cold, hard eyes. 'You're going inside.'

Hutch's hands began to shake and his beer sloshed over the side of his glass. Winter put a hand on Hutch's shoulder in a father-like gesture of concern.

Hutch shook him away. 'Don't touch me,' he hissed.

THE SOLITARY MAN

NIKOLAI KONOVALOV WIPED HIS forehead with a grubby handkerchief. He doubted that he'd ever get used to the heat and humidity. Or the mosquitoes. He'd studied for his degree in Kiev and completed his PhD in St Petersburg and he was more used to sub-zero temperatures and snow drifts than he was to the unrelenting sauna that was the Golden Triangle. He tucked the wet handkerchief into the pocket of his lab coat and checked the timer on his workbench. Fifteen minutes. Long enough for the morphine and acetic anhydride to bond together. Simple chemistry, the sort of process he'd done at school, never mind university. A child with a chemistry set could do the same, provided he had access to morphine. Konovalov had access to morphine, enough morphine to keep a thousand people in euphoria for a year.

He turned off the gas burner and waited for the mixture to cool. The heat of the burner made the air inside the hut almost unbearable. The walls and ceiling were of corrugated iron, and while there were large holes cut in the walls to allow ventilation, it was still an oven. A floor-mounted fan at the end of the bench did its best to keep the air moving, but it was fighting a losing battle. Konovalov picked up the fan and put it closer to the huge glass flask containing the mixture to speed up the cooling process.

When the flask was cool enough to touch, he called for his assistant, a young Thai boy who was waiting outside. Together they wrapped a thick cloth around the neck and swivelled it down, carefully pouring the contents through a carbon filter to remove the impurities. It was ironic, Konovalov thought as he watched the clear liquid bubble through the filter, that he was going to such trouble to keep contaminants out. By the time the drug reached its end users, it would probably have been adulterated with chalk, talcum powder, brick dust, or any one of a dozen other substances. That was no reason for him to take any less care. Nikolai Konovalov was a professional, and he took a pride in his work.

The boy removed the filter and put it in a bin in the corner of the hut. He helped Konovalov lift the twenty-gallon glass flask off the floor and on to the bench. Konovalov had already weighed out the sodium carbonate and he nodded for the boy to proceed. The boy sprinkled the crystals into the liquid and stirred it with a long wooden pole. Konovalov peered at the flask, watching as the crude heroin particles solidified and dropped to the bottom. More basic chemistry, he thought. A child could do it. In fact, he hoped to get to the stage where his young assistant did most of the work. The boy was eager to learn, and he had steady hands. Konovalov nodded and the boy grinned, pleased at the approval.

· Together they waited until all the heroin had been deposited at the bottom of the flask, then they poured the mixture through a large filter. Konovalov used a stainless-steel spatula to scrape off the crystals and deposit them in another flask, this one containing a slurry of alcohol and charcoal, another step in the purification process. He filtered out the charcoal then put the flask on the burner.

There was an extractor fan set in the roof above the bench and Konovalov flicked on the switch. The fan growled and began to spin and only then did he light the burner. The alcohol fumes could be explosive in a confined space, and more than one of Zhou Yuanyi's jungle laboratories had gone up in flames before Konovalov had arrived on the scene. That was why he was earning fifty thousand dollars a month, paid into a Swiss bank account; not to carry out basic chemistry, but to ensure that the conversion from opium to injectable heroin went off without incident. Konovalov worked for eighteen hours a day, seven days a week, and he'd been in the jungle for eight months without a break. He didn't resent the long hours, not when he was being paid so well. As an industrial chemist in Russia it would have taken him ten years to earn fifty thousand dollars. It had taken him only minutes to accept the offer made by Zhou's representative in a bar in St Petersburg. Konovalov was single, his father had died of liver cirrhosis years earlier and his mother had remarried and moved to a Moscow suburb. He had no reason to stay, and fifty thousand reasons to go.

It took an hour for the alcohol to evaporate, during which time he prepared a new flask of morphine and acetic anhydride, ready to start the process again. The laboratory functioned as a production line – it had to if the Russian was to keep up with Zhou's demands for the finished product. Zhou had three such laboratories at different locations within the area of the Golden Triangle he controlled.

At the far end of Konovalov's laboratory were the drums of chemicals Konovalov needed, most of them with Chinese labels, the quality as good as anything he'd be able to buy in Russia. In some cases Konovalov reckoned the Chinese chemicals were better than he'd be able to buy in his own country because black marketeers in Russia weren't above adulterating their wares in the same way that street pushers diluted their drugs with whatever was available.

With the alcohol gone, Konovalov was left with white granules of heroin. The final stage in the preparation of No. 4 heroin was the most dangerous. It involved dissolving the granules in alcohol once more and then carefully adding hydrochloric acid and ether. Ether vapour was even more explosive than alcohol and had to be carefully handled. The boy stood at Konovalov's shoulder as he poured in the acid. White flakes began to form in the mixture. Konovalov put out his hand and without being asked the boy gave him the wooden pole, like a nurse assisting a surgeon. As Konovalov stirred, more flakes began to form, like a snowstorm. All that remained was for him to filter and dry the flakes and he'd have another batch of pure heroin. So far that day he'd produced five kilograms and it wasn't even midday.

HUTCH LOOKED AT HIS watch. It was almost three o'clock. Bird was coming around to the guest house at four. He paced up and down at the end of the bed. The room was claustrophobic and the lack of a window made it feel like a prison cell. He wondered if that was why Winter had booked him in that particular guest house. Hutch shuddered.

'Seven days,' he whispered to himself. 'It's only seven days.' He'd done two months in solitary confinement after an early escape attempt from Parkhurst, and he'd got through that. It hadn't been easy, but he'd done it.

He stood with his back to the door and gently banged his shoulders against the wood. 'Seven days,' he said. Like Winter had said, he'd be able to do it standing on his head.

He couldn't face waiting alone in the room with its cheap furniture and blood-flecked sheets any longer so he went downstairs. He wandered aimlessly through the hot, crowded streets, his mind in turmoil. He kept thinking about the boy he hadn't seen for more than eight years, and his wife Kathy, who he'd loved with all his heart and who'd dropped him like a stone when he'd been given his life sentence.

He walked by a line of small stalls where women were diligently threading orchids and flowers into garlands. As he turned a corner he came across a small outdoor temple. Worshippers, mainly women, lit sticks of sickly-sweet incense and prayed, and half a dozen young Buddhist monks in saffron robes were engaged in earnest conversation at the entrance. A group of motorcyclists was ranged in front of a red traffic light, and while most gunned their engines impatiently, several had their hands together in prayer as they stood astride their machines.

Hutch peered through the black and gold railings which surrounded the temple. It was a long time since Hutch had prayed. A long time. And he doubted that a prayer to any god would solve his present problems. Nevertheless, he was touched by the intensity with which the Thais went about their worship, totally focused on the shrine and the trappings of their religion and ignoring the heat and noise and pollution. He held on to the railings with both hands as he watched the Thais at prayer.

A few paces along to his left, close to the entrance to the

temple, an old woman sat next to a metal table on which was a stack of small red-painted wooden cages containing tiny birds. A good-looking woman with a Chanel bag on her arm handed the old lady some money and was given one of the cages. She carried it into the grounds of the temple and opened it. The birds flew skywards and the woman watched them go before handing the empty cage back. Hutch guessed that releasing the birds was some sort of tribute or celebration.

The old woman saw him looking at the caged birds and she smiled, revealing a gap where her two front teeth had been. She said something to him in Thai but Hutch knew as little of the language as he did the religion. He returned her smile and went over to her table. There were six cages in all, each containing six birds.

'How much?' he asked, picking up one of the cages.

The old woman's smile widened and she held up five fingers. Hutch had no way of knowing if she meant five, fifty or five hundred baht. He took out his wallet. The woman pointed at the cage he was holding. Hutch shook his head and waved a hand over the table. 'All of them,' he said. The old woman frowned, not understanding. Hutch pointed at the cages one at a time. She nodded enthusiastically. Hutch gave her a handful of banknotes, then he picked up the first cage and set its occupants free. He smiled as they flapped upwards in a flurry of brown feathers, chirping furiously. He opened the second cage, and the third, releasing the birds.

'You're wasting your time,' said a voice behind him.

Hutch whirled around. It was Bird, smiling good naturedly.

'Are you following me?' Hutch asked.

Bird shrugged but didn't answer. 'They put something in the food that they get addicted to. Like heroin. The birds return to her and she puts them back in their cages and sells them again.'

'Yeah?' Hutch looked at the three remaining cages. He picked one up. He realised that it didn't matter. He wasn't doing it for them, he was doing it for himself. He opened the lids and set the last of the birds free. They flew upwards and he shielded his eyes with his hands to protect them from the glare of the sun as he watched them go.

'What is it, Bird? Did Billy tell you to keep an eye on me? Did he tell you I'd run?'

'It's time to go,' said Bird. He was wearing a light blue safari suit with short sleeves.

Together they walked back to Hutch's guest house and up to his room. Bird took a plane ticket from his inside jacket pocket and gave it to Hutch.

'Is Billy coming?' Hutch asked.

'No. He doesn't want to be seen here. The police will come around later and ask questions. We don't want anyone to tell them that you had a farang visitor.'

Hutch looked at the ticket. It was to Hong Kong. 'What if the police don't put me into the prison?' Hutch asked. 'What if they give me bail?'

'They won't,' said Bird. 'They take drug smuggling very seriously here, more seriously than murder. You will be carrying what appears to be a kilogram of pure heroin. They will discover that you have been staying here, and they know that this guest house is often used by drug gangs as a recruiting centre for couriers. You won't get bail.'

'And what do I tell them?'

'You can say that you were here on a short holiday, or

for a business meeting. You stayed here to save money. And you've no idea how the drugs got in your bag. You play the innocent tourist. Of course, they will not believe you.'

Hutch wrapped his arms around his waist as if he were hugging himself. 'How can you be sure they'll put me in with this guy Harrigan?'

'We can't, but you'll be able to find him.' Bird took a photograph from his jacket pocket and showed it to Hutch. 'This is Ray Harrigan.'

Hutch studied the picture. It was six inches by four inches but it looked like a passport photograph, and the pale blue eyes stared out blankly as if the man's thoughts were elsewhere when it was taken. He had black, curly hair that was drapped across a broad forehead, and a narrow, almost pointed chin. The lips were thin and tightly set, and the over-riding impression Hutch had was that it was a cruel face, the face of a man who would enjoy inflicting pain.

As Bird took the photograph back, there was a knock at the door: three taps close together followed by a pause, then two more taps. Bird opened the door and let in a small wiry Thai wearing a Calvin Klein sweatshirt, shorts and flip-flop sandals. He was carrying a white plastic bag. He handed the bag to Bird, who dropped it on to the bed and opened it.

'Is that it?' asked Hutch, peering inside. He reached out his hand but Bird pulled the bag away. 'You musn't touch it, we don't want your fingerprints on it. That's why he's here. He's the one who's going to call the police, and then confess later.'

Hutch looked across at the man in the Calvin Klein sweatshirt. The man smiled at Hutch and nodded several times. 'He doesn't understand English,' said Bird.

'And he's happy about taking the fall for this?'

'Taking the fall?' repeated Bird, frowning.

'He's going to confess to planting the stuff, right? How does he feel about going to prison?'

Bird burped, a long, loud belch that seemed to fill the tiny room. 'Like we said, he'll probably just get fined. And if he does go to prison, we'll look after his family and he'll be well paid. Where's your bag?' asked Bird.

'Under the bed,' said Hutch. He knelt down and pulled it out. Bird spoke to the man in Thai who put the package of white powder in the bottom of Hutch's holdall.

'Anything else to go in it?' asked Bird.

Hutch shook his head. Bird said something else to the man, who nodded and zipped the bag closed.

'Don't open it again,' said Bird. 'For any reason.'

Hutch looked at the ticket again. The flight left in three hours. They didn't want him to have time to think, to change his mind.

'You have your passport?'

Hutch patted the back pocket of his jeans. 'Are you coming to the airport with me?'

'No. Billy says you are to go alone.'

Hutch picked up the bag. 'I'll be seeing you, then.'

Bird held up a hand. 'We must leave first. Wait ten minutes and then catch a taxi to the airport.'

Hutch dropped his bag on the floor. Bird put his palms together in a prayer-like gesture and pressed the fingertips to his chin, bowing his head slightly. It was a wai, the Thai way of saying hello or bidding farewell. *'Chaw-di,'* he said. 'Good luck.'

'All the luck I've had so far has been bad, Bird. I don't expect it to get any better. Now fuck off and leave me alone.' He turned his back on the two men and stared at the wall until their footsteps had faded down the stairs and all he could hear was the street sounds outside.

RAY HARRIGAN SAT WITH his back up against the cell wall, his knees drawn up against his chest. Something buzzed by his ear but he was too tired to swat it away. He had been working all day in the prison's leather factory, sewing bags by hand, and he was bone tired.

'You okay, Ray?' asked the Canadian.

Harrigan shrugged. 'I've been better.'

'Rough day at the office?'

Harrigan snorted. It was as close as he could get to a laugh. 'I'm knackered,' he said.

The Canadian sat down next to Harrigan and coughed throatily. 'I don't know why you don't buy your way out of the factory,' he said, and spat on the floor.

'Nah, I'd rather work. What else would I do all day?'

'There are ways of passing the time,' the Canadian said. He pulled a cloth bag out of his shirt pocket and undid the drawstring.

'Not fifty years,' said Harrigan.

The Canadian took a syringe out of the bag. 'It goes faster this way,' he said.

'Jesus, it was drugs got us put in here. Why would I want to inject the stuff into my veins?'

The Canadian chuckled. 'Because it feels good.'

Harrigan watched as the Canadian prepared his heroin. 'How long have you been using?' he asked as the Canadian wrapped his shoelace tourniquet around his arm and popped up a vein.

'Eight years, I guess. I started sniffing, you know, chasing the dragon. Guy in Hong Kong showed me how.' The Canadian began to cough again, a dry, hacking cough that made his whole body shake. He held the syringe away from his body until the coughing fit subsided.

Harrigan ran his fingers through his dirty hair. 'How come heroin's so easy to get in here?' he asked. 'It doesn't make any sense to me.'

The Canadian rubbed his nose with the back of his hand, the syringe needle narrowly missing his right eye. 'This is Thailand,' he said. 'They send you to prison for possessing the stuff, then the guards sell it to you.'

'The guards?'

'How do you think it gets in here?' the Canadian asked. He shoved the needle into the raised vein and slowly withdrew a small amount of blood. Harrigan watched, fascinated, as the blood swirled into the heroin mixture. The Canadian sighed and slowly depressed the plunger, pushing the drug into his system.

'Doesn't it hurt?' asked Harrigan.

'A bit,' admitted the Canadian. 'But it's nothing compared with the buzz. You've never tried? Not even smoked the stuff?'

'Not me,' said Harrigan.

'Like I said, it'll help pass the time.'

'I don't want to pass the time,' said Harrigan venomously. 'Anyway, they said they'd get me out. They promised.'

The Canadian's eyes began to blink. 'What are you talking about?' The empty syringe fell from his fingers and clattered on the floor.

'They promised,' repeated Harrigan quietly. 'They fucking promised.'

BILLY WINTER DREW DEEPLY on his large Cuban cigar and watched a blonde girl in her twenties rub suntan lotion along her smooth, shapely legs. She looked up and saw him staring at her. Winter raised his cigar in salute but she pretended not to notice. Winter grinned and put the cigar back in his mouth. A poolboy hovered and Winter pointed at his empty glass. 'Brandy and Coke,' he said, his eyes still on the girl. 'A double. With ice.' The poolboy scurried away.

The blonde's bikini was the flimsiest of things: the top was barely enough to conceal her full breasts, the bottom little more than a thong. Her tan was already a deep, golden brown, and the sun had bleached her hair almost white. Winter blew a tight plume of smoke through pursed lips. He was lying in the shade of a spreading umbrella, wearing a pair of swimming trunks and with a white towel draped over his lap.

Another blonde, a few years older and wearing a bright blue swimsuit, pulled herself out of the pool and walked over to the girl on the sunlounger. Without asking she took the bottle and poured a little of the lotion into the palm of her hand. The younger girl rolled on to her front and unhooked her bikini top. The older blonde began to massage in the lotion, using both hands. Even from the other side of the pool, Winter could see that her fingers were pushing deep into the girl's flesh. The girl on the sunlounger opened her legs, allowing the older girl to rub the inside of her thighs. Winter was reasonably certain that they were doing it for his benefit.

He'd seen the older of the two blondes in the hotel elevator that morning. Then she'd been wearing a short cotton dress, skin-tight in all the right places and a blue almost as vibrant as her swimming costume. Winter was sure she was on the game. She had a hooker's eyes, pale green and almond-shaped, and she hadn't avoided his stare as he'd asked her what floor she'd wanted. Winter had spent a lifetime paying for sex and he was as expert at recognising prostitutes as they were at identifying prospective clients. Winter had been tempted to ask her then and there if she'd go to his room with him, but the elevator had stopped and a young couple had got in. The blonde had given Winter a small shrug, as if recognising that an opportunity had been lost.

Winter knew that women didn't find him instantly attractive; even when he'd been in his prime he hadn't had the face or the physique that pulled women towards him, and he'd never had a good line of chat. It wasn't that he was shy, or lacked confidence, but he'd always despised small talk. Winter knew that women didn't open their legs for him because they fancied him, but because he had money and power, and he also knew that these were far greater aphrodisiacs than a strong jaw and rippling biceps.

The older woman wiped her hands on a towel, lay back on her sunlounger and put on a pair of sunglasses. She raised her knees slightly and opened a magazine. The other girl said something and they both laughed like schoolgirls. Winter could feel himself growing hard. He took a long pull on his cigar. As he exhaled he saw Bird walking through reception. Winter gave him a half-wave and Bird came over, his gold bracelet and neck chain glinting in the sun. Winter was always amused by the tasteless jewellery favoured by Bird and his fellow Thais; they had all the class of an East End used-car dealer, and even the gold seemed a brighter yellow than he was used to seeing back in Europe.

'Everything okay?' he asked as Bird walked up and sat down on the neighbouring sunlounger.

'No problems,' said Bird.

'What about the stuff?'

'He was a bit worried, like you said he would be. He wanted to check it. I told him that he couldn't touch the package. Because of fingerprints.'

'And he was convinced?'

'I think so.' Bird looked at his diamond-studded gold Rolex. 'He should be at the airport soon. The plane leaves in one hour.'

Winter nodded, satisfied. 'He's going to go apeshit when he finds out,' he chuckled.

'Apeshit?' repeated Bird.

'Apeshit. Crazy. Very unhappy.' He punctuated each word with a jab of his cigar.

'How do you know he won't tell the police what happened?'

Winter looked at Bird over the top of his sunglasses. 'Because I know him, Bird. I know how he thinks, I know how he reacts. I spent twelve months banged up with him, he's an open book to me.' Winter flicked ash from his cigar on to the floor, ignoring an ashtray on the table next to him. He swung his legs off the sunlounger and leaned towards Bird. 'Let me tell you about Chris Hutchison,' he said, his voice a soft growl. 'Throughout his life he's had one philosophy, one creed that he lives by.' He paused for a few seconds, checking that he had Bird's undivided attention. 'There is no problem so big, no situation so unpleasant, that Mrs Hutchison's little boy can't run away from it.' Winter raised his eyebrows and smiled. 'That's how he's lived his whole life. He ran away from home when he was fifteen. His father used to knock him about a bit, his mother was an alcoholic. His first serious girlfriend dumped him and he ran away to the navy. He served five years, mostly as an electrical engineer, and when he left went through a succession of jobs. None lasted for more than a year. Every time he had a problem, he'd quit.'

Bird pulled a face. 'He's a coward?'

Winter shook his head. 'No, he's not a coward. If he has to fight, he fights. He killed a man in prison, stabbed him in the throat. It's nothing to do with cowardice, it's to do with avoiding unpleasant situations. It's to do with escaping. And you're right, under normal circumstances he'd do a deal with the cops, but that's not an option for him now. His son is his weak spot, he has no choice but to do what I say. He'll hate it, he won't stop thinking of ways of getting away from the situation, but so long as I know where the boy is and he doesn't, I've got him by the short and curlies.'

Bird frowned, but before he could ask for an explanation of 'short and curlies', the poolboy returned with Winter's brandy and Coke. The poolboy put the glass down on the table next to Winter's sunlounger and picked up the empty one.

'See those girls over there?' Winter asked, nodding in the direction of the blondes.

'Yes, sir,' said the poolboy.

'Take them over a bottle of champagne. The best you've got, right?'

'Yes, sir.'

Winter swung his legs back up on the sunlounger as the poolboy dashed away. 'Bird, it don't get much better than this, do it?' he asked, and sucked on the end of his cigar like a baby feeding.

HUTCH PAID OFF THE taxi driver and walked inside the terminal. He stared up at one of the departure screens, looking for his flight. Several flights had been delayed but his was on time. He rubbed his chin as he stared up at the list of destinations: London, New York, Paris, Sydney. Places far, far away, cities where a man could hide and never be found, where new identities could be bought and old ones lost, where a man could start again if he didn't have a young son who wanted to play for Manchester United when he grew up.

'Damn you, Billy,' he muttered to himself. His hands were sweating and he put the holdall on the floor and wiped them on his jeans. Two policemen in brown uniforms walked by. One of them looked at Hutch, but he was listening to his companion and his face was an expressionless mask. Hutch bent down and picked up his holdall again. He figured that the phone call had probably already been made. The police would have been tipped off: his name, a description, and the fact that he had a kilo of heroin in his bag. It was just a matter of time before they grabbed him. He looked over his shoulder at the two policemen, but they were heading out of the terminal, still deep in conversation.

Hutch took his passport and ticket from his jacket pocket and went over to check in. He waited behind an Indian family who seemed to have packed the entire contents of their house into cardboard boxes. An elderly man in a grubby white turban was arguing with two young Thai girls about an excess baggage charge, but eventually he handed over a wad of banknotes, grumbling loudly. Hutch was checked in with a minimum of fuss. They looked at his passport, took his departure tax from him, and gave him his boarding card. He looked at his wristwatch. There was still an hour to go before his flight was due to board. He could feel his pulse racing and his forehead was bathed in sweat. He took several deep breaths and went over to immigration control.

The immigration officer who took his passport was a middle-aged man with skin the colour of malt whisky. He looked at Hutch, then at the photograph in the passport, then back at Hutch. Hutch smiled but his lips seemed to drag across his teeth and he knew that it was more of a snarl. The immigration officer flicked through the passport, seemingly at random. Hutch looked away. Two policemen were standing at the entrance to immigration control, and they were both staring at him. Hutch's heart began to pound and he felt light headed as if he was about to pass out. He took off his glasses and polished them on the edge of his shirt, concentrating on cleaning the lenses in an attempt to take his mind off his predicament. He couldn't understand why he was so nervous, because there was no way of changing what was about to happen. It would go down exactly as Billy had said: the police would stop him, they'd find the package, he'd be arrested and thrown into prison, and a week later he'd be released. When he looked back at the immigration officer his passport was already on the shelf in front of him. Hutch nodded, picked it up, and walked through.

The departure area was packed and there was hardly a vacant seat to be found. He wandered through the duty-free area, past shelves piled high with cigarettes, alcohol and perfume, and threaded his way through a crowd of Japanese tourists to a cafeteria. He joined the queue and helped himself to a cup of coffee, then found an empty table where he sat and sipped it. A group of Cathay Pacific stewardesses walked by, giggling, and one of them flashed him a shy smile. She reminded him of Chau-ling, and his mind flashed back to Hong Kong and his kennels. He wondered what Chau-ling was doing, and what she'd think when she discovered that he'd been arrested on drug-smuggling charges. His friends, too; how would they react when they heard the news?

Hutch stared at the holdall as he sipped his coffee. He wondered how the professional drug couriers managed to control their nerves. He was only carrying a kilogram of innocuous powder and facing a week in prison; the real smugglers knew that they'd be behind bars for fifty years or more if they got caught. It almost defied belief that anyone would risk a life sentence for a few thousand dollars. His hand shook as he lifted the coffee cup to his lips. A week. He could manage a week.

Hutch wondered how far they'd let him go before they arrested him. They could have taken him when he'd checked in, or at immigration. He doubted that they'd wait until he was on the plane. He looked at his wristwatch again.

Forty-five minutes before the plane was due to leave. Some time within the next three-quarters of an hour they'd come for him. He sipped his coffee again. It was tasteless. Hutch slumped back in his seat and closed his eyes. The tension was painful; he felt as if he had a strap across his chest, so tight that he could barely breathe. He wiped his hands on his trousers.

'Passport.' Hutch opened his eyes. A Thai police officer in his fifties stood in front of Hutch, his hands on his hips. His right hand was only inches from a large revolver in a black leather holster. The dark brown uniform was immaculate and the silver badge on his chest gleamed under the fluorescent lights of the cafeteria.

Hutch heard the squeak of a boot behind him and he looked over his shoulder. Two younger policemen stood there, and behind them two men in polo shirts and jeans. Hutch looked back at the senior officer. He handed over his passport and boarding card and the policeman scrutinised the names on both.

'You are Warren Hastings?'

'Yes.'

'Come with us.' The policeman nodded at his colleagues and they stepped forward. Hutch reached for his holdall but one of the men in polo shirts rushed forward and beat him to it.

'That's my bag,' said Hutch.

'We will take care of it,' said the officer. 'Come with us.'

Hutch pushed back his chair and stood up. 'What's wrong? Is there something wrong with my passport?' It was important that he played the part of the bewildered innocent, so that when they eventually discovered that the package didn't contain drugs everything would be in character. Heads began to turn in Hutch's direction. He felt his cheeks flush red with embarrassment.

'Come with us,' said the officer, his hand sliding over the butt of his gun. He thrust his square jaw forward as if daring Hutch to argue.

Hutch's arms were seized just above the elbows.

'Okay, okay, there's no need to grab me,' said Hutch. He tried to shrug off the hands but they gripped tighter. People were openly staring and a sudden hush fell over the cafeteria.

The two policemen who were holding Hutch twisted him around and marched him away from the table. 'Look, there's been some mistake,' Hutch protested.

They took him out of the cafeteria, up an escalator and along a corridor. At the far end of the corridor was a door with a small glass window at head height. One of the policemen opened the door and went in first. Hutch felt a hand push him in the small of the back and he stumbled across the threshold. A man in a white coat moved nimbly to the side to avoid Hutch and said something to the policemen. All the Thais laughed, and Hutch knew it was at his expense.

In one corner of the room was an X-ray machine, as tall as Hutch, with a control panel on one side. One of the uniformed policemen positioned Hutch by the machine and stood by him while the man in the white coat fussed over the controls.

'This is a waste of time,' said Hutch, but nobody was listening.

The man in the white coat nodded and the policemen moved away. Hutch smiled grimly. They were obviously afraid of the damage the radiation would do to their private parts. He stopped smiling as he realised that he'd be receiving a much bigger dose than them.

'No move, please,' said the man in the white coat. There was a click and a buzzing noise. 'Okay.'

Hutch's arms were grabbed once more and he was manhandled out of the room and along the corridor again. He was taken into a second, smaller office, this one with two metal tables which had been pushed together to form a right angle. Three brown-uniformed policemen were sitting at the tables. There was nowhere for Hutch to sit and he stood in front of them, his hands at his side. His palms were sweating and he wiped them on his jeans. 'It's only talcum powder,' he kept repeating in his mind. 'Seven days. Seven days then it'll all be over.'

The policeman in the middle was the oldest of the three, with metallic-grey hair and a scar on his upper lip as if he'd had surgery there many years earlier. He had a sheet of paper in front of him and was scrutinising Hutch's passport. He meticulously looked at every page in the passport, even those which were blank. He looked up at Hutch and studied him with impassive, almost bored, eyes.

'You are Warren Hastings?'

Hutch nodded.

The policeman tapped a silver ballpoint pen on the table. 'You are Warren Hastings?' he repeated.

'Yes,' said Hutch.

The policeman nodded and began writing. The door opened behind Hutch and the man who'd picked up Hutch's bag walked over to the tables. He had an identification badge clipped to his shirt. He put the bag on the table and unzipped it, then took out the contents, piece by piece, holding each one out so that the grey-haired policeman could get a good look at it. The first item was Hutch's wash-kit and there was a long discussion in Thai as the two men obviously tried to work out how to describe it. Eventually they reached a conclusion and the policeman wrote something down on the form. The man in the polo shirt pulled out the polythene-wrapped parcel, using both hands. He wasn't wearing gloves. The three seated policemen all nodded and the grey-haired one continued to fill out the form.

When the entire contents of the holdall were spread out across the tables, the form was pushed in front of Hutch and he was handed the pen. The grey-haired policeman tapped a space at the bottom of the sheet of paper. 'Sign,' he said, brusquely.

Hutch attempted to pick up the piece of paper, but the uniformed policeman standing to Hutch's right grabbed his arm. 'I just want to read it,' said Hutch.

The grey-haired policeman tapped the form with his finger. 'Sign,' he repeated.

Hutch leaned forward and looked at the form. It was all in Thai and totally incomprehensible. He had no way of knowing if he was signing to acknowledge that the bag and its contents were his, or if he was putting his name to a confession. He shook his head. 'I can't sign this.'

'Sign,' said the policeman, and this time there was a hard edge to his voice.

'I can't read it,' said Hutch. 'I can't sign something that I can't read. Get someone to read it to me in English, then I'll sign it.' He folded his arms across his chest.

The grey-haired policeman stood up slowly, as if it were an effort. He stared at Hutch for several seconds. The slap, when it came, was all the more shocking because it was totally unexpected. Hutch took a step backwards and was immediately restrained by the uniformed men on either side of him. Hutch opened his mouth to speak but no words came out. He felt his left cheek redden.

'Sign,' said the policeman, raising his hand again.

Hutch looked around the men in the room. They were all looking at him with emotionless stares, like shop-window mannequins. It was the first time he'd ever seen so many unsmiling Thai faces. The Land of Smiles was how the travel agents described Thailand, and generally it was true that most of its people did seem to go about their everyday lives smiling, but the men in the room were showing Hutch a different side to Thai culture; a cruel, violent side that few tourists ever saw. He knew without a shadow of a doubt that if he didn't sign the piece of paper they would beat him to a pulp, or worse. He reached for the pen and signed it: Warren Hastings.

The grey-haired policeman took the form away from Hutch, scrutinised it, then spoke to the uniforms. Hutch's arms were forced behind his back and he felt handcuffs being snapped around his wrists. He was taken out of the office and led down the corridor to another door. This one was locked and one of the policemen had to fish a key out of his pocket before they could open it. Hutch was pushed inside without a word and the door closed behind him.

It was hot and airless and in total darkness; the only light in the room came through a narrow gap at the bottom of the door. Hutch couldn't even tell how large the room was, or if there was anyone else there. He felt his heart begin to race and he struggled to stay calm. He edged towards the door, then put his forehead against the plaster wall and felt around until he found a light switch. It took several attempts before he could press the switch with his nose, but he managed it and an overhead fluorescent light flickered into life. Hutch sighed with relief as he turned around and leaned against the wall. The room was about three paces wide and four paces long with pale green walls and a bare tiled floor. There was no furniture, no sign that the room was ever used.

The handcuffs were hurting his wrists: they'd been put on too tight. From the treatment he'd received so far, he suspected that the police had done it deliberately. He slid down the wall and sat on the floor. There had been no interrogation, no questions; it was as if he was part of a bureaucratic process that had no interest in his guilt or innocence. He banged the back of his head against the wall. A week. A week and it would be all over.

The fact that the policeman who took the drugs out of his holdall hadn't been wearing gloves worried Hutch. It was as if they didn't care about forensic evidence. They had their tip-off and they had the drugs and that was all they needed, Hutch smiled to himself. They'd get a shock when the results came back from the laboratory and they realised that it wasn't heroin in his bag.

Hutch couldn't see his wristwatch so he had no idea how long the police left him alone in the room, but eventually the door was thrown open and Hutch looked up expectantly. There were half a dozen uniformed policemen there, including two who'd taken him to be X-rayed. They pushed two large black men in flowered shirts and cut-off denim shorts into the tiny room.

'What's going on?' Hutch asked the police. The one who'd opened the door shrugged and started to close it again. Hutch struggled to get to his feet, pushing himself up against the wall. 'Hey, come on, you can't leave three of us in here,' pleaded Hutch.

The policeman either didn't speak English or didn't care what Hutch had to say. He closed the door in Hutch's face.

'At least take my handcuffs off!' Hutch shouted, 'I can hardly feel my fingers.' The door remained resolutely closed.

Hutch turned around to face the two new arrivals. They were big men, fleshy rather than muscular, with jet-black skin. Their faces were fearful and they were sweating. Hutch realised they were probably as uncomfortable as he was.

'So what are you guys in for?' Hutch asked.

The two men looked at each other. The bigger of the two was sweating profusely, and as he wiped his forehead with the sleeve of his multi-coloured shirt Hutch realised that neither man was handcuffed. The two men spoke to each other in a language Hutch didn't recognise.

The smaller man grinned at Hutch, revealing a gold incisor. 'Heroin,' he said. He pointed to his ample stomach. 'Condoms.'

Hutch couldn't help smiling. They'd obviously been caught with the evidence inside their stomachs and the police were waiting for nature to run its course. He just hoped they'd let the men out to use the toilet when necessary.

'You are English?' said the man.

Hutch nodded. 'You?'

'Nigerian. What happens to people they catch? Do you know?'

'With drugs?'

The Nigerian nodded. His sweating friend dropped down on to the floor and sat with his back against the wall, his head in his hands. He was totally bald and his entire scalp glistened with moisture.

'Don't you know?' asked Hutch.

The Nigerian shook his head.

'Prison,' said Hutch.

'How long?'

Hutch was astounded at the Nigerian's ignorance. 'Twenty five years,' he said. 'Maybe longer.'

The Nigerian's jaw dropped. He spoke to his companion and the bald man groaned.

Sweat was dripping from Hutch's brow and he tried to wipe it on his shoulder but he couldn't reach. The Nigerian realised what Hutch was trying to do and he used his own shirt sleeve to mop Hutch's forehead. Hutch smiled his thanks. The room wasn't big enough for three people; there was no air-conditioning and no window. He could feel another panic attack building and he took deep breaths. The feeling of claustrophobia intensified and he closed his eyes. He tried to imagine that he was back home in Hong Kong, sitting in his study, Mickey and Minnie at his feet. He tried to picture the furniture, the overhead fan, the window and its view of the garden, but even with his imagination working overtime he could still smell the sweat and the fear of the two Nigerians.

JENNIFER LEIGH SWIRLED THE ice around her gin and tonic with her finger, then licked her red-painted fingernail. 'It's the best drink in the world,' she said to her companion. His name was Rick Millett and he was an American journalist who was stringing for several US papers and magazines and, unless he did something incredibly stupid, was the man she'd probably end up bedding before the night was out.

'Yeah?' said Millett. 'I've always been a whisky drinker myself.'

'No comparison,' said Jennifer, lifting her glass. 'It's refreshing, doesn't give you a hangover, doesn't make your breath smell, and its packed with vitamin C. Plus, you can always count the slices of lemon to find out how many you've drunk.' She raised the glass to him and then drank deeply. Millet watched her, an amused smile on his lips.

It was Jennifer's third night in Bangkok, and she was determined to enjoy herself. The days had been filled with trips up the river to floating markets, seemingly endless visits to temples, and on the first two evenings she'd been forced to endure interminable exhibitions of traditional Thai dancing and handicrafts, and meals with boring hotel executives and airline officials. That was the downside of accepting a free trip, but she'd managed to escape for her third and last night in Bangkok and had found her way to the Foreign Correspondents' Club. Millett was the best-looking guy in the club, and she'd sat herself down on the bar stool next to his and introduced herself. At thirty-eight years old and with two broken marriages behind her, Jennifer Leigh didn't believe in wasting time.

Millett was about six years younger than she was, and about half as bright, but he had a good body and delicate hands and while he took himself a little too seriously, Jennifer figured he'd be enthusiastic enough between the sheets. She was wearing a loose white shirt, open to halfway down her not inconsiderable cleavage, and black ski pants, and within twenty seconds of striking up a conversation she'd seen his glance drop down to take in her breasts, which was always a good sign. In her experience, once a guy had looked down her cleavage, he was lost.

He'd asked her about her journalistic experience in the United Kingdom and had been impressed by the papers she'd worked for. Jennifer knew that she had an impressive CV, almost as impressive as her breasts, and she used both to her advantage as they drank and talked. She'd glossed over the fact that it had been some time since she'd covered hard news and that she now worked for the features department. She told him stories about covering the Falklands conflict and the Gulf War, and neglected to tell him about her most recent piece: a feature on snooker players' favourite recipes. His eyes kept dropping to her chest and she knew he was hers.

'So, I suppose you've got a Thai girlfriend?' Jennifer asked after he ordered the fifth round of drinks.

Millett shrugged. 'One or two.'

'Yellow fever?'

Millett flashed an embarrassed smile. 'It's more that they outnumber the farang women.'

'Farang?'

'It means foreigner. We're all farangs.'

'Is it derogatory?'

'It depends on who you ask. It comes from the Thai word for Frenchman, but it does carry connotations of inferiority.'

'So it's just a question of numbers, then? You've nothing against farang women?'

'Nothing at all,' said Millett, taking another furtive look at her breasts. Jennifer smiled. She might not have the perfect skin or lustrous hair that the Thai women all seemed to have, but she had other attributes, and she could see that he was eager to get his hands on them. She'd show him what a farang woman could do, and God help him if he didn't return the favour.

She reached over and put her hand on his arm, and was just about to suggest that they go back to her hotel room for a nightcap when his pager began bleeping. She had a sudden urge to tell him not to answer it, but that would have been over-keen. As he went over to a telephone she lit a cigarette and studied herself in the mirrored gantry behind the bar. Jennifer had a journalist's eye for detail and she could be uncompromisingly harsh on herself when it came to assessing her looks. She tilted her head up a fraction so that it tightened the muscles of her neck. That was her worst feature, she knew, and recently she'd begun to wonder if cosmetic surgery might be the answer to the folds and wrinkles. Her skin was generally good, though she knew it would look a great deal better if she hadn't drunk and smoked so much, but around her neck it hung in unsightly folds if she lowered her chin. She smiled at her reflection. Her teeth were gleaming white, despite all her smoking and coffee-drinking, and her eyes were clear and blue, though her eyelashes had always needed mascara to look halfway decent. Her hair was as blonde as when she'd been a teenager, though these days it needed the help of chemicals. It wasn't as glossy as it had been, either, though the Thai humidity had definitely softened it. It hung in slight waves down to her shoulders and she moved her head from side to side to see how it swung. She blew her reflection a kiss. 'Rick, boy, you don't stand a chance,' she whispered to herself.

'Say what?' said Millett, behind her.

'Just wondering what to do with the rest of the night,' she said, turning to face him. She smiled and took a long pull on her cigarette, watching him through slightly narrowed eyes but making sure that she kept her chin up.

'Yeah, well, I know what I'm going to do,' he said. 'I've gotta go,' he said. 'The cops have called a Press conference to show off a drug courier they've just arrested. You might be interested, he's a Brit.'

Jennifer exhaled. 'Sure,' she said, keeping her eyes on him. 'I'll come along for the ride.'

He held her look for several seconds, then grinned like a child who'd been promised a bicycle for Christmas. She followed him out of the club and stood by his side as he flagged down a taxi. One stopped within a minute and Millett opened the front passenger door and spoke to the driver in Thai. After a few words he opened the rear door for Jennifer.

'Where are we going?' she asked.

'The Narcotics Suppression Division. It's in the old Chinatown, not far from the river.'

The roads were still busy but nowhere near as packed as they'd been during the day. She lit a cigarette. She'd been meaning to give up for years but figured there was no point in even trying in Bangkok – tobacco smoke paled into insignificance compared with the traffic fumes and industrial waste that she was already drawing into her lungs with every breath. She offered the pack to Millett but he shook his head. 'Don't smoke, huh?' she asked.

'My mother died of lung cancer,' he said.

Jennifer exhaled, wondering if the American was being sarcastic but decided that he was just being honest. 'Would you rather I . . . ?' she said, holding out the cigarette, but Millett shook his head.

'They're your lungs,' he said.

Jennifer smiled tightly and put out the cigarette in the ashtray set into the taxi door. Millett stared out of the window, his thoughts elsewhere.

'This guy, do you know his name?' Jennifer asked.

'Nah. He's a Brit, from Hong Kong. That's all I was told.'

A motorcycle swerved in front of the taxi and the driver braked sharply. Millett instinctively reached over to hold Jennifer back in the seat and his arm brushed her breasts. 'Sorry,' he said, blushing.

'You saved my life,' she replied. 'Now you're responsible for me for evermore.' He frowned, confused. Jennifer had yet to meet an American with a sense of irony. She patted him on the knee. 'Joke,' she said, smiling sweetly.

The taxi lurched to a halt. 'This is it,' said Millett. He paid the fare as Jennifer climbed out of the taxi. They'd stopped in front of a rundown, nondescript building in a bustling side street. 'This way,' said Millett. He led her through an archway, across a passageway and through a second archway where a small shop sold cigarettes, soft drinks and soap. Millett showed his Press credentials to a uniformed receptionist and spoke to her in Thai. The receptionist looked at Jennifer, said something to the American journalist, and Millett replied. The receptionist nodded and made a waving motion with her hand.

Millett took Jennifer along a passageway to a large room where there were already more than two dozen

Thai journalists standing around. They were facing a long wooden table behind which was ranged a line of five empty chairs. Technicians were setting up television cameras and microphones. As Millett and Jennifer sat down a door opened at the far end of the room and two Thai men in T-shirts and jeans walked in. They had badges pinned to their shirts, the only sign that they were policemen. One of the men was carrying a black holdall. They were followed by the Brit, his hands manacled and his legs in chains. He stumbled as he entered the room and the policeman carrying the bag steadied him.

The Brit was in his early thirties with short mousy-brown hair and wearing steel-framed spectacles with round lenses. He had the build of a runner, tall and thin, wiry rather than well muscled. He kept his head lowered so Jennifer couldn't see his features clearly. Camera flashes were going off in quick succession like a strobe light and he turned away. He was wearing a light green shirt with the sleeves rolled up to his elbows, black Levis and Reeboks. The policemen forced him to sit in the middle of the five chairs. As he dropped into his seat, Jennifer saw his face clearly for the first time. He had brown eyes with long black lashes either side of a long, thin nose and his forehead was lined with deep creases as if he spent a lot of time frowning. There were dark patches under his eyes, a sign of the strain he was under. His mouth was set in a nervous half-smile as if he was trying to reassure himself that everything was going to be all right. The strain was evident in his face and his hands were trembling. He clasped them together on the table and bowed his head so that his features were hidden once more. The uniformed policemen sat down either side of him. They had large handguns in black leather holsters on their hips and transceivers clipped to their belts.

The policeman with the holdall put it on to the table and unzipped it. He took out a plastic-wrapped package of white powder about the size of a housebrick. He held up the package and the flashes started again. The policeman grinned and slowly twisted around so that all the photographers could get a good shot. When the flashes had subsided he put the package down next to the bag and took out a passport which he put on the table and then sat down. An older uniformed officer with hair as grey and shiny as burnished steel began to speak to the reporters in Thai. At one point he held up a sheet of paper and there was another flurry of photographic flashes.

Millett put his head on one side as he listened intently, and from time to time he wrote in his notebook. Jennifer craned her neck to see what he was writing. Among his shorthand she saw the name 'Warren Hastings' and 'Hong Kong'.

There was a flurry of questions, all in Thai, which the grey-haired policeman answered. Jennifer tapped Millett on the shoulder. 'What are they saying?' she whispered.

'Just giving us the basics. Who he is, how much heroin there was, where's he from. I'll give you the details later.'

'Can I ask a question?'

'Sure, go ahead,' said Millett. 'The head cop there understands English. Just speak slowly.'

Jennifer raised a hand and the officer nodded at her. 'I'd like to know what Mr Hastings has to say for himself,' she said. 'How does he explain the drugs in his bag?'

Hastings kept his head down.

'Does he plan to plead guilty?' Jennifer pressed. Still there was no reaction from Hastings.

The door behind the table opened again and another uniformed officer appeared carrying a sheaf of papers. He began to hand them out to the reporters.

'What about your family, Mr Hastings? Are you married? Are your parents still in England?' She knew that she needed a local angle for her paper to give the story a decent show. It was a good start that Hastings had a British passport, but what she really needed was a mother and father back in the UK able to give her a quote along the lines of 'he was always such a good boy, we don't know where he went wrong'.

Hastings said nothing. One of the Thai reporters began to ask a question in Thai. Jennifer sat back in her seat, frowning. If he intended to plead not guilty, then now was the time to be protesting his innocence.

Millett leaned closer to her. 'He's already signed a confession, of sorts,' he whispered. 'That sheet of paper the older cop was holding up, it's an inventory of what was in his bag when he was detained. He signed to say that he was in possession of the drugs. Even if he does say he's innocent, his signature on that form is enough to convict him.'

There were more questions from the Thai reporters. A photocopy of the inside pages of Hastings' passport was thrust in front of Jennifer and she took it. His date of birth made him thirty-two. She looked at the photograph of the man who was sitting at the table, head bowed. He didn't look like a drug smuggler, more like a university lecturer. She wanted to ask him for personal details but it was clear that Hastings wasn't saying anything and that she'd be wasting her time.

'What do you think?' Millett asked her.

'Ten pars. Maybe more if I could get some background on recent drugs cases here.'

'I'm your man,' said Millett, grinning widely.

Jennifer slid her notebook into her handbag. 'Why don't you come back to my hotel, Rick? We can both file our stories and have a drink at the same time.'

Millett jumped to his feet as if he were spring-loaded and Jennifer resisted the urge to laugh.

CHAU-LING SAT ON THE sofa with her feet curled up underneath her, She was wearing just a T-shirt and bikini pants and had the windows open. She hated air-conditioning, and even on the hottest nights she preferred to rely on the fan mounted in the ceiling to keep her cool and the netting across the windows to keep the mosquitoes out. Mickey and Minnie were sprawled on the floor, tongues lolling out of the sides of their mouths as they panted. Occasionally Mickey would raise his head off his paws in a silent plea for her to switch on the air-conditioner but Chau-ling pretended not to notice. Like her, they were natives of Hong Kong, but Warren had spoiled them.

The television was on but she had the sound muted. She flicked through the cable channels with the remote control, only half-watching. She was hoping to find a decent movie, but all she could find were Australian soap operas, sports events and cartoons, par for the course in Hong Kong; it wasn't a city where people regarded an evening in front of the television as decent entertainment.

Suddenly she saw something that grabbed her attention. She sat bolt upright. The dogs realised something was wrong and they sat up, ears erect. Chau-ling fumbled with the remote. She missed the volume control with her thumb and accidentally switched channels. She cursed and frantically tried to find the original channel: a football match; a music video; Warren, sitting behind a desk, flanked by two men in uniforms. She looked down at the remote, this time making sure she pressed the volume button. An American voice was saying that Warren Hastings had been arrested at Bangkok International Airport with a kilo of heroin in his possession. Chau-ling's mouth fell open. 'What?' she said, out loud.

Mickey growled. The reporter went on to say that he was the fourth drug courier apprehended in the last month by Thai police as part of the country's ongoing crackdown on heroin smugglers. The camera went in close on Warren. Chau-ling slid down off the sofa and crawled over to the television until she was only a few feet away from the screen. He looked terrible, his eyes were ringed with dark patches as if he hadn't slept and his hair was in disarray. The clothes he was wearing were the same ones he'd had on when she last saw him. 'Warren?' she whispered.

Minnie padded over to Chau-ling and licked her face. Chau-ling pushed the dog away, her eyes fixed on the screen. It didn't make any sense. As far as she knew, Warren had never had anything to do with drugs. He didn't even smoke. She sat back on her heels. The news broadcast went on to cover an inquiry into a ferry collision in the harbour. She tapped the remote control against her cheek as her mind raced. Warren was in trouble. She had no doubt that there had been a terrible mistake.

She got to her feet and went over to the phone. She tapped in a number and muted the television volume as she waited for the phone to be answered. It took three rings.

'Daddy,' she said, her voice trembling, 'I need your help.'

THE BUFFALO BOY SMACKED one of the slower buffaloes on the rump with his stick. There were a dozen animals, and only the Buffalo Boy, his father and his older brother to keep them moving. The boy's father was talking to two uniformed border guards, laughing and offering them cigarettes. They had made the crossing many times. Sometimes three times a week. There were good profits to be made selling the buffaloes in Thailand; they fetched a much higher price than in Burma. The Buffalo Boy was only fifteen years old, but he'd been working with his father since he was eight and he knew that the profit they could make from the sale of just one buffalo was enough to feed their family for a month. There was a tax to be paid, and bribes of cigarettes, brandy and money to be given to the officials on both sides of the border, but the journey was still worth making, even without the heroin.

The Buffalo Boy was twelve before he'd been told about the heroin, except then it hadn't been heroin but opium that had been hidden inside the buffaloes. The Buffalo Boy's father had explained that heroin was much more expensive than opium, and that the man they worked for, Zhou Yuanyi, wanted to make as much profit as possible. The boy knew about profit. Profit was the difference between living in a hut without electricity and a big house; profit meant good food, clothes, maybe one day a car. A Mercedes, perhaps. He'd seen a picture of a Mercedes in a magazine one of his cousins had bought in Bangkok and he'd decided that one day he'd own one of his own. Life was all about profit, and in Burma it was heroin that made the biggest profit.

The drugs were put into condoms, tied several times so that they wouldn't come undone accidentally, and forced down the throats of the animals. Each condom contained about four ounces of heroin, and it was possible to get a single buffalo to swallow fifty. Two hundred ounces in every buffalo, and there were twelve buffaloes. The Buffalo Boy did the multiplication in his head: twelve times two hundred was two thousand four hundred. How many pounds was that? The boy frowned as he tried to divide by sixteen, but before he could do it, his father jolted him out of his reverie.

'Somsak, what are you doing? Keep them together!'

The Buffalo Boy ran to catch an errant buffalo and slapped it on its rump until it rejoined the herd. His brother laughed and waved his stick and the Buffalo Boy looked away, embarrassed. He beat another buffalo, harder than was necessary. The animal snorted as if it realised the treatment was unjust.

The Buffalo Boy's father brought up the rear as they crossed the border into Thailand. More guards were there, this time wearing Thai uniforms. The guards waved the animals across. They never inspected the buffaloes. The

Buffalo Boy knew why. They were paid by Zhou Yuanyi, paid more each month than they earned from their salary. Paid not to ask questions. That was something else that profit bought you, thought the Buffalo Boy. Power over others. If you had enough money, you could get people to do what you wanted. Profit meant power, and the most powerful man in the Golden Triangle was the warlord Zhou Yuanyi. The Buffalo Boy had seen him once, astride a huge white horse.

The herd crossed into Thailand. A man in an Isuzu pickup truck watched them walk down the road. The Buffalo Boy pretended not to notice him, exactly as his father had instructed. The man in the Isuzu worked for Zhou Yuanyi – once the heroin-filled condoms had passed through the water buffaloes, he would take the condoms to Chiang Rai, and from there to Bangkok. Meanwhile it was the Buffalo Boy's job to watch the buffaloes and to fish out the condoms from the shit they left behind. It would be at least another day before the condoms began to appear. Sometimes it took as long as four days for all of them to come out. The Buffalo Boy had to poke through the shit with his stick until he had all two hundred, then he had to wash them clean in stream water. He hated doing it, but he did the job thoroughly. One day, in a few years perhaps, the Buffalo Boy would try to join the warlord's army. He wouldn't be like his father, content to make a small profit from selling buffaloes and smuggling drugs. The Buffalo Boy wanted to be near the source of the power, at the centre. He wanted to serve Zhou Yuanyi, and to profit from that service.

He jumped up and sat on one of the smaller buffaloes, his legs either side of the animal's neck, imagining for a moment that he was Zhou Yuanyi, master of all he surveyed. He kicked the buffalo with his heels, the way he'd seen the warlord spur on his horse. The buffalo ignored him; it barely felt the kicks from his spindly legs.

THERE WERE EIGHT OF them in the tiny cell and it was all Hutch could do to stop himself from screaming. He'd been inside half a dozen prisons in Britain but he'd never experienced anything as primitive as the conditions in the cell the police had put him in. It was barely fifteen feet square, three of the walls were bare brick and the fourth was composed of floor-to-ceiling bars and overlooked a narrow corridor. There was no furniture, and the sanitary facilities consisted of a metal bucket. A red plastic bucket was half-filled with drinking water in which there floated a polystyrene cup. Four of the prisoners were Thai and they had all managed to get hold of sleeping mats. Hutch and the three other Westerners had to sit or lie on the bare concrete floor. The only consolation was that at least the guards had taken off the handcuffs and leg irons with which they'd constrained him for the Press conference.

The Press conference had come as a complete surprise, and not a pleasant one. He'd tried to keep his head down to avoid the photographers and the cameramen, but he wasn't sure how successful he'd been. And he had a bad feeling about the English woman who'd started asking questions. He hoped that she worked for one of the Bangkok English-language newspapers and that she wasn't planning to file the story back to Hong Kong or the United Kingdom.

When they'd loaded him in a police van at the airport he'd assumed that they were taking him to Klong Prem prison, but they'd continued along the expressway towards the city. The van had eventually driven down a bustling side street and into a car park in front of a single-storey building.

There had still been no interrogation. Other than to be asked if his name was Warren Hastings, he hadn't faced a single question since he'd been arrested at the airport. In fact, he wasn't even sure if he'd actually been arrested. He certainly hadn't been cautioned, unless it had been in Thai and he hadn't realised it.

'My name is Toine,' said a voice at Hutch's side. 'Toine Altink.' Hutch turned to face a tall, well-muscled man in his early twenties. 'I am from Holland.'

His smile seemed genuine, though Hutch had been in enough prisons to know that appearances could always be deceptive and that an easy smile could just as easily be followed by a knife in the ribs.

'Warren,' said Hutch. 'From Hong Kong.'

Toine slid his arms through the bars and leaned his forehead against the metal. 'This is a nightmare,' he said in his heavy Dutch accent. 'How much were you carrying?'

'I wasn't carrying anything,' said Hutch. He had no way of knowing whether or not Toine was trying to earn a reduced sentence by informing on his fellow prisoners. Until it was over, Hutch would give away as little as possible.

'Yeah? I wasn't carrying five kilos,' said Toine. He banged his forehead against the bars making a dull ringing sound. 'How could I have been so stupid?' The question was clearly rhetorical so Hutch didn't reply. 'I only wanted to earn enough to be able to come back and take care of my girlfriend,' continued Toine. 'She wants to stop working in the bars, but her father's sick and they need money for the farm. One trip, that's all, she said, one trip and we'd get married.' Hutch didn't know what to say. 'They shoot drug smugglers, you know,' said Toine. He sounded as if he was close to tears.

'Not any more, they don't,' said Hutch. 'It's always commuted to life imprisonment.'

'Great,' said Toine bitterly. He banged his head harder against the bars.

The Dutchman's mouth was set tight as if he was grinding his teeth and he had a faraway look in his eyes. Hutch had seen the same look on a thousand faces before, the faces of first-timers who had still to get used to the fact that they were going to spend a good part of their lives behind bars.

'What is this place?' asked Hutch.

'Narcotics Suppression Division,' said Toine.

'How long have you been here?'

Toine snorted. 'Five days,' he said. 'Five days and they haven't let me shower once.'

'Five days?' repeated Hutch. 'Are you sure?' Billy had said that he'd be transferred to the main prison almost immediately.

Toine stopped banging his head. 'What do you mean, am I sure?'

'I mean, how long do they keep us here?'

'I don't know,' said Toine. 'They only speak Thai. Or they pretend to only speak Thai. You can't tell with them.'

'Seven days,' said an American voice behind Hutch. The speaker was an anorexically thin man in his mid-to-late twenties who was sitting with his back to the far wall, his

150

legs straight out in front of him. 'Then they have to put you in front of a judge.'

'A week?'

'That's the law,' said the American. 'But the seven days doesn't start until you get here.'

'But it could be less than seven, right?' said Hutch.

The American shrugged dejectedly. 'Sure. But I've been here six days and they don't seem in any rush.'

Hutch's throat felt dry and swollen. He went over to the water bucket and filled the plastic cup. Small dead flies floated on the surface and he fished them out with his finger before drinking.

The American smiled grimly. 'Wait until you see the food,' he said. 'A few flies is nothing. My name's Matt, by the way.'

'Nice to meet you, Matt,' said Hutch. 'I'm Warren.'

Hutch dropped the cup back in the plastic bucket. He was dog-tired but the only space large enough to lie down was next to the metal bucket and the smell from it was more than he could bear. He went back over to the bars and stood next to the Dutchman.

A uniformed guard walked down the corridor and stopped outside the neighbouring cell. He was carrying a clipboard and he ran his finger down it. 'War-ren,' said the guard, leaving a gap between the two syllables. When there was no response from the occupants of the cell, he repeated the word, louder the second time as if he was more sure of himself.

'That's you,' said Toine.

'Huh?' said Hutch. He hadn't been listening, he'd been thinking about Billy Winter and wondering how he'd managed to be so wrong about the Thai police procedures. According to Billy, he should be in Klong Prem prison by now, making contact with Ray Harrigan and putting together an escape plan. If they kept him in the detention centre for seven days, the forensic laboratory would discover the drugs weren't real and he'd be released without ever having set foot inside the prison.

'That's your name. Warren. He's calling your name.'

Hutch stuck his hand between the bars and waved at the guard. 'Here!' he called. 'I'm Warren Hastings.'

The guard walked over and held the clipboard up so that Hutch could read the name written there. Hutch nodded eagerly. 'That's me,' he said.

The guard unlocked the barred door and motioned for Hutch to get out of the cell. Hutch waited impatiently as the guard relocked the door. Maybe this was it, he thought, maybe he was going to court straight away and then off to the prison.

The guard walked down the corridor and Hutch followed him. The cells were separated from the general office and reception area by more floor-to-ceiling bars, but before they reached the bars the guard opened a wooden door and led Hutch through into a long, narrow room. The right-hand side of the wall was composed of thick vertical steel bars over which was a double layer of chicken wire. It was a visiting room, Hutch realised, and he cursed under his breath. Through the wire, Hutch could see the office area where half a dozen uniformed guards were sitting at desks. Most of them weren't doing anything, though one was pecking unenthusiastically at a typewriter.

About a yard away from the bars on the office side was a horizontal metal rail at waist height, presumably to keep visitors at a safe distance so they couldn't pass across any contraband.

'I want to go back to the cell,' Hutch said to the guard.

The guard closed the door and stood with his back to it, the clipboard clutched against his chest.

'Fine,' muttered Hutch, and he turned back to the chicken wire.

He heard a scraping sound to his right, out of his vision. It sounded as if something was being dragged along the ground, and it was accompanied by an occasional grunt. A man appeared in a dark suit, walking with the aid of a stick. His legs were strangely disjointed and his head was at an angle to his body as if his neck was causing him pain. He walked by swinging one leg from the hip, then supporting himself on the stick before moving the other leg. It was a laborious way of walking and the man had a pained smile on his face as if apologising in advance for keeping Hutch waiting.

'The name's Wilkinson,' he said as he made his way to the rail. 'Simon Wilkinson. From the British Embassy.' He had the clipped tones and commanding voice of a former army officer and appeared to be wearing a regimental tie over a rumpled white shirt. He was a good-looking man with a shock of unruly jet black hair and piercing blue eyes. He reached the bar and leaned against it gratefully. When he stopped moving, the stick was the only sign of his disability. 'Sorry I didn't get here earlier, the traffic's hell.' He hung his stick on the bar and nodded curtly at Hutch. 'So, got ourselves in a bit of a pickle, haven't we?'

'We?' said Hutch.

'Well, you know what I mean,' said Wilkinson. 'Have you got a lawyer?'

'No.'

'I can recommend a few names,' said Wilkinson.

'I don't need a lawyer,' Hutch insisted.

'I'm afraid you will,' said the Embassy official. 'All court proceedings and documents will be in Thai and they don't provide translations. Even if you're going to plead guilty, you'll still need a lawyer.'

'I won't be pleading guilty,' said Hutch. 'I won't be pleading anything. There's been a mistake.'

Wilkinson raised his eyebrows. He had an amused smile on his face but his eyes were flat and hard. Hutch had the distinct impression that Simon Wilkinson didn't care one way or the other what happened to him.

'It's up to you, of course,' said Wilkinson. 'The Thais will quite happily try you without you having a lawyer. Is there anyone you want me to contact?'

'What do you mean?'

Wilkinson shrugged. 'Family, friends, business colleagues.'

Hutch shook his head. 'No. No one.'

Wilkinson pursed his lips, then shrugged again. 'Up to you,' he said. 'But you're going to need money.'

'What for?'

'Food. Toilet paper. Soap. The basics. They all have to be paid for. Conditions are pretty Draconian here, as I'm sure you've discovered.'

'I have to buy toilet paper?'

'You have to buy everything, Mr Hastings. Life can be unpleasant in a Thai jail, or it can be bearable. The only thing that makes a difference is money. Now if you have someone in Hong Kong or England that I can contact, I can explain what's happened and arrange for them to transfer funds to the Embassy, which we can then pass to the authorities.'

'No. There's no one. Is it right they can hold me here for seven days?'

Wilkinson nodded. He leaned against the horizontal bar and gripped it with his left hand and then shifted his weight as if his hip was troubling him. 'Seven days then you have to be in front of a judge. The police will run through their evidence, and if the judge is satisfied, you'll be held in custody.'

'At the prison, right? Klong Prem?'

'That's right.'

'But it might not be seven days, it might be sooner?'

'I'm not sure what you're hoping for, Mr Hastings. From what the police have told me, I don't think you should hold out any hope of an early release. Or bail, for that matter.'

'Why do you say that?' asked Hutch.

'Well, for a start, the confession you signed doesn't exactly help your position,' said the Embassy official.

'Confession? What confession?'

'The form you signed. It was a list of everything found in your possession at the airport, but at the tail end of it was a statement that you were trying to take the drugs out of the country.'

'It was in Thai,' hissed Hutch angrily. 'How the hell was I supposed to know what it said?'

'You should have waited until you'd received a translation,' said Wilkinson. He spoke slowly and patiently as if he thought that Hutch would have difficulty understanding him.

Hutch exploded. 'You don't know what the fuck you're talking about!' he shouted. 'You weren't there, you didn't have half a dozen uniformed thugs breathing down your neck!'

Two guards rushed down the corridor to the visiting area, but Wilkinson waved them away with his walking stick and a few words in Thai.

'There's no need to shout,' Wilkinson said to Hutch. 'One of the things you're going to have to learn is that you won't make any progress by losing your temper. That goes for me as well as the Thais.'

Hutch struggled to control his temper. The Embassy official's sanctimonious tone had infuriated him, but Hutch knew that there was no point in antagonising the man. He raised his hands in surrender. 'I'm sorry,' he said. 'I'm under quite a bit of pressure, as you can imagine.'

Wilkinson's smile returned, but there was still no warmth in his eyes. 'I do think you should consider hiring a lawyer,' he said.

Hutch shook his head emphatically. 'I can handle this myself.'

'I admire your confidence, but I can assure you that it's misplaced,' said Wilkinson. He tapped his stick on the floor. 'But it's your decision. I'll come and see you again in a few days.'

'There's no need to go to any trouble,' said Hutch.

'It's no trouble,' replied Wilkinson. 'It's what I'm paid for.' He pushed himself away from the rail and walked away, the sound of his uneven gait echoing off the walls

THE SOLITARY MAN

JENNIFER LEIGH TOWELLED HER wet hair and walked over to her hotel room window. Far below, long, thin boats powered along the Chao Phraya River leaving frothy wakes in the murky brown water. Jennifer didn't know if the colour of the water was due to pollution or silt but she'd have put money on the former. Almost everything she'd seen in Bangkok had been polluted: the air was foul with exhaust fumes, the water that came from the taps was undrinkable, and the food sold by the hawkers on the streets was covered with flies. Not that she'd mention that in the articles that she was going to write for her newspaper's travel pages, of course: she'd been in the business long enough to have learned that there was no point in biting the hand that fed her. She was a guest of the Thai Tourist Authority, and had flown first class on Thai Airways, and the suite they'd fixed up for her in the Shangri-La was almost as big as her Islington flat. Skipping over the unpalatable facts of life in the Land of Smiles was a small price to pay for a free luxury holiday.

She tied the towel around her chest, padded over to the television and switched it on. She tuned it to CNN. A copy of the *Bangkok Post* lay on the floor by her door and she picked it up. There was little of interest on the front page: several convoluted and badly written political articles, a picture of the King meeting hilltribe farmers, and a bus accident which had killed three schoolchildren. The Warren Hastings story was on page three, a photograph across three columns and half a dozen paragraphs. The paper obviously didn't regard a kilogram of heroin as a big deal. There was nothing in the piece that she hadn't included in her copy that she'd filed to London. She looked at her wristwatch. London was seven hours behind Bangkok which meant that it would be two o'clock in the morning there. She picked up the phone and dialled the direct line for the news desk.

It was answered by Neil Morris, a young, thrusting Oxford graduate who'd only been on the paper for eight months. Jennifer had heard that his mother was a close friend of the proprietor, which explained his promotion to night news editor with next to no journalistic experience. 'Jenn, so nice to hear from you. How's Bangkok?'

'Hot and sweaty, Neil,' she said. She had a sudden urge to add that it was just like his armpits, but Morris was touchy about his perspiration problem so she bit her tongue. The way young Morris' career was progressing, he'd probably be editor before long. 'I was just calling to see what sort of a show my piece got.' The presses started running just after midnight, so the first editions should already be on his desk.

'Piece?' said Morris. 'What piece?'

Jennifer mouthed a silent 'shit' and took a deep breath. 'A guy from Hong Kong caught smuggling drugs out of Bangkok airport.'

'Didn't see it, love. They were expecting it, were they?'

'I checked with Robbie, he said he'd pass it on to foreign. He told me it'd get a good show.'

'A chink caught with dope? It doesn't set my pants on fire, Jenn.'

'He's not Chinese, he's a Brit.'

'From where?'

'I don't know, they just said from Hong Kong. And he wasn't talking.' Jennifer heard the sound of pages being turned.

'I don't see it,' said Morris. 'Space is tight tonight, maybe it didn't make it.' Jennifer's heart sank. 'What was it slugged?' Morris asked.

'Heroin,' said Jennifer.

There was silence for a few seconds. 'Yeah, I've got it. It's in the foreign hold queue.'

'So it's not been used?'

'Afraid not. Sorry about that.'

'Do me a favour, Neil, have a word with the foreign desk, will you, see if you can squeeze it in for the second edition?'

'I'll do my best, Jenn, but I don't think they'll have room. What are you doing chasing fire engines anyway? I thought you were there on a freebie.'

'Yeah, I am. But there's something not right about the guy, he's not the normal sort of drug courier, you know? I want to run with the story.'

'You'll have to check with Robbie, I can't okay that.'

'I'll call him tomorrow,' said Jennifer.

'You're having a good time, though?' he said. He had a patronising way of talking to all the reporters, especially the ones who hadn't been to public school.

'Just great, Neil.'

'I thought it was a bit of a waste sending a girlie, myself. I mean, you're not really able to take full advantage of all the opportunities on offer, are you?' He chuckled suggestively.

Jennifer felt a sudden rush of anger. 'Well, Neil, maybe

they just wanted someone who didn't think with his dick,' she snapped.

'Hey, there's no need to snap, Jenn. I just meant—'

'Yeah, I know what you meant. Go fuck yourself, you sweaty little shit.' She slammed down the phone, fuming. Her anger faded after a few seconds to be replaced by a sick feeling of impending doom. Morris was too well connected to have as an enemy, especially when she was trying to get back to hard news reporting. She'd tried to be nice to him, she really had, but she loathed his accent, his patronising tone and his perspiration-stained handmade shirts. And the fact that he was fifteen years younger than she was.

'Problems?' asked Rick Millett, who was sprawled across the bed, his face half-buried in a pillow.

'They're not using my piece on Hastings.'

'Sorry about that,' Millett said, sleepily. He rolled over and looked at her with half-closed eyes. 'What time is it?'

'Why? Are you in a hurry to go?'

'I've gotta get to the office some time this morning, that's all.'

Jennifer undid her towel and let it fall to the floor, remembering at the last second to tighten her stomach muscles and lift her chin.

'Jennifer, I've really gotta go,' said Millett, raising himself up on one elbow.

Jennifer knelt on the bed and leaned over him, letting her breasts brush against his chest. She lowered her head slowly and kissed him on the lips. He resisted for about two seconds, then lay back and slipped his arms around her.

HUTCH LAY ON HIS back, his arms folded behind his head. He stared up at the ceiling with unseeing eyes. He could hear far-off shouts and from time to time a metal door would slam shut, the vibrations travelling up through the concrete floor. Toine had said that a sleeping mat would cost five hundred baht but the police had taken Hutch's wallet off him when he was arrested. No matter which way he lay he couldn't get comfortable. His back ached and his hips burned and his right arm had gone to sleep. A mosquito had bitten him on his neck and he had to fight the urge to keep scratching. There was no window in the cell and none of the prisoners had been allowed to keep their wristwatches, so there was no way of telling what time of day it was. Hutch figured it was probably mid-morning. He'd been in the cell for at least twelve hours.

Hutch couldn't stop thinking about Billy Winter, and how he'd managed to get it so wrong. Winter had been so sure that he'd be taken straight to the prison, and every hour that he remained in the detention centre was an hour lost, an hour when he could have been briefing Harrigan and working out how he was going to get him out of the prison.

He was having to use every ounce of concentration to stop himself banging on the bars with his bare hands and screaming for them to let him out. His stomach growled. All he'd had to eat was rice and fish sauce which had been served in a piece of newspaper, and a plastic bag filled with lukewarm water. He wondered what the food would be like in prison. He doubted it would be up to the standards of British prison fare – he'd put on almost a stone in weight while at Parkhurst and that was despite using the gym as often as possible.

A guard walked down the corridor, rattling a key chain. Hutch heard his name being called. He sat up, grunting with discomfort, and he massaged his tingling arm. 'Okay,' he said. 'That's me.'

The guard glowered at Hutch through the bars as if he was a convicted child molester. 'Visitor,' he said.

'Is it the guy from the Embassy again?' Hutch asked as the guard unlocked the barred door.

The guard said nothing. He escorted Hutch along the corridor to the visiting room. Wilkinson wasn't waiting for him on the other side of the bars and chicken wire. Standing there was a middle-aged Thai man in a dark suit carrying a leather briefcase.

'Mr Hastings?' the man said.

Hutch frowned. The visitor didn't look like a policeman, and none of the officers he'd come into contact with had called him 'Mr'. He was tall for a Thai, with greying hair and a slight paunch across which was stretched a gold watch chain.

'Who are you?' Hutch asked.

'Your lawyer,' said the man. He proffered a business card that was so blindingly white that it appeared to glow. 'My name is Khun Kriengsak.'

The lawyer spoke to one of the guards on his side of the bars. The guard took the card, walked around the rail, and poked it through the wire.

Hutch took it. 'I don't need a lawyer,' he said, reading the card.

Kriengsak smiled benignly. He had charm, but it was a cold, clinical charm that Hutch felt the man could turn on and off at will. 'Oh yes you do, Mr Hastings. I don't think there's a man in Bangkok right now who needs a lawyer more than you do.'

Hutch shook his head. 'Look, there's been a mistake,' he said. 'I haven't asked for a lawyer. I don't need a lawyer. I don't know what sort of ambulance-chaser you are, but I don't have the money for—'

'Please don't misunderstand, Mr Hastings. My fee has already been taken care of. By Mr Tsang Chai-hin.'

Hutch held out Kriengsak's card but the guard had already moved away. 'I don't know any Mr Tsang,' said Hutch.

'He's certainly taken an interest in you. I have been paid a retainer already and told that money is no object in the preparation of your case.'

Hutch pulled a face. 'Well, you've been paid for nothing, because I don't need a lawyer. Who is this Tsang? Is he a Thai?'

'He has extensive business interests in Thailand, but Mr Tsang is Hong Kong Chinese. You know his daughter, I believe.'

Realisation dawned. 'Chau-ling's father?' he said.

'Indeed.'

Hutch exhaled deeply. 'The answer's still no. This has been a mistake, and once the police realise it's a mistake I'll be released.'

Kriengsak smiled thinly. 'This is Thailand,' he said. 'Things are rarely so straightforward. Guilty or innocent, there are procedures that must be followed, and it would be beneficial for you to have a lawyer acting for you. You do not speak Thai, I understand, and the Thai legal system is full of pitfalls that can entrap even an innocent man.'

Hutch tapped the business card against the chicken wire. 'I don't want to keep repeating myself, Khun Kriengsak, but at the risk of appearing to be rude, I really would prefer to be left on my own.'

Kriengsak bobbed his head. 'Very well,' he said. 'But please keep my card. Just in case you change your mind.'

Hutch was about to argue, but decided against it. He slipped the card into the pocket of his jeans. Kriengsak turned to leave.

'You could do one thing for me,' said Hutch.

'By all means,' said the lawyer. 'My bill has been paid in full already.' He took a slim gold pen and a small leather-bound notebook from the inside of his jacket.

'You could get me something to sleep on. The floor's murder.' He scratched the bite on his neck. 'And cream for mosquito bites.'

THE GIRL WAS CRYING, curled up on the bed, her legs up tight against her chest, her hands over her face. The mamasan tutted impatiently. It had been a month, and still the girl was crying. They usually stopped crying after the first week, once they realised that there was no point, that tears got them nowhere. She walked over and stood at the bottom of the metal-framed bed.

'Stop your tears,' she said. The girl's only reaction was to curl up in a tighter ball. The chain that fastened her left ankle to the bed rattled and then went still.

There were ten beds in the room, three of them empty. Threadbare curtains hanging from the ceiling separated the beds, offering some privacy. Not much, but then the men who visited the room didn't stay long. The mamasan heard grunting from the next bed and the squeaking of tortured springs, then a muffled curse.

'Stop crying,' said the mamasan. 'Stop crying or I'll beat you.' The girl sobbed into her hands.

She heard the man visiting the next bed zip up his trousers and pad out of the room. As his footsteps echoed down the wooden stairs, a bell rang. The mamasan left the crying girl and went into the hallway. There was a sagging sofa there, a wooden stool and a small desk. A man in his early twenties came upstairs. He was a regular customer, and came to the brothel at least once a day, sometimes twice. He already had his hundred-baht note in his hand and he gave it to the mamasan.

'Ying,' he said.

'Ying isn't feeling well,' said the mamasan. 'Why don't you try Bit? Bit is very pretty, very young.'

The man shook his head emphatically. 'I want Ying.'

The mamasan licked her lips. She didn't want to offend a regular customer, but the girl was in no fit state to entertain anybody. 'Can you wait?' she asked.

The man looked at the plastic watch on his wrist. 'How long?'

The mamasan waved at the sofa. At one end was a pile of sexy magazines. 'Not long,' she said.

The man sat down and began leafing through one of the magazines. The mamasan unlocked the cash box in the desk drawer, put away the hundred-baht note, and relocked it.

The girl was still crying. The mamasan sat down on the edge of the bed and patted the girl on the shoulder. 'Ying, there is a customer here for you.' The girl pulled away from the mamasan's hand and continued to cry.

The mamasan folded her bony arms and glared at the girl. Four weeks of tears. The other girls had been complaining about the noise. They'd shouted to Ying, imploring her to stop, telling her that there was no point in crying, that she had no choice but to accept her fate. The mamasan had explained to Ying that her parents had accepted the money, and that Ying had to repay the debt in the only way she could. Ying had wailed and begged to be allowed to go home, but the mamasan had told her that she had no home to go to. Even if she could break the chain, even if she could escape from the brothel, even if she could get back to her village in the north, there was no escape. Her parents had accepted the money and they would simply send her back.

The mamasan stood up. 'If you don't stop crying, I'll give you your medicine,' she said. When there was no response, the mamasan went back to the hallway. The man looked up expectantly but she shook her head. 'A little longer,' she said. The man went back to his magazine, scratching his scrawny neck as he flicked through the pictures.

In the drawer next to the cashbox was a syringe and the equipment the mamasan needed to prepare the heroin. She sat on the wooden stool as she got the drug ready and filled the syringe. There was a needle in the drawer that had only been used a few times. She wiped it clean with a cloth and screwed it on to the syringe. It was so much easier in the old days, when she would give the girls opium to smoke. The opium pipe was simple to prepare and it didn't leave ugly marks on the girls' arms the way the needle did. But opium was almost impossible to get in Chiang Mai; it was only heroin that was now coming out of the Golden Triangle. The warlord Zhou Yuanyi had seen to that. The mamasan had a sister who lived near the border and she'd told her that Zhou wouldn't even allow the hilltribe people who harvested the poppies to grow their own opium. The warlord's laboratories took all the opium for processing and even the hilltribe people were being forced to use heroin instead. They had to steal the opium they smoked. The mamasan's sister said that some of the local farmers had tried to defy Zhou, and they had been killed as a warning to the others. There were rumours that they had been impaled alive. The mamasan doubted that anyone could be so cruel, but there was no denying the fact that there was no opium to be had in Chiang Mai at any price.

She carried the syringe back into the room and along to the curtained-off bed where the girl still cried. The mamasan kept the needle pointing away from her own body, careful not to prick herself. She sat down on the bed and gripped the girl's leg, just above the manacle around her ankle. There was a line of sores running along a large vein, sores that didn't seem to be healing. The mamasan found an untouched section of vein and inserted the tip of the needle. The girl's leg jerked but the mamasan had a tight grip. She eased the plunger down. The leg went still in her hand. She pulled out the needle. A dribble of blood ran down the girl's ankle and stained the sheet.

The mamasan seized the girl's shoulder and pulled her

on to her back. This time there was no resistance. There was a faraway look in the girl's eyes. She was a pretty young thing, with soft skin and glossy hair, budding breasts and a narrow waist. The mamasan stroked the girl's cheek, still damp with tears. She wouldn't stay fresh for long, the mamasan knew. They wilted like cut flowers once they became addicted. She stood up and went back to the hallway.

'Ying is ready now,' she said, putting the syringe back in the drawer.

The man grinned and stood up. As he walked into the room he was already unbuckling his belt.

TIM CARVER SLAMMED SHUT the car door. His driver had already reclined the front seat and had his eyes closed. Thais seemed to have a natural ability to catnap, no matter how uncomfortable their surroundings. Carver had seen motorcyclists sleeping while sprawled on their bikes parked at the roadside, beggars asleep on crowded streets, and schoolchildren with their eyes closed strap-hanging on buses, dead to the world. Carver ran his hands through his hair as he headed for the entrance to the prison. The Bangkok air was so filthy that even the short time he'd spent walking from the DEA office to the car had left his hair greasy. He tended to shower three times a day, but even that wasn't enough and he never felt truly clean while he was in the city.

He showed his credentials to the two guards at the entrance and was waved through. A guard with a large key chain escorted him to the cells where the police interrogated prisoners. The guard's uniform was several sizes too big for him and the collar of his shirt hung around his collarbone. The guard opened the cell door and nodded for Carver to go through.

The DEA agent sat down on one of the two wooden chairs that were placed on either side of a white-topped metal table and settled down to wait. He had no way of telling how long it would be before the guards brought the prisoner. Sometimes it was right away, sometimes they made him wait two hours. He pulled his red and white pack of Marlboro from his shirt pocket and tapped out a cigarette. A cockroach scuttled across the concrete floor and up the wall by the door. Carver lit his cigarette and sat back in his chair. If he'd learned nothing else during his four years in Thailand, he'd learned to be patient. Nothing was ever gained by getting angry or demanding that things be done faster. The Thais had their own pace, and they wouldn't be hurried. Any attempt to spur them along would only result in further delays. Carver practised blowing smoke rings as he waited.

A guard, older than the one who'd shown him to the cell, appeared carrying a glass of water which he placed in front of Carver. The DEA agent thanked him with a smile. He hadn't asked for the water, and he'd never been offered a drink on previous visits. Carver had long since stopped being surprised by Thailand – now he just expected the unexpected.

He was smoking his fifth cigarette when he heard the rattle of leg chains and snuffling sandals in the corridor outside. A Thai in his late twenties, short and stocky with a crew cut, was led into the cell by a guard. The prisoner stood staring sullenly at Carver and scratched his pockmarked right cheek.

'*Sawadee krup,*' said the DEA agent.

The prisoner nodded curtly but didn't return the greeting.

Carver smiled at the guard. 'It's okay, you can leave him with me,' he said. Carver's Thai was virtually perfect: he'd spent a year studying the language at the American University alumni school in Bangkok and had lived with a Thai family outside Chiang Mai for three months, honing his accent and getting his tones just right. He had a natural affinity for the language and had yet to meet a farang who could speak Thai better.

'Shall I wait outside?' asked the guard.

'If you wish, but I'd like the door closed, please,' said Carver, smiling.

The guard left the cell and locked the door behind him.

'What do you want?' asked the prisoner. He had the mahogany-brown skin and guttural accent of an easterner. According to his file, Park had been born in Surin, a town not far from the border with Cambodia.

Carver offered Park the pack of cigarettes. The prisoner took the pack, pulled a cigarette out with his lips, and leaned forward so that Carver could light it for him with his Zippo. 'Keep the pack,' said Carver.

Park slipped the pack into the back pocket of his trousers. His wrists were cuffed so he had to put both hands up to his mouth to take the cigarette out. 'I've nothing to say to you,' he said.

'Sit down, please. I just want to talk.'

'You're wasting your time.'

Carver shrugged. 'The government pays me to waste my time.'

Park stared at Carver for several seconds, then he grinned. He sat down. 'Can I have that?' he asked, nodding at the glass of water.

'I got it for you,' Carver lied.

Park drank, using both hands to hold the glass. His nails were bitten to the quick, Carver noticed.

'So, how long's it been?' asked Carver.

'Twelve months.'

'So you've got forty-nine years to go?'

Park put down the glass. He shrugged as if the length of his sentence didn't matter to him one way or the other. 'It could have been worse,' he said.

'It could be easier,' said Carver.

'I'm doing fine.'

'You'll be an old man by the time you get out.'

'Wisdom comes with age,' said Park. His voice was devoid of emotion. He might have been discussing the weather and not the fact that he faced a lifetime behind bars.

'So you'll be a smart old man.' Carver took a long pull on his cigarette and blew a perfect smoke ring up at the ceiling. 'Why not be a smart young man?'

Park's eyes hardened. He clenched his fists and put them on the table. He had big hands with strong fingers, scarred across the knuckles. Carver had read the man's files and discovered that in his youth he'd been a champion kickboxer. 'Why are you here?' His voice was as hard as his eyes.

Carver blew another perfect smoke ring before answering. 'Zhou Yuanyi,' he said. 'You worked for him.' Park said nothing. 'You were working for him when you got caught.

It was his heroin that you were running down from the Triangle.' Park looked away. Carver leaned forward so that his mouth was only inches from the prisoner's left ear. There was scar tissue there, the result of years of kicks and punches to the side of the head. 'You don't have to do the full fifty years, Park. I can get you out of here. All you have to do is to help me.'

Park stabbed out his cigarette on the table. 'No,' he said.

'I can give you a new identity. I can get money for you. A new life.'

Park snorted softly through a nose that had been broken several times. 'What about my mother? My father? My grandmother? Her husband? I have five brothers and three sisters. I have twelve nephews and fourteen nieces. Can you protect them all? Can you give us all new identities? Where do you plan to hide us all? Laos? Cambodia? Maybe you can fly us all to Disneyland and we'll live with Mickey Mouse. Is that what you're offering? Disneyland?'

Carver massaged the back of his neck. He could feel the tension building up in the muscles there. He knew that Park was right. There was no way the DEA could protect his whole extended family, and family was everything to a Thai.

'Do you know what happened to the last man who tried to betray Zhou Yuanyi? Park asked quietly.

Carver knew. 'I'll protect you,' he said, though even he could hear the hesitation in his own voice.

'He died with a pole up his arse,' said Park. 'Zhou impaled him. It took him a long time to die, I hear. It's not too bad here if you've got money, and money is sent in regularly. I can buy decent food, I don't have to sleep near the toilet,

I have a mattress, clean clothes, medicine when I get sick. My family gets money. I'm a hero to them. A live hero. That's got to be better than being a dead informer. What do you think?'

When Carver didn't reply, Park stood up. He pulled the cigarettes from out of his back pocket and threw them on to the table, then turned and banged on the cell door with both fists.

JENNIFER LEIGH WAS CLIMBING out of the shower for the second time when the telephone rang. There was a handset on the wall by the toilet and she picked it up as she pulled back her wet hair. It was Gerry Hunt, the paper's features editor and her boss.

'Bloody hell, Jenn, what did you say to Neil Morris?' asked Hunt.

'Good morning, Jenn. How are you, Jenn? Thanks for the two-thousand-word feature you filed, Jenn,' said Jennifer, juggling the phone as she wrapped a towel around her waist.

'Yeah, yeah, yeah, all of the above,' said Hunt. 'You sure know how to win friends and influence people, don't you?'

'He's a little shit.'

'He's going to be editor before he's thirty.'

'He's still a little shit. Anyway, it was nothing to do with features, it was about a piece I filed for news.'

'It was Robbie Ballantine who asked if I'd give you a call. He's not a happy bunny, Jenn.'

Jennifer cursed soundlessly and glared at her reflection in the mirror. If Robbie Ballantine had turned against her, she'd never be able to get back on to hard news reporting. 'I just wanted to make sure the piece got a good show, that's all. Hell's fucking bells, I work my butt off to file and it doesn't even get in. What's the point, Gerry?'

'The point, darling, is that you're there to file features for the travel pages. The arrest of a small-time drug courier they can take off the wires.'

'There's more to it than that,' said Jennifer. Water was pooling around her feet on the white marble floor. 'He doesn't look like your normal drug courier. And he wouldn't say anything at the Press conference.'

'So?'

'So they always protest their innocence, don't they? They always say they were set up or they were just carrying a package for a friend. This guy didn't say a dicky bird.'

'Maybe he's guilty.'

'Maybe he is, but even if you plead guilty here you still get sent down for fifty years.'

'Forget it, Jenn. Your flight's tomorrow, right?'

'I wanted to talk to you about that, Gerry.'

'No.'

'You don't even know what I'm going to say.'

'Yes, I do, and the answer's no.'

'This one's worth following up, Gerry.'

'What part of no don't you understand, Jenn?'

'The part that says you don't trust my news judgement. The hairs on the back of my neck are standing up, I know there's something not right here. The guy didn't want to be photographed, didn't want to talk to the Press, it's like he had something to hide.'

'He'd just been caught with a bag full of dope, of course he didn't want to be photographed.'

'So maybe he's connected to someone famous. Maybe his father's a big wheel in the City, a politician maybe.'

'Fantasy Island, Jenn. You're trying to turn chicken shit into *coq au vin* and it won't work.'

'Yeah, well, we won't know unless I dig a little, will we? Look, what have you got to lose?'

'The services of a features writer who should be back in this office on Wednesday morning.'

'Yeah? Doing what? Another celebrity recipe special, huh? Come on, Gerry, let me run with this. At the very least I'll give you a feature on drug couriers; there's more than a dozen Brits in prison here serving long sentences. I'll go in and get interviews, you know it'll be a good read.'

There was a short silence on the line and for a moment Jennifer thought that the connection had been cut.

'Are you sure you can get inside?' Hunt asked.

Jennifer could tell that his interest was aroused. 'Sure, I've got a contact here who says he can get me in. Interviews, pictures, the works. It'd be a great spread, Gerry. And I'll keep on at this Hastings guy.'

There was another silence on the line for several seconds as Hunt considered what she'd said. Jennifer said a silent prayer.

'You've got an open ticket?' he asked eventually.

Jennifer's heart leaped. 'It's a freebie, I can go back whenever I want.'

'Two days, Jenn.'

'Thanks, Gerry. Really.'

'Just get me the story. And file your travel stuff by tonight, okay?'

'It's a deal.'

'And be nice to Morris, will you? You might not be around when he turns thirty, but I plan to be.'

'Sorry, Gerry, the line's breaking up, I can hardly hear you. Talk to you later.' Jennifer hung up the phone and punched the air in triumph.

THEY CAME FOR TOINE and two of the Thais some time in the morning. Hutch had no way of determining the time, all he knew for certain was that it was after the shit bucket had been emptied and before the prisoners had been fed. An elderly policeman in a too-tight uniform had struggled over the pronunciation of a list of names of prisoners who were to be taken to court. Hutch's heart had sunk when the policeman got to the end of the list without calling his name. Toine had shaken Hutch's hand and wished him well. Hutch had just shrugged and said that they'd probably meet up again at Klong Prem prison. He was sad to see the Dutchman go; he and the American, Matt, were the only two other English-speakers in the cell and talking was the only way of relieving the monotony. Still, at least it meant that he had more room to stretch out. The stench in the cell didn't seem to turn his stomach as much as it had done when he'd first been thrown there, though he was still grateful for the chance to move a few feet away from the bucket.

He lay down on the reed mat that Chau-ling's lawyer had obtained for him and stared up at the ceiling, trying to make out shapes in the network of hairline cracks that ran through the aged plaster. His body felt restless so he took off his shirt and began to do sit-ups in an attempt to burn off his excess energy. Two young Thais sat with their backs against the bars and watched him with amused grins on their faces. Hutch increased the pace and his stomach muscles began to burn. The exercise helped ease his hunger pains. The food had never varied: a fist-sized ball of rice and fish sauce in newspaper and a plastic bag of water. Hutch's last rice ball had contained a dead cockroach.

There were slow footsteps in the corridor and the two Thais scuttled away from the bars like frightened crabs. A guard in a chocolate-brown uniform appeared at the entrance to the cell, looking over his shoulder as if he didn't want to be seen by his colleagues. He made a shushing sound and waggled his fingers at Hutch. Hutch got to his feet and wiped his hands on his jeans. The guard motioned for Hutch to approach the bars. The guard looked over his shoulder again and then thrust an envelope through the bars. It dropped to the floor and Hutch bent to retrieve it. By the time he was upright again, the guard was already at the other end of the corridor.

Hutch ripped open the envelope. He expected it to be from Billy, but the letter inside was handwritten on hotel notepaper and he didn't recognise the name on the bottom: Jennifer Leigh.

Dear Mr Hastings,

You don't know me but my name is Jennifer Leigh and I'm a reporter with the Daily Telegraph. *I've tried several times to contact you, but the police won't allow me to see you unless I have your permission in writing. Without seeing you, I can't ask your permission. It's*

*a crazy system, I know, but all they'll let me do is to
write a letter to you.*

*I'd like to write an article on your predicament. I
think publicity at this stage could only help your case.
On previous occasions, appeals for clemency from MPs
and family back in the UK have resulted in reduced
sentences and even early releases for people convicted
of drug smuggling. I can guarantee that my article
would be sympathetic, and I'd be happy to pay for the
interview. I'm sure the money would come in handy to
help pay for legal representation.*

*If you are agreeable to an interview, please inform
the police and I'll make arrangements to see you as
soon as possible.*

The signature at the end of the letter was almost illegible but
she'd written her name underneath it. Hutch read the letter
again, not because he was interested in what the reporter had
to say, but because he was so bored that he just enjoyed the
feeling of reading something. The prisoners in the detention
centre weren't allowed any reading material.

'What is it?' asked Matt, craning his neck to get a
better look.

'Nothing,' said Hutch. Publicity was the last thing he
needed, especially back in the United Kingdom. He was
pretty sure that even if his picture were published there
he wouldn't be recognised, not even by his former wife.
He'd shaved off his beard before leaving England, lost two
stone since he'd moved to Hong Kong, and had started
wearing glasses, but he didn't want anyone digging into his
past because he wasn't sure how well his passport would
stand up to scrutiny. When Eddie Archer had sold him the

passport seven years earlier, it had been with the warning that he shouldn't try to renew it, or use it to travel to the United States. Archer had never explained why, and Hutch had never had any trouble travelling throughout South-east Asia, but the warning still worried him and he didn't want a reporter from the *Daily Telegraph* on his case.

He folded up the letter and shoved it into his back pocket. There was nothing Jennifer Leigh could do for him.

THE RECEPTIONIST CALLED TIM Carver's office and told him that he had a visitor.

Jennifer Leigh was standing with her back to the elevator, her legs slightly apart, her weight on her right leg. There was something overtly sexual about her stance; it was confident, aggressive almost, and he had the distinct impression that it was a pose for his benefit. She must have heard the elevator doors hiss open, but she didn't turn around. She was wearing black high heels, dark tights or stockings and a mauve skirt that only just reached her knees. She had good legs, strong calves and trim ankles. Carver's eyes travelled upwards to a slim waist and a black jacket. Her hair was blonde and hung down to her shoulders. She turned her head quickly and caught him looking at her.

'Hi,' he said, smiling easily. 'I'm Tim Carver.'

'Tim, so good of you to see me,' she said, turning and extending her hand. She was in her late thirties, he guessed, as he concentrated on her face. There were deep lines at the corners of her eyes and she was wearing a little too much mascara, like a schoolgirl who had yet to learn the value of subtlety when it came to make-up. There were small lines around her lips and again she had a little too much lipstick and it was just a little too red. She was a good-looking woman, though; there was no denying that. Ten years ago she would have been stunning.

Carver shook her hand. It was a good firm grip, the sort he'd expect from a man with something to prove, and as she took it away he saw that the nails were a dark red, the colour of a day old scab. 'Let's go up to my office,' he said, and stepped to the side to allow her to go into the elevator first. As she walked by he couldn't stop himself looking down at her breasts. The top two buttons of her mauve shirt were open and he could see a good two inches of cleavage. A gold crucifix nestled between her breasts. He didn't think she'd seen the surreptitious glance, but then he saw that she was smiling and he realised that she must have done. 'So, Richard Kay gave you my name?' he said, to cover his embarrassment.

'Yeah, he said you knew what was going on here,' she said. Her eyes crinkled at the corners and he had the impression that she was secretly pleased that he'd stolen a look at her breasts. 'You gave him a lot of help with his drugs feature, he said.'

Carver raised an eyebrow. 'He didn't quote me, I hope.'

Jennifer smiled reassuringly. 'The only direct quote was attributed to a drugs investigation official. He didn't even say it was from the DEA.'

The elevator arrived at Carver's floor and he took her along to his office. There was a water cooler in one corner and he filled two paper cups. He put one down in front of Jennifer and went behind his desk.

'Thank God,' said Jennifer, indicating the ashtray that nestled between the files that covered most of his desk area. 'Another smoker.'

'Yeah, I'm afraid so,' said Carver, pushing it towards her as she took a pack of Rothmans from her brown leather handbag.

'Hey, don't apologise,' she said. 'We're a dying breed.' She offered him a cigarette.

'Literally,' said Carver ruefully. He flipped the top of his Zippo and lit her cigarette, then his own. 'You wouldn't believe how many times I've tried to quit.'

'Don't bother,' she said, leaning back in her chair. 'Just enjoy it.' She exhaled and sighed with pleasure.

Carver risked another look at her breasts. They rippled under the shirt as she leaned back in the chair. He pulled his eyes away and tried to keep them on her face. 'So, what is it you want to know?' he said.

Jennifer reached into her handbag again and took out a notepad and pen. 'Okay if I take notes?' she asked.

Carver held up his hands as if warding off an attack. 'Only if it's off the record,' he said. 'An unattributable briefing, no quotes, no names.'

'No problem,' she said. 'I'm putting together a feature on drug smugglers. Who they are, how they operate, what happens to them when they're caught. It's background I'm after, that's all.'

Carver nodded and sipped his cup of water. 'Okay, fire away.'

'I'm tying it in to this guy Warren Hastings that was arrested at the airport.'

'Yeah, I read about it in the papers.'

Jennifer put her head on one side and narrowed her eyes. 'You mean the DEA wasn't involved?'

'It was a kilo, right? That's a drop in the ocean, Jennifer. We're after bigger fish.'

'So Hastings is a minnow?'

'He's either a low-ranking courier, or a freelance doing it for himself. Might even have been a decoy.'

'A decoy?' said Jennifer. She drew on her cigarette, emphasising the lines around her mouth.

'Yeah, that's how it goes sometimes. Say you're trying to move a hundred kilos and it's a rush order so you can't put it on a freighter. You split the consignment into ten, and recruit ten couriers. The stuff goes into their suitcases, electrical equipment, wooden statues, the usual sort of places. Then you give a one-kilo package to the decoy, except of course he doesn't know he's the decoy. An hour before the flight, you ring the cops and tip them off about the decoy. The cops pull him off the plane, they find the drugs, it's medals and pats on the back all round. Especially if it's a farang.'

'Meanwhile, the rest of the couriers get through?'

'Exactly. The cops don't care, they've got a high-profile bust: another farang they can put on trial to show the world they mean business. The man setting up the deal is happy – he's only lost one per cent of his consignment. It's cheap insurance.'

'Everyone wins but the decoy?'

Carver nodded. 'That's the way it goes. Sometimes a 747 to Hong Kong can have as many as a dozen couriers on board.'

'And you think Hastings was set up?'

'Like I said, I haven't seen the file, but it sounds like it.'

Jennifer made notes in her pad as she smoked. Her hair fell over her eyes and she flicked it away. 'How do they recruit these couriers?'

'The farangs they usually pick up at cheap guest houses or hostels. Word spreads on the backpacker grapevine. There's always someone who's run out of money and who thinks it's worth taking the risk. The Thai and Chinese couriers are a different breed – they're well organised, they travel on false papers and usually make several trips a month. The going rate is about two thousand bucks a kilo. And if they get caught their families are taken care of. It's like a pension scheme.'

'But they execute the ones they catch, don't they?'

Carver shook his head. 'They get a death sentence for large amounts, but the King invariably commutes it to a life sentence.'

'And they risk that for a couple of thousand bucks?'

Carver shrugged and tapped the ash from his cigarette into the ashtray. 'They know that the odds are on their side. The chances are that they won't get caught. There are about a thousand foreigners in Thai prisons for drug offences, but for every one in jail, there's probably twenty that get away with it.'

'Other than the decoys being thrown to the wolves, how else do they get caught? Do they use dogs or X-ray machines or what?'

'Intelligence, mainly,' said Carver. 'The Thai police keep known suppliers under surveillance and they have a network of informers. At the airport it's usually a matter of searching those travellers who fit the profile of a typical courier.'

'Which is?'

'Usually male, usually in their twenties or thirties, often travelling alone with hand luggage and a stack of visas in their passport. From what I saw of the Press conference on television, your guy seems to fit the profile. That might be why they pulled him in.'

Jennifer made notes in her scratchy shorthand, then looked up at the DEA agent. 'There is one thing that worries me,' she said. 'At the Press conference, he didn't say a word.'

'A lot of them don't. The amateurs are usually in shock, the professionals are paid to keep their mouths shut. Besides, there's nothing they can say that'll have any effect on the Thais.'

'Sure, but they usually protest their innocence, don't they? Even the guilty ones.'

Carver shrugged. 'It didn't strike me as unusual.'

'And he didn't have a lawyer.'

'Early days.'

'What, they can put him on show like that, with the drugs and everything, and he doesn't have the right to legal representation? It prejudices the trial, doesn't it? Everyone who saw him on TV is going to assume he's guilty.'

Carver smiled thinly. 'This is Thailand. The Thais have their own way of doing things, and you just have to go with the flow. You can't fight it. Thailand is the one country in South-east Asia that's never been colonised, did you know that?'

'Which says what about the place?'

'That it can't be changed by Western ways or attitudes. They invite you to their country, they want you to spend your money here, they'll even allow McDonald's and Pizza

Hut to set up shop here, but at the end of the day, this will always be Thailand and they'll carry on doing things their own sweet way. Hastings will get a lawyer, and a trial. And probably a fifty-year prison sentence, unless he co-operates. Then you and the rest of the media will forget all about him.'

'Maybe,' said Jennifer. 'But I still think there's a good story to be done on this guy. I'm going to try to get an interview with him.' She leaned forward showing another inch of cleavage. 'Can you do me a favour? Can you find out for me how he was caught?'

'No problem.' He tried to keep his eyes from wandering down to her cleavage and concentrated on the bridge of her nose.

Jennifer scrawled the telephone number of her hotel on a blank page of her notebook, ripped it out and handed it to him.

'Good hotel,' said Carver, recognising the number.

'It's a freebie,' said Jennifer. 'You should come over and check it out.'

Jennifer extinguished her cigarette. 'The heroin that Hastings had, where would it have come from?'

'Probably the Golden Triangle. That's the major source. It produces something like two and a half thousand tonnes of raw opium each year, equivalent to about one hundred and ninety tonnes of heroin.'

'Which would be worth how much?'

Carver leaned back in his chair and looked up at the ceiling. He pursed his lips and sighed. 'Hell of a question, Jennifer. It depends at what stage you're looking at it.'

'I don't follow you.' She lit another cigarette with his

Zippo then offered him the packet. He took a cigarette which she lit for him.

'The hilltribe people who grow the poppies get about a hundred dollars for every kilo of opium,' he said. 'So the total crop would be worth somewhere in the region of two hundred and fifty million US dollars. It's then processed into heroin and by the time it's reached Bangkok it's worth about eight thousand dollars a kilo.' He reached for a calculator on his desk and tapped on the keys. 'That would make the whole crop worth about one and a half billion dollars.'

Jennifer scribbled the numbers into her notebook.

'That's only the start of it,' he said. 'The dealers here buy it for eight thousand dollars a kilo, they spend a couple of thousand bucks on the courier, and by the time it gets on to the streets of New York or London or Amsterdam or wherever, it's worth almost half a million bucks, and when it's been cut with whatever additives they've got access to, then that same kilo is worth three million dollars. Total street value of the heroin coming out of the Golden Triangle . . .' He tapped a few more keys. 'Five hundred and seventy billion dollars.'

Jennifer's pen stopped dead. 'That's impossible,' she said.

'No. That's a fact. But not all of it gets to the West. There's wastage, there's the drugs we seize, and a lot is used in the region. Thailand has six hundred thousand addicts, and we reckon there's two million in China. But about twenty tonnes of heroin gets to America each year from the Triangle. Street value, sixty billion dollars. So you can see why I don't get excited about your guy and his kilo of smack.'

'You're not going to win, are you?'

'The war against drugs? So long as people want drugs, there'll be people making and selling them. There's just too much money at stake. We can shut down areas of supply, we can hit distributors, we can lock up the users, but you're right. Off the record, of course. Totally off the record.' He took a sip of water and licked his lips.

'What would you do, if you were calling the shots?'

Carver thought about her question for several seconds. 'I don't know,' he said eventually. 'We have to do something, but it's a question of supply and demand. We have to change hearts and minds, we have to convince people that drugs are a bad thing.'

'Tough job.'

Carver shrugged. 'What drugs have you taken?' he asked.

Jennifer smiled. 'That presupposes that I have taken drugs, of course,' she said. Carver didn't say anything. Jennifer nodded slowly. 'Marijuana, obviously,' she said.

'Obviously?'

'Sure. Everyone tries it, right? I did coke, a few times. Never heroin, I'd never touch heroin. I tried ecstasy once, but it didn't do anything for me.'

'But you don't have any moral convictions about drugs?' he asked.

'I didn't say that,' said Jennifer. 'But I can handle them, there was never any question of me becoming addicted.'

'You might be right. But if you take the view that drugs are okay, and a lot of people do, then we're wasting our time.'

'Like prohibition was doomed to failure, you mean?'

'Maybe.'

'So maybe the best way to get it under control would

be to treat heroin and cocaine in the same way as we treat tobacco and alcohol. Legalise it, tax it, and point out the risks. Then let people make their own choices.'

'It'll never happen,' said Carver. He held up his half-smoked cigarette. 'If anything, it'll go the other way. Maybe these'll become illegal eventually.'

'Yeah? And if they do outlaw cigarettes, you think that'll stop people smoking? I don't think so.'

'Me neither,' said Carver. 'But I'm just a foot soldier. I don't get to make decisions, I just . . ,'

'. . . follow orders,' Jennifer finished for him. She smiled. There was a smear of lipstick on her right canine, Carver noticed. It glistened like fresh blood. 'I've just realised that I've confessed to a DEA agent that I've taken drugs.'

'That's okay, I won't bust you.'

'Oh, I don't know,' said Jennifer. 'It might be fun.' She put her notebook into her handbag and stood up. 'Thanks for the info. I won't take up any more of your time. Give me a call if you turn up anything on Warren Hastings.' She leaned forward and stabbed out her cigarette in the ashtray, giving him another lingering look at her cleavage. 'Or even if you don't.'

Carver picked up the piece of notepaper and ran it through his fingers as he watched her walk out of his office.

HUTCH WAS DOING SIT-UPS on his sleeping mat when one of the Nigerians was put into the cell. Hutch stopped exercising and nodded a greeting.

The Nigerian looked around the cell despondently. 'Where do I sleep?' he asked.

'The new guy sleeps by the bucket,' said Matt. He grinned at Hutch.

The Nigerian walked over to the metal bucket. He peered down and wrinkled his nose in disgust. 'Shit,' he said.

'Sure is,' said Matt.

'You can sleep here,' said Hutch, shuffling to the side to make room.

The Nigerian walked over and stuck out his hand. 'Joshua,' he said.

'Warren,' said Hutch. They shook. Hutch's hand was dwarfed by the Nigerian's.

Joshua looked at the other occupants of the cell. 'Does anyone else speak English?' he asked Hutch.

Hutch shook his head. 'Just you, me and Matt,' he said. 'Matt's the one with the sense of humour. There was a Dutchman here, but he went to court.'

Joshua sat down with his back against the wall. He wrapped his arms around his stomach.

'Are you okay?' Hutch asked.

'They gave me something to make me shit,' said Joshua. 'To get the drugs out. Julian is managing to keep it all in, but it went straight through me.' He eyed the bucket. 'How often do they empty it?' he asked.

'Once a day. If we're lucky.'

A deep rumbling noise emanated from Joshua's stomach. 'Do you think they'll let me see a doctor?' he asked.

'I doubt it,' said Hutch. 'How much did you have inside you?'

'A kilo.'

'And you swallowed it all?'

The Nigerian grinned. 'Not at once,' he said. 'It was packed into condoms. About eighty. It took all day to get them down.' He held up his right hand, his thumb and first finger a couple of inches apart. 'Each condom was about this big. They gave me some green stuff to swallow while I was doing it. It numbs the throat and makes them slide down. Like oysters. Have you ever eaten oysters?'

'Yeah, but not eighty at one go. What did it feel like?'

'Like I'd eaten eighty oysters.' Joshua rubbed his stomach. 'Whatever the Thais gave me to flush them out, some of it's still in there. I've got to use the bucket.' He stood up and went over to the bucket. 'This isn't going to be pleasant,' he warned, and dropped his trousers. The Thais shuffled away, muttering to each other. Hutch averted his eyes. If there was one thing worse than using the bucket, it was watching someone else use it.

THE WOMAN CLUTCHED THE baby to her chest and made soft shushing sounds even though the baby showed no signs of waking. The stewardess smiled. 'Such a good baby,' said the stewardess. 'Is it a boy or a girl?'

The woman didn't know. 'A boy,' she said.

'He didn't cry once. Is he always this well behaved?'

'Always,' said the woman. She stepped out of the plane and walked down the stairs to the waiting bus. A Chinese businessman gave up his seat for her and she smiled her thanks. She held the baby close to her chest. On one arm she carried a bag filled with things a baby might need on a long flight: disposable nappies, a bottle of milk, tissues. The bottle was untouched.

The bus drove quickly to the terminal. It would soon be over, but the woman couldn't relax because the most crucial stage was still to come. The bus parked and the doors hissed open. The passengers rushed out, eager to be first to reach immigration control. The woman walked slowly, a benign smile on her face.

She joined a queue and waited patiently. When it was her turn to show her passport she whispered into the baby's ear.

The immigration officer was a Chinese woman with purple lipstick. She examined the woman's passport, then frowned. 'The baby's passport,' she said.

For a moment the woman was flustered. Then she realised it was still in her bag. 'I'm sorry,' she told the immigration officer. She fumbled in her bag and found the passport.

The immigration officer checked the photograph in the brand new passport and then nodded at the baby. 'Can I see the baby's face, please?'

The woman smiled. She turned the baby around and pulled the shawl away from its face. The immigration officer smiled for the first time, showing chipped and uneven teeth. 'He's a very quiet baby,' she said. She was in her late forties and there was no wedding ring on her finger.

'He's always very well behaved,' said the woman. 'I think he likes flying.'

The immigration officer looked at the baby for a few seconds, and then stamped both passports and gave them back to the woman.

The woman waited at the luggage carousel. Her suitcase was small with a yellow strap around it. As she reached for it an American teenager stepped forward and lifted it off the carousel. 'Let me help,' he said.

'Thank you,' said the woman in hesitant English. She took the case from him, holding the bag and the baby with her other hand.

'Can you manage?' he said.

The woman frowned, not understanding.

'Let me help you,' said the teenager, taking the case for her. He had a large blue nylon rucksack on his back. The American walked with her to the Customs area.

A Customs official wearing a light green uniform waved them over. 'Where have you come from?' he asked.

'Bangkok,' said the American boy.

'Bangkok,' said the woman.

The Customs officer pointed at the suitcase. 'Is that yours?' he asked the American.

'It's hers,' he said. 'I'm just carrying it for her.'

'Open it, please,' the Customs officer said to the woman.

She held the baby close as she opened the case with her free hand. The Customs officer checked the contents half-heartedly. Threadbare clothes, a washing kit, some Thai magazines, and a small plastic bag of green chillies.

'Okay,' he said, as if disappointed not to have found anything. He waved them through.

The American carried her bag through the main arrivals area. A Chinese man in T-shirt and jeans walked over and spoke to the woman in Thai. She replied and the man took the bag off the American. 'Thank you for helping my sister,' he said in heavily accented English.

'No sweat,' said the American and he walked off in the direction of a taxi rank.

'That was stupid,' hissed the man.

'I couldn't stop him,' said the woman.

'Don't do it again,' said the man. 'Use a trolley if you have to, but you carry your own bag.' He walked with her out to the car park. A driver was already at the wheel of the blue Nissan. No one helped the woman get into the car, she had to open the passenger door herself.

They drove in silence to a housing estate and into an underground car park. A small girl and her mother were in the lift, and they both smiled at the baby.

'He's so quiet,' said the mother. She looked down at her daughter. 'I wish you'd been that quiet when you were a baby. You cried all the time.'

It was only when the two men and the woman got into the flat that the woman let out a long sigh of relief. She put the baby on to the kitchen table and massaged the back of her neck. The driver went into the lounge. The other man took a long knife from a drawer under the kitchen sink. He went over to the baby and unwrapped its shawl. A red line ran down the centre of the baby's torso, an old cut that was held together with white stitches. The man used the knife to cut through the stitches one by one. The skin popped apart. The woman turned away.

'Not squeamish, are you?' grunted the man. 'You carried it all the way from Bangkok.'

The woman shuddered. It wasn't her baby, and it had been dead when she collected it from the house on the outskirts of Bangkok, but that didn't make her feel any better about what she'd done.

The man reached into the baby's body cavity and took out a plastic package the size of his fist. It was splattered with blood. He put it into the sink. There were another four packages inside the dead baby. Almost two kilos of pure heroin. The man rinsed them under the cold tap.

The woman went into the lounge and poured herself a glass of whisky. She gulped it down. It was the tenth time she'd made the trip, the tenth time she'd carried a dead baby through Customs. She never asked where the babies came from, whether the mothers had been paid for them or whether they'd been stolen. That they had been killed solely for the purpose of smuggling heroin out of Thailand, she had little doubt. The tiny corpse would be incinerated, the drugs fed into the distribution network, and she'd be back in Bangkok within twenty-four hours with her thirty-thousand-baht fee. It was a lot of money, more money than she could earn in six months in Thailand.

'Whose idea was this?' she asked the driver.

'This?'

'The babies.'

The man beamed. 'Brilliant, isn't it? It's never failed. They never examine the babies.'

The woman refilled her glass and stared into the amber liquid as if seeking an answer to her question there. 'The man who thought of it, he must be mad.'

'Oh no, he's not mad. And he'd better never hear you call him that. Zhou Yuanyi is a very dangerous man.

JENNIFER LEIGH WAS READING through a stack of photocopied newspaper cuttings that Rick Millett had given her, about the heroin trade and foreigners in Thai prisons, when there was a knock at the door. She looked up from her desk, an annoyed frown on her face. She'd left a 'Do Not Disturb' sign hanging on the doorknob as she'd wanted some peace and quiet while she read. The knock was repeated, louder this time.

'Can't you read?' she yelled.

'Er, it's me,' said an American voice.

'Me who?' shouted Jennifer.

'Me, Tim Carver. I've got something for you.'

Jennifer got to her feet. There was a mirror hanging on the wall above the desk and she checked herself in it. Damn it, why hadn't he phoned first? She was wearing a sweatshirt and a pair of baggy shorts. She growled in frustration as she realised that she wasn't even wearing a bra.

'Yeah, hang on, Tim, will you?' she called. 'Sorry,' she shouted, as an afterthought.

She ripped off the sweatshirt, pulled one of her bras from a drawer and fumbled with it as she looked at her open suitcase for something decent to wear. She chose a pale green silk shirt and left the top two buttons undone. The shorts would have to stay, she realised. She ran a comb through her hair, grinned at the mirror to check that there were no remnants of her club sandwich lunch sticking to her teeth, and went over to open the door.

Carver was wearing a beige linen suit that was rumpled at the knees and his hair was tousled as if he'd just got out of bed. He looked, thought Jennifer with a slight tightening of her stomach muscles, good enough to eat.

'Hi, come in. Sorry about that.'

Carver shrugged good naturedly. 'This is Thailand,' he said. 'I'm used to waiting. Time moves at a different pace here, as you've probably discovered already.'

'Tell me about it,' said Jennifer, closing the door. 'Why

do they walk so slowly? Three abreast so that they block the pavement?'

'Just one of the mysteries of Thailand,' said Carver, looking around the room. 'Like, why do they put salt in their orange juice? This is a great room, Jennifer. Practically a suite.'

'Yeah, like I said before, it's a freebie, so make yourself at home. Do you fancy a drink?'

Carver sat down on a plush sofa and crossed his legs. 'Just water,' he said. He took out a pack of Marlboro and his lighter. 'Do you mind?'

'Do I mind? I've just smoked the last of my duty frees, so I'm gasping,' she said.

She took a bottle of Perrier water from the minibar, opened it and handed it to Carver. For a moment he looked as if he was going to ask for a glass, but then he drank straight from the bottle and put it down on the table next to the sofa. He lit two cigarettes and handed one to Jennifer.

'Didn't Humphrey Bogart do that in a movie?' she asked.

'What, drink Perrier?'

Jennifer looked at Carver through slightly narrowed eyes, wondering if he was joking or not. 'The thing with the cigarettes,' she said. Carver looked confused and when he opened his mouth to ask her to explain, Jennifer waved a hand to cut him off. 'Forget it,' she said. She sat on the edge of the bed. 'You said you had something for me?'

'Information,' he said.

Jennifer smiled. That was a good sign, because he could have telephoned her. The fact that he'd turned up on her doorstep meant that he was interested. She leaned forward slightly. 'I'm listening.'

'Warren Hastings. It was a tip-off. Anonymous, which is unusual.'

'Why unusual?'

'Because the police generally pay for information leading to arrests. Most of their tip-offs, and ours, come from our regular informants. This one came out of the blue. I've checked with our Hong Kong office and Hastings isn't known there, though that might just mean that he hasn't been caught before. He runs a kennels there, trains dogs, looks after them while their owners are away, that sort of stuff.'

'Have you got an address?'

Carver grinned and pulled an envelope out of his jacket pocket. 'I knew you'd ask, so I've put it all down on paper for you.'

Jennifer took it eagerly. She opened it and slid out a single sheet of paper. 'Perfect,' she said, quickly running her eyes over the typed information. 'You've worked with journalists before. This is just what I wanted.'

He threw her a mock salute. 'The DEA is here to serve, ma'am,' he said.

'Do you know how he's going to plead?'

Carver shrugged and ran a hand through his untidy hair. 'He'd be crazy to do anything but plead guilty. He's not co-operating, though, from what I've been told. He's sitting tight and saying nothing. He even turned down a lawyer.'

Jennifer raised an eyebrow. 'Why would he do that?'

'Jennifer, I wish I knew,' he said. 'Hastings turned down the services of one of the best lawyers in the city, a guy called Khun Kriengsak.'

Jennifer grabbed for a pen and asked Carver to spell the lawyer's name. 'Is Kriengsak his family name?' she asked.

'No, that's his first name. Khun is the equivalent of mister or miss, it's used by both sexes.'

Jennifer nodded. 'Who was paying this Kriengsak?'

'No idea. So you haven't managed to speak to Hastings yet?'

'Sore point,' she said. 'My journalist friend didn't come through. He said the cops wouldn't play ball, the best I could do was to get a letter to him, and that cost me a thousand baht. I don't even know if Hastings got it, he certainly didn't get back to me. I might have more luck once he's been transferred to Klong Prem.'

'You could just try offering more money. When the Thais say that something isn't possible, more often than not they mean that you haven't offered a big enough bribe.' Carver looked around for an ashtray, holding his cigarette upright.

Jennifer got one from on top of the television cabinet and handed it to him. He smiled his thanks.

'Why are you so keen on this story?' he said. 'The guy doesn't want publicity, he's facing a long prison sentence and he's turned down a lawyer. I'd have thought there were better things you could be working on.'

Jennifer wrinkled her nose and shook her head. 'I've got a hunch on this one, Tim. There's something not right about the way Hastings is behaving, as if he's trying to hide something.'

Carver drew on his cigarette and exhaled slowly. 'It could be that he's been told not to say anything. By the people he's working for.'

Jennifer nodded. 'Maybe. But I think there's more to it than that.' She waved the sheet of paper in his face. 'He's a dog trainer, for God's sake. Why would a dog trainer get involved in drug smuggling?'

Carver stabbed out the stub of his cigarette and stood up. 'Beats me,' he said.

'You're not interested?' she asked.

'Like I said before, it's such a small amount, relatively speaking; it's not worth my time. The DEA is after bigger fish. I'll wait to see what the lab says.'

Jennifer frowned. 'What can they tell you? Heroin is heroin, right?'

'It's more complicated than that. They can do a detailed breakdown of the drug so that we can tell where it came from. Each batch is different, depending on the raw materials used and the way the heroin is manufactured. The lab can even tell which scientist was in charge of production. They all have their own way of doing things and they leave their own signature. Even the way the heroin is wrapped can give us an idea of who was handling the distribution.'

'So it might lead you to Mr Big?'

Carver grinned boyishly. 'It might tell us which Mr Big is behind it, but that doesn't get us any nearer arresting him. Most of the Mr Bigs are up in the Golden Triangle and they're pretty well untouchable.' He looked at his wristwatch. 'I'm sorry, I have to go,' he said.

Jennifer's face fell. 'Oh, I was hoping we could have dinner . . . or something.'

Carver looked at his watch a second time. 'I'm afraid I've got someone to see.'

'A pretty Thai girlfriend?' she asked, unable to keep the bitterness from creeping into her voice.

'No,' he said.

'Not Thai?' said Jennifer.

'Not a girlfriend,' said Carver. He looked at her levelly. 'Boyfriend.'

Jennifer narrowed her eyes. 'Oh,' she said. She hesitated for a second as realisation dawned. 'Oh,' she said again, quieter this time. 'I'm sorry.'

Carver smiled broadly. 'There's no need to be. Anyway, I've got to run. The traffic's hell outside.'

Jennifer opened the door for him. 'Thanks for the info,' she said as he left. 'And if you change your mind . . .' She flinched as she heard what she'd said, and closed the door before he could say anything.

She leaned against the wall, her face reddening as waves of embarrassment washed over her. 'I thought it was the Mounties who always got their man,' she muttered to herself. She grinned. 'What the hell, there's plenty more fish in the sea.'

CHAU-LING WAS PUTTING BOWLS of dog food in front of Mickey and Minnie when Naomi yelled at her from the office. 'Telephone,' she called, and mimed putting a phone to her face. The Dobermanns stuck their muzzles into the bowls and wolfed down their food.

'Who is it?' Chau-ling asked as she got to the office door.

'Some Thai guy,' Naomi replied in Cantonese. 'Wouldn't say what it was about.'

'Thanks,' said Chau-ling. 'Can you finish the feed for me? This might take some time.' Chau-ling waited until Naomi had left the office before picking up the receiver.

It was Khun Kriengsak. He briefly explained what had happened during his visit to the detention centre. 'I am sorry, but I appear to have wasted my time,' he said.

'I don't understand,' said Chau-ling, sitting on the edge of a desk. 'Does he have another lawyer? Is that it?'

'No. He said that he doesn't require any legal representation.'

'But that's crazy.'

'That is what I told him, Miss Tsang. But he was adamant.'

Chau-ling's forehead creased into a frown. It didn't make any sense. Warren hadn't tried to get in touch with her, and she'd checked to see if he'd contacted his lawyer in Hong Kong. He hadn't. There was no reason she could think of that would explain why he was refusing her help.

'What will happen next, Khun Kriengsak?' she asked.

'He'll appear before the Criminal Court in Ratchad-raphisek Road. The police will present their evidence, and if the judges are satisfied that there's a case, he'll be sent to prison.'

'Prison? Oh my God.'

'Believe me, Miss Tsang, conditions in prison are no worse than where he is being held at the moment.'

Chau-ling sighed mournfully. 'What can I do, Khun Kriengsak?'

'Until the police have finished their investigation, nothing,' said the lawyer. 'Bail is never allowed in drugs cases. Mr Hastings can present his own evidence to the judges, but to be frank, Miss Tsang, I doubt that there is anything he could say that would prevent him from being held in custody. He was found with a kilogram of heroin in his possession.'

'But Warren would never . . .' began Chau ling, but she didn't finish the sentence. It wasn't the lawyer she had to convince of Warren's innocence. 'What about character witnesses?' she asked. 'Could I speak at the hearing?'

The lawyer didn't reply immediately and Chau-ling sensed from his hesitation that he didn't think Warren's prospects were good. 'Perhaps,' he said, and his tone confirmed her first impression.

'So what do we do?' she asked. Her father had told her that Khun Kriengsak was one of the best lawyers in Bangkok and she was prepared to accept his judgement.

'I will continue to monitor the case,' he said. 'I have contacts within the police who will be able to advise me of the strength of the case within a day or so. Until then, all we can do is wait.'

'Okay,' said Chau-ling despondently. 'But as soon as you know when he's going to appear in court, please call me. I want to be there, even if it's just to offer him moral support.'

Chau-ling's voice began to shake and she ended the call quickly. Tears rolled down her cheeks and she wiped them away with the back of her hand. There was a scratching at the office door and Mickey pushed his way in, his stub of a tail wagging furiously. Chau-ling bent down and hugged the dog as she wept.

IT TOOK JENNIFER LEIGH six attempts before she managed to speak to Khun Kriengsak on the telephone. He was polite, and while he didn't actually refuse her request for an interview, he insisted that pressure of work meant he wouldn't be available in the foreseeable future.

'Can you at least tell me if you'll be representing Warren Hastings at his trial?' asked Jennifer.

'Mr Hastings has made it clear that he doesn't require my services,' said the lawyer curtly.

'Doesn't that strike you as unusual?'

'Unusual? In what way?'

'He's not a lawyer, is he? And presumably he understands the seriousness of his situation. Surely he'd be only too keen to have a lawyer representing him, especially a lawyer of your calibre.'

'One would have thought so, yes.'

'So, did he give you the impression that he already had a lawyer? Or that he had something else in mind?'

'Such as?'

'Oh, I don't know. Co-operating with the police, maybe. Offering information in exchange for a shorter sentence, that sort of thing.'

'He would be foolish in the extreme to attempt that without a lawyer.'

'Could he plead not guilty without a lawyer? Could he represent himself in court?'

'Not unless he speaks fluent Thai and had legal training. And I don't think either applies in his case.'

Jennifer toyed with the telephone cord. Warren Hastings rejecting the services of a lawyer didn't make sense, no matter how he intended to plead. 'Khun Kriengsak, who exactly is paying your fee for this case?'

'As things stand, Miss Leigh, the matter of a fee is hardly relevant. Other than to make a couple of telephone calls and visit Mr Hastings twice, I have done no work at all on the case.'

'But you were hired by someone, obviously.' There was a long silence on the line as if the lawyer was deciding what to say next. Jennifer had the feeling that if she didn't break the silence, he wouldn't answer her question. 'I'm just trying to get some background information on Mr Hastings,' she said. 'I won't be quoting you, or even mentioning you in the article. But it would be a big help if I could speak to people who know him so that I can find out what sort of person he is and why he would get involved in heroin smuggling.'

'I don't think the man who hired me knows Mr Hastings personally,' said the lawyer. 'His daughter works for him. But I think I have said too much already, Miss Leigh.'

Jennifer had a sudden image of Kriengsak sitting in the witness box while she interrogated him and she smiled. To do their jobs well, both lawyers and journalists had to be able to extract information from unco-operative witnesses. And while Kriengsak wasn't exactly being unco-operative, information was hardly pouring out of him.

'Her father must be a very wealthy man to be able to afford your fees,' said Jennifer. 'A lawyer of your reputation doesn't come cheap.'

'Miss Leigh, I can tell you now that flattery won't work with me,' said the lawyer. 'Now, please . . .'

'Oh, I wasn't trying—'

He didn't let her finish. 'I know exactly what you are trying to do, and you're wasting your time. I'm afraid I've already told you more than I should have done. I don't want to be rude, but I think I've said all that I have to say. Goodbye.'

The line went dead in Jennifer's ear. She put down the receiver and considered her options. Warren Hastings wouldn't speak to her, neither would the lawyer who had been hired to represent him. Rick Millett had been no help, and she figured that she'd got all she could out of Tim Carver. She smiled. More's the pity, she thought. She already had enough background information to write an article on heroin smuggling, but the nagging feeling that there was more to the story kept worrying her, like a bothersome child tugging at her sleeve. Her airline ticket was lying on the desk and she picked it up. The only line she had to follow was the girl in Hong Kong, the girl who worked for Hastings. Jennifer didn't have a name, but she did have the address of the kennels. If she was going to keep on digging, she'd have to go to Hong Kong. The question was, would the trip be justified?

She knew it was pointless to confer with the paper's news desk; they'd simply tell her to get on the next plane home. Jennifer knew that she had to follow her hunch. She tapped the ticket against the side of her face. The ticket was a freebie, compliments of the airline, so she doubted that there'd be any problem persuading them to fly her via Hong Kong. She could go and speak to the girl in person. A day at most, that's all it would take, and she'd know whether or not it was worth continuing with the story. She nodded to herself, her mind made up. It wouldn't be a waste of time, her journalistic instincts had never failed her before.

RAY HARRIGAN ROLLED OVER on his sleeping mat. The Canadian was staring at him with vacant eyes. 'What? What are you looking at?' asked Harrigan.

The Canadian blinked several times. 'You were talking in your sleep.' He coughed and cleared his throat noisily.

'Yeah? What was I saying?' Harrigan pushed himself up into a sitting position. It was late at night and through the windows he could hear the clicking of insects and the barking of far-off dogs.

'I couldn't make it out. Something about getting away.'

Harrigan rubbed his eyes. 'Chance'd be a fine thing. I'm starting to think I'll be in here for ever.'

'Nah,' said the Canadian, sitting up. 'Only fifty years.'

Harrigan laughed harshly. A mosquito landed on his leg and he slapped it. It splattered on his skin, a mixture of black and red.

The Canadian unscrewed the top off a plastic bottle of mineral water and drank. He wiped his mouth with the back of his hand and gave the half-empty bottle to Harrigan. He grinned when he saw Harrigan look at the bottle neck. 'First of all, I haven't got AIDS, and second of all, you can't get it from a bottle,' he said.

'I wasn't . . .' Harrigan began, but the Canadian silenced him with a wave of his hand.

'Yes, you were. You had the same look in your eyes that you have whenever I shoot up.'

'Sorry,' said Harrigan, and he drank as the Canadian watched, amused. Harrigan handed the bottle back. 'There's a lot of Thais with AIDS in here, you can see why I'd be worried,' he said.

'Only if you share your works or let them fuck you up the arse,' said the Canadian. 'And I don't do either.'

'What does it feel like?' Harrigan asked.

'Being fucked up the arse?'

Harrigan flashed a two-fingered gesture at the Canadian. 'Heroin,' he said.

The Canadian pursed his lips. 'Remember what it was like the first time you had sex?'

'Jesus, I can barely remember the last time I had my hole, never mind the first time.'

'Well, it's like sex, but it lasts longer. It's a rush, it's like you're firing on all cylinders.'

'But what does it feel like?' Harrigan pressed.

'Like an orgasm. But deeper. It's not just in your head or your dick, it's everywhere. And it goes on and on and on.' He cocked his head on one side. 'Are you thinking of trying it?'

Harrigan shrugged. 'I'm going out of my head in here,' he said. 'You said before that it was like an escape.'

The Canadian nodded. 'It is, man. It's like your mind is somewhere else.'

Harrigan shuddered. 'Forget it,' he said. 'I can't stand needles.'

'You don't have to inject,' said the Canadian. 'It's a better rush, for sure, but you can smoke it. Fifty baht for a hit, that's all. You've got fifty baht, right?'

Harrigan settled back on his sleeping mat and put his hands behind his head as he stared up at the ceiling. 'I dunno,' he said, almost to himself. 'Maybe.'

JENNIFER LEIGH SWORE UNDER her breath. The female immigration officer seemed to be working in slow motion, as if the fact that there were a couple of dozen people waiting in line was of absolutely no concern to her. When she finally reached the front of the queue, the immigration officer peered up at her through thick-lensed spectacles. Jennifer flashed her a cold smile. The woman examined Jennifer's passport and the immigration form she'd filled in on the plane.

'How long will you be staying in Hong Kong?' the woman asked. She had yellow teeth, Jennifer noticed. Not cream coloured, not off-white, but the yellow of old newsprint.

'One day. Maybe two.'

The immigration officer stamped the passport with what seemed to Jennifer to be excessive vigour and handed it back, already looking past her to the next person in line.

'Welcome to Hong Kong,' Jennifer muttered as she walked over to collect her luggage. She had waited so long to get through immigration that her bag was already on the carousel and she loaded it on to a trolley and went over to the Customs area. The queues there were even longer than the ones at immigration had been. 'Shit,' she said under her breath.

Half an hour later she was at the information desk in the arrivals area. They had a copy of the Hong Kong *Yellow*

Pages and she found half a dozen dog-training centres and kennels listed. She found Hastings' address among these and copied the number down into her notebook. She changed some traveller's cheques into Hong Kong dollars and obtained change for the telephone from a newspaper stall.

A girl answered when Jennifer called the kennels number. 'Can I speak to Warren, please?' said Jennifer.

'I'm afraid he's not here at the moment. Can I help?' said the girl.

Jennifer said a silent prayer of thanks. 'Who am I talking to?' she asked.

'This is Chau-ling. I'm looking after the kennels until Mr Hastings gets back.'

In about fifty years, thought Jennifer acidly. Chau-ling sounded like a Chinese name, yet the English accent was faultless. 'You train dogs, don't you?' asked Jennifer.

'That's right.'

'I have a dog that needs training. Can I come around later this week?'

'Of course. I'll give you directions. Do you have a pen?'

Jennifer tapped her notebook. 'I certainly do,' said Jennifer. She wrote down Chau-ling's instructions, and then hung up. She rubbed the back of her neck. The tingle had returned. She was sure that she was going to get something from the girl.

THE UKRAINIAN SLAPPED HIS neck with the palm of his hand but the mosquito was too quick for him and had already flown away, laden with blood. He scratched the spot where he'd been bitten and cursed venomously.

The Chinese mercenary riding the horse in front of him turned and grinned. The Chinese never seemed to get bitten, the Ukrainian had noticed. Maybe it was something to do with their diet, or the cigarettes they were always smoking. Or maybe it was just that Ukrainian blood was sweeter. He waved at the mercenary, letting him know he was okay. The man spoke no Russian or English and all communication had been with gestures and smiles. The mercenary slipped a bottle of Coca-Cola from his belt and drank from it.

The Ukrainian's mule stumbled and he grabbed at the saddle as a small avalanche of red dirt scattered down the hillside. He had grown to hate the bad-tempered animal, which kept its head resolutely down and whose hoofs seemed to find every tree root and hidden rock in the trail. Last time he'd made the trek to Zhou Yuanyi's camp he'd been given a horse. Admittedly it hadn't been much of a horse, but it had been a hundred times more comfortable than the mule. There was a water bottle tied to the pommel of the antiquated saddle and the Ukrainian unscrewed the metal top and drank from it. The liquid was hot, almost too hot to drink. He wiped his forehead with his sleeve. The peaked cotton cap he was wearing shaded his face from the sun's rays, but the heat was all-pervasive and his khaki shirt and trousers were soaked through with sweat. He hated the climate almost as much as he hated the mule.

The Ukrainian wasn't exactly sure where they were going. Zhou Yuanyi changed his headquarters on a regular basis. He had many enemies, which was one of the reasons he was so keen to buy what the Ukrainian had to sell.

THE SOLITARY MAN

The mule stumbled again and the Ukrainian kicked its flanks. He might as well have been kicking a log. He looked over to his right and immediately wished he hadn't. The hillside plunged precipitously away and far below was a muddy brown river peppered with jagged rocks. To his relief, the convoy turned away from the ravine and into the relative safety of the jungle. The trail they were following wound its way through the vegetation, most of which was dripping with water, and soon the Ukrainian couldn't see the sky, so thick was the tree cover overhead. He could understand why Zhou Yuanyi found it so easy to hide in the jungle.

He twisted around in his saddle, keeping his right hand on the pommel to maintain his balance. Behind him were another twenty mules, several with riders, Chinese and Thai mercenaries with rifles strapped to their backs, others loaded with wooden boxes. He had travelled with the boxes on a freighter to Samut Sakhon, a port close to Bangkok, and then on a truck overland to the border, then on a boat up the Mekong River to another truck, and when the roads had petered out they'd taken to the godforsaken mules and crippling saddles. He'd camped overnight with the boxes, never letting them out of his sight, but now he was nearing the end of his journey. He was taking a risk, heading into the jungle with men who would kill for the contents of his wallet, let alone for what was in the crates, but the Ukrainian knew that the mercenaries feared Zhou Yuanyi and would never disobey him.

A dragonfly, its body a brilliant blue, buzzed by his face and he jerked back in surprise. He hated insects, almost as much as he hated the mule and the climate, but at least dragonflies didn't bite. His mule walked under a tree with spreading branches, and leaves brushed against his face. The Ukrainian shuddered at the slippery touch of the vegetation. It felt like the tentacles of some slimy sea creature. The image made him think of the snakes that could be hiding in the branches of the trees all around him and he reached for the handle of the machete that hung from the saddle.

The trail wound around a massive tree trunk that rippled with vines as thick as his leg, and then the vegetation began to thin out. The Ukrainian sniffed. He could smell smoke. Ahead of them was a fence of bamboo stakes, half as tall again as a man, and set into it was an open gate, guarded by two men wearing traditional Burmese longyi, sarong-style trousers, and chewing on cheroots as they cradled modern M16 rifles in their arms. They waved at the Chinese mercenary and said something to him, but the Ukrainian couldn't even tell what language they were using, never mind understand what they were saying.

To the right of the entrance was a wooden pole on top of which was a gleaming white mask. The Ukrainian peered at it as he rode by, and he realised with a jolt that it wasn't a mask, it was a human skull. He shivered, but knew better than to show any sign of weakness. He turned his attention to the M16s carried by the guards, and wondered where Zhou had got them from. They seemed almost new, and the guards had bands of cartridges around their waists and shoulders. It looked as if Zhou now had another supplier, which was going to make negotiating a price that much harder. Not that the Ukrainian was worried. He had an ace in the hole. Four aces in fact.

The caravan moved slowly into the compound, past clusters of thatched huts towards a much larger building which had been constructed of wood hewn from the jungle. It was built on thick wooden stilts and wide planks formed stairs running up to a large door made of bamboo stakes. It had a sloping roof made of rusting sheets of corrugated iron over which had been strewn camouflage netting. Behind the building were two metal towers like electricity pylons, atop of which were several aerials and satellite dishes.

The bare soil around the building had been stamped hard by countless feet and hoofs. Half a dozen horses, big and well nourished with gleaming hides that put the caravan's horseflesh into the shade, stood tethered to the left of the building. One of them was a magnificent animal, a tall white stallion.

The Chinese mercenary slid smoothly off his horse and motioned for the Ukrainian to do the same. The Ukrainian grunted as he climbed down. They took their mounts over to a corral behind the main building where a small boy was using a bright yellow plastic bucket to fill a trough with water. The Ukrainian tied his mule to a wooden rail, well away from the trough. He grinned and slapped the sullen animal on the neck. He'd make sure that Zhou gave him a real horse for the ride back to civilisation. It would be the least he could do for the four aces the Ukrainian had brought with him.

He wiped his hands on his trousers. He felt as if the dirt from the two days' travelling through the jungle had become ingrained into his skin, and he knew that he must smell pretty bad. He wanted a shower or a bath, but he also wanted to spend as little time as possible in the compound. It was a dangerous place, he knew. Many who visited never left. Some ended up as skulls on the top of bamboo poles.

He walked around to the front of the building. Two more

armed guards stood at attention at either side of the wooden stairs, their M16s held in front of them. They stared at the Ukrainian as if daring him to try to get past them.

'My friend, my friend, how was your journey?' asked a booming voice from the top of the stairs. The Ukrainian looked up. Zhou was standing there, his legs apart and his hands on his hips. He was wearing a black silk shirt that appeared to have been freshly laundered and gleaming black riding boots over spotless beige jodhpurs. Zhou had put on a little weight over the two years that had passed since the Ukrainian had last seen the warlord, but his smooth-shaven, round face didn't appear to have aged. He was wearing sunglasses, a different pair to the ones he'd had on last time they'd met. The Ukrainian had never seen the warlord's eyes and, for some reason, he never wanted to. He was happier having his own reflection staring back at him. It seemed somehow safer.

'Long and uncomfortable,' said the Ukrainian. 'But hopefully profitable.'

'We shall see,' boomed Zhou, beckoning the Ukrainian up the stairs.

As the Ukrainian walked slowly up the wooden steps, a group of Zhou's soldiers came around the side of the building carrying the boxes that had been tied to the backs of the mules.

'You have everything we spoke of?' asked Zhou, patting the Ukrainian on the back.

'And more,' said the Ukrainian. He stepped across the threshold into the cool interior. There was one large room, with two wood-bladed fans turning softly in the ceiling. Giant loudspeakers stood either side of a matt black stereo system. To the right was a teak-framed kingsize bed shrouded in mosquito nets, its sheets in disarray. A figure lay on the bed, but all the Ukrainian could see through the fine mesh was the outline of a young girl lying face down, her head resting on her arms. Next to the bed stood a large-screen television set and a video recorder, and a double-doored refrigerator. Much of the furniture was in the traditional Thai style, but there was a massive ornate desk that looked like a French antique and behind it an equally fussy gilded chair. An IBM computer sat on the desk and an extension cord trailed across the teak floor and out of a window like an escaping snake. From behind the building came the pulsing throb of a diesel generator.

Zhou dropped down on to a teak bench piled with silk cushions and waved the Ukrainian to a large cushion under the slowly circulating fan. The Ukrainian felt exposed as he sat down: there was nothing behind him except for two wooden doors that led off to the rest of the building. Zhou's seat, however, was up against a wall. The warlord was deliberately trying to make him feel uneasy, the Ukrainian knew. It had happened last time he'd visited, and he was happy to play the game. If Zhou ever decided to turn against him, it wouldn't matter where the Ukrainian was sitting.

'A drink?' Zhou asked.

'Whisky would be good,' said the Ukrainian.

Zhou spoke to an elderly servant wearing a white jacket and black pants. A bottle of Black Label whisky was produced on a silver tray along with a full ice bucket, a pair of silver tongs and a glass. The ice impressed even the Ukrainian, who was by now well used to Zhou's eccentricities. There couldn't have been many ice-making machines in the jungle.

'Coke? Or ginger ale?' Zhou indicated the refrigerator.

'Water will be fine,' said the Ukrainian.

Zhou spoke to the servant again. The bottled water was French.

The Ukrainian took a small package from his pocket and handed it to Zhou, who opened it eagerly, ripping away the wrapping paper and letting it fall to the ground in his excitement. It was a compact disc. Zhou beamed at the Ukrainian. 'Billy Ray Cyrus. Excellent. Thank you.'

The Ukrainian nodded. The warlord loved country music and the Ukrainian had made a special trip to a music store in Bangkok to buy the CD.

'Do you mind?' asked Zhou, holding up the CD.

'Of course, go ahead,' said the Ukrainian.

Zhou went over to his stereo and slotted the CD in. He adjusted the volume, listened to the first few bars, and then went back to join his visitor. 'Billy Ray Cyrus is one of my favourite singers, did you know that?'

The Ukrainian nodded again. He knew. Last time he had visited the warlord, he had had to sit through his rendition of 'Achy Breaky Heart'. Outside, he could hear the wooden crates being stacked up.

'AK-47s?' asked Zhou.

'All brand new,' said the Ukrainian. The servant retreated to the far end of the room and stood there stock still, his head bowed, like a marionette waiting for a puppeteer to bring him to life.

'I have M16s now,' said Zhou, pushing his sunglasses further up his nose with a perfectly manicured finger.

'So I saw.'

'They are good weapons, M16s.'

The Ukrainian shrugged carelessly. 'Talk to me again in six months,' he said. 'After the jungle has got to them.'

Zhou lit a cigarette with a gold lighter and exhaled before speaking. He held the cigarette between the thumb and first finger of his right hand, delicately, as if he feared that it might break. 'My men know how to take care of their weapons,' he said.

'I didn't mean to imply otherwise. But M16s don't compare to the AK-47 in terms of reliability, not in the jungle. They'll jam.' He grinned. 'Trust me, they'll jam. Why do you think so many of the American Special Forces used Kalashnikovs in Vietnam? They couldn't wait to ditch their M16s.'

Zhou flicked ash into a huge crystal ashtray at his elbow. 'You might be right,' he said coldly. 'How many did you bring?'

'One hundred and twenty. With one hundred thousand rounds of ammunition.'

'I need more,' said Zhou.

'More guns? Or bullets?'

'Both.'

'I'll see what I can do. I've brought fragmentation grenades. Eight dozen. And anti-personnel mines, Czech made. Plastic so they can't be detected.'

Zhou nodded and pursed his lips. 'Mines are good,' he said. 'And your price is as agreed?'

'As agreed,' said the Ukrainian. 'And I'll take it in heroin. But first, I have something else. A surprise.'

He got to his feet and went over to the door. The Chinese mercenary was standing by the wooden boxes. The Ukrainian pointed to one of the crates and the mercenary yelled at two soldiers in camouflage uniform, who carried the crate up the steps and into the building.

Zhou stood up and watched as the Ukrainian used a screwdriver to prise open the box. The warlord whistled softly as the Ukrainian removed the lid and pulled away the polystyrene packing material.

The Ukrainian sat cross-legged on the floor. 'Made in the Soviet Union when it was a union,' he said.

'How many?' asked Zhou.

'Four.'

'And you can show me and my men how to use them?'

'Of course. But you just point and pull the trigger. The missile does the rest. It goes straight for a heat source. Providing it's aimed at a helicopter or a plane, that's where it'll go.'

'Range?'

'Ten kilometres. Just over six miles.'

Zhou knelt down beside the Grail SA-7 portable ground-to-air missile launcher and stroked it as if it were his only son. 'How much?' he whispered.

The Ukrainian rubbed his nose with the back of his hand and sniffed. 'Expensive,' he said. 'But you can afford it.'

The warlord's head jerked around and the dark lenses stared at the Ukrainian, his lips set in a tight line. For a moment the Ukrainian feared that he'd gone too far, but then the lips curled back into a cruel smile and Zhou began to laugh. He slapped the Ukrainian on the back, hard, as his laughter echoed around the building.

THE WROUGHT-IRON GATES to the kennels were open but Jennifer Leigh told the taxi driver to wait outside. He protested in broken English and told her that he wanted to get back to the airport, but Jennifer hadn't seen any other taxis in the vicinity and she didn't want to be stranded. 'Keep the meter running,' she said. 'I'll pay for the waiting time.'

'Huh?' he grunted.

Jennifer pointed at the meter. 'Meter,' she said. 'I'll pay. Okay?'

The driver looked as if he wanted to argue but Jennifer didn't give him the opportunity. She slammed the door and walked through the open gates, past a large wooden sign with the name of the kennels and underneath, in block capital letters: 'Warren Hastings, Prop.'

Jennifer had changed into a two-piece cream suit at the airport and left her suitcase at the left-luggage counter. In her handbag was a small tape recorder with enough tape for half an hour. She looked at her wristwatch and noted the time. She didn't expect it would take longer than thirty minutes, but she could always say she needed to use the bathroom before the machine was due to click off. Her high heels crunched as she walked along the gravel path towards the two-storey house with its whitewashed walls and red-tiled roof. From behind the house she could hear excited barks and yelps and she headed towards the noise.

There were two kennel buildings, each with adjacent

runs. In one of the enclosures a young Chinese girl with a ponytail was putting down bowls of food.

Jennifer went over to the wire fence. 'Excuse me, are you Chau-ling?' she asked.

The kennel maid straightened up. An exuberant Boxer jumped up and splattered her T-shirt with its muddy paws and the girl pushed it away. 'No, she's in the office,' said the girl.

Jennifer looked in the direction the girl was pointing. Linking the two kennel buildings, like the centre bar of the letter H, was a brick building with large windows. Through the windows Jennifer could make out a couple of desks and a noticeboard studded with coloured pins.

'Thanks,' said Jennifer, but the girl had already gone.

Jennifer walked over to the office and knocked.

'Yes. Hi. Come in.' It was the voice on the phone.

Jennifer smiled, took a deep breath, and pushed open the door. 'Hi. My name's Jennifer Leigh,' she said.

Chau-ling was chewing the end of a pen. 'You don't know anything about provident fund contributions, do you?' she asked, brushing a strand of long black hair from her face.

'I'm afraid not,' said Jennifer. 'I'm a journalist, not an accountant.'

'Well, our accountant's in Macau playing the roulette tables and these have to be filled in by the end of the week.' She put the pen down. 'Anyway, that's my problem. How can I help you? She stood up and Jennifer noticed with a twinge of envy how trim the girl's figure was. Early twenties, Jennifer reckoned, maybe twenty-four, but with the skin tone of a teenager and the cheekbones of a supermodel. Her hair was a glossy black that Jennifer had never seen outside of a shampoo commercial, and even the faded Harvard sweatshirt and baggy blue jeans she was wearing didn't detract from her prettiness.

'I'm a reporter,' said Jennifer. 'I'm doing a story on Warren, and the trouble he's in.'

A worried frown crossed Chau-ling's face. 'Did you call earlier today?' she asked.

'No,' Jennifer lied smoothly.

'Your voice sounds familiar, that's all.'

Jennifer shrugged carelessly. 'I've come straight from the airport. I spoke to the lawyer you hired. He suggested I speak to you.' The lie tripped easily off Jennifer's tongue. It wasn't the first untruth she'd told in pursuit of a story, and she was sure it wouldn't be the last.

'Khun Kriengsak? He gave you my name?'

'He agrees with me that publicity might help.' Another lie. This one came as easily as the others.

Chau-ling looked at Jennifer thoughtfully, then nodded decisively. 'We have to do something, that's for sure. Do you want a coffee?'

'A coffee would be great, thanks.'

'Let's go through to the house. I want to put some distance between me and these damn forms.'

She led Jennifer out of the office and over to the house. A back door led into a modern, well-equipped kitchen. Chau-ling waved at a table by the window. 'We can sit here,' she said. Jennifer sat down as Chau-ling busied herself with a coffee filter. 'Who do you work for?' Chau-ling asked. 'One of the local papers?'

'The *Daily Telegraph*.' Jennifer took a quick look at her watch. Twenty-five minutes to go before the tape ran out. She put her handbag on the table.

'In London?'

'That's right.'

'And they're interested in the story?'

'You sound surprised. Warren is British.'

'But he's been in Hong Kong for almost seven years. Milk?'

'Please. No sugar. The fact he's British makes it a story for the *Telegraph*. Besides, there's a lot of interest in heroin and the drugs trade at the moment. There's a big drugs problem back in the UK.'

Chau-ling put a mug of steaming coffee down in front of Jennifer and sat down opposite her. She stirred two large spoonfuls of sugar into her own mug. Jennifer smiled. Chau-ling obviously wasn't a girl who needed to worry about her weight. Close up, Jennifer could see that there were bags under the girl's eyes as if she hadn't slept much. Jennifer wondered how close Chau-ling had been to Warren Hastings.

'Warren's not married, is he?' Jennifer asked.

Chau-ling shook her head.

'Not divorced?'

Another shake of the head. 'Why do you ask?'

'Well, a single man in his thirties, you know. Most of them are married or divorced. Or something.'

'Something?' A smile flashed across Chau-ling's face. 'Oh no, he's not gay.'

'Is that from personal experience?' Jennifer put the question lightly, and smiled encouragingly, hoping to give the impression that it was a chat between friends and not an interview. That was why Jennifer was relying on the hidden tape recorder and not using a notebook; only when the story appeared in print would

Chau-ling realise that everything she said was on the record.

Chau-ling blushed. 'What do you mean?' she asked.

'Well, he's a good-looking guy, and you're . . .'

'We were never boyfriend-girlfriend, if that's what you're getting at,' said Chau-ling, but Jennifer felt that the denial came a little too quickly.

'I'm sorry, I just assumed that . . . you know . . . because you hired the lawyer and everything . . .'

'He's a friend, and right now he needs all the friends he can get.'

Jennifer nodded sympathetically. 'What about family? Where do his parents live?'

'They're both dead.'

'Brothers or sisters?'

Chau-ling shook her head. 'He never mentioned any.'

'What about his birthday? Did he get any cards from relatives? An aunt or uncle back in England? Someone I could talk to.'

The girl shook her head again. Her jet-black hair swung freely, rippling like silk. 'Warren was funny about birthdays,' she said. 'It was usually me who had to remind him. I arranged a surprise party for him two years ago here at the kennels. He didn't even know what it was for until we showed him the cake. He said his family had never really celebrated birthdays.'

'Do you know where he's from? Originally?'

Chau-ling wrapped her hands around her mug. 'Manchester, I think.' She frowned. 'Actually, I'm not sure. He never said. I think I just got the impression that he was from the north of England. Why is that important?'

'Because if he's got a strong UK connection, say a relative

or something, we can go to the local MP. Remember the two girls that got long sentences a few years back? They were pardoned after the Prime Minister intervened. It all helps. Now what about before he moved to Hong Kong? What did he do back in England?'

Chau-ling tilted her head and gave Jennifer a long look. 'Why are you asking me all this?' she said. 'Couldn't you ask Warren himself?'

Jennifer smiled and gave a helpless shrug. 'I wish it was as easy as that,' she said, 'The Thais are being difficult about access. I was at the Press conference after he was arrested, but they didn't give me a chance to ask for personal details. Like, for instance, did he have a kennels back in the UK?'

Chau-ling continued to look at Jennifer for a few seconds, then sat back in her chair. 'I don't know. He didn't talk about England much. But he sure knows a lot about dogs.'

'Does he breed them?'

Chau-ling grinned. 'Dobermanns,' she said. 'They're the love of his life. Sometimes I think he likes them more than people.'

'So tell me, do you think he did it?' Jennifer asked.

Chau-ling's jaw tightened. 'Absolutely not. Absolutely one hundred per cent not. He's always been anti-drugs. He won't even take aspirin when he gets a headache. And he doesn't need the money. I've been through the books, the kennels are doing just fine.'

'No vices? Gambling? Stuff like that?'

'He goes to the racetrack occasionally, but he's not a big gambler, no. Swimming and walking are about his only regular hobbies.'

Jennifer glanced down at her wristwatch. Twenty minutes

of tape left. More than enough. 'So if you believe he's innocent, what do you think happened?'

Chau-ling sighed. 'I don't know, I really don't know. At first, I thought there'd been a terrible mistake, you know? That maybe he'd picked up the wrong bag at the airport. But then he refused even to talk to Khun Kriengsak. That just didn't make any sense.'

'Why was he in Bangkok?'

'Yes, that's something else that doesn't seem right. It happened all of a sudden, and he didn't even say why he was going.' She leaned forward. 'He only had one bag, a holdall, but he said he'd be away for a week, maybe longer. It wasn't a holiday, he'd have given me more notice if it was.'

'A business meeting, maybe?'

'That wouldn't take a week. He'd talked about setting up a kennels in Thailand, but it was just talk, there was nothing concrete. Not as far as I know, anyway. And that wouldn't take a week, would it?'

'What about enemies? What about someone who wanted to get Warren into trouble?'

Chau-ling frowned and chewed the inside of her lip. She shook her head emphatically. 'No. Everyone liked him. He didn't go out of his way to make friends, but he didn't make enemies, either. He has about four real friends, and that's it. He's always kept himself very much to himself. He's not an easy man to get close to.' Chau-ling's eyes went suddenly distant, and then she abruptly shook herself. 'No. No enemies.'

'Have you spoken to him at all? Since he was arrested?'

Chau-ling sighed despondently. 'I tried telephoning, but it wasn't any use. I'm thinking of flying over, but I don't know what to do about the kennels. Warren left me in charge, and I don't want to let him down. Do you think it would help? Do you think I should go?'

'I'm not sure,' said Jennifer. 'I think he's rejecting everyone at the moment. You might be wasting your time.'

Chau-ling nodded. 'That's what I thought. I told Khun Kriengsak to let me know when the trial is. I might go over for that. I can offer Warren moral support, if nothing else.'

Jennifer wondered if Hastings knew that Chau-ling was in love with him. Probably not, she thought. 'I need a favour,' said Jennifer. 'Do you have a recent photograph of Warren? One that I could use with the article I'm writing. The ones taken at the Press conference weren't much use, he has his head down in most of them.'

Chau-ling ran her hands through her hair and pulled it back into a ponytail. Her eyes were moist as if she was close to tears, but she managed a smile. 'He hates his picture being taken. The only photographs I've seen of him are in his passport and on his identity card.'

'Yeah, well, we all hate the camera as we get older,' said Jennifer, though she doubted that Chau-ling had ever been afraid of a camera's lens. 'But there must be some. Holiday snaps, that sort of thing.'

Chau-ling let go of her hair and it spilled around her neck. 'No. Nothing.'

'No publicity photographs, for the kennels? At dog shows? Winning awards?'

'He's almost paranoid about it. He always turned his head away if there was a camera anywhere near him. Shy, I guess.'

'There's no reason for him to be. He's a good-looking guy.'

'I know,' said Chau-ling, quickly. Her cheeks reddened and she looked away, as if she'd just revealed a dirty secret.

There was a scratching at the door and two large Dobermanns forced their way in, stubby tails wagging furiously. Chau-ling grinned and slid down off her chair to hug the dogs. 'Mickey and Minnie,' she said, by way of introduction. 'They're Warren's favourites.'

Jennifer crossed her arms protectively across her chest. She hated dogs, especially big ones. 'I'd better be going,' she said. She picked her handbag up off the table and clutched it to her chest. One of the dogs stopped fussing over Chau-ling and stood staring at Jennifer, panting. Jennifer backed towards the door. The dog took a step forward, its head on one side.

'It's okay,' said Chau-ling, sensing Jennifer's discomfort. 'They won't hurt you.'

'I'm sure they won't,' said Jennifer, uncertainly. She'd been badly bitten by a Jack Russell when she was a child, and still had a small white scar on her left leg, just below her knee. 'Thanks for your time. Is there any message you want me to give Warren? I'm going to try to see him again in Bangkok.'

Chau-ling reached for the Dobermann's collar and pulled the dog back. 'Just tell him that I . . .' She hesitated. 'No. It's all right. I'll tell him when I see him.'

Jennifer backed to the door, then slipped through and closed it behind her. She walked quickly back to the taxi. The driver pointed to the meter and said something to her in Cantonese. 'Yeah, yeah, yeah,' she said. 'You'll get your money.'

The driver repeated whatever he'd said, louder this time. Jennifer gave him an artificial smile, her lips pulled so far back that it was almost a grimace. 'I said you'll get your money, you little shit,' she said. 'Now shut the fuck up and let me think.' From inside her handbag there was a metallic click as the tape recorder switched off. She told the driver to go straight to the airport.

After checking in for the next flight back to Bangkok, she went over to a row of callboxes. They were all occupied and more than a dozen people, mainly Chinese, were eyeing each other warily as they waited for the phones to become free.

There seemed to be no queuing system. Eventually she managed to grab a callbox by shoulder-barging a Chinese businessman out of the way as they both rushed for the same one. The businessman glared at her, but Jennifer shrugged. If Hong Kong rules meant every man for himself, she was more than happy to comply.

She flicked through her notebook as she waited for her call to go through. There were several clicks, then a ringing tone. Richard Kay answered the phone. 'Where are you?' he said.

'Hong Kong,' said Jennifer. 'The airport. Let me run something by you, okay? There's this guy, name of Warren Hastings.'

'As in the battle of?'

Jennifer ignored him. 'Hastings was picked up at Bangkok airport with a kilo of heroin in his bag. He does everything he can to avoid having his picture taken, and he turns down the services of one of Bangkok's top lawyers. Free services, that is. A girl who works for him was going to foot the bill. He refuses to speak to me—'

'Now why would he do that? I wonder—' Richard began.

'Don't be a prick all your life, sweetie,' Jennifer interrupted. 'He puts a big X in the no-publicity box, and sits in police custody as meek as a lamb. Now, this guy lives in Hong Kong, he's been there for seven years or so. He has no next-of-kin, no family, he gets no Christmas cards. But he's not a loner, he has friends in Hong Kong and the girl who works for him would open a vein if he asked her to. This guy never talks about his life before he arrived in Hong Kong, and he's camera shy. And before you say anything, I can assure you he's not ugly. Oh yeah, and the kicker is, he can't remember his date of birth.'

'Ah,' said Kay. 'I see.'

'So I want you to run his passport number by the Home Office and see if alarm bells ring. And then I want you to check his birth certificate and then see if you can find a matching death certificate.'

'That could take days, Jenn. They're not computerised yet, it's all in ledgers. I'd have to check every—'

Jennifer ignored his protests. 'Also, get one of your cop friends to check out the Warren Hastings name through CRO, just in case it is genuine. Try the Kennel Club, too. He breeds Dobermanns.' Jennifer read out the passport number and date of birth and had Kay repeat them. 'I'm going back to Bangkok,' she said. 'I'll call you from there.'

'Okey-dokey. How did you get on with Tim Carver, by the way?'

'He was okay. Gave me plenty of background. Did you know he was gay?'

'Gay? What? Are you sure? Oh shit, hang on, Gerry wants a word,' said Kay.

'Shit,' mouthed Jennifer.

'Jenn, where the hell are you?' asked her boss.

Jennifer ripped a sheet of paper out of her notebook. 'Gerry, hi, how are you?'

'Short of one reporter,' said Hunt. 'Get your arse back here ASAP.'

Jennifer crumpled the paper next to the receiver and spoke through the crackling noise. 'Gerry . . . you're breaking up . . . can't hear you . . . I'll call you back later.' She hung up. Hunt would be mad at her, but he'd get over it, especially when he got the story she was planning to file. She looked up at a monitor announcing departures. Her flight to Bangkok was boarding and the back of her neck was tingling again.

HUTCH SCRATCHED THE TWO reddening mosquito bites on his left arm. He'd been bitten some time during the night and now the itching was driving him to distraction. He'd already applied some of the antihistamine cream that Kriengsak had sent in to him, but the bites still itched. Hutch knew that scratching the bites would only make them worse, but the itching was incessant and the temporary relief was better than no relief at all.

A young Thai with a tattoo of an elephant on his right forearm was squatting over the metal bucket, a look of quiet contemplation on his face. The Thais seemed to have no problem going to the toilet in full view of the rest of the prisoners. Hutch had used the bucket several times, but only when he'd been unable to contain himself any longer, and it had been with a feeling of intense shame. He wondered how he'd cope when the inevitable stomach bug struck. He rolled over on his sleeping mat and tried to get comfortable. The smell from the bucket was nauseating and he pulled his shirt up over his mouth and nose. He hadn't washed in four days but even his body odour was preferable to the stench from the bucket.

There was a rattle from the bars and Hutch opened his eyes. There was a guard standing there, looking left and right as if he was worried about being seen with the prisoners. He pointed at Hutch. Hutch got up off his mat, and scratched his bites as he went over to the bars. The guard unlocked the cell door and took Hutch along to the visiting room.

There was a woman waiting on the other side of the wire, a thirty-something blonde smoking a cigarette. She smiled when she saw Hutch, as if she'd just thought of something funny, something that she wasn't prepared to share with him. The guard closed the door and stood with his back to it, his eyes half-closed.

'Warren Hastings, I presume,' she said. Her voice was deep and throaty, almost masculine. 'I'd just like you to know that this meeting's costing me five thousand baht. It's the first time in my life that I've paid for a date.'

Hutch narrowed his eyes. 'Jennifer Leigh?' he said.

'How sweet. You remembered.' She flicked ash on the floor. 'What's it like in there? Pretty rough, I suppose.'

She was wearing a beige jacket and a brown skirt that ended just above her knee, and high heels, but the feminine attire was at odds with her stance. She stood like a man, with her legs shoulder-width apart, her hip to one side. Her cigarette was in her right hand, held away from her face, and her left arm was across her body, supporting her right elbow. It looked to Hutch as if she was posing for him, using all her body language to impress on him what a tough cookie she was. Dogs did the same to try to assert their dominance: their hackles would go up, they'd hunch their shoulders and they'd show their teeth. More often than not it was an act. A menacing-looking dog could almost always be faced down. A truly aggressive animal didn't bother showing its teeth and growling, it just went for the throat.

'I've nothing to say to you, Miss Leigh.'

She smiled tightly. Her lipstick was a vibrant shade of pink. It had been applied thickly and was smeared over the filter of her cigarette. 'Oh, you can call me Jennifer,' she said. She took a long pull at her cigarette, then exhaled and watched him through the smoke. 'Now, what should I call you?' They stood looking at each other for several seconds. 'Cat got your tongue?' she said eventually.

'I'm not sure what you mean,' said Hutch.

Jennifer arched an eyebrow. 'Don't give me that, Warren, or whatever your name really is. You know exactly what I'm talking about.' She walked closer to the wire netting and looked at him with pale green eyes that seemed to stare deep inside him. 'You can trust me,' she said.

Her voice carried all the sincerity of an undertaker consoling the recently bereaved. Hutch stared back at her. He didn't believe her for one second. She was a reporter for a Fleet Street newspaper, and jobs like that weren't given to soft-hearted pushovers. 'Leave me alone,' he said. 'There's no story here for you.'

She took another pull at the cigarette. The smile vanished but her eyes continued to bore into his. 'Oh, I think there is. I think that's why you're sweating, Mr Whatever-your-real-name-is. I think that look in your eyes tells me that you know that I know. I think you're clenching your fists because you're scared shitless.'

She smiled again, and if Hutch didn't know better he would have been taken in by its warmth and sincerity. Whatever else she was, Jennifer Leigh was a real pro.

He relaxed his hands. 'What do you know?' he asked quietly.

Jennifer studied the burning end of her cigarette. 'I know you're not Warren Hastings,' she said.

'That's ridiculous.' Hutch's heart began to pound. How did she know? And more importantly, how much more did she know?

The journalist shrugged. 'Yes, well, you would say that, wouldn't you? Why are you so camera shy?'

The question took Hutch by surprise. 'What?' he said.

'Why are there no photographs of you in your house?'

'You've been to my house?'

'Why don't you get any Christmas cards from the UK? Why can't you remember your own birthday? Why have you turned down the services of one of Bangkok's top lawyers?'

Hutch's jaw dropped. 'You've been to my house?' he repeated.

Jennifer dropped her cigarette on to the floor and ground it out with her left foot. 'What's your real name?'

Hutch took a step back from the wire. He looked across at the guard. The guard was looking at the ground, his eyes half-closed as if he was dozing.

233

'I can find out, you know.'

Hutch's head jerked around. 'Leave me alone,' he spat.

'I'm having your passport checked out,' she said. 'I'm having your birth certificate pulled. I'm digging, Mr Whatever-your-name-is. How long do you think your new identity is going to stand up to scrutiny?' She snorted softly. 'I can see from the look on your face that you don't think it'll be too long,' she said.

Hutch massaged his neck. The tendons there were as taut as steel wires. 'You don't know what you're doing,' he whispered.

Jennifer's smile widened. 'Oh yes I do. I know exactly what I'm doing.'

Hutch closed his eyes and shook his head. He felt as if he was about to pass out. Everything was going wrong. Everything.

'The best thing you can do is to talk to me,' said Jennifer, her voice as smooth and slippery as castor oil. 'I'm going to find out anyway, but if you co-operate, I promise that I'll at least give you a fair hearing. I'll put your side of the story. Look, we might even be able to write it from your point of view. I think I can persuade my paper to come up with money. How does that sound?'

Hutch opened his eyes. 'You don't have children, do you?' he asked quietly.

Her lips tightened. 'No. I don't have children.' She frowned quizzically. 'Do you?'

Hutch turned away. He headed towards the door and the guard hurried to open it.

'You can't run away from me,' said Jennifer. 'You're going to have to face me some time.'

Hutch walked through the door and down the corridor, the guard following in his footsteps.

'You can't run away from me!' she shouted after him.

Hutch quickened his pace. 'Just watch me,' he muttered through gritted teeth.

SOMCHAI HUMMED TO HIMSELF as he walked towards the payphone. It wasn't such a bad job, being based at the detention centre. Sure, there wasn't much action, but action was for heroes and heroes often ended up in hospital, or worse. It was a quiet life, more like being a prison officer than a policeman, but the pay was better. There weren't as many perks as there were in the traffic division, where unofficial on-the-spot fines could quadruple an officer's salary, but then Somchai didn't have to spend all day breathing the filthy polluted air or risk being run over by a bus driver high on amphetamines. Besides, he didn't have the necessary exam grades or family connections to get into traffic. Traffic was for people with connections, and Somchai's family were farmers near Ubon, one of the poorest parts of Thailand. He was lucky to have the job he had, and he knew it.

He was even luckier to have met the man called Bird. There weren't many opportunities to make a bit of extra money in the detention centre. He'd occasionally smuggle out a letter, or take contraband in, but it was for small money, nowhere near as much as a traffic policeman could get for catching a Mercedes making a wrong turn. The big money went to the officers, and there was little chance of Somchai being promoted. The five thousand baht the reporter had paid for the unofficial meeting with the farang called Warren had gone straight to the inspector on duty. Somchai doubted that he'd see more than five hundred baht of the bribe. Maybe not even that. But Bird had promised him the equivalent of more than a month's salary if he told him about any visitors the farang had. More if he could tell Bird what they spoke about. Bird had been as good as his word when Somchai had told him about the visit from the lawyer. Bird had handed over the cash in a hotel envelope, all new notes as if they'd come fresh from the bank. Somchai hadn't even told his wife about the money. He was keeping it hidden in his locker, under a pile of old newspapers, until he decided what to do with it. Maybe a gold bracelet for his mistress. He smiled to himself. Maybe another mistress. He fished into his trouser pocket and took out a five-baht coin.

Somchai hadn't been able to eavesdrop on the conversation the farang had had with the lawyer, but he'd heard every word that had passed between the prisoner and the woman journalist. He hadn't understood everything, but his English was good enough to allow him to follow the gist of what was said. The woman thought that the prisoner wasn't who he said he was. She thought he was lying. And she wanted to write a story for her newspaper. Somchai hitched up his belt. Bird would pay a lot for that information. It wasn't a bad job at all, being in the detention centre.

BILLY WINTER OPENED HIS mouth and the young girl sitting on his left fed him a steamed prawn. He chewed with relish and grinned at Bird. 'It don't get much better than this, do it?' Winter said in his gruff Newcastle accent.

Bird nodded and peered at the laden plates on the table in front of them. Winter had over-ordered madly and there was enough food for a dozen people.

Winter and Bird were in a private room, sitting on cushions, with four girls in white kimonos that opened to reveal that they were naked underneath. They had two girls each, one at either shoulder, feeding them and holding their drinks to their lips whenever they wanted a drink. The restaurant's gimmick was that the diners never had to use their hands. Not to eat, anyway.

'I wonder what Hutch's having for dinner tonight?' mused Winter. He laughed harshly. 'Bread and water, you think? Is that what they give them in clink here, bread and water?' He used a finger to open the kimono of the girl sitting on his right. Her breasts were pert and firm and her skin the colour of light oak. She smiled engagingly, showing small, even teeth. They reminded Winter of baby teeth.

'Rice,' said Bird. 'Rice and soup. Some fish, maybe.'

'Yeah, well, it'll give him an incentive to get out, right?'

'Right,' agreed Bird.

'Yeah, he's always needed an incentive, has Hutch.' Winter opened the kimono wider. 'How old is this one, Bird?' he asked.

Bird spoke to the girl in Thai. 'Eighteen,' he said.

'Eighteen? She looks about twelve.'

'A lot of them lie about their age,' said Bird. 'They have to, to work.'

'So how old do you think she really is?'

Bird looked at the girl carefully. 'Fifteen. Maybe sixteen.'

Winter fondled the girl's breasts. 'Jailbait,' he whispered. 'Anywhere else in the world she'd be jailbait.' Her smile widened in anticipation of a large tip. 'I can smell smoke, I think the place is on fire,' Winter said. He grinned. The girl smiled at him and fluttered her eyelashes. Winter looked at the other girls. 'Can anyone else smell smoke?' He met with blank faces.

'I told you, they don't speak English,' said Bird.

'Just checking,' said Winter. He opened his mouth and accepted a piece of beef and a sliver of ginger. 'So what did you want to talk about?'

Bird stroked the thigh of the girl on his right. She opened her legs invitingly and held his glass to his lips. Bird sipped his beer. 'There's a woman journalist who has been asking questions about Hutch.'

Winter's eyes narrowed. 'About Hutch or about Warren Hastings?'

'Hastings,' said Bird, realising his mistake. 'She's been in Hong Kong, to his kennels. She's been to the detention centre twice. And I'm told that she's been talking to the DEA.'

'Shit,' said Winter. 'Does she know anything?'

'I don't think so, nothing definite anyway. Just suspicions. But if she keeps interfering . . .'

'Yeah, I get the picture.' He stroked the girl's soft, glossy hair. It reached her waist, jet black and perfectly straight. 'How much for the two of them?' he asked.

'A thousand baht each should do it. Unless you want to get rough.'

Winter laughed. 'Not me, Bird. I never went for the rough stuff. A thousand baht each, huh? That's about the price of a bottle of Johnnie Walker, right?'

Bird nodded. 'Red Label. Black's a bit more expensive.'

'What about you, Bird? Fancy giving them one? My treat.'

Bird shook his head. 'No thanks, Billy.' One of the girls wiped his chin with a napkin while the other delicately shelled a cooked prawn.

Winter bit into a chunk of crab proffered by the girl on his left. 'What's this one called again?' he said.

'Nood,' said Bird. 'The other one's Need.'

'Nood and Need. Love it. This journo, what's her name?'

'Leigh. Jennifer Leigh.'

'Chinese?'

Bird shook his head. 'A farang.'

'We can't have her making waves.'

'Making waves?' Bird repeated, not understanding.

'Rocking the boat. Screwing things up. If she keeps asking questions, she might find that Warren Hastings isn't what he claims to be. You're going to have to take care of her, Bird. And quickly.'

Bird grinned. 'Is it all right with you if I have a little fun with her first?'

Winter opened his mouth and the girl on his right popped in a morsel of chicken. 'So long as you take care of the bitch, you can do what the fuck you want, Bird,' he said.

JENNIFER LEIGH WAS SITTING on her hotel bed in bra and pants going through her notes when the telephone rang. She picked up the receiver.

'Miss Jennifer?' The voice was Thai, male.

'Yes,' she said, hesitantly.

'You have been asking about Warren Hastings.'

'Yes. Who's speaking?'

'I have some information for you.'

'About Warren Hastings?'

'Yes. But I want money.'

'How much?'

The man was silent for a few seconds. 'Perhaps a lot.'

Jennifer picked up her notebook, her heart racing as she realised that this could be the break she was looking for. 'What is the information?'

The man chuckled. 'If I tell you, Miss Jennifer, the information has no value.'

'But my newspaper won't pay unless we know what we're buying.'

There was a longer silence. Jennifer could hear a Thai pop song in the background, and the sound of glasses clinking, as if the man was calling from a bar.

'I must talk to you,' said the man eventually. 'Face to face.'

'That sounds like a good idea,' said Jennifer. 'Why don't you come to my hotel?'

'No. I must not be seen with you.'

'Why?'

'Because it is dangerous. For me. No one must know I have talked to you.'

'Okay, okay,' said Jennifer eagerly. The man sounded genuinely frightened and she feared that he might change his mind and hang up. 'I'll come to you. Anywhere you want.'

'I will send a taxi for you.'

'Give me your address and I'll get a hotel car.'

'The address is difficult. Better I send a taxi. Wait outside the hotel in one hour.'

'But . . .' Before she could finish, the line went dead.

Jennifer stripped and showered and watched CNN while she blow-dried her hair. She envied the on-camera reporters, flying around the world covering the big stories, reporting from the trouble spots. If she could just break the Warren Hastings story, if she could find out what the hell it was all about, it might be the ticket that would get her back on the road again. She'd do anything to get off the features desk and back to real reporting. Hell, if the guy's information was good, she'd damn well pay him out of her own pocket.

She opened her suitcase and wondered what to wear. Trousers or a dress? Skirt and top? A dress would be best, she decided. She'd seen Thai men in the streets staring at her breasts and knew that she had a better figure than most Thai women. They might have great skin and glossy black hair, but there was no way they could compete with good old British breasts. She picked up a blue linen dress and held it against herself, then dismissed it for being too wrinkled. It made her look good but she didn't have time to get it pressed. She took out a yellow cotton dress, cut to just above her knees. Perfect, she decided. Demure enough at the top so that it only suggested what lay beneath, but short enough to show off her legs, her second-best feature. She slipped on the dress and admired herself in the mirror. She had no doubt that between her legs and her breasts, she'd beat the guy down to a sensible price for whatever information he had.

She turned her back on the mirror and looked over her shoulder. 'Not bad for a thirty-eight-year-old,' she said to herself, then grinned at her reflection. She put her notebook and pen in her handbag and went downstairs.

A bellboy in a red jacket and white pants and wearing a peaked cap held the door open for her. In front of the glass doors was a blue taxi.

The driver, a middle-aged man with a large black mole on his chin, looked at her expectantly. She raised her eyebrows and he nodded. 'Miss Jennifer?' he said.

'That's me,' she said. 'Where are we going?' she asked the driver as he put the car in gear.

'No English,' he said gruffly as he joined the traffic which was crawling along outside the hotel.

The air-conditioner was on its lowest setting and the atmosphere was stifling. She pointed over the driver's shoulder at the air-conditioner control. 'Colder,' she pleaded. The driver nodded and increased the setting.

They turned left at a main intersection and drove for thirty minutes, during which time Jennifer estimated they covered perhaps two miles. The whole city appeared to be gridlocked. The only vehicles that made any progress were the motorcycles that weaved in and out of the cars. Virtually without exception the drivers of the cars left enough room for the motorcycles to pass by, and the thoughtfulness was frequently acknowledged with nods and smiles.

They turned off the main road into a single-lane street,

devoid of traffic, and then turned again and rattled along a narrow alleyway. Suddenly the taxi stopped. Jennifer looked around anxiously. The alley was gloomy and strewn with rubbish. There was nobody around.

'Are we here?' Jennifer asked. The driver shook his head. Jennifer couldn't tell whether or not he understood her. 'Is this it?' she asked. Before the driver could reply the passenger door opened. 'I'm still using this cab,' she protested, but a large Thai man slipped in to sit beside her.

'I am the man you have come to see,' said the man. 'My name is Bird.'

He was broad shouldered and had thick forearms as if he lifted weights a lot. Most of the Thais Jennifer had seen were short and slight; this man wouldn't have looked out of place in a London gym. He had a thick neck around which he wore a gold chain that appeared to be almost tight enough to choke him, as though he'd been wearing it since he was a child.

Jennifer held out her hand. 'Jennifer Leigh,' she said. 'But you know that already.' They shook. His hand was huge and engulfed hers entirely, but his grip was surprisingly gentle. He wore several large gold rings, and a diamond-studded gold Rolex. He was, Jennifer realised with an electric jolt, very attractive. As he turned his head she saw that he had a thin scar that ran from his left ear to the side of his nose.

Bird spoke to the driver in Thai and the car drove off. 'I am sorry to be so secretive,' said Bird. 'You will understand later. When I've told you what I know.'

'And what do you know?' Jennifer asked.

'Not here,' said Bird.

The taxi drove along to the end of the alley and turned

on to a street. By now Jennifer was totally disorientated. 'How did you know where to find me? How did you know who I was?'

'I heard that you were asking questions about Warren Hastings.'

'But so are the police. Why did you come to me?'

'The police don't pay as much as newspapers. Certainly not as much as British newspapers. But please, can we talk later?' He folded his arms across his chest.

They drove in silence. The taxi had to wait ten minutes before turning off the street and on to a four-lane highway. Despite the wider road, traffic was still moving at a snail's pace.

'Where are we going?' she asked. It had been more than an hour since she'd left the hotel.

'Not far.'

Flecks of rain peppered the windscreen and the driver switched on the wipers. The shower swiftly became a downpour and even on full power the wipers were unable to cope with the cascade of water. The traffic came to a standstill.

'Is it always like this?' Jennifer asked.

'It's the monsoon season,' said Bird.

'How long does it go on for?'

Bird shrugged and pulled a face. 'Until it stops,' he said. His face was impassive and Jennifer had no way of telling if he was joking or not. She smiled anyway.

The traffic began to move and the taxi turned off the main road. They made a series of turns, seemingly at random, and Jennifer had the distinct impression that the driver was deliberately trying to confuse his route. Eventually they stopped in front of a bar with black tinted windows.

'We are here,' said Bird. The driver pulled an umbrella from under the front passenger seat and handed it to Bird. They climbed out of the taxi and Bird used the umbrella to shelter them both.

The bar seemed to be closed and Bird rapped the door with his knuckles. They heard footsteps, and the sound of a key being turned and bolts being drawn back, then the door opened a fraction. Bird said something in Thai and the door opened further. Behind them, the taxi pulled away from the kerb and drove off into the rain.

Bird motioned for Jennifer to go first. Jennifer was suddenly apprehensive. She didn't know Bird, she had no idea where she was, or what she was getting in to. She suddenly remembered that she hadn't told the office where she was going. Bird smiled. It was an honest and open smile. Jennifer considered herself a good judge of character, and she felt that she could trust him. She returned the smile and stepped across the threshold, her misgivings forgotten.

It was dark inside and it took her eyes several seconds to get used to the gloom. To the left was a line of booths, all empty. To the right, a scattering of Formica tables and chairs, also deserted. There were several television sets suspended from the ceiling and a small podium with banks of speakers on either side. The door closed behind her and she jumped. The man who'd opened the door for them was small and had a withered arm that he kept pressed close to his chest as if it was hanging in an invisible sling. He slipped past her and went over to a well-stocked bar where a barman in a stained sweatshirt was half-heartedly polishing a glass.

Bird shook the umbrella and slotted it into a stand by

the door. He waved Jennifer over to one of the booths. 'Please sit,' he said.

Jennifer looked at her watch pointedly. 'I can't stay long,' she said.

'I understand,' he said pleasantly. 'But you can surely have a drink while I talk, yes?'

He seemed genuinely eager to please and Jennifer nodded. 'Gin and tonic,' she said. 'Ice and lemon if you've got it.'

Bird spoke to the barman in Thai and joined Jennifer in the booth. Jennifer was facing the door and she noticed that the door had been bolted. She swallowed as the feeling of apprehension returned.

Bird turned to see what she was looking at, then smiled reassuringly. 'For privacy,' he said, as if reading her mind.

'Sure,' she said, more confidently than she felt. 'So, what have you got to tell me?'

'It's about Warren Hastings,' said Bird, leaning forward conspiratorially. 'He's not who he says he is.'

Jennifer leaned forward, too, intrigued. 'Yes?'

Bird nodded. 'Warren Hastings isn't his real name.'

Jennifer took her notebook and pad out of her handbag and flicked through to an empty page. 'And his real name is . . .' she said, urging Bird on.

The man with the withered arm returned, balancing a tray with his good hand. He put Jennifer's drink down in front of her and gave Bird a bottle of Singha beer. Bird raised the bottle in salute. 'Cheers,' he said, then more slowly added, 'Bottoms up,' as if he was unsure how to pronounce the phrase.

'Cheers,' said Jennifer, and she clinked her glass against

his bottle. It was hot and airless in the small bar and Jennifer drank gratefully. Bird watched her over the top of his bottle.

Jennifer put down her glass. 'What is his real name?' she asked.

Bird smiled thinly. 'I think that is information you should pay for.'

'Do you have proof?'

Bird nodded. 'Yes. I have proof.'

'Documents? Photographs? What exactly do you have? My newspaper won't pay for rumour or innuendo.'

Bird picked up his bottle again. He waited for her to lift her glass, then toasted her. 'Cheers,' he said.

'Cheers,' she said. They both drank. Jennifer was beginning to feel light headed. There was a tumbler full of paper napkins on the table and she pulled one out and wiped her forehead.

'Are you feeling all right?' Bird asked.

'Just a bit hot,' she said. Her hands were sweating and she was having trouble keeping a grip on her pen.

'You are very pretty,' he said.

'What?' she said, confused by the sudden change of subject.

Bird reached over and stroked the back of her wrist. 'You're a very sexy farang,' he said, grinning. There was something unpleasant about the smile, she realised. Something predatory, a wickedness that hadn't been there before. She was suddenly afraid and pulled her hand away.

'Let's stick to the Hastings business,' she said.

'I think that business is now over,' he said. She saw him look over her shoulder and she turned quickly. Her head swam and she fought back a feeling of nausea. As her eyes focused she saw that two more men had joined the barman. They stood leaning against the bar, hands in their pockets. The man with the withered arm was sitting on the podium, staring at her. Jennifer shivered. She could barely keep her eyes open.

'We're going to have so much fun with you,' said Bird, reaching for her hand again.

Jennifer tried to get to her feet but the effort was too much for her and she slumped forward, her arm sweeping her glass from the table. She heard it shatter on the floor and then she passed out.

THE PAIN SHAFTED THROUGH Ray Harrigan's stomach like a lance and he grunted. 'Jesus Christ,' he said.

The Canadian looked up from his food. 'What's up?'

'Stomach cramps,' he said. He winced again and squatted down on his heels. 'Jesus, it hurts.'

The Canadian held up a spoonful of rice. 'Food poisoning, you reckon?'

Harrigan rolled on to his bed and hugged his stomach. 'I don't know, but it hurts like hell.'

The Canadian looked at his spoonful of rice for a few seconds, then he shrugged and swallowed it.

'I need a doctor,' groaned Harrigan.

'Yeah, and I need cable TV,' said the Canadian. Harrigan continued to moan so the Canadian put down his plate and went over to him. There were beads of sweat on Harrigan's forehead and his hair was damp. 'You're burning up,' said the Canadian.

'Is that a professional opinion?' Harrigan grunted. 'Fuck, fuck, fuck.' He drew his knees up against his chest into the fetal position. He began to breathe in short, sharp gasps like a weightlifter preparing to lift. 'You've got to give me something,' said Harrigan.

'I haven't got anything,' said the Canadian.

Harrigan grunted. The pain seemed to be getting worse, though it was already more than he could bear. 'You have to give me something.'

'Ray, I keep telling you, I haven't got any medicine.'

'What about your smack? That'll kill the pain, won't it?'

'You want heroin?'

'I can smoke it, you said. It's a painkiller, right?'

The Canadian rubbed the back of his neck. 'Sure.'

'So I'm in pain.' He moaned and shook his head from side to side as if to emphasise the point.

'I can see that, Ray. But you can't smoke it. I haven't got any foil.'

'What? What's that got to do with it?'

'You have to put it on a piece of foil, and then hold it over a flame. That's how you get the smoke.' He put a hand on Harrigan's shoulder. Harrigan put his hands between his legs and bit down on his lower lip as he grunted with pain. 'I'm sorry, man,' said the Canadian.

Harrigan didn't reply. His shirt was soaked and rivulets of sweat dripped down on to his mat.

'Look, Ray. If you want, I can, you know, give you some smack.'

'You said . . .'

'You can inject. I've got a clean needle. Never been used. Pristine.'

'I hate needles,' said Harrigan through clenched teeth.

'Yeah. You said.'

Harrigan rolled over so that he was facing away from the Canadian. He began to shiver uncontrollably. 'Okay,' he said eventually.

'Okay what?'

'Don't fuck me around.' Harrigan's teeth began to chatter. 'Get the stuff ready.'

JENNIFER HEARD VOICES, INDISTINCT as if far away at the end of a long, long tunnel. Whispering, then laughing. She felt as if she were enveloped in a feather quilt, as if everything around her were soft and fuzzy. She swallowed and there was a funny taste in her mouth. It was hard to breathe, something was pressing down on her chest, something heavy. Something that moved. Something hard and wet forced itself between her lips. She began to choke but then suddenly she could breathe again. She was lying on her back and she tried to roll on to her side but something was preventing her. She tried to move her arms but they felt as if they'd turned to stone. There was no feeling, no response when she tried to raise them. The weight returned to press against her and she felt her legs being pushed apart.

The voices became louder but she couldn't make out what was being said. There was more laughing. She was hot. Very hot. She wanted a drink of water. Something was pounding against her, moving quickly, thumping into her groin. It didn't hurt, in fact it was quite pleasant, and

Jennifer smiled to herself. She was dreaming, she realised. She was in bed, safe and warm, and she was dreaming. Her hair was over her face and she wanted to brush it away but still her hands wouldn't move. She swallowed again. There was something bitter in her mouth. Her eyelids flickered. It was light. She must have overslept. She wondered what the voices were. Maybe she'd fallen asleep with the television on. She tried to drift back to sleep, back into the dream, but the light was insistent and so were the voices. Men's voices. The pounding between her legs became faster, more frantic, and she felt something deep inside.

She opened her eyes. There was a face looking down at her, a face contorted into a grimace of pain. It was a man, with two gold teeth at the front of his mouth. His eyes were closed and his nostrils flared as he snorted For the first time she became aware of his breath, rancid and stale like old cheese. She turned her face away. There was another man there, holding her arm. And behind him another man, bare chested and smoking a cigarette. The man on top of her went suddenly still, then laughed. It was a bark of triumph. The room seemed to spin and she closed her eyes. The man rolled off her and she tried to close her legs. Something was stopping her. She opened her eyes and looked down towards her feet. Bird was there, grinning and holding her left leg. The barman was gripping her other ankle with both hands.

The barman said something to Bird and they both looked at her. Bird let go of her leg and walked out of her vision. The man with the withered arm sat down on the bed. He reached out with his good arm and stroked her breast. Jennifer was aware of what he was doing but she couldn't feel anything. It was as if it was happening to someone else.

Bird appeared at her side. He was holding a bottle in one hand, and a cloth in the other. 'What are you doing?' she tried to ask, but she was unable to form the words and all that came out was a low moan. Bird said something to her but his voice sounded a million miles away.

Another man, big with rippling forearms, stood next to Bird, unzipping his jeans. Jennifer shook her head, but even as she did she knew she was powerless to resist. Her stomach lurched. There were a dozen Thai men in the room, maybe more. They were all around her, laughing at her, pointing at her. The big man climbed on top of her and this time she felt a sharp pain between her legs. Tears sprang to her eyes, tears of frustration. The feeling was starting to return to her left leg and she tried to kick him away but she was too weak and he was too strong. He moaned as he pushed himself deeper inside her. He arched his back and grunted, and then it was over and he lifted himself off her.

Bird thrust the cloth over her face and she breathed in sickly sweet fumes. She threw her head to the side but Bird's fingers gripped her cheeks and forced her back on to the bed. She tried holding her breath but it was futile. Bird waited until she'd taken half a dozen breaths before taking the cloth away. She gasped for fresh air but she could feel consciousness slipping away. Bird took off his trousers and stood at the end of the bed, holding his erection and laughing at her. He said something in Thai and she felt herself being rolled over on to her stomach. She realised what Bird was going to do and she tried to beg him not to but the words wouldn't come. Her head was twisted to the side and all she could see was the man with the withered arm, grinning at her. Bird climbed on to the bed. She was suddenly embarrassed. No man had ever done that to her before. Ever. She'd never let a man even touch her there. She felt Bird lie on top of her and then force himself inside. There was surprisingly little pain, she realised, and then she passed out again.

HUTCH WOKE TO THE sound of the cell door being opened. Four uniformed police threw a man in and then clanged the door shut. They watched him through the bars as he got unsteadily to his feet. It was the second Nigerian.

Joshua was lying next to Hutch, fast asleep. Hutch shook him by the arm. Joshua opened his eyes and grunted. When he saw his friend he began to laugh. It was a deep, booming sound that echoed around the cell. The two men embraced and slapped each other's back. They spoke to each other in their own language and Joshua laughed even louder.

'You won't believe what Julian did,' said Joshua.

The policemen went back down the corridor. Hutch sat on the floor and the two Nigerians followed his example.

'They gave him the same stuff they gave me,' Joshua continued. 'But the Thais didn't watch him closely enough. The condoms kept coming out, and Julian kept swallowing them. The Thais couldn't work out what was going on.'

Julian grinned. He looked around for a sleeping mat. When he realised there was none to be had, he lay down on the bare floor, seemingly unconcerned by his surroundings.

'Why?' asked Hutch. 'Why did he bother? They'd get the stuff eventually.'

Joshua shrugged. 'I don't know. He's crazy.'

Julian's eyes were closed and he appeared to be asleep already.

'He said we're going to be in court tomorrow.'

Hutch sat up straight. 'How does he know?'

'We have a lawyer. The lawyer told him.'

Hutch's heart began to race. If the Nigerians were going to court, maybe they'd be taking him, too. He'd been arrested at the same time as them. Maybe Winter's plan would work after all. If he was transferred to Klong Prem prison tomorrow, he might still have a chance of getting to Harrigan and finding a way out before the police discovered that he wasn't carrying drugs and he was released.

THERE WAS SOMETHING PRESSING against Jennifer's knees, something hard and unyielding. She tried to open her eyes but it felt as if the lids had been sewn shut. In the distance she heard a deep growling noise, like some huge prehistoric animal proclaiming its dominance. She swallowed but her mouth was painfully dry and her tongue seemed to have swollen to twice its normal size. She heard voices, and an engine being revved. Her neck was sore and she tried to arch her back but there was something hard behind her, something that prevented her from moving. Images flashed through her mind: Bird in the bar; the men in the room; the cloth against her face. The horror and the shame flooded over her and she opened her eyes. Eighteen inches from her face was a curved metal surface. She turned her head and felt the bones in her neck grind together. She was rammed in a circular metal container, with her knees up against her chest. She closed her eyes again. It was a dream, a horrible dream. Maybe it had all been a nightmare, right from the start. Maybe she was still in her hotel room, asleep in the queensize bed. Maybe the American was even in bed beside her.

The growling roar intensified and she felt its vibrations come up through her backside. She opened her eyes again. It was no dream. She tried to move her arms but they were jammed against the metal. She forced her head back as far as it would go. There was sky above her head, grey clouds moving slowly against a black background, and to the right was the towering skeleton of a building under construction: girders and scaffolding and concrete beams.

Jennifer opened her mouth to call for help. Maybe she'd been in an accident. A car crash, perhaps. She was okay, she was alive, somebody would come and rescue her eventually, she just had to stay calm.

A man appeared above her, his head silhouetted against the clouds. She shook her head, clearing the hair that had fallen across her face, and peered upwards.

'Help me,' she said. Her voice was little more than a croak. The head disappeared. Jennifer groaned and tried to move her hands again. She was naked, she realised. Totally naked. It didn't make any sense, she thought. What had happened to her clothes? Where was she?

She looked up again. High overhead flew an airliner, a red light flashing from one wing. Another head appeared. She recognised the face. It was Bird. He was grinning.

'Help me, please,' she gasped.

Bird turned away and gestured with his hand, motioning for someone to come closer. The roaring noise wasn't an animal, she realised, it was machinery. An engine, and tyres crunching across gravel.

There was a bad taste in her mouth and she tried to clear her throat. Her whole body ached, and she felt a searing pain deep inside her, as if the flesh there had been torn apart. Something warm and liquid dribbled from between her legs and she had no way of telling if it was blood or urine. She began to cry, more from helplessness than from the pain.

Bird shouted and the engine noise reduced to a low throb, then there was a rattle of metal and a two-foot-wide chute appeared above Jennifer's head. Bird held it steady with one hand as he peered down at her.

'Please, don't,' she begged through her tears. 'Please.' The man had drugged her, raped her, done God knows what else to her, but he was the only hope she had. She looked up at him, her eyes wide and fearful. 'I'll do anything,' she said. 'Anything.'

Bird's grin widened. 'You already have done,' he said. 'And you weren't that good. Too old.'

He turned away and waved at someone she couldn't see. The unseen engine roared and the chute began to tremble in Bird's hand. Something cold and wet spewed out, spraying over her. She closed her eyes and clamped her mouth shut and tried to breathe through her nose as the gritty cement coated her hair and ran thickly down her neck. She felt it pool around her backside and rise up around her waist. The deluge intensified, and the sheer weight of it forced her head down. It poured into her nostrils and she began to choke. Cement began to seep into her mouth and she coughed and spluttered. Her lungs ached for air but she resisted the urge to breathe, knowing that her next breath would be her last, wanting to cling on to life until the last possible moment. The cement clogged her ears but she could still hear the roar of the engine and Bird's laughter. Her lungs began to burn, and as she opened her mouth and it filled with cement, the last thought that passed through her mind was that she didn't even know why she was being killed.

HUTCH SAT ON THE hard wooden bench and stared straight ahead. Through the bars in front of him he could see a raised podium on which were three desks. To his right were the two Nigerians; to his left was a young Thai man in a torn T-shirt and cut-off jeans. Behind him were more benches, with more than twenty prisoners in all, including the American. They'd been handcuffed and herded into a coach by armed police early in the morning and driven out of the city. Hutch had been given his wallet and his watch but they hadn't allowed him to take his sleeping mat, and when he'd asked what had happened to his other belongings he'd been met with blank faces. The guards hadn't said where they were going, but Hutch was certain he was in the Criminal Court for his first appearance before a judge.

Hutch looked over his shoulder. There were half a dozen uniformed guards holding shotguns, their fingers on the triggers. There were more guards inside the court itself, their backs against the walls.

There was no air-conditioning and Hutch was drenched with sweat. The mosquito bites on his body now numbered more than twenty and the itching was almost unbearable. He wiped his forehead with the sleeve of his shirt.

'Warren?' said a trembling voice.

Hutch looked up sharply. There were two people standing on the other side of the bars: an Oriental girl and a Thai man. For a second he couldn't place their faces. When he did recognise Chau-ling, he felt suddenly embarrassed by his dishevelled appearance. She was wearing a dark blue two-piece suit and matching high heels, a far cry from the sweatshirts and faded jeans she favoured while working at the kennels, and she wore a thin gold necklace that he'd never seen before.

'Warren,' she said. 'You look terrible.'

She stepped forward and held the bars as if it was she who was the prisoner. Behind her was Khun Kriengsak, the highly paid lawyer employed by her father.

Hutch glared at her through the bars. 'What the hell are you doing here?' he asked.

She was surprised by the intensity of his anger. 'I've come to help you,' she said, her voice trembling.

'Chau-ling, if I'd wanted your help, I'd have asked for it.'

'Warren, you're in trouble and I want—'

'I can take care of it,' he said. 'I'd rather you stayed and looked after my business.'

'The kennels are fine,' said Chau-ling earnestly. 'Naomi and Man-ying are there, they can handle it.'

'I left you in charge,' said Hutch. He turned on the lawyer. 'And I already told you that I don't need a lawyer. Do you have a problem with English?'

Kriengsak's eyes hardened. 'No, Mr Hastings, my English is perfectly adequate. Miss Tsang has come a long way to see you, and if I were you I'd be more grateful for her concern. A friendship such as hers does not come along too often. And your attitude so far suggests to me that you are not worthy of it.'

Hutch felt his cheeks redden as he realised that the lawyer was right. 'I'm sorry, Chau-ling,' he said. 'I just want to take care of this myself.'

'Warren, to be honest you don't seem to be doing too good a job right now.'

Hutch stood up and went over to the bars. She saw him glance down at his chained hands and his shame deepened. 'It's going to be all right,' he said. 'The best thing you can do is to go back to Hong Kong. Look, this has all been a terrible mistake, and once the police realise that, I'll be on the next plane home. How are Mickey and Minnie?'

'Pining,' she said. 'They send their love.'

Hutch smiled. 'Thanks,' he said. 'You look great, by the way.'

She returned his smile, albeit hesitantly. She reached up to brush a strand of hair from her eyes. There was a gold Cartier watch on her wrist. Chau-ling had been working at the kennels for almost a year before Hutch had discovered who her father was and that she was sole heir to one of the biggest fortunes in Hong Kong. She drove a six-year-old Suzuki Jeep and the only jewellery he'd ever seen her wearing was a Swatch wristwatch. Hutch was genuinely surprised by her sudden exhibition of wealth and good taste.

'Is it bad, where they're holding you?' asked Chau-ling.

'It's not exactly a four-star hotel,' Hutch replied. He looked at Kriengsak. 'I go from here to the prison, right?'

'Yes. They will hold you there until the trial.'

Hutch shook his head emphatically. 'There isn't going to be a trial,' he said.

Kriengsak and Chau-ling exchanged looks. Something unspoken passed between them. Kriengsak narrowed his eyes and stared at Hutch. 'Mr Hastings, is there something you want to tell me?'

'You sound more like a psychiatrist than a lawyer,' said Hutch.

'Warren, we're only trying to help,' said Chau-ling. 'We have to prepare your case before you go to trial.'

Hutch gripped the bars, his eyes intense. 'Chau-ling, this isn't going to go to trial. It's all been a mistake and when the police realise that, I'll be out of here.'

Kriengsak frowned. 'In what way has there been a mistake?' he asked.

Hutch sighed in exasperation. 'The drugs they found. They're not drugs. Once they've been tested, they'll have to let me go.'

The lawyer and Chau-ling exchanged glances again.

Hutch realised there was something they weren't telling him. 'What?' he said. 'What's wrong?'

The confusion was obvious in Chau-ling's eyes. 'Warren, the results of the tests came back this morning. You were carrying ninety-eight per cent pure Number Four heroin.'

Hutch's jaw dropped and he felt suddenly weak at the knees. His knuckles whitened as he gripped the bars tighter. The room seemed to spin and he closed his eyes.

'According to a friend of mine in the prosecutor's office, they will be looking for a speedy trial,' he heard Kriengsak say. 'And the prosecution will be pressing for the death penalty.'

Hutch's shoulders sagged. He let go of the bars and massaged his temples with the palms of his hands. 'What? What are you talking about?' He found it difficult to talk and the strength had drained from his legs.

The lawyer repeated himself, but Hutch barely heard the words. He sat down heavily. His head felt as if it was about to explode. It didn't make any sense. None of it made any sense. Pure heroin? How in God's name had the laboratory come to that conclusion? Something had gone wrong, badly wrong. Maybe the Thai police had set him up. Maybe when the lab had shown that the white powder wasn't heroin, the police had decided to take matters into their own hands and had substituted the real thing.

'Warren, it's okay,' said Chau-ling. 'They don't execute foreigners here. The King always commutes the sentence to life imprisonment. Not that . . . I mean . . . you know . . . it's not going to come to that.'

Hutch wasn't listening. It had all gone wrong from the start. According to Billy, Hutch should have been sent to the main prison straight away, he shouldn't have been locked up in a police cell for three days. How had Billy managed to be so wrong? Hutch realised he was panting: his breath was coming in short, ragged gasps like a heart attack victim. He held his breath for several seconds and fought to stay calm. Panic wouldn't serve any purpose. He forced himself to breathe slowly and he clenched and unclenched his hands.

'Warren? Warren, are you all right?'

Hutch ignored her. Maybe Billy had set him up? But that didn't make any sense because if Billy wanted to cause him grief, all he had to do was to make one telephone call to the police in the UK. And if Billy wanted Hutch dead, then

Billy knew people, very heavy people, people who'd quite happily pull the trigger on a sawn-off shotgun without the need for laboratory analysis or a trial. But that didn't make any sense either, because Hutch had never crossed Billy. In fact, in Parkhurst they'd been friends. And Hutch had agreed to help him get his colleague out of prison, albeit reluctantly. Why would Billy then go and double-cross him? Whichever way he looked at it, it didn't make any sense.

Perhaps it wasn't Billy who'd set him up; perhaps Bird had substituted the drugs. Maybe Bird was working against Billy and this was some sort of plot to destroy Billy's operation. But if Bird had betrayed Billy, then why hadn't Billy been in touch? And what about the man who'd delivered the drugs, the man who was supposed to step forward and take the blame so that Hutch could be released? Maybe he'd had a change of heart; maybe he'd set Hutch up so that he wouldn't have to go to prison.

Hutch put his hands up to his face and covered his eyes with his palms. Bird. Billy. The police. Bird's contact. Someone had gone to a lot of trouble to set him up. There had to be a way out. There had to be something he could do to get out of his predicament.

'Warren. Pull yourself together.' Chau-ling spoke urgently and Hutch snapped out of his reverie.

'I'll be okay, Chau-ling,' he said. He looked up but he had trouble focusing. He shook his head and blinked several times.

She stared at him, her concern obvious in her eyes. 'Let Khun Kriengsak help you,' she said, her voice little more than a whisper. 'Let him at least present your case.'

Hutch stood up again and walked hesitantly towards her. He felt suddenly faint and put his forehead against the bars. Chau-ling reached out to touch him but an armed policeman barked at her and she pulled her hand back as if she'd been stung. 'Chau-ling, you have to listen to me,' he said. 'You have to listen to me, and you have to do what I say.'

'Anything, Warren.'

'Go home. Forget about me. Forget everything.'

She shook her head quickly. 'No. You can't make me go.'

Behind her, a black-robed judge and three women carrying files entered the courtroom and took their places. Clerks scurried about and several uniformed policemen walked in, carrying more files and talking in hushed voices.

'It is about to start,' said Khun Kriengsak. 'The proceedings will all be in Thai, so I shall have to translate for you.'

'Okay,' said Hutch. 'But I don't want to say anything.'

'You won't be asked to say anything,' said the lawyer. 'At this stage, all the judge wants to know is that the police have a case against you. It's nothing more than a formality.'

A gavel banged and the lawyer jerked as if he'd been pinched. He nodded curtly at Hutch, signalling that they'd have to be quiet. He went over to the sparsely filled public benches with Chau-ling and they sat down together. Chau-ling kept looking over at Hutch with anxious eyes but he ignored her and stared straight ahead.

TIM CARVER WAS STANDING by the water cooler when he heard his name being called. It was Ed Harris, a young agent on attachment from the DEA's New York office. 'Tim, call for you. London.'

Carver drained his paper cup, crumpled it and bounced it off the wall into a wastepaper basket. 'Yeah, two points, the crowd goes wild,' he muttered to himself. 'Okay, Ed,' he called down the corridor. 'I'll take it in my office.'

His phone was already ringing when he pushed open his office door. He sat down and picked up the receiver. It was Richard Kay, a British journalist he'd met only once but with whom he'd struck up an immediate rapport. They chatted for a while, reminiscing about Kay's recent fact-finding trip to the Far East, then the journalist came to the point.

'Tim, have you seen Jennifer Leigh recently?'

'A few days ago.'

'But not within the last forty-eight hours?'

'No. Why?'

'She's gone AWOL and the feature editor's doing his nut.'

'Sorry I can't help,' said the DEA agent. 'I gave her some background on a Brit who got caught with a kilo of heroin, but I haven't seen her since.'

'Warren Hastings?'

'That's the guy. She had some conspiracy theory, a hunch that something wasn't kosher.'

'Yeah, it turns out that she might be right.'

Carver tensed and reached for a pen. 'What makes you say that, Richard?'

There was a moment's hesitation as if the journalist was considering how much to tell Carver. 'I checked out the passport number she gave me. It's genuine. Issued just over seven years ago. So far so good. But then I went to look up his birth certificate. There isn't one.'

'You mean it's missing?'

'I mean that no one called Warren Hastings was born on the date in the passport. Nor during the months either side.'

Carver doodled on his notepad. 'How can that be?' he asked. 'It's the same procedure in the UK as in the States, right? You have to produce a birth certificate to get a passport.'

'That's right. The usual way of setting up a false identity is to use the birth certificate of someone who died without ever getting a passport, ideally an infant.'

'Same in the States,' said Carver. 'So you're saying that this Hastings guy got a passport without a birth certificate?'

'Uh-huh. There've been a couple of bad apples in the Home Office over the past few years, selling passports for cash to rich Chinese and Nigerians and the like. Two rings were busted and some of the passport numbers they sold are known, but most aren't. I'm assuming that Hastings or whatever his real name is bought one of them.'

'Have you told the Home Office yet?'

'Bit of a sticky wicket, there,' said Kay. 'There's a guy I pay for information, and I can't tell them officially without tipping them off that I've got an inside source. So mum's the word.'

Carver wrote the name Warren Hastings on his notepad and underlined it three times.

'Also, Jenn told me that Hastings avoided having his photograph taken,' continued Kay. 'And he had no relatives, none that he talked about, anyway.'

Carver put down his pen and pulled a half-empty pack of Marlboro from his shirt pocket. He tapped a cigarette out and lit it. 'So her hunch was right,' he said. 'Hastings isn't his real name, he's hiding from something. Or somebody.'

'Yeah, that's the way it looks. Jenn went to Hong Kong to sniff around, and then she was on her way back to Bangkok. But since her last phone call from Hong Kong, we haven't heard from her.'

'Does she always keep in touch with the office? I got the feeling she was a bit of a maverick.'

'She's a bit headstrong, but she's always professional,' said Kay. 'And she wanted the information I've got, so she'd call for that if nothing else.'

'Where was she staying the last time she was here?'

'The Shangri-La. And she was flying Thai. She might have spoken to them about reconfirming her ticket.'

Carver wrote the name of the hotel and the airline on his notepad. 'I'll check around, Richard. Give me your number and I'll get back to you.'

Kay gave him the office telephone number. 'Hey, by the way,' said the journalist. 'What's this about you telling her you were gay?'

Carver chuckled. 'She told you that, huh?'

'Could have knocked me down with a feather. Didn't seem to gel with what the two of us got up to in that massage parlour you took me to, but I didn't put her right. Did she hit on you?'

'Like a ten-ton truck. Suggesting that women didn't turn me on seemed to be the most diplomatic way out. She's dangerous, that one.'

'A maneater,' agreed Kay. 'But I hope she's okay.'

THE JUDGE SAID NOTHING for almost an hour. One by one files were handed to him and he read them silently, occasionally making notes on a pad. He was middle aged and overweight with a high forehead, bulging eyes behind thick lenses and jowls under his chin that wobbled as he turned his head. He looked for all the world like a brown-skinned frog contemplating his next meal. Eventually he looked up, put his pen down on his pad, and interlinked his fingers. One of the female officials, the eldest and clearly the most senior, called out a name. One of the Thais stood up. The judge asked a policeman several questions and then said something to the prisoner. He began to reply but the judge silenced him with an impatient wave of his hand. Two guards took the prisoner away and led him through a back door.

Warren Hastings was the next name to be called. Hutch got to his feet and stood straight, his chained hands in front of him. Immediately Khun Kriengsak stood up and addressed the judge. The judge nodded, and then began to talk to a uniformed policeman.

Kriengsak went over to the bars and motioned for Hutch to come forward. As the policeman read from a file, Kriengsak translated in a hushed voice, so quietly that Hutch had to strain to hear. The policeman had related the details of the arrest at the airport and the results of the lab test on the heroin that was discovered in his bag. The policeman took a sheet of paper and held it up. The judge motioned for the woman with Hutch's file to hand it to him. He polished his glasses and flicked through the paperwork and pulled out a sheet of paper which he studied carefully.

'The police say that you signed a confession, admitting that the heroin was yours,' whispered the lawyer.

'Under duress,' said Hutch.

'Nevertheless . . .' said Kriengsak, but he didn't finish. He listened to what the policeman was saying. 'They say the arrest was the result of a tip-off from a regular informant.'

The judge nodded gravely and then looked at Hutch, blinking behind the thick lenses. He spoke for less than a minute, then put the file aside and waved at the senior assistant to continue with the next case.

'You are to be held in custody for twelve days,' said Kriengsak. 'No bail.'

'Where?'

'Klong Prem.' A uniformed guard took a sheet of paper from the judge and passed it through the bars to Hutch. 'You must sign that,' said Kriengsak. He handed Hutch a slim gold pen.

Hutch fumbled to hold them both with his handcuffed hands. He scanned the sheet. It was all in Thai. 'What is it?' he asked.

'You sign it to say that you understand that you are being remanded for twelve days. After twelve days they'll bring you back here. And for every twelve days thereafter until your trial. You'll have to sign a form like this each time they take you to prison.'

'Just a thought,' said Hutch. 'What would happen if I didn't sign?'

'Then they'd keep you in the holding cell,' said the

lawyer patiently. 'Without food or water or a place to sleep.'

Hutch signed. He almost made the mistake of using his real name, and struggled to make the C that he'd begun to write look like the W of Warren. He handed the paper and the pen back to Kriengsak. 'Now what happens?' Hutch asked.

Before the lawyer could answer, Hutch's shoulders were seized and he was pulled away from the bars. He looked over his shoulder. Chau-ling had got to her feet, her face creased in anguish.

He was taken through the door at the back of the seating area, along a corridor and through a second door. Behind the second door was another corridor, with cells on both sides. He was put in the first cell on the right. It was barely twenty feet square with green-painted walls and floor-to-ceiling bars on the side facing the corridor. There were already more than thirty men there, most of them in brown sleeved shirts and short pants and almost half with chains on their legs. They sat on a dirty cement floor or stood at the bars shouting to prisoners in the cell opposite. Hutch walked to the back of the cell, but stopped when the smell of the toilet hit him. There was an open sewer stinking of urine behind the squat toilet. He returned to the front of the cell and found a place to sit while he waited. After an hour Matt was put into the cell and he sat down next to Hutch.

'Klong Prem,' sighed the American.

'Yeah, me too,' said Hutch. 'Was your lawyer there?'

'For all the good that it did me. I paid him thirty thousand baht and he didn't even have a copy of the arrest report. He'd been drinking, too. I could smell it on his breath. I asked him to translate what the judge was saying, but all he kept telling me was that it was routine, that the judge would be angry if I held him up by asking for everything he said to be translated. Then he asked me for another fifty thousand baht.' He closed his eyes and banged his head on the wall again.

Hutch drew his legs up against his chest. He didn't like the look of the chains that the men were wearing, and the brown uniforms suggested that they had already spent time in the prison. Did that mean that he too would be put in chains?

There were footsteps in the hallway, but Hutch didn't look up. 'Khun Warren?' It was Kriengsak, holding his briefcase in one hand.

Hutch got to his feet and went over to the bars. 'Thanks for translating,' he said.

The lawyer accepted Hutch's thanks with a slight smile. 'I am only sorry that you would not let me do more, Khun Warren. Do you still insist that you do not require my services?'

Hutch had a sudden impulse to beg the lawyer to do whatever it took to stop him being sent to prison, but he knew it was pointless. He shook his head.

'Very well,' said Kriengsak. 'I wish you the best of luck.' He turned to go.

'Wait!' said Hutch. 'You've been inside Klong Prem?'

'Not personally,' said the lawyer, without any sense of irony. 'But I have had several clients who have had the misfortune to spend some time there, despite my best efforts.'

Hutch put his head closer to the bars. 'Klong Prem,' he said. 'What's it like? What can I expect?'

'It will not be pleasant.' The lawyer took a deep breath as if preparing himself for a courtroom speech. 'First, you must understand that prisons in Thailand do not operate as they do in the West. Prisoners here do not have the same rights, even prisoners such as yourself who are on remand. We assume that if the police say a man is guilty, he is. You will be chained as soon as you reach Klong Prem. The chains will stay on for at least a month, perhaps longer, but if you are prepared to bribe your guards, the chains can be taken off sooner. The food you will be given will be worse than you can possibly imagine, but you will be able to buy better food, fruit and vegetables. You will be put in a cell with up to twenty other prisoners, but if you are prepared to pay, you can be moved to a better cell.'

'I can buy myself a better cell?' asked Hutch in astonishment.

'In Klong Prem, you can buy almost everything,' said the lawyer. 'Except your freedom.'

Hutch groped for his wallet. He opened it. There was only two thousand baht inside.

'I'm sure Miss Tsang will deposit money for you,' said Kriengsak.

Kriengsak stepped aside to allow two guards to open the door to the holding cell. The two Nigerians were ushered in and the door relocked. Joshua gave Hutch a gentle pat on the back and mumbled something that Hutch couldn't quite catch.

'And I have to stay in prison until the trial?' Hutch asked Kriengsak.

'I'm afraid so, yes.'

'Which will be how long?'

'Three months. Four. Trial dates are unpredictable in Thailand.'

Hutch rested his forehead on the bars. A group of brown-uniformed policemen walked in twos down the corridor. One of the guards shouted at the prisoners and gestured for them to stand up. Hutch looked at Kriengsak expectantly.

'You are to be taken to the prison now,' said the lawyer. 'All I can do is to wish you the best of luck. If you should change your mind about representation . . .' He didn't give Hutch time to reply, as if he already knew what his answer would be. He smiled sympathetically and walked away, leaving Hutch feeling more alone than he'd felt since he'd arrived in Thailand.

THE PHONE ON TIM Carver's desk trilled like an injured bird and he picked it up. It was a Thai scientist at the police forensic laboratory. His name was Chat, and though Carver had never met the man he spoke to him several times a month. Their conversations were always in English. Carver's Thai was as fluent as a Westerner's could be, and it was considerably better than Chat's English, but the scientist refused to speak to the DEA agent in Thai. Carver wasn't sure if it was because the scientist felt threatened by Carver's grasp of the language, or if it was simply that Chat wanted to practise his English, but whatever the reason, the conversations were punctuated with pauses and hesitations as Chat sought to get his grammar and vocabulary in order.

'Mr Tim, we have received now the results of the heroin test,' said Chat, labouring over each word.

'That's good,' said Carver, flicking a cigarette out of its packet with one hand.

'It is from heroin that we have had before,' Chat continued.

Carver lit his cigarette and settled back in his chair. 'Even better,' he said.

'What?' said Chat.

Carver realised his words of encouragement had only confused the scientist. 'Nothing,' said Carver. 'Please go on.'

'Yes, good,' said Chat. 'It is identical to a batch we tested last year. From Chiang Mai. I have a reference number. Do you have a pen?'

Carver reached for a ballpoint. 'Yes,' he said. Chat gave him the reference number used by the Thai police. It wasn't familiar, but then Carver dealt with hundreds of cases every year. 'Chiang Mai, you said?'

'The big one last year. Fifty kilos. From Zhou Yuanyi.'

Carver remembered the bust, one of the biggest that year. It had been handled by the Thais, and the DEA hadn't been informed until after arrests had been made. One of those arrested had been Park, the man Carver had gone to see in Klong Prem prison. He wrote, 'Zhou Yuanyi' on a sheet of paper and underlined it. 'Fax me the report, will you, Chat? I'd like to see it as quickly as possible.'

'Of course, Mr Tim,' said Chat. 'Right away.'

Carver smiled as he replaced the receiver. The fax could arrive any time within the next week or so. The Thai definition of 'right away' was flexible, to say the least.

THE PRISONERS WERE SHEPHERDED on to a coach by brown-uniformed guards with shotguns. It wasn't one of the pristine white coaches that Hutch had seen parked outside the prison: it was shabby with blue rusting paintwork, though it did have similar metal screens on the windows. There were more prisoners than seats and Hutch and the two Nigerians had to stand during the two-hour journey to the prison. The main road leading out of town was almost blocked solid with traffic and they moved at a snail's pace. Two guards with shotguns rode at the back of the bus, another rode up front with the driver.

Hutch looked down at the manacles on his ankles. They were shiny stainless steel, almost brand new, with a lock on each shackle. The chain allowed him to take steps about three-quarters of his normal stride. Several of the prisoners had tied strips of cloth to the middle of their chains which they held to keep the chain from dragging on the ground as they walked. Hutch managed to get a close look at the manacles on the legs of a Thai man in prison uniform and what he saw scared him: there appeared to be no locking mechanism, just pieces of metal which had been curved around the ankles. He hoped they weren't standard wear in the prison. Chau-ling's lawyer had said that he would be forced to wear chains for the first month. If the manacles had locks, at least he stood a chance of getting them off: the chains worn by the Thai prisoner could only be removed by forcing the metal link apart, something that would require superhuman strength or, more likely, some sort of machinery.

The bus turned off the main road and rattled over the railway lines, exactly as Hutch and Bird had done in the Capri. Hutch tried to remember how long ago that had been. He couldn't be exact about the number of days, they had all begun to merge into one during his stay at the detention centre. That was one of the first things to go in prison: the sense of time passing. The sentence became a limbo, marked only by the meals that arrived and the switching on and off of the lights.

'Is that it?' asked Joshua, bending to peer through the mesh-covered window. He was bathed in sweat and his body odour was overpowering. 'Is that Klong Prem?'

'Yeah,' said Hutch.

'I've got friends there,' said Joshua. 'What about you?'

Hutch shook his head. The coach turned sharply to the left and he had to hold on tightly to keep his balance. It drove around the roundabout and came to a sudden halt in front of the main entrance. The rear doors opened and the guards began to usher the prisoners out. Hutch could barely believe what he was seeing: they were being asked to walk into the prison under their own steam. The sun was blinding and Hutch kept his head down as the prisoners were recounted and made to line up in pairs. When the guards were satisfied, the prisoners were walked forward, through the archway and along a gloomy hallway. Corridors led off to the left and right, and ahead of them was a huge white-painted metal gate. As they approached it, a small door set into the gate was opened by a guard with a look of boredom on his face.

Once through the door they were made to squat while

another head count was taken in a courtyard, the likes of which Hutch had never seen in a prison. There were neatly trimmed bushes, flower beds laid out as formally as a royal park, and grass that would have done a bowling green proud. There was a building that looked as if it was an administration centre and another large gate set into an inner wall. It looked more like a holiday camp than a prison. A man in a blue uniform cycled past on a gleaming bicycle without giving them a second look.

When the count was finished, the prisoners were divided into two groups and those wearing the brown uniforms were marched away. Hutch and the rest of the remand prisoners were taken into the administration building.

In a large reception area a middle-aged Thai guard barked at them, reading from a clipboard. 'He's telling us when we eat, when we wash, the work we'll be doing, stuff like that,' Matt whispered to Hutch. He was cut short by a guard, who hit him on the back of the head with the flat of his hand.

'No talking,' grunted the guard. It was the first time that Hutch had heard a guard speak English. Hutch flashed Matt an apologetic smile. It had been his fault that the American had received the blow.

To the left of the reception area were two tables. One was piled high with cardboard boxes. The men were marched up in pairs and ordered to hand over their belongings. Hutch handed over his wallet. It was put into a box which he was surprised to see already contained his holdall and clothes taken from him at the airport. There was no sign of his sleeping mat or the rest of the things he'd left at the detention centre.

The men were made to line up again and a guard

wearing gold-rimmed sunglasses removed their handcuffs and manacles, handing these to another guard who put the chains in wooden boxes. There were more shouted commands and Matt began to undress. Hutch followed his example. The prisoners squatted naked as the guards went through the clothing, then they were made to stand and bend over for an internal search. It was only perfunctory, and Hutch was grateful for small mercies. A guard used a large pair of shears to cut the sleeves off the shirts and hack the trouser legs off just above the knee before handing back their clothes. The prisoners were marched off to another room, smaller than the first but painted in the same drab green.

One by one the prisoners were taken to a table where a young Thai in blue T-shirt and shorts took their thumbprints and made them sign their name on a form filled with Thai writing. Hutch was weighed, his height was measured, and he was marched back out into the main reception area where he was made to squat again. Squatting was something that Thais did naturally, but for a Westerner it was an agony, and his muscles burned after just a few minutes.

Once all the prisoners had been processed a guard reached into a sack and began putting manacles on the table. Hutch's heart fell. They were similar to the ones he'd seen on the man on the bus: no locks, just a steel plate that was bent around the ankle by an antiquated vice operated by another blue-shirted Thai. The guard checked that Hutch couldn't slip his feet out of the manacles then pushed him to the side. The rough steel was like a cheese grater against his ankles and Hutch winced with each step. He bent down to pull up his socks and a guard screamed at him. One thing was for sure, Hutch realised: with the chains on, escape would be next to impossible.

The Thai prisoners were separated out and taken away. Hutch and the rest of the foreigners were marched through another large steel gate, and then another, and then into another walled courtyard. The further away from the main gate they got, the more austere their surroundings became. The second courtyard was a square of dried grass about half the size of a football pitch with a cluster of green two-storey blocks with bars on the windows.

Hutch realised that the lack of security he'd seen on the outer wall was deceptive. There was no reason to have a large perimeter wall with high security measures because there were so many internal walls to cross, all of which were guarded by men with shotguns. Still, there were no closed-circuit television cameras and he saw no motion detectors or other sensors on the wires running along the top of the walls. Klong Prem would be a difficult prison to break out of, but not impossible, given enough time.

They were taken over to one of the blocks and ushered inside. The block was on two floors, lined with cells on all sides. The cells on the ground floor overlooked a concrete-floored courtyard and there was a metal catwalk with waist-high railings running around the upper level. It was noisy, hot and airless, and as close to hell as Hutch could imagine a place to be. He could barely breathe, and the sound of shouts and arguments was mind numbing. Matt looked across at him and grimaced. The door clanged shut behind them.

Half a dozen men in blue T-shirts and shorts gathered around. There were no signs of the brown-uniformed guards who'd escorted them from the administration building. They were divided into three groups, apparently arbitrarily. Matt, Joshua and two Taiwanese teenagers were pushed together with Hutch. Two of the Thais in blue took them up a metal stairway to the upper level, along the catwalk and into a cell about twenty feet square with two fluorescent strip lights in the ceiling, and a metal-bladed fan. There were already a dozen men there, sitting with their backs against the wall or lying on the floor. There was a window high up in the far wall, covered with a mesh screen that had probably been put up to keep out mosquitoes but was so tattered as to be useless. Apart from a line of wooden lockers under the window, there was no furniture in the cell. In one corner a cement wall, just under three feet high, hid a foul-smelling squat toilet and a tub of water. The new arrivals stood in the centre of the cell, uncertain what to do next.

One of the Thais in blue stepped forward and introduced himself as Pipop. He was in his early forties with skin so dark that it was almost as black as Joshua's. He was slim but well muscled and had a nose that looked as if it had been broken several times. Pipop explained in halting English that the men wearing blue were trustys, prisoners like themselves but with added responsibilities. 'Anything you want, we will get for you,' said Pipop. 'Any money you have is registered with the front office. You can use that money to buy food from the outside. You tell us and we will have it brought in for you. Stamps, writing paper, soap, we can supply anything for you. You do not ask the guards for anything. You ask us. Do you understand?'

The prisoners nodded.

Matt said something to the trusty in Thai.

Pipop nodded. 'You will get ten baht a week for working in the furniture workshop.'

'Ten baht?' exclaimed Matt. 'That's nothing.'

Pipop smiled cruelly. 'That is right. You will have to have money sent in from outside. You will be woken at six. You start work at seven.'

Hutch looked around for somewhere to sit. The only floor space was close to the toilet. He caught Joshua's eye and the two men grimaced together. 'Toss you for it?' said Hutch.

Joshua grinned. 'Help yourself. I'm gonna stand for a while.'

A guard appeared and he talked to Pipop before reaching for a key chained to his belt. Hutch stepped towards the bars and watched as the guard locked the cell door. He stared at the key as the guard withdrew it, trying to imprint the shape on his memory.

The guard and trustys walked along the catwalk, laughing together. Matt joined Hutch at the bars. They stood together, looking out over the catwalk at the cells opposite. In virtually all the cells sheets or blankets had been put up along the bottom of the bars to give the prisoners a measure of privacy.

'Ten baht?' repeated Matt incredulously. 'Ten baht a week?'

'Haven't you got people who can send you money?' Hutch asked.

'No way,' said the American. 'I split from my family years ago, and my Thai girlfriend won't hang around. I'm up shit creek.' He went over to the concrete wall next to the toilet and sat down.

Hutch watched the guard and trustys go downstairs and walk across the courtyard, then turned around. Joshua was deep in conversation with another Nigerian. Matt had his eyes closed. An old Oriental moved his blanket to the side to make room for Hutch. There was barely enough floor space for everyone to lie down at the same time. Hutch smiled his thanks and sat down on the hard concrete floor. A mosquito whizzed by his left ear. The noise from the surrounding cells was almost deafening, an incomprehensible mixture of languages and accents, mixed with shouts and screams and moans. He put his hands over his ears and closed his eyes. He wasn't looking forward to his first night in Klong Prem.

CHAU LING RESTED HER HEAD against the side of the plane and felt the vibration deep inside her skull. The seat next to her was empty and she was grateful for the space: the last thing she wanted was for someone to attempt to engage her in conversation. Go back to Hong Kong, Warren had said. Forget about him. She banged her fist against her leg. Forget about him? How the hell did he expect her to do that? There wasn't a day that had gone by since they'd first met that Warren Hastings hadn't occupied her thoughts. Why did he think she'd stuck at the job so long? It wasn't as if she needed the money, he knew that. She'd taken the job originally because she loved dogs and had wanted to start breeding Golden Retrievers. Working for Warren had seemed an obvious way of picking up the necessary knowledge: his kennels and the quality of his Dobermanns were renowned through the territory. She'd made it clear from the start that she only intended to work for him for six months or so and that her eventual aim was to set up her own kennels. But that had been almost two years ago and she had made no attempt to leave. She'd found him attractive right from the start, and his apparent lack of interest only added to his appeal. Chau-ling was used to being pursued. She was well aware of her looks, had been since she was a teenager, and she'd had a succession of boyfriends while she was at college in the United States, but always it was they who chased her. In Hong Kong her pursuers were all the more persistent, because her father's wealth was well known, and in Hong Kong money often counted for more than looks. But Warren Hastings had never asked her out, hadn't even asked her if she had a boyfriend.

A stewardess asked her in Cantonese if she wanted a drink. Chau-ling shook her head. She massaged her temples with her fingertips. 'Headache?' asked the stewardess.

Chau-ling forced a smile. 'I'm fine,' she said.

'I could get you something.'

'Really, I'm fine,' she said. Chau-ling never took painkillers, or any form of Western medication. On the few occasions in her life when she'd fallen sick as a child, her parents had consulted a traditional Chinese herbalist, and now that she was an adult she continued the practice.

The stewardess moved away to attend to a Thai businessman who was having trouble opening his packet of peanuts. Chau-ling looked out of the window. The sky was a brilliant blue, the clouds below a pure white. They looked almost solid enough to walk on. She wondered what Warren was doing. He'd looked terrible in the courtroom. He hadn't shaved, he hadn't washed, and there was a look in his eyes that she'd never seen before. It was the look of a trapped animal.

Chau-ling ran her hands through her hair and tucked it behind her ears. It didn't make any kind of sense. If Warren was innocent, why wouldn't he accept Khun Kriengsak's help? And why had he been so convinced that he'd never go to trial? She was certain that there had been a mistake; there was no way that a man like Warren would ever get involved with drugs. But the evidence was overwhelming, and she couldn't see how he'd expect to avoid a trial. The way his shoulders had sagged when she'd told him about the laboratory results had almost broken her heart. She wanted to take him in her arms and hold him, to comfort him and tell him that whatever happened she'd always stand by him. There had to be something she could do, some way in which she could help. Her lower lip began to tremble and she fought back the tears.

She'd gone to the prison with Khun Kriengsak and tried to see Warren, but had been told that Thursday was the only day she could visit. The lawyer had shown her how to deposit money so that Warren could make himself a little more comfortable. She had had to queue with him in the searing sunshine outside a window set into the prison perimeter, close to a cafeteria serving cooked meals and soft drinks. Two beige-uniformed guards sat on the other side of the window. Putting money in Warren's prison account had been surprisingly easy: she handed over twenty thousand baht and her passport and a piece of paper with Warren's name on it. In return she was given a receipt. It was a small thing, the least that she could do. No, she corrected herself, it was *all* she could do, for the moment at least. Khun Kriengsak had insisted that nothing would happen until Warren's next court appearance, and that she might as well wait in Hong Kong. She knew that the lawyer was right, but that didn't make leaving any easier. The tears began to fall and she turned her head to the window, not wanting anyone to see her grief.

THE SONG WAS 'MY WAY', the singer a tall girl with shoulder-length permed hair and a sky-blue evening dress that reached almost to the ground but did little to conceal her ample breasts. She stood in front of a large-screen television which showed pictures of a young Thai couple walking hand in hand through the streets of Paris while the words to the song scrolled across the bottom.

'Decisions, decisions,' said Billy Winter, swirling his brandy and Coke around his tumbler. 'I really don't know which one to choose, mamasan.'

The mamasan was in her sixties, wearing a sequined dress that tried but failed to bolster her sagging figure. She smiled, showing gleaming white teeth that belied her age, and put a bony hand on his arm. 'Why choose just one, Khun Billy?' she said.

Winter cackled and sucked on his cigar. 'Why indeed, mamasan? Why indeed?' He drained his glass and surveyed the half a dozen girls in vibrant-coloured evening dresses who were sitting at a neighbouring table. 'Who else would you recommend?' he asked.

'Som is always popular,' said the mamasan, nodding at a girl in a skintight red dress with waist-length hair that would have done credit to any shampoo commercial, and a cleavage that could have trebled brassière sales. She had the face of a schoolgirl, unlined and innocent, and she covered her mouth with a petite hand as she giggled at something on the television screen.

'How old is she?' asked Winter.

'Eighteen,' said the mamasan.

Winter grinned. Som was fifteen, at most. 'I hope she's not too popular,' said Winter, the cigar clenched between his teeth.

'All our girls are checked regularly,' said the mamasan. 'They have a general check every month, and they're tested for AIDS every three months. If the girls are sick, they cannot work.'

'So, what about the girl who's just started singing? Tell me about her,' said Winter.

The mamasan looked at Winter for a few moments, then turned to look at the new singer, who was struggling to keep up with the words on the screen. She had short hair with a fringe and was wearing a tight black dress cut low at the front that only emphasised how boyish her figure was. She wasn't the type that Winter normally went for, but there was a fearful look in her eyes that appealed to him. 'Ah. Geng. She is a new girl. She only started work last month.'

Winter took the cigar out of his mouth and jabbed it in the girl's direction. 'How old is she?'

'Eighteen.'

Winter grinned. 'Pretty little thing,' he said. Geng stumbled over her words and tried frantically to catch up with the music.

'Inexperienced,' said the mamasan. 'I have had complaints. Sometimes she isn't very enthusiastic.'

The lift doors at the far end of the bar opened. All the girls in the bar immediately brightened and turned on their smiles. It was Bird, carrying a notebook. He ignored the display of young flesh and headed straight for Winter's table.

Winter raised his brandy glass in salute. 'Bird, pull up a hooker and join us,' he said brightly. 'You're just in time to help me choose.'

Bird handed the notebook to Winter, sat down and ordered a Singha beer from the mamasan, who spoke to him in Thai. They continued to talk as Winter flicked through the notebook. Most of it was in spidery shorthand but there were several notes in capital letters. The mamasan poured Bird's beer and then went over to talk to the cashier.

Winter looked up from the notebook. 'She was thorough. The DEA, the cops, the detention centre, Hong Kong. And she's getting his passport checked out.'

'Yes. I saw that.'

'And the lawyer. Kriengsak or whatever his name was. He's still around?'

A waitress walked over with a dish of salted peanuts which she put down next to the bottle of brandy. Bird stayed silent until she was out of earshot. 'He's taking a close interest in the case. He was at the hearing. The girl who works for Hutch was there, too.'

Winter picked up the notebook again. He opened it and found the page he was looking for. 'Chau-ling Tsang?'

'Tsang Chau-ling,' said Bird. 'The family name comes first. She's back in Hong Kong now, at Hutch's kennels.'

Winter nodded. 'Hutch has tried to dissuade them from poking their noses where they're not wanted?'

'Yes. But the girl is continuing to pay the lawyer's fees.'

'We can't have the lawyer screwing things up for us. The

time might come when Hutch decides he wants to find a legal way out of his predicament. We have to make sure that he doesn't have that option.'

Bird whistled softly through his teeth and shook his head. 'Khun Kriengsak has connections in Bangkok,' he said. 'Political, social and legal. He is very well known, very influential. His brother-in-law is a general in the army; he is related by marriage to the Royal Family; two of his brothers are high up in the police. Getting rid of a farang journalist is one thing; a man of his status . . .' Bird left the sentence unfinished.

'Money isn't a problem,' said Winter. 'Whatever it takes.'

'It's not a question of money,' said Bird. 'Khun Kriengsak is untouchable. I wouldn't be able to find anyone to do it.'

Winter looked at Bird through narrowed eyes. 'What about you?'

Bird avoided Winter's glacial stare.

'Well?' Winter pressed.

'I wouldn't do it either,' Bird said after a pause of several seconds. 'They'd move heaven and earth to find out who did it. A murder like that wouldn't go unpunished.'

Winter stared at Bird, and then smiled. It was a baring of the teeth, as artificial as the smiles of the girls at the neighbouring table. 'So if we can't get the lawyer, we get the person who's paying his bills. I've never yet met a brief who worked for free.'

Bird nodded slowly. 'I can send someone,' he said.

'Soon?'

'Tomorrow.'

'Soon enough,' said Winter. He patted Bird on the

back and waved his cigar at the mamasan, pointing at Bird's empty glass once he'd attracted her attention. 'Have another beer, then help me choose my playmates,' he said. He jabbed his cigar in the direction of the singer. 'What about her?' he asked. 'What do you think?'

Bird nodded. 'Pretty girl.'

Winter pointed at another young girl who was sitting straight-backed and smiling for all she was worth. 'What about her? Apparently her body massage drives you wild. I can't make up my mind between the two.'

Bird grinned and scratched the scar on his cheek. He looked across at the mamasan and then back at Winter. 'It's a guy, Billy.'

Winter stared at him in astonishment for several seconds, then he shook his head. 'Nah,' he said. 'You're pulling my chain.' He narrowed his eyes and stared at the girl. She pointed between her cleavage. 'Look at those breasts,' he said. 'You can't tell me that's a guy.' Bird shrugged. Winter drew on his cigar and exhaled slowly. He looked at the singer, then back to the girl. 'How can you tell?' he asked.

'Thai girls are short. He's tall. The hands are big, too.'

Winter looked. They were long and elegant with perfectly painted nails. But Bird was right, they were big. They weren't a woman's hands. He nodded.

'And the breasts are too good. They're definitely implants.'

Winter sat back in his chair. 'Bloody hell,' he said. He drained his brandy glass and slammed it down on the table. 'Looks like it's going to be Geng, then.' He waved over at the mamasan and pointed at the singer, who had given up trying to sing and was now humming along to the music.

'What about Hutch?' asked Bird. 'When are you going to talk to him?'

Winter flicked ash from his cigar on to the carpeted floor. 'A day or two,' he said. 'I want him to sweat for a little while longer.'

HUTCH WOKE UP WITH a raging thirst and three more mosquito bites on his left arm. He'd left the antihistamine cream in the detention centre and had no idea when he'd be able to get more. He sat up and stretched. His back ached and the skin around his ankles was red raw. The fluorescent lights had remained on all night and he'd had to pull his shirt over his head to get some relief from the brightness. Many of the prisoners had strips of cloth which they draped over their eyes, so Hutch figured that the lights were never switched off. He sat up and rubbed his eyes with the back of his hands.

Joshua was already awake, sitting with his back to the wall. The Nigerian waved a greeting. 'Sleep well?' he asked playfully.

'How come you're so cheerful?' asked Hutch.

Joshua shrugged. 'This is gonna be my home for fifty years or so, so I might as well make the best of it.' He had a plastic bottle of water by his side which he tossed to Hutch.

Hutch drank gratefully. 'Where did you get this from?' he asked.

Joshua nodded at the big Nigerian sleeping next to him. 'Baz. He's a friend of a friend,' he said.

'How long's he been here?' asked Hutch.

'Eight years.'

Hutch looked around the cell. Eight years, he thought. How could a man spend eight years in a hellhole like Klong Prem and remain sane?

'My lawyer said I could buy myself a better cell. Is that right?'

Joshua nodded. 'Baz says there are private cells. The prisoners buy them and pay a monthly rent. Then they can choose who they want to share with them.'

Hutch exhaled through his teeth. The way the prison was run made no sense at all.

'It's Thailand,' said Joshua, as if reading his mind. 'Money gets you anything here. My friend was telling me that at the old prison, rich Thai prisoners would pay other men to serve their time.'

'What about money? How do I get it?'

'You don't. You get vouchers every day to buy stuff, but the rest of it stays in the book. The trustys arrange to transfer it between accounts, and they take a cut.'

Hutch's stomach growled. He had to use the toilet, and soon. He stumbled to his feet and carefully threaded his way between the legs of sleeping prisoners. The squat toilet was covered with a layer of dirty brown crud and Hutch wrinkled his nose in disgust. He had to hold on to the concrete wall to balance himself over the toilet. The smell was nauseating and he tried to hold his breath as long as possible. Joshua laughed at his predicament but Hutch failed to see the funny side. His shit came out in a liquid stream. Afterwards he splashed water on himself but he still didn't feel clean. He pulled his cut-off jeans back up and hobbled back to his place. Before he could sit down there were cries of 'Kao, kao' from the lower level.

'Breakfast,' explained one of the Hong Kong Chinese prisoners. 'Kao is Thai for rice.'

Two trustys appeared at the door to the cell. They passed eggs through the bars of the cell, one for each man, and then slid a tray of plastic bowls through a narrow gap at the bottom of the bars. Hutch picked up a bowl and sat down with it. It was greenish water with a spoonful of rice in it. 'This is it?' he asked Joshua.

Joshua spoke to the other Nigerian in his own language. 'We get this or something like this twice a day. That's why they said we should buy our own.'

Hutch sipped the soup. It was lukewarm and tasted of nothing. The egg was raw. He cracked it open on the side of the bowl and tipped it in, then stirred the mixture with his finger. The broth wasn't hot enough to cook the egg and the semi-congealed mixture made his stomach heave. He put the bowl on the floor. One of the Hong Kong Chinese pointed at it eagerly. 'Okay?' he asked, nodding furiously.

'Go ahead,' said Hutch.

The Chinese grabbed the bowl and bolted the soup down as if afraid that Hutch would change his mind.

Matt woke up and rubbed his eyes. 'What's happening?' he asked. 'What time is it?'

'Six o'clock. Breakfast.'

Matt stood up and walked painfully over to the bars. There was one bowl left on the tray, but it was empty, and there was no sign of his egg. He cursed and kicked at the tray, forgetting that his legs were chained. He stumbled and grabbed at the bars to keep from falling. Tears welled up in his eyes and he began to sob. Hutch looked away, embarrassed.

A brown-uniformed guard walked along the catwalk, swinging his key chain. Pipop followed him. Hutch made his way over to the bars and leaned against them. He kept his eyes down and stared at the key as the guard inserted it into the lock. Pipop shouted in Thai and the prisoners began to gather up the empty bowls and stack them on the tray. All around the catwalk prisoners were spilling out of their cells, carrying towels and soap. Hutch and the rest of the prisoners were counted out by Pipop, and they joined the rush down the stairs and out of the building, hurrying as fast as they could in their chains.

The bathing area was behind the building, and prisoners were already sluicing themselves down with water from large tubs. Hutch found a plastic bowl which he used to throw water over his arms and legs. He took off his glasses and put them in his shirt pocket, then sloshed water over his face. The sun was already burning hot and he was soon dry. He still felt dirty, though. The water had washed away the sweat but not the grime that he'd picked up from the cell floor. Joshua came over to him, taking small, mincing steps. The chain linking his ankles appeared to be several inches shorter than Hutch's. Joshua handed him a bar of white soap with a grin. Hutch was impressed with how quickly the Nigerian had got to grips with the system. He even had a threadbare towel slung around his massive shoulders.

Hutch washed again, gave the soap back to Joshua, and rinsed himself. A trusty with gold braid on one arm of his T-shirt appeared and barked commands. The prisoners began to stream back into the building. Hutch was one of the last to get back to the cell.

Matt was still standing by the bars in exactly the same position as when Hutch had left. Hutch patted him on the back, but couldn't think of anything to say to the man.

The prisoners put away their washing gear and squatted down by the cell door. Pipop and another trusty arrived and took a head count, then led them back down the stairs and out of the building. Hutch kept stopping to pull up his socks so that they would provide some relief from the rough manacles. Each time he did one of the trustys would scream at him in Thai.

The prisoners were shepherded into another building. Inside the factory, stacks of timber were piled up next to rows of ancient wood-turning machines, lathes and saws To the right were semi-finished articles of furniture: desks, chairs, dining tables and bookcases. The floor was covered with a thick layer of sawdust. Most of the prisoners went immediately to their assigned places but Hutch and the rest of the new arrivals stood around, not sure what to do. Pipop came over and brusquely ordered them to different parts of the factory. This time he spoke only in Thai.

Hutch's assigned job was with a group of mainly Thai men who were rubbing chairs smooth with pieces of sandpaper rolled around blocks of wood. A balding man of indeterminate age, whose skin was as brown and hard as the wood they were working on, handed a sanding block to Hutch and mimed working on one of the chairs. 'Hi ho, hi ho, it's off to work we go,' said Hutch. The Thais smiled uncomprehendingly. Hutch took the block and set to work.

TIM CARVER SPREAD THE photocopies of the Thai arrest sheets out and studied them. They were written in Thai but Carver could read and write the language almost as well as he could speak it and he had no problem understanding the contents. There was nothing to suggest that Warren Hastings was anything other than a low-level courier who'd taken one chance too many. Carver tapped the photocopied sheets with his cigarette lighter. He wondered if it was worth going to see the Brit, to see if he knew where the heroin had come from, but Carver decided that he'd be wasting his time. As he'd told Jennifer Leigh, one kilo wasn't even a drop in the ocean. Hastings had probably never even heard of Zhou Yuanyi.

Carver lit a cigarette and smoked it thoughtfully. It might be worth keeping an eye on Hastings, though, just in case he had any visitors. He wondered if there was any connection between Hastings and the men who'd been arrested up in Chiang Mai. That had been a dead end, too. Park and the rest of the Thais had refused to co-operate, understandably in view of Zhou Yuanyi's reputation, and the Irishman Ray Harrigan hadn't said a word since he'd been arrested. According to the file on the Chiang Mai bust, Harrigan was smallfry, too. He'd deteriorated in prison and probably couldn't talk sense now even if he wanted to.

Carver leaned back in his chair and blew an almost perfect smoke ring towards the ceiling. Time was running out. Jake Gregory had stressed the importance of finding a direct link to Zhou Yuanyi, and soon. Carver was determined not to let him down.

HUTCH SHUFFLED OUT INTO the sunlight and shaded his eyes from the blinding sun. It was just after midday and work had stopped. He wasn't sure how long the break would be, or even if they'd finished for the day. He looked around the courtyard. Joshua was sitting in the shade of one of the cell buildings with Baz, his Nigerian cellmate, so Hutch shuffled over to join him. He dropped down beside Joshua and stretched out his legs.

'How are they?' Joshua asked, indicating the manacles.

'Painful.'

'Yeah. Mine too.'

'Do you reckon they just do it to torture us?' asked Hutch.

'Probably. What have they got you doing?'

'Sanding,' said Hutch. He held out his hands. They were red raw from the work. 'You?'

'Labouring. Moving the wood stocks around.'

They were joined by Matt, who sat down next to Hutch. 'I'm sure this is against the Geneva Convention or whatever law it is that governs prisons,' he said. 'It's slave labour, and we haven't even been tried yet.'

'You can't argue with them,' said Joshua. 'They'll just gang up on you and give you a kicking. The only way to get out of it is to bribe them.'

'Yeah, well, I would if I had any money.'

'What about you?' Joshua asked Hutch.

Hutch shrugged. 'Some's been paid into my account, I think. How do I get at it?'

'You can get vouchers from the block office, just to the right of the entrance. You have to go at shower time. They allow you so much a day to buy meals. If you want to buy stuff from outside, you have to do as Pipop said and do it through the trustys.'

'What about the manacles? How much to get them off?'

Joshua whistled softly. 'A lot. Ten thousand baht maybe. Have you got that much?'

Hutch pulled a face. 'I don't know. Maybe. If I get the money, what happens then?'

'You speak to the block boss. The big guard in the office.'

Matt had stripped off his training shoes and socks and was examining his feet. 'Athlete's foot,' he said. 'How do I get to see a doctor?'

Joshua's companion burst into deep-throated laughter. 'A doctor? For foot rot?'

Matt scowled at the Nigerian. 'It spreads if you don't treat it.'

Baz continued to chuckle. 'Foot rot, groin rot, armpit rot, we've got it everywhere. They'll only let you see a doc for really serious stuff. TB. AIDS. Cholera.' As the American put his socks back on the Nigerian stopped laughing. He could see that Matt was close to tears again. 'You can buy talcum powder from the trustys,' said the Nigerian.

'I haven't got any money,' said Matt.

'I can lend you some powder,' said Baz.

The American smiled gratefully but he still looked upset.

Hutch stiffened. Two men were walking across the far side of the courtyard. One of them was Ray Harrigan.

'What's up?' asked Joshua.

'I think I know that guy. The one with the beard.'

'British guy,' said Baz. 'He's in our block.'

'British or Irish?' asked Hutch.

Baz sniffed. 'What's the difference?'

'Do you know his name?'

'Ray, I think. He's in a private cell on our level. The other guy's his cellmate. A Canadian.'

Hutch watched the two men sit down in the shade of one of the buildings on the far side of the courtyard, then got to his feet, grunting as the scabs on his ankles opened again. He hobbled across the courtyard. A guard on the compound wall watched him uninterestedly. The wall was no barrier to escape: Hutch could climb it with a rope and hook or a piece of timber from the factory, but not with his legs chained. He hoped that Chau-ling had put enough money into his account to pay for their removal.

Harrigan had his eyes closed by the time Hutch reached the two men. The Canadian looked up and frowned.

'Hi, how are you doing?' asked Hutch.

'Not bad,' said the Canadian.

'Just arrived,' said Hutch. He bent down closer to Harrigan. 'Are you Ray Harrigan?' he asked.

Harrigan opened his eyes sleepily. He squinted at Hutch. 'Do I know you?'

'We've a mutual friend.'

'Yeah?'

'Billy Winter.'

Harrigan's eyes widened. 'How do you know Winter? Did he fuck you over, too?' He sniggered. 'I suppose he must have done, huh? Why else would you be in here?'

'Just lucky, I guess.'

Harrigan closed his eyes again. He didn't appear to care one way or the other who Hutch was or why he was standing in front of him.

Hutch bent down and touched him lightly on the shoulder. 'Can I have a word, Ray?'

Harrigan's eyes remained firmly closed. 'I'm listening,' he said.

Hutch turned to look at the Canadian. 'Can you give us a few minutes, in private?' The Canadian grinned good naturedly, then stood up and walked away. Hutch waited until he was out of earshot before sitting down next to Harrigan. Harrigan still refused to open his eyes.

'Ray, I'm here to get you out,' said Hutch.

Harrigan said nothing.

'Did you hear me?'

'Billy Winter sent you?'

'Sort of.'

'And you're going to help me escape?'

'That's the idea.'

'You're out of your mind,' said the Irishman.

'I'm serious.'

Harrigan opened his eyes sleepily. 'And who the fuck are you?'

Hutch decided that it would be safer not to tell Harrigan who he really was. There was something wrong with the Irishman. He seemed to be having trouble focusing his eyes and his mind appeared to be elsewhere. 'Hastings. Warren Hastings.'

'Well, Warren Hastings, the way I see it, you're the one

with his legs chained. How the hell do you plan to get me out of here?' Harrigan scratched his left arm. There was a line of bites close to his wrist as if a mosquito had had several attempts at tapping a vein.

'I haven't worked that out yet,' Hutch admitted.

Harrigan closed his eyes again. 'Well, Warren, when you have worked it out, come back and we'll talk.'

Hutch was about to ask Harrigan what his problem was when the Canadian ambled back. 'All done?' he asked.

'I guess so,' said Hutch. He struggled to his feet. 'I'll talk to you later, Ray,' he said. Harrigan didn't reply but the Canadian gave him a friendly wave. As Hutch hobbled across the courtyard, a trusty blew a whistle and the men began to pour back into the factory.

THE MAN CALLED WONLOP studied the menu. He was sitting in the business-class section of a Cathay Pacific 747. Basically the choice came down to beef or chicken. Wonlop was a vegetarian, and had been ever since he'd become a monk at the age of fifteen. He'd given up the saffron robes and life of chastity when he'd turned eighteen, but had never again eaten meat. He slipped the menu into the pocket in the seat in front of him, and closed his eyes. He could eat afterwards. There would be plenty of time.

Twelve rows behind Wonlop in the economy section sat his assistant, Polcharn. They had checked in separately and had studiously ignored each other. Polcharn was in his late thirties, a decade younger than Wonlop. They had worked together on a number of jobs over the years, and functioned well as a team. Polcharn had been Wonlop's first choice when Bird had given him the contract on the Chinese girl, not least because he spoke fluent Cantonese.

Wonlop was travelling on one of several passports he owned, all of them containing different names, dates of birth and professions, and he had other documentation to back it up. He wore a grey suit with a blue and grey striped tie and highly polished black shoes, and in the overhead locker was a briefcase which contained nothing more innocuous than a few files, a clean shirt and a copy of the *Bangkok Post*. He would collect the weapons in Hong Kong from a contact who'd never let him down before. Wonlop would have to pay a premium because of the short notice, but the money Bird was paying would more than cover the cost.

HUTCH'S ARMS ACHED, HIS fingers ached, practically every muscle in his body ached. The sanding team had finished the chairs and moved on to a set of bedside cabinets. The air was thick with dust and Hutch had managed to find a piece of cloth to tie over his face. He could only imagine the damage the dust was doing to his lungs. The Thais he was working with were friendly enough. One of them spoke a little English and Hutch tried to learn a few Thai words as they worked. Once an hour a prisoner took around a bucket of water and they were allowed to help themselves with a plastic cup.

There were a dozen or so trustys lounging around the factory, and two guards. No one in authority inspected their work, but the sanding team worked slowly and methodically and took a pride in its work. The old man who'd given Hutch his sanding block was Thep, the leader of the team. He checked each piece before it was taken over to the varnishing department, and refused to approve any work which was below his exacting standards. Hutch wiped his cabinet with a cloth and nodded to Thep that he was ready for inspection. Thep came over and peered at the cabinet, running his fingers along the side, pulling open its single drawer and examining it carefully. Eventually he nodded his approval. Hutch felt a surge of pride that his work had been given a seal of approval, even if that approval came from a convicted drug dealer who had spent most of his adult life behind bars.

He shuffled over to the varnishing area and placed the cabinet on the ground beside a dining table. Thais with strips of cloth tied across their mouths and noses were applying varnish with small brushes. They worked as carefully as the sanders.

Hutch took a quick look around. The guards were talking by the doorway and there were no trustys close by. Instead of going back to the sanding area, Hutch hobbled towards the wood-turning machines. The noise was deafening but the men operating the lathes had been given no ear protection. Several of the prisoners had stuffed pieces of cloth into their ears in an attempt to protect their hearing, but most of them hadn't bothered. The air was thick with dust and Hutch coughed as he threaded his way through the machines.

Once the wood was cut and shaped it was carried over to the carpenters, the most highly skilled of the factory workers. Hutch had asked Matt to find out from the Thais how the carpenters were selected, and according to the American they were prisoners who had worked as carpenters outside or who were serving long sentences. They assembled the furniture and had access to various tools, which were stored on racks. Hutch walked slowly by the racks, looking for what he needed. The Thai carpenters looked up from their work as he passed. Hutch saw what he was looking for, but before he could reach it, Pipop came over. He shouted at Hutch in Thai, and pointed back to the sanding area. Hutch turned away, and as he did, Pipop punched him in the small of the back. Hutch pitched forward and sprawled on the floor. Before he could get to his feet, the trusty stepped forward and kicked Hutch in the ribs. Hutch rolled over and glared at Pipop.

'Okay, okay!' Hutch shouted. He shuffled backwards, using his hands and feet. The trusty pointed at Hutch and continued to scream. Once he was out of range of Pipop's feet, Hutch stood up and hobbled back to the sanding team.

WONLOP ADJUSTED HIS TIE. The briefcase lay flat on his knees and he put his hands on it like a pianist preparing to play. He sat in the back of the rented Toyota while Polcharn drove. Polcharn was a careless driver who rarely used his mirrors and consistently left braking until the last possible moment. Wonlop was reluctant to criticise his associate. Besides, Polcharn hadn't been hired for his driving skills.

The traffic was heavy but it was moving smoothly, unlike Bangkok where two-hour traffic jams were common and traffic lights sometimes stayed red for as long as fifteen minutes. Polcharn stamped on the accelerator and the car leaped past a minibus. They were driving through the tower blocks of the Central business district on Hong Kong Island, edifices of glass and steel so close together that Wonlop couldn't see the sky.

Polcharn guided the Toyota into an underground car park, stopping to take a ticket from the automatic dispenser. He drove down to the third level. The Mercedes was already there, its engine still running. As Polcharn brought the Toyota to an abrupt halt next to the Mercedes, the briefcase slid forward and bumped against the back of the seat in front of Wonlop. Wonlop said nothing. He opened the door and walked over to the Mercedes. The windows were tinted and all he saw was his own reflection. For all he could tell, he could be looking down the barrel of a gun. Or several guns.

As he reached the Mercedes, the rear door opened. The occupant of the rear seat slid over to make room for Wonlop, and he climbed in, pulling the door shut behind him. There were two big men in the front of the car but they didn't turn around.

The man in the back seat was an obese Chinese wearing a grey suit that barely managed to contain his spreading stomach. He held out a damp hand. 'Welcome to Hong Kong again, Khun Wonlop,' he said.

Wonlop took the offered hand and shook it. He didn't like the Western-style greeting, in fact he disliked most forms of physical contact, but he had no wish to cause offence. 'You look well, Mr Lee,' he said. Both men spoke halting English. It was the only language they had in common. Wonlop took back his hand and placed it on his briefcase. He resisted a sudden urge to wipe his palm.

'You too,' said Lee, beaming. Lee was in his early fifties with an oval head that disappeared into his shirt with no sign of a neck. He had small eyes either side of a pug nose, and fleshy lips. He toyed with a large gold ring on the middle finger of his right hand as he spoke. 'It's good to see you back so soon.'

Wonlop gave a small shrug. It had been three months since he'd last worked in Hong Kong, but he didn't care to be reminded of it. Lee charged high prices, and for that Wonlop expected a discretion that bordered on amnesia. It was unprofessional of Lee to have referred to the previous contract. 'Do you have what I asked for?' he said.

Mr Lee looked wounded by the suggestion that he might have turned up empty handed. He opened his hands and turned them palms upwards. 'But of course,' he said. He spoke in Cantonese to the man in the front passenger seat and a cloth-wrapped parcel was passed over. Lee took it and handed it to Wonlop. 'Exactly as you requested,' said Lee.

Wonlop unwrapped the package. There were two guns, both Chinese-made automatics, and two bulbous silencers. Wonlop picked up the guns and checked them.

'Both clips are full. Do you require more ammunition?' Lee asked.

'This will be enough,' said Wonlop as he ejected the clip from one of the guns.

'My standard arrangement applies, of course,' said Lee. 'I will buy them back from you at half the price you pay if they are not fired.'

Wonlop sighted down the barrel of the handgun. 'I shall

not be returning them,' he said. He attached the silencer with a few deft twists, then removed it. He sniffed it to check that it had not been used. A used silencer was worse than no silencer at all.

'As you wish,' said Lee. He rubbed his hands together as Wonlop stripped and checked the second weapon. 'Is there anything else I can do for you, Khun Wonlop?'

'Not this time, thank you,' said Wonlop. He rewrapped the guns and silencers and put them in his briefcase. He took out a brown envelope and handed it to Lee before clicking the briefcase shut.

'It has been a pleasure doing business with you,' said Lee, 'I hope to see you again soon.'

Wonlop nodded and climbed out of the Mercedes. He had already decided that he would not be buying any further weapons from Mr Lee.

CHAU-LING WAS SITTING IN the office going through the kennel accounts when the intercom buzzed. She frowned and pressed the talk button. 'Hello?' she said hesitantly. The intercom was connected to the front gate and she wasn't expecting any visitors. No one spoke. She looked at the clock on the wall. It was eleven o'clock at night. 'Who is it?' she said. She swivelled around and looked at a black and white monitor on a shelf above the filing cabinets. It had been switched off all day and she'd forgotten to turn it on after she'd locked the gates.

'My car has broken down,' said a man in Cantonese. 'Can I use your telephone, please?'

'Do you want a breakdown truck?' Chau-ling asked, switching to Cantonese, her first language.

'Can I use your telephone?' the man asked again.

'I'll call a truck for you,' said Chau-ling. 'Where is your car?'

'I'm not sure, it's dark. I had to walk quite a way to get here. Can you open the gate, please?'

'Just a minute,' said Chau-ling. She stood up and switched on the closed-circuit TV. Mickey lifted his head off his paws and watched her. The screen flickered and then she saw a man in his late thirties wearing a polo shirt and jeans. He looked up at the camera and waved. He looked respectable enough, but apart from the Filipino maid in the servants' quarters, she was alone in the compound and was reluctant to admit a stranger after dark. Chau-ling went back to the intercom. 'Wait there, I'll call a mechanic,' she said. 'He can pick you up at the gate.'

The man rubbed the back of his neck and stared directly into the camera. 'Can I call my wife? She'll be worried about me.'

Mickey growled softly as if sensing that something was wrong. Chau-ling's brow creased into a frown. The man was polite enough, but she didn't like the way he kept insisting on being allowed to use the telephone. Minnie got to her feet and walked stiff-leggedly over to join Mickey. The two Dobermanns stood looking at Chau-ling, their ears at attention. Chau-ling clicked her tongue a few times and then reached for the telephone. It wouldn't hurt to give the local police a call. Besides, they might be able to help get the man's car started. She put the telephone to her ear but there was no dialling tone. She looked back at the closed-circuit television monitor. The man had gone. Chau-ling clicked the receiver several times but the telephone was dead. She put down the handset and stood up.

Mickey and Minnie followed her outside. It was a hot night and the air was filled with the sound of clicking insects. Chau-ling stopped and listened. A dog in the kennels to the right of the office barked, and soon there was a cacophony of howls and yelps. 'Come on, guys,' she said to the Dobermanns and walked briskly to the house.

The back door was unlocked and she went into the kitchen and picked up the wall-mounted telephone. This time she did hear a dialling tone. The telephone had a long lead and she walked with it over to the refrigerator where there was a list of important numbers held on to the door with a magnet in the shape of a slice of pizza. She tapped out the number of the local police station, but before she reached the last digit the line went dead. She stared at the telephone. Mickey growled and padded over to the kitchen door.

'What's wrong, Mickey?' asked Chau-ling. The door was ajar and she went over to lock it. Before she reached it she saw a man walking in the direction of the house. It wasn't the man she'd seen on the monitor, this stranger was older and heavier and wearing a suit. He was smiling, but it was a tight, nervous smile and his eyes were hard as he walked purposefully towards her. His right arm seemed unnaturally stiff and as he got closer she realised that he was holding something pressed against his leg. A gun.

Chau-ling's heart raced. She rushed to the door and locked it with fumbling hands. The man broke into a run and brought the gun up. She ducked as he fired and one of the panes of glass in the door exploded. A shard of glass cut her cheek but she barely noticed the pain as she scrabbled across the linoleum floor towards the hall. Mickey and Minnie were barking furiously. As she crawled into the hall, Chau-ling realised that she'd left the key in the kitchen door. All the intruder had to do was reach in through the broken window and he'd be able to let himself in. She cursed herself for her stupidity. There were no guns in the house, and the only knives were in the kitchen.

The dogs continued to bark aggressively. She turned around and called them and they trotted obediently to her side. From where she was kneeling she couldn't see the kitchen door. She leaned forward cautiously. The man had his hand through the window and was reaching towards the key. Chau-ling clicked her fingers to get Mickey's attention. He looked at her, ears up. Both dogs were trained to obey hand signals as well as voice commands. Chau-ling pointed at the arm and made a clenched fist gesture. Immediately the Dobermann sprang into the kitchen. Minnie stayed where she was, watching Chau-ling intently.

Mickey leaped at the arm and gripped it with his teeth, his paws crashing against the door. The weight of the dog pulled the arm on to the jagged glass that was still in the frame and the man screamed. He jerked his arm back but the Dobermann hung on.

Minnie growled but Chau-ling silenced her. 'Trousers,' she said. The dog stopped growling but took a step towards the kitchen, keen to help her mate. Something crashed in the living room and Chau-ling whirled around. It sounded as if a window had been smashed. There were more crashing noises, then the sound of splintering wood. Someone was forcing their way into the front of the house.

Chau-ling began to tremble. A knife, she had to get a knife from the kitchen. She got to her feet, restraining Minnie by her collar. The knives were on a rack fixed to the wall to the left of the sink, in the corner furthest away from the back door, where Mickey was still holding on to the intruder for all he was worth. Through the smashed window, Chau-ling could see the man outside, his face contorted with pain and rage as he tried to free himself from the dog's grip.

'Come on, Minnie,' said Chau-ling, and she half-led, half-pulled her towards the sink. She'd only taken three steps when the man used the gun in his free hand to smash another pane of glass. Chau-ling ducked as the man thrust the gun through the hole. He fired but the bullet went wide, shattering a toaster. The gun made surprisingly little noise, more of a cough than a bang. She dragged Minnie back into the hallway. As she reached the relative safety of the hall, she looked back over her shoulder. The intruder had pointed the gun down so that it was aiming at Mickey's flank.

'No!' screamed Chau-ling, but it was too late. The man pulled the trigger and the gun coughed again. The bullet blew a chunk out of the dog's side and blood sprayed across the linoleum. Chau-ling screamed hysterically. Mickey was still hanging on to the man's arm but his back legs had stopped moving. The man fired again, there was more blood, and the Dobermann finally released its grip and slumped lifelessly to the floor. The man's bloody hand began to search for the key again.

Chau-ling ran down the hallway, towards the front door. She was at least five paces away from it when the door to the living room opened. It was the man who'd been at the front gate, now holding a handgun. Chau-ling screamed again.

Minnie growled and leaped forward. The man took a step backwards, raising his gun, but Minnie was too quick for him. She cannoned into his chest, her teeth snapping at his throat. The gun dropped from the man's hand as he tried to push the Dobermann away. Minnie bit his ear and shook her head savagely. Blood poured down the side of his neck and over his shirt. Minnie snapped again and this time she caught his throat. Her jaws clamped shut and the man went down with the dog on top of him.

Behind her, Chau-ling heard the kitchen door crash open. She ran for the stairs. She tripped on the bottom stair and banged her elbow as she fell. Minnie lifted her head, her teeth smeared with blood. The man on the floor was still alive, but his eyes were closed. Chau-ling heard footsteps running across the linoleum and she used the banisters to pull herself up. She scrambled up the stairs. When she reached the top she looked down. Minnie was still standing over the man. The gun was to the dog's left, lying close to the front door. Chau-ling pointed at the gun, then placed her hand over her heart. The dog reacted immediately. She dashed over to the gun, picked it up gingerly, then raced up the stairs to Chau-ling.

'Good girl,' said Chau-ling, grabbing the weapon and holding it in both hands. She'd never fired a gun before, never even held one, but she assumed that the man had taken the safety off and that all she'd have to do was to pull the trigger. The man in the suit came running down the hall. Chau-ling slipped her finger inside the trigger guard. Her hands were trembling.

The man in the suit jumped over his prostrate colleague and turned to go up the stairs. He stopped dead when he saw Chau-ling. His eyes narrowed as he weighed up the situation, then he fell into a crouch and aimed his gun at her chest.

Chau-ling pulled the trigger. It wasn't like it was in the movies, she realised. There was hardly any recoil and the intruder didn't fly backwards through the air. He didn't even cry out, he just sagged against the banisters as if all the strength had gone from his legs, then he slowly crumpled to the floor. Chau-ling sat down, keeping her gun aimed at him. He was breathing heavily, his eyes half-closed. He turned his head to look at her. There was a small hole to the left of his tie, black in the centre, from which blood gushed, thick and treacly and not at all how Chau-ling imagined blood would look like. It wasn't as red as it was in the movies. The man looked as if he wanted to say something, but when his mouth moved, no sound came out. He swallowed, coughed, and then his head fell forward and he went still. Chau-ling waited until she was sure that he was dead before putting down her own gun and hugging Minnie to her chest. She began to cry, huge sobs that wracked her whole body. Minnie whined and licked the tears as they ran down her cheeks.

HUTCH LAY ON THE concrete floor, curled up on his side, his head resting in the crook of his left arm. There was no position in which he was comfortable for more than a few seconds. His fingers were red raw from the day's sanding, his ankles burned and every time he moved his legs the scabs opened. The scraps of rags he'd wrapped around the inside of the manacles were soaked in blood and he knew that if he didn't get hold of antiseptic or clean dressings his ankles would soon be infected. Overhead the metal-bladed fan spun noisily, but it provided little relief from the unrelenting heat and humidity. The air was thick with the scent of human bodies and the stench of the open toilet. The fluorescent lights burned through his closed eyelids, making sleep impossible.

A rising feeling of panic kept threatening to overwhelm him and he forced himself to relax. He filled his mind with calming images, memories of happy times. He thought of his son, whom he'd last seen in the flesh when he was barely two years old. He thought about walking his dogs, watching the rugby, his early morning swims, anything to take his mind off the bars and the walls and the guards with shotguns. But no matter how he tried to occupy his mind, he kept returning to Billy Winter and the betrayal that had set him on course for a fifty-year sentence. It didn't make any sense to Hutch; he could think of no reason why Winter would have gone to such trouble to set him up.

Hutch turned over, trying to find some relief from the hard floor. One of the first things he intended to buy was something to sleep on, a mat or a piece of foam rubber. And food. The food served to the prisoners was inedible. After they'd been locked in their cells in the late afternoon, they were given their second meal of the day: scraps of chicken, barely two ounces per man including the skin and bone, and the same rice soup they'd been given for breakfast. A dog wouldn't be able to survive on the basic prison diet, let alone a human being. Some of the prisoners had paid for extra food and it was delivered after the meal: boiled rice wrapped up in newspapers, baked fish in foil, and fruit. Joshua's friend Baz had even bought a bottle of Thai whisky.

Hutch thought about Ray Harrigan. He couldn't understand why the Irishman hadn't been more enthusiastic about his arrival. Maybe Harrigan had become as disillusioned with Winter as Hutch had. Hutch hadn't been able to say much before Harrigan's Canadian cellmate had returned, but even so, the Irishman didn't show any interest in Hutch at all. Hutch ran the conversation back in his mind. Maybe he hadn't expressed himself properly; maybe Harrigan hadn't understood what Hutch had said. No, Hutch had explained that he was a friend of Winter's and he'd told him that he was there to help him escape. There could have been no misunderstanding.

Hutch had met prisoners who had become so institutionalised that they were unwilling or unable to live outside of prison, men who'd served such long terms that they knew no other home, but that didn't apply to Harrigan as he'd been inside for less than a year. Whatever the reason for Harrigan's lack of interest, it wasn't that he'd gone stir crazy. He had made one good point, though: until Hutch came up with some sort of workable plan there was little point in discussing escape with the Irishman.

One of the Hong Kong Chinese began coughing on the other side of the cell. It was a throaty cough that sounded like the onset of something serious. Disease was rampant throughout the prison, where the lack of ventilation and sanitation facilitated the spread of germs. Hutch had seen at least a dozen men who were little more than walking skeletons, victims of some wasting disease that could well have been AIDS, and he'd seen rashes and skin infections on the majority of prisoners. His own groin itched and he rubbed it. He'd been wearing the same clothing for more than a week. That was something else that he planned to buy as soon as possible. Joshua had told him that he'd have to buy himself a brown T-shirt and shorts for court appearances. The prisoners were allowed to wear whatever they wanted while in the prison, so long as the shirts had short sleeves and the trousers ended above the knee, but they had to be in uniform when they were in court. The guards would provide a uniform if Hutch didn't have his own, but the communal ones were old and worn and were never washed. Hutch balked at the thought of having to pay for his own prison uniform, but he hated even more the thought of wearing clothes that had been handed from prisoner to prisoner.

He shifted position again. Sleep wouldn't come, and the more he tried to force it, the less sleepy he became. He put a hand over his eyes, trying to blot out the light. He pictured the prison, starting from the outside. He imagined himself walking under the arched entrance, through the main gates and into the garden courtyard. He pictured the walls, and the guard towers, and then he imagined himself going through the second set of gates, and into the compound containing the cell blocks and the factory. In his mind he walked into the cell block, up the metal stairway and along the catwalk until he was standing at the door to the cell, looking in at his own body, lying on the floor like an animal in a cage. At some point during the imaginary journey, he fell asleep, and was unable to tell which was the real man: the one in the floor or the one outside the cell door, looking in.

CHAU-LING SAT IN THE back of the limousine, her arms folded across her chest. The tears had stopped but she was still in a state of shock and had no idea where they were going other than that she was away from the house and the men with the guns. Minnie was on the seat with her. Her father had wanted to leave the dog behind but Chau-ling had insisted. Just then it seemed terribly important that Minnie stayed close by. Minnie had saved her life. Mickey, too, but Mickey had died. There had been no room on the back seat for Chau-ling's father so he'd ridden in the front, next to the driver. From time to time he turned around to see how she was but she avoided eye contact with him.

Minnie sniffed and nuzzled Chau-ling's leg. She reached over and stroked her absentmindedly. There was something wet on the dog's head and she looked down. It was blood. The man's blood. She took her hand away and wiped it on the seat. Her father twisted around in his seat to see what she was doing.

'I'm sorry,' she mumbled. 'I've got blood on the seat.'

'It doesn't matter,' he said.

'I'm sorry,' she repeated, then the tears started again.

The limousine was following a white van with the name of one of her father's companies on the side. There were two big men in the front of the van, men that Chau-ling had never seen before but whom her father seemed to know well. There were two more men in the back of the van, one barely alive with a hastily applied bandage to his neck, the other dead.

TSANG CHAI-HIN SWITCHED OFF his mobile phone and handed it to Ricky Lim. 'Wake him up,' said Tsang. Lim slid the telephone into the leather holster on his belt. Tsang stood with his arms folded as Ricky went over to the man who was tied to the wooden chair in the centre of the office. Blood was seeping through the bandage on the man's neck and it occasionally dripped on to newspapers that had been placed on top of the sheet of thick polythene spread over and around the chair. Tsang was using his own office and he had no wish to stain the carpet.

Ricky Lim was a big man for a Chinese: he stood well over six feet and had the broad shoulders and well-muscled arms of an American football linebacker. Lim had been born in Chicago and had benefited from an American diet and health system before moving back to Hong Kong with his parents in the early 1980s. He had strong white teeth, a wide jaw with a dimple in the centre and spiky black hair cut close to his scalp.

Tsang in contrast had spent his early years in the north of China and was barely five feet seven inches tall and beanpole thin. He had a receding hairline and most of his teeth had long ago been crowned, porcelain at the front of his mouth, gold at the rear. Every year one of the local Chinese newspapers printed a list of the top one hundred richest men in Hong Kong. It had been more than twenty years since Tsang Chai-hin had not been in the top half of the list, but the one thing his wealth could not buy him was a new body. To compensate, he surrounded himself with men like Ricky Lim. Not that Tsang Chai-hin needed to use their muscle to get what he wanted: his money and reputation were enough for that.

Lim slapped the man across the face, quite gently considering the size of his shovel-like hands.

Another big man, Terry Hui, stood with his back to the door. Not that Tsang expected to be disturbed. It was just after midnight and the building was deserted. They had come up in the private elevator that led up from the underground car park. Only Tsang had access to the elevator, and it was not connected to the closed-circuit television system that enabled the building's security staff to monitor the rest of the building. Tsang was not an infrequent nocturnal visitor and he had no wish to have his comings and goings monitored. Nor did he have to, not when he owned the thirty-storey tower block along with several acres of prime Kowloon real estate around it.

Tsang went over to the massive rosewood desk that dominated the far end of the office. All of the ornate Chinese-style furniture in the office was made from the same dark reddish-brown wood, including the chair behind the desk. There was no cushion on the chair – Tsang believed that sitting comfortably was not conducive to thinking. On the desk were two Thai passports and two wallets, the contents of which were spread out on the blotter: some banknotes, Hong Kong and Thai, return tickets to Bangkok, a receipt for the rental car. Nothing personal, no family photographs, no scribbled addresses or telephone numbers. Not that Tsang expected to find anything: the men were clearly professionals.

Tsang put his hands on the desk and leaned forward. Through the floor-to-ceiling window he could see hundreds of navigation lights in the harbour below, and beyond the inky blackness of the water were the tower blocks of the Central business district, most of them topped with bright neon advertising slogans. Toshiba. Canon. Fosters. Tsang was angry, angrier than he'd ever been in his life, but outwardly there was no sign of the emotion that raged within. He had long ago learned to control his feelings. It had been a necessary survival tool during the years of the Cultural Revolution and one of the keys to his success upon his arrival in Hong Kong. He turned to face the man tied in the chair, his face impassive.

The man's eyes were flickering and he didn't appear to be able to focus. Lim went over to a sideboard on which there stood a crystal decanter filled with water and several glasses. He took the decanter to the bound man and slowly poured the water over him. It cascaded over his shoulders and soaked into the newsprint. The man shook his head and winced as the wound in his neck pained him.

Tsang walked over and stood in front of the man, his feet inches away from the newspaper and plastic sheeting on the carpet. 'Do you have any idea what you have done?' he asked. He used Cantonese, the language which his daughter said the man had spoken. It was Tsang's second language – he was happier using Mandarin Chinese – but he didn't want to use a translator.

The man didn't reply. He averted his eyes but Lim grabbed him by the hair and forced him to look at Tsang.

'She is my only child. My only living relative. You tried to take the life of my daughter.' Tsang shook his head as if trying to clear his thoughts. 'The name in the passport is Srisathiantrakool. Is that your real name?' The man stared fixedly ahead, his lips together in a tight line. Tsang waved a thin, liver-spotted hand dismissively. 'It is your choice. If you wish to die using another's name, so be it. Your name does not concern me. Nor does the name of your dead companion.' The man's eyes widened. Tsang realised that the man hadn't known that his companion had been killed. Not that it mattered. There was no need for Tsang to play games.

Tsang took a deep breath. He was finding it difficult to stay calm. He had an overwhelming urge to step forward and hit the man hard, very hard. He wanted to hurt him, to make his blood flow, to beat him to a pulp with his bare hands. But Tsang knew that to do so would be to lose face in front of the men who worked for him, and that was not a price he was prepared to pay. 'I have protected my daughter from the evils of life,' he continued, his eyes fixed on the bound man. 'She has known nothing but peace and harmony, and you have stolen that from her. My daughter took a life tonight. She killed a man. Do you have any idea what that means? She is not of your world, yet you have dragged her in, you have tainted her, you have stained her with blood that will for evermore be on her hands. Not a day will go by when she will not think of what she has done, what you made her do. For that alone you are going to die.'

The man pulled at his bonds but he was securely tied. The exertions increased the flow of blood from his neck and Tsang motioned for Lim to adjust the bandage. He did not want the prisoner to die prematurely. There were things he had to know, first.

'Yes, you are going to die, here in this room. There is nothing you can do about that. But before you die you will tell me who paid you to kill my daughter. The sooner you tell me, the sooner your suffering will end. The choice is yours.'

Tsang nodded at Lim. Lim reached into his leather jacket and took out an ice-pick, a long metal spike with a pale wooden handle, worn glass-smooth from years of use. Tsang walked slowly around his desk and sat down on the rosewood chair. He steepled his fingers under his chin and watched with eyes as hard as pebbles as Lim went about his task.

HUTCH WAS SANDING DOWN a wooden chest when Pipop came up behind him and tapped him on the shoulder. 'Visitor,' he said.

Hutch frowned up at the trusty. 'Who is it?'

'Come,' said Pipop.

Hutch put down his sanding block and wiped his dusty hands on his shorts. Pipop started walking towards the exit. Hutch followed, using a strip of cloth that Thep had given him to keep the chain from dragging on the floor. Pipop waited for Hutch at the compound gate, and took him across the main courtyard to the administration block.

'Where are we going?' Hutch asked Pipop in Thai. He'd learned a few words from Thep and the rest of the sanding crew, because most of the guards didn't speak Thai and those that knew English often refused to use it when speaking to prisoners. Pipop didn't reply. Hutch knew that the visiting area was next to the main gate, but that wasn't where the trusty took him. Pipop led him into the administration block and along a corridor. Hutch became apprehensive.

He'd heard stories about prisoners being beaten to death by guards, sometimes to obtain confessions, sometimes just for their amusement.

A cockroach scuttled across the floor and disappeared under a door. Hutch wished he could escape as easily. A sharp pain stabbed through his stomach. He'd spent most of the morning crouched over the toilet with a burning case of diarrhoea. He was hot and thirsty and he was sure he had a temperature. He shuffled after Pipop, the manacles rubbing against the open sores on his ankles. Joshua had given him some fresh rags to stuff around the manacles, and the padding had helped, but every step was still agonising.

Pipop stopped in front of a brown-painted wooden door. He opened it and pushed Hutch through. The door slammed shut. A Thai man in a grey suit was sitting behind a small wooden desk that looked as if it belonged in a school classroom. There was an empty chair on the near side of the desk. Hutch turned and looked at the closed door.

'He has been paid to ensure that we can speak in private,' said the man. He spoke slowly with a heavy accent and a slight lisp.

'Yeah? Who are you?' Hutch asked as he faced the man.

'I am Khun Bey,' he said. 'I am a lawyer. Please, sit down.' He indicated the empty chair.

Hutch shuffled over to the chair and sat down. Bey took out a pack of cigarettes and offered one to Hutch. Hutch shook his head. 'I don't smoke,' he said.

'Take the pack,' said Bey. 'You can use them as bribes.'

Hutch considered the offer for a few seconds and then

reached for the pack and slipped it into the pocket of his shirt. 'Thanks,' he said, 'but I still don't need a lawyer.'

'I'm not working for you, Khun Chris.'

Hutch narrowed his eyes. So far as the authorities were concerned, his name was Warren Hastings. Billy Winter was the only one who knew his true identity. He leaned forward over the desk, his hands clasped together. 'Billy sent you?'

'I am working for Khun Billy, yes.'

'What the hell's he playing at?' Hutch hissed.

'You can talk to him yourself,' said Bey. He had a gleaming brown leather briefcase on the floor and he picked it up and placed it on the desk. He opened it and took out a portable telephone. After tapping in a number he handed it to Hutch. Hutch held it to his ear and listened to the ringing tone. Winter answered on the fifth ring.

'Billy, what the fuck's going on?'

'Hutch, how's it going? How's the food?'

Winter's casual tone infuriated Hutch. 'Fuck you, Billy. Fuck you. I'm going to go down for fifty years, how do you think it's going? Have you any idea what it's like in here?'

'Hutch, I know you're upset . . .'

'Upset! *Upset!* I'll be in here for life, you bastard!' Hutch was screaming and Bey moved his chair back as if fearful of being too close to him. 'Why did you do it? Why did you set me up?'

'Relax, Hutch. Take it easy.'

Hutch was gasping for breath, almost hyperventilating. Another wave of pain rolled across his stomach and he felt light headed, as if all the blood was draining away from his brain. 'Relax?' Why, Billy? Just tell me why. I did what you wanted, why did you lie to me?'

'If you don't stop yelling at me, I'll hang up.'

'Fuck you, Billy. Fuck you.'

'Last chance, Hutch. You can either shut up and listen or you can go back to your playmates in the cell.'

If Winter had been in the room with Hutch, Hutch would have grabbed him around the throat and squeezed the life out of him, but he knew that the phone was the only link he had with the outside world and he couldn't afford to have that link broken. He had no choice but to listen to the man. He bit down on his lip, hard enough to draw blood.

'That's better, old lad,' said Winter. 'Now we can get down to business.'

'I'm listening, Billy. But I want to know why. Why did you set me up? Wasn't it enough that you threatened my kid?'

'Do you know the difference between involvement and commitment?' Billy asked.

Hutch frowned, not understanding. 'What are you talking about?'

'What did you have for breakfast this morning?'

'What?'

'Breakfast. What did you have?'

'A raw egg. And soup that tasted like dishwater.'

'Yeah? I had a full English breakfast. Eggs, bacon, the works.'

'Get to the point, Billy.'

'It's about commitment, Hutch. Take my breakfast: eggs and bacon. The hen is just involved. But the pig, hell, the pig's committed.' There was a pause and for a moment

Hutch wondered if he'd lost the connection, but then Winter spoke again. 'That's what you are now, old lad. Committed. You've got to get out. And you're going to bring the Harrigan boy with you.'

'And if I don't?'

'If you don't get out, you'll die there. And if you get out without the Harrigan boy, then we're both dead.'

'So it looks as if you're committed, too.'

'Just do what you do best, Hutch. Escape. Then all our problems are over. Talk to Bey. He'll get you anything you need.'

The line went dead and this time Hutch realised that the connection had been cut. Winter had hung up on him. Bey held out his hand for the telephone. Hutch gave it to him. Bey put it into the briefcase and took out a wad of banknotes. 'Khun Billy sent this. It will make things easier for you. Keep it hidden from the guards. You are not supposed to have money in the prison.'

'I know,' Hutch snapped. He wanted to fling the money in the man's face but he resisted the urge and slipped it into his pocket. If he was ever going to get out, he'd have to stay calm and use every advantage he had. 'There are things I might need from the outside. Can you get them for me?'

'Within reason,' said Bey. 'Money is no problem, and the guards will allow me to give you food and medicine. Weapons are out of the question. I am searched before I come in, but I might be able to conceal small objects.'

Hutch gestured at the manacles on his legs. 'First, I need you to get these off for me. Find out who has to be paid and how much they want and get it done. I can't go anywhere with these on. Then I need lockpicks. Something that will pick handcuffs, and the locks on the lockable leg-irons that they use. Billy knows what'll work.'

Bey took a small cardboard-bound notepad and a cheap plastic pen from his jacket pocket. He wrote down Hutch's requests. 'Anything else?'

'Gold chains. Stuff I can use as bribes. Make sure they're long so that this shirt'll hide them.'

'I understand. What else?'

'There's a guy called Matt. An American. He came in with me. Put some money in his account. And a guy called Joshua. A Nigerian.'

'Surnames?'

Hutch glared at Bey. 'I don't know. But I'm sure you can find someone who'll tell you. I want their manacles taken off, too.'

'That will be expensive.'

'Tell Billy it's part of my plan. As for the rest, I'll have to think. How do I get hold of you if I need you?'

Bey put the pen and notepad away. 'I will come back in two days.'

Hutch nodded. 'Put more money in my prison account,' he said. 'As much as you can. Billy can spare it.' He went over to the door and banged on it with both fists.

'Good luck,' said Bey, behind him.

'Thanks,' said Hutch. 'Thanks for nothing.'

TSANG CHAU-LING SAT IN the outer office and stared at the aquarium. Her father didn't like tropical fish but the feng shui man had told him that fish in the far corner of the office would bring him good luck, and her father was not the type to disregard the advice of the feng shui man. Her father's secretary was on the telephone, but she'd acknowledged Chau-ling's arrival with a quick smile and nod. On the wall behind the secretary were large framed photographs of Tsang Chai-hin's business empire: office blocks in the city's high-rent districts; container ships that crisscrossed the Pacific; electronics factories over the border in Shenzhen. Her father always made a point of telling Chau-ling that one day it would be hers, that he wanted to pass the company on to her, but she was reluctant to take on the responsibility. Not because she didn't think that she was capable, far from it. Her fear was that if her father were ever to give up his company, he would give up on life itself. Since the death of his wife, Chau-ling's mother, ten years earlier, Chai-hin had devoted every waking hour to his businesses, as if he was unwilling to give himself time to grieve.

The secretary finished her call and pressed the intercom to tell Chau-ling's father that she was there to see him. The door to Tsang Chai-hin's office opened almost immediately.

'What are you doing here?' he asked.

'Can't I visit my own father?' she chided.

Tsang waved his hands apologetically. 'I'm sorry,' he said. 'I thought you were at home.' By home, Chau-ling knew, he meant his home. She'd been taken there and been under almost constant guard since the night of the attack. Tsang looked around the office. 'Where are your bodyguards?'

Chau-ling resisted the urge to smile. Her father had insisted that two heavy-set men stay with her at all times, but she had given them the slip while out shopping. 'I wanted to be on my own for a while,' she said.

Tsang's features stiffened. He stood to the side and motioned for her to go through to his office. He waited until they were both inside and the door was closed before speaking to her. 'This is not a game, Chau-ling,' he said.

'I know, Father, but I felt ridiculous walking around with two huge men following me everywhere.'

'They are not following you, they are protecting you.'

There were four rosewood chairs grouped together around a circular table to the right of the door and Tsang put a hand on her arm and guided her towards them.

'I'm not an invalid,' she said in exasperation. 'You don't have to treat me as if I'm going to break.'

'Just humour an old man,' he said. Chau-ling went to sit in one of the chairs but Tsang pulled her away. 'No, not that one,' he said quickly. 'Here. Sit here, by me.' He kept a grip on her arm until he was seated, then he sat down next to her.

He looked old, thought Chau-ling, older than he'd looked in a long time. 'You are working too hard,' she said softly.

'A man can never work too hard.' The telephone on his desk rang and he patted her on the knee before going to answer it. He put the receiver to his ear and watched her as he listened. 'Yes, she is here,' he said. 'We shall speak of this later.' He put down the phone. Chau-ling thought he was about to scold her again, but his face creased into a smile. 'The lingerie department?' he said. 'You left them in the lingerie department of Lane Crawford?' He chuckled and went over to sit by her again. 'Do not do that again,' he said. There was a seriousness in his eyes that broached no argument.

'I won't,' she said. 'I promise.' Her father nodded,

satisfied. 'Not in the lingerie department, anyway,' she added.

Tsang raised a finger to admonish her but then realised that she was joking. He nodded slowly, and smiled again. 'Why does everyone respect me but my own daughter?' he asked. 'What do I do so wrong in my life that I am cursed with such an offspring?' His smile widened and his eyes were full of such love and adoration that Chau-ling felt a sudden rush of sadness.

'I'm sorry,' was all she could think of saying. She slid off the chair and rested her head in her father's lap, the way she'd done when she was a child.

Tsang stroked her hair. 'You are all I have left,' he whispered. 'I promised your mother that I would take care of you.'

'You do,' replied Chau-ling. 'No one has a better father. No one.'

They sat together in silence for several minutes. It was Chau-ling who spoke first. 'Why?' she said.

'Hush,' he said. 'It's over. I will handle it from now on.'

Chau-ling's eyes were damp but there were no tears. 'It was me they were after. I deserve to know why.'

'I don't know why,' said her father. 'I only know who, but that is enough. Now that I know who, I will be able to find out why. But I don't want you to think about it any more. Perhaps you should go on holiday. Anywhere you want. The United States, perhaps. You could go and visit your college friends there.'

'It was you who wanted me to stay in Hong Kong,' she reminded him. 'It was you who wanted me close by. Now you're pushing me away.'

'I am only suggesting that you take a holiday.'

Chau-ling sat up and shook her head emphatically. 'No. I am not running away,' she said. 'Who were they, those men?'

'Their names are unimportant,' said Tsang.

'Father, don't play games with me. I'm not a child any more.'

Tsang looked at her, then slowly reached over and tousled her hair. 'You will always be a child to me.'

Chau-ling raised her eyebrows sternly. Tsang's eventual nod was almost imperceptible.

'They came from Thailand,' he said. 'From Bangkok.'

'And were they trying to kill me? Or did they want to kidnap me? Were they trying to get to you through me?'

Tsang pursed his lips and shook his head. 'They had been paid to kill you.'

Chau-ling frowned. 'Why? Why should anyone in Thailand want to kill me?'

'As I said, I do not know why. Not yet.'

'But you know who, you said.'

'A man called Bird. A Thai. He is involved in the drug trade, but so far that is all I know about him.'

'It's to do with Warren, I'm sure it is. There's been something wrong right from the start. He had no reason to go to Thailand in the first place, and he's totally anti-drugs. Yet he wouldn't say more than a few words to me and he refused to have anything to do with Khun Kriengsak.'

'You are jumping to conclusions, Chau-ling.'

'Don't you see, Father? I tried to help Warren, and this Bird is worried. I'm a threat to him. Why? Because he knows that Warren is innocent, and for some reason he doesn't want anyone else to know.'

Tsang leaned forward and took her hands in his. They were almost the same size, though there was a lifetime's difference in the texture of the skin. 'You cannot know that,' he said.

Her eyes flashed fire. 'A journalist came around to the kennels, asking questions about Warren. She seemed to think there was something strange going on, too.'

'I will make inquiries,' said Tsang.

'It's to do with Warren, I know it is. I'm going to Bangkok.'

'No.'

'You said I can go anywhere. I want to go to Thailand.'

'No,' Tsang repeated.

'He needs my help.'

'What is he to you, this gweilo?'

Chau-ling withdrew her hands. 'I don't know,' she said. 'I don't know how I feel about him.'

Tsang looked at her through watery eyes. 'I can see how you feel about him, daughter. You wear your feelings on your face.'

Chau-ling shrugged. She felt herself blush and she looked away.

Tsang stood up and looked down at Chau-ling. 'I want you to promise that you will not go to Thailand,' he said.

She shook her head. 'I cannot,' she said.

Tsang made a tut-tutting noise with his tongue and folded his arms across his chest. Tsang Chai-hin was not a man used to being disobeyed, but he knew he had met his match in his daughter. Half of her genes were his, and it appeared to Tsang that she had inherited all the stubborn ones. 'I will do a deal with you, wilful daughter.' She looked up at him expectantly. 'Let me make some inquiries. Then if it is safe I will allow you to go to see the gweilo. With suitable protection. Do I have your word that you will do nothing until then?'

Chau-ling nodded. 'Cross my heart,' she said, speaking in English for the first time.

PIPOP TOOK HUTCH BACK to the furniture factory. He rejoined the sanding team and spent the best part of an hour working on the chest. When he had finished he showed it to Thep. The old man nodded his approval and Hutch took it over to the varnishing section. Once he'd stacked it with the rest of the furniture awaiting varnishing, Hutch hobbled over to the carpenters. He looked around to reassure himself that the guards weren't watching him and went over to the racks of tools. He picked up a small file and examined it. It was perfect.

The leader of the team was a big Thai with his hair tied back in a ponytail. He was screwing the legs on to an ornate coffee table but he stopped and glared at Hutch. *'Tham a-rai?'* he asked. Hutch waved him over. The carpenter loomed over Hutch, a large screwdriver in his hand. *'Tham a-rai?'* he repeated.

Hutch held up the file. The carpenter reached for it, but Hutch pulled it away. Before the carpenter could say anything, Hutch took a handful of banknotes out of his pocket. The carpenter's eyes glinted. He looked at the money, then at the file, then at the money again. He held out his hand for the money. Hutch gave it to him. The file was about eight inches long, including a wooden handle which made up half its length. Hutch wrapped it in the cloth he used to keep the chain off the ground, and limped over to the woodworking machines. An elderly Thai was bent over one of the circular saws, cutting a table leg. Hutch pointed at the saw, then at the file. Then he showed him two of the banknotes and the pack of cigarettes that Bey had given him. The Thai nodded immediately, as if being bribed for the use of his machine was a regular occurrence. He stood back as Hutch used the saw to cut off the wooden handle. Hutch threw the bits on to a pile of off-cuts, then slipped what remained of the file into his left training shoe.

He went back to the sanding area. Pipop was standing there, speaking to Thep. Hutch bent down and began to work on a chest of drawers.

TIM CARVER PRESSED THE stop button. He ejected the cassette and tapped it thoughtfully against his cheek.

'You were right,' said Nikom.

'Yeah, wasn't I just,' said Carver. 'Who else knows about this?'

'Just you and me. The warden and a couple of the guards know that we bugged the room, but no one else heard what's on the tape. They met in private.' Nikom grinned. 'They paid the guards a stack of money.'

'And this guy Bey. Where did he go?'

'The Oriental. He went to see a Brit called Billy Winter. The Billy who spoke to Hastings, I guess.'

'Description?'

'Late fifties, early sixties. Grey hair, slicked back. Medium build, looks as if he works out. Oh yeah, he was smoking a big cigar. A really big cigar.'

Carver nodded. 'Okay, Nikom, thanks. Good work.'

'Anything else I can do?'

Carver dropped the cassette into his desk drawer. 'This Winter. How long is he booked in for?'

'Two weeks.'

Carver pushed the drawer shut. 'Okay, so we won't put a tail on him just yet. Let me do a little digging then I'll get back to you.'

Carver settled back in his chair as Nikom left his office. Nikom was Thai and had worked for the DEA for the best part of four years. He was a freelance, but totally trustworthy, and Carver used him whenever he wanted to get information without having to file a report, paying him from the DEA's substantial informers' fund. The fewer people who knew about Warren Hastings, the better. Carver wondered what the man's real name was. Chris something. The man Bey had called him Khun Chris. And Billy Winter had called him Hutch. Chris Hutch? Chris Hutchins? Chris Hutchinson? There couldn't be too many possibilities, assuming that Hutch was a nickname. Carver picked up a pen and wrote the various surnames down on his notepad.

He doodled as he replayed the tape in his mind. The man called Hutch was planning to escape, that was clear enough. And he was going to take another prisoner with him. Harrigan. Carver knew of Ray Harrigan; he was the Irishman who'd been arrested in the Chiang Mai bust. He'd been found in possession of fifty kilos of Zhou Yuanyi's top grade heroin. Carver recalled the conversation he'd had with Nung from the police forensic laboratory: the heroin that had been found in Hutch's bag was from the same batch. Carver wrote down Zhou Yuanyi's name in capital letters. A smile spread slowly across his face, like dawn breaking over a harsh landscape. He drew a circle around the possible Hutch surnames, and then drew a thick arrow connecting it to the name of the drug warlord.

HUTCH OPENED THE PLASTIC bag and sniffed appreciatively. Fried chicken. He put it down on his newly acquired sleeping mat and opened the second bag. Sliced fresh pineapple. The third bag contained boiled rice. He put half the chicken and the rice into a red plastic bowl and gave the remainder to Joshua and Baz.

'Thanks, man,' said Joshua, picking up a chicken leg and gnawing on it.

'Least I can do,' said Hutch. He saw Matt looking at the chicken and offered him a piece. The American took it and wolfed it down. The money Hutch had told Bey to put in his account had yet to work its way through the system.

'Hey, you don't owe me nothing,' said Joshua. He lay back and waggled his legs in the air. 'Getting those things off my feet was the best present you could give me.'

'Tell me about it,' said Hutch, stretching his legs out. Two trustys had arrived at their cell soon after they'd been led in from the factory. One of them was the man who'd attached the cursed manacles to their ankles on their arrival at Klong Prem. This time he had a large vice-like apparatus which he used to unbend the metal manacles. One by one he freed Hutch, Matt and Joshua. Along with the food, Hutch had received a tube of antiseptic ointment which he'd smeared over his injured ankles, and more antihistamine cream which he'd dabbed on his mosquito bites. He was starting to feel halfway human again. The sleeping mat made a big difference, too. It was barely an inch thick but after a week sleeping on the bare concrete floor it felt like a double-sprung mattress.

Later, when he was sure that his cellmates were asleep, he sat up with his back to the wall and took the file from his training shoe. He slipped his fingers inside a small slit he'd made in his foam rubber sleeping mat and pulled out a piece of metal he'd taken from the furniture factory. It was thin steel, about three inches long and an inch wide with four holes drilled into it. The carpenters had been using similar pieces to strengthen joints in bed frames they were assembling.

Hutch closed his eyes and tried to visualise the key that the guards had used to lock the cell door. He'd seen it more than a dozen times and from several angles. He began to work on the metal, slowly and methodically, alert for any sign that the noise was disturbing his cellmates.

TSANG CHAI-HIN HAD TURNED his chair around so that he could look out of his window. The view was spectacular at any time of day, but he enjoyed it most during the early afternoon when the sunlight glinted off the steel and glass towers of Central. To Tsang's eyes, Hong Kong was the most beautiful city in the world, a monument to capitalism at its most rampant, where tycoons both Chinese and British had competed to build the biggest and best edifices that money could buy. Tsang Chai-hin owned several of the skyscrapers that he could see, and two of them he had built from scratch. When he had finished the first of his tower blocks, he had considered moving his headquarters on to the island, but he had decided that such a move would have been a betrayal of his origins. Forty years earlier Tsang had been a near-penniless street trader, buying and selling plastic flowers among the sweatshops and rancid alleys that had long ago been replaced by high-priced tourist shops and five-star hotels.

The intercom on his desk buzzed. 'Yes?' he said, his eyes fixed on the view.

'There is a Mr C. K. Lee here to see you,' said his secretary. 'He does not have an appointment, but . . .'

'Show him in, please,' said Tsang. He twisted his chair around so that it was once more facing the desk.

The door opened and the obese frame of C. K. Lee waddled into the office. 'Mr Tsang, it is good of you to see me,' said Lee. He was sweating profusely and wiping his hands on a large, white handkerchief. Tsang remained seated and waved at a chair. Lee forced himself into it, his midriff bulging against the wooden arms. He stuffed the handkerchief into his top pocket. 'I have come to apologise, Mr Tsang. I have come to make amends.'

Tsang frowned and waited for Lee to continue.

'I am sorry about what happened to your daughter. Most unfortunate, most unfortunate.'

That Lee had heard of the attack on Chau-ling did not come as a surprise to Tsang; Lee had connections that ran the gamut of the Hong Kong and Chinese underworld. He steepled his fingers under his chin and studied Lee the way an entomologist might examine a rare beetle.

'I wanted to talk to you before ... well, before your investigations go any further. To explain, and to offer my assistance.'

Tsang nodded slowly as he realised why Lee was so frightened. 'I thank you for your courtesy,' he said. 'Please continue.'

Lee toyed with the large gold ring on the middle finger of his right hand and blinked his small eyes several times. 'I had no idea what they intended to do,' he said. 'If I had known, it goes without saying . . .'

Tsang waved his hand dismissively, wanting his visitor to get to the point.

Lee took the hint. 'I sold two guns and silencers to a man from Bangkok. The man's name was Wonlop. His assistant I had not seen before. Wonlop is a paid killer, a very expensive killer.'

Tsang nodded. That much he already knew. The man Ricky Lim had interrogated had told them about Wonlop before he had died.

'I have spoken to people in Bangkok and they tell me that a man called Bird offered the contract to Wonlop.'

Again, it was nothing that Tsang didn't know. 'You have worked with this Wonlop before?'

'I don't work with him, Mr Tsang. I am not a murderer. I only supply the tools.'

'I understand,' said Tsang. 'Do you know why this Bird wanted my daughter dead?'

'No, but he is working for a gweilo,' said Lee, continuing to play with his ring. 'A gweilo called Billy Winter.'

It wasn't a name that Tsang had heard before. 'This gweilo is also involved with drugs?'

Lee swallowed nervously and licked his fleshy lips. 'He imports heroin into Europe. He has been active in Bangkok for the past three years.'

'And his heroin, where does he get it from?'

'From Zhou Yuanyi. In the Golden Triangle.'

Tsang had heard of Zhou Yuanyi, one of the most powerful warlords in the region. If the gweilo was connected to Zhou Yuanyi, he was not a smalltime drug smuggler. From what Lee had told him, Tsang was becoming convinced that his daughter was right, that the attack on her was in some way connected to her employer, Warren Hastings.

'Did you hear about the gweilo who was arrested at Bangkok airport recently?' Tsang asked Lee.

Lee nodded quickly. 'A smalltime courier, Mr Tsang,' he said. 'No one seems to know who he was working for.'

'I would appreciate it if you would find out,' he said.

The request was made in a polite, almost diffident voice, but Lee nodded quickly as if it had been a direct order. 'Of course, I shall make it my highest priority.'

'You have good connections in Thailand?'

'Oh yes, I do a lot of business with the Thais.' He flushed and looked away, not wishing to remind Tsang that he had sold the guns to Wonlop.

Tsang leaned forward and put his hands flat down on the desk, his fingers spread wide. 'I thank you for bringing this information to me, Mr Lee. And I accept your apologies. I do not blame you for the use to which your guns were put. If my daughter had been harmed, perhaps my feelings would be different, but . . .' He left the sentence hanging.

Lee stood up. His grey suit had creased badly around the knees and there were damp patches under the arms. 'Thank you, thank you,' he said, and backed away to the door, his oval head bobbing from side to side like a metronome.

Tsang had lied to the weapons dealer. He had already traced the guns to Lee, but had been biding his time. It was better that Lee had come to see him of his own volition, but it would make little difference to the end result. Tsang did blame Lee for the damage done to his daughter, and at some point in the future Tsang would wreak his vengeance. But first he wanted to find out what the gweilo called Billy Winter was up to, and why he had wanted to kill Tsang's only child.

TIM CARVER WAS BLOWING his twenty-second smoke ring up at the ceiling when the guards showed Hutch into the room. His legs weren't shackled, Carver noticed. The man whom Billy Winter had sent to the prison obviously had good contacts. The requisite bribe had been paid and the shackles had come off.

'Who are you?' Hutch asked, rubbing his eyes. It was late at night and he'd obviously just been woken up.

Carver smiled easily and blew another smoke ring. His twenty-third. 'The question is, Mr Hastings, who are you?' He waved at the plastic seat on the opposite side of the table. 'Sit down, please.'

'Please?' said Hutch, his voice loaded with sarcasm.

'You can stand if you'd rather,' said Carver. He tossed his packet of Marlboro across the table.

'I don't smoke,' said Hutch.

'No vices, huh?' said Carver. 'Other than trying to smuggle a kilo of Number Four heroin out of the country. Sit down. You're going to have to listen to what I've got to say anyway.'

Hutch looked as if he was going to argue, but then he sat and stared coldly at Carver. The DEA agent spoke to the guards in Thai and asked for them to leave him alone with the prisoner. They went without saying a word and closed the door behind them. Carver sensed that they were unhappy at the night-time visitation but there was nothing he could do about that. The fewer people who knew that the DEA agent was in the prison, the better.

Carver stared at Hutch for almost a minute. Hutch glared back. Neither man was prepared to look away first. Carver's smile widened. 'I know who you are,' he said.

Hutch showed no reaction, at least none that Carver could discern.

'And I know why you're in here.'

Hutch shrugged carelessly. 'I'm in here because I was caught with drugs in my bag. It's a mistake. I was set up.'

Carver stubbed out the remains of his cigarette in a battered aluminium ashtray. 'Yes, you were.'

'Who are you?' asked Hutch.

'Carver. Tim Carver. I'm with the Drug Enforcement Administration.'

'I thought it was Agency.'

'What?'

'Agency. I thought DEA stood for Drug Enforcement

Agency.' Hutch scratched his face. 'I don't suppose you've got a badge.'

'It's Administration. And we don't carry badges.' Carver lit another Marlboro. He inhaled and blew a smoke ring up to the ceiling.

'You do that well,' said Hutch.

'I've had a lot of practice,' said Carver. He leaned forward and clasped his hands together, the burning cigarette pointing towards Hutch like the barrel of a gun. 'There are times when I don't know everything, you know? I have to try and prise out the information I want. Sometimes I have to use threats, sometimes I offer money, occasionally I have to use little tricks. But this time, I know everything. It's a great feeling, Chris.'

Hutch licked his lips. It was the first sign of nervousness that he'd shown. He waited for Carver to continue.

'Your name is Chris Hutchison, and you've been dead for seven years. You assumed the identity of Warren Hastings shortly before you arrived in Hong Kong and you're being forced to engineer the escape of Ray Harrigan.'

Hutch visibly paled and his mouth dropped open. 'Jesus H. Christ,' he said under his breath.

'Billy Winter is threatening to kill your son if you don't help get Harrigan out.'

'How?' said Hutch. 'How do you know?'

Carver smiled and raised an eyebrow. 'I can read minds, Chris. I can see right inside your head. You're a very special man. One in a million. You escaped from one of the highest-security prisons in the United Kingdom. Before that you managed to get out of two other prisons, neither of which were exactly holiday camps, but you were recaptured. Once I read your record, it was obvious why Winter wanted you.'

341

There were beads of sweat on Hutch's brow and he wiped his forehead with his sleeve. 'Bey,' he said. 'You had the room bugged.'

Carver smiled tightly. 'I admit it's not as impressive as mindreading, but it works.'

'Who else knows?'

Carver took another pull on his cigarette before answering. 'That's a sensible question to ask, Chris. It shows you're thinking. They do call you Chris, right?'

'Hutch. Everyone calls me Hutch. Who else knows?'

'Just me.'

'But you checked with the UK authorities. So they know, too.'

Carver shook his head slowly. 'I'm not stupid, Hutch. I got our Miami office to run a check on you and Winter, along with half a dozen other names, all Brits. It'll appear to be routine, no red flags will be raised, believe me.'

'There was a woman, a reporter . . .'

'Jennifer Leigh. I don't think she's going to be a problem.' Carver was fairly sure that Jennifer Leigh was dead. Her luggage had turned up in a hotel by the river and she'd signed an American Express chit before disappearing. He'd arranged for the local hospitals to be contacted just on the off-chance she'd been involved in an accident, but Carver knew he was just going through the motions. Life was cheap in Thailand, cheaper than almost anywhere else in the world.

Hutch fell silent, as if he'd run out of questions. He looked down at the tabletop.

Carver could practically hear the man thinking. He flicked ash into the ashtray. 'I think at this point you're supposed to say, "What is it you want?" or something like that.'

Hutch looked up. 'What is it that you want?' he said. His voice had gone suddenly hoarse.

Carver stood up and walked over to the door. He stood with his back against it. 'I need your help,' he said.

'What, are you trying to escape, too?'

Carver smiled. 'Good to see you haven't lost your sense of humour,' he said. 'Do you have any idea what you're going to do, assuming that you get Harrigan out?'

Hutch didn't say anything for a few seconds, then he nodded. 'He's going over the border into Burma.' He smiled coldly. 'I guess I was supposed to go with him. Billy's got connections there, he said.'

'I'll say he has. Harrigan was found with fifty kilos of heroin produced by a Chinese warlord up in the Golden Triangle. I'm pretty sure that this Winter's going to take you and Harrigan to him. I can't see how else he's going to get you out of the country. What else did he say?'

'He said we'd go to a place called Fang. Some town up north.'

'I know it,' said Carver. It was a Wild West town, the haunt of drug dealers and backpackers. It was a dangerous, lawless place.

'He said we'd get a guide there, some guy who'd take us across the border.'

Carver studied the end of his cigarette. 'You can help us, Hutch. You can help us big time.'

'How?'

'The DEA wants to find out where this warlord's base is.'

'So what am I supposed to do? Phone you when I get there?'

Carver's smile vanished. 'You can leave the details to

343

me,' he said. 'At this stage all I need to know is that you agree to co-operate.'

Hutch stared at the DEA agent. 'And if I don't?' he said eventually.

'What do you mean?'

'I mean, you're the third person to threaten me this month. I'm getting used to the format. First you tell me what you want, then you tell me what you'll do if I don't help you.'

Carver pushed himself away from the door and went back to the table. He put his hands on the surface and leaned forward so that his face was only inches away from Hutch's. 'I don't want to threaten you, Hutch. I don't want to put electrodes on your balls or whack the soles of your feet with a baseball bat. I don't want to do any of those things. I want you to help me because you'll be doing the right thing. You'll be helping to put away the man who's directly responsible for turning kids into heroin addicts, the man who's ruining my country and who'll be doing the same to yours before long.'

'And if I say no?'

'I hope that you won't, Hutch.'

'So all you're going to do is to appeal to my better nature? I don't think so.' He sat back in his chair, his chin tilted up defiantly. 'I want to hear you say it. I want the words to come out of your mouth.'

'Don't make me put it into words, Hutch. Let's not spoil a beautiful friendship.' He straightened up and stubbed out the remains of his cigarette.

Hutch said nothing. He just stared coldly at the DEA agent.

'Okay,' said Carver. 'First of all, I can just call the UK

authorities and have you sent back to your cell on the Isle of Wight. Or I can just let things run their course here. You'll get fifty years, minimum. And you can forget any chance of escaping because I'll make sure that you spend the whole fifty years in solitary, handcuffed and manacled. There's no prisoners' rights in this country, Hutch. Bey won't get near you, you won't have any visitors. You'll rot here, you'll rot until you die. And Harrigan will be in the cell next to you.'

Hutch nodded slowly, his eyes hard and emotionless.

'I'm not sure what Winter will do to your kid. Maybe nothing. I hope so, I wouldn't want anything to happen to him. What do you think, Hutch? Do you think Winter's a good loser?' Carver picked his pack of Marlboro off the table and lit another cigarette. 'Are you happy now?' he asked.

Hutch took a deep breath. 'Happy doesn't exactly describe my state of mind, no.'

'It's not all bad news,' said Carver. 'If you do help, there are things the DEA can do for you. Things that even Winter can't offer you.' He sat down and rested his elbows on the table. 'I can put you into the DEA's witness protection programme. We can give you a new identity, a passport, a Social Security number. Money in the bank, a job if you want it. The DEA can give you a new life.'

'I quite liked the old one,' said Hutch.

'Whichever way this works out, your life is never going to be the same again,' said Carver. 'If you help me, Zhou Yuanyi and his people are going to be after your blood. If you refuse . . .' Carver let the threat hang in the air.

'Between the devil and the deep blue,' said Hutch.

'A rock and a hard place,' agreed Carver. 'But at least the DEA can offer you a way out.'

'Assuming I can trust you.'

Carver blew a smoke ring above Hutch's head. It hung there like a halo.

'Can I trust you, Carver?' said Hutch. 'Can I?'

Carver flicked his fringe out of his eyes. 'Thing of it is, Hutch, can you afford not to?'

Hutch nodded slowly. 'What is it you want me to do?'

HUTCH WAITED UNTIL THE guard's footsteps had faded into the distance before slipping the piece of metal from its hiding place in the foam rubber mat. He'd shoved the file in the mat when the guard had come to take him for the late-night visit, but he realised with a jolt that it was missing. He looked around the cell frantically. Joshua was awake, lying on his side and grinning at Hutch.

'Don't fuck about, Joshua,' Hutch said.

Joshua sat up and tossed the file over to Hutch. 'You're breaking out, aren't you?'

'Oh sure. I'm digging a tunnel. Wanna come?'

'Where did you go?'

'I had a visitor.'

'At night? You can't have visitors at night. And it isn't Thursday. Foreigners are only allowed visitors on Thursdays.'

'Blood hell, Joshua, are you bucking for trusty status or what?'

Joshua went over to Hutch and sat down next to him. 'I want to go with you,' he whispered.

Hutch started filing the piece of metal. 'You can't,' said Hutch.

'I can help.'

'I don't need your help.' He brushed away the metal filings and examined the progress he'd made.

'How? How are you going to get out?'

'I'm not sure yet.'

'But you're making a key?'

'No, this is a CD player. Of course it's a key.'

'So you've got a plan?'

'Yeah. I've got a plan. But it doesn't involve you, Joshua. I'm sorry.'

The Nigerian drew his knees up against his chest. He watched Hutch work away at the piece of metal. 'How are you doing that? How do you know what shape to make it?'

'I've had a good look at the key they use. All I'm doing is making an approximate copy. Then I'll fine tune it.'

'So then you can get out of the cell. Then what? You've got the guards, the walls, the wire. How are you going to get out?'

Hutch stopped filing and blew the metal dust away. 'Can you keep a secret, Joshua?'

The Nigerian leaned forward, his eyes bright. 'Sure.'

'Good. So can I.'

For a moment or two the Nigerian didn't get it, then he began to chuckle. Hutch motioned for him to be quiet. He didn't want the rest of the cell waking up. Joshua slapped Hutch on the knee. 'Okay, man, I'll help you.' He got to his feet.

'Like I said, I don't need your help.'

'I can keep watch for you. I'll tell you if the guards come up.'

The guards tended to stay on the lower level during the night and most of the time they were asleep in the office, but occasionally one would walk lethargically around the cells. Joshua went to stand by the door, threading his arms through and resting his head against the bars. Hutch bent his head down and began filing again.

TIM CARVER'S DRIVER DROPPED him outside the block which housed the DEA's offices and pointedly looked at his watch.

Carver smiled. 'Okay, I won't be needing you again,' he said. In fact he would have preferred the driver to take him home after he'd finished what he had to do, but it was already past midnight and the man had a family to go to. The driver acknowledged Carver with a slight nod. He was offended, Carver realised, and he wondered what exactly he'd done or said. Thai sensibilities were a minefield, and no matter how carefully he trod, a Westerner would always make mistakes. It could have been asking the driver to work late that had upset him, or the fact that he hadn't told him how long he was expected to wait outside the prison. Or it could have been something Carver had said a week ago. Trying to work out what made a Thai tick was akin to solving quadratic equations blindfolded, an almost impossible and pointless task. 'Thank you,' he added. As he climbed out of the car, Carver suddenly realised that he'd spoken to the driver in Thai. The driver was an accomplished English speaker and overly proud of his linguistic ability. By addressing him in Thai, Carver was inadvertently suggesting that the driver's English was less than perfect and that communication would be easier in his first language. That was probably what had offended him. Carver made a mental note to use only English the next time he was in the car.

He showed his identification to the uniformed security guard and went up to the sixth floor. He ran his security card through the reader at the door to the DEA offices and tapped in his PIN number. The DEA offices were deserted. He got himself a black coffee from the machine in the corridor and went through to his office. His computer was already switched on and winged toasters were drifting aimlessly across the VDU. He lit a Marlboro and clicked the mouse, selecting his Internet connection. The modem clicked and dialled and once he was connected he sent a brief coded message to Jake Gregory's e-mail address.

AFTER TWO NIGHTS OF working on the key, Hutch was ready to try it. One of the Hong Kong Chinese had stomach problems and was getting up every half-hour to use the toilet and Hutch had to wait until the man was asleep before creeping over to the door.

Joshua was leaning against the bars, peering down into the courtyard below. He was half asleep and he jumped as Hutch tapped him on the shoulder. 'What?' he said, through half-closed eyes.

'Time to give it a go,' said Hutch. He put his hand through the bars and slotted the key into the lock. He turned it. It met resistance almost immediately. He pulled the key out. Disappointment was written all over Joshua's face. Hutch took a box of matches from his shirt pocket. 'Hold this,' said Hutch, handing the key to the Nigerian. Hutch lit a match and ran it up and down the makeshift key, blackening the bright metal with the smoke. It took five matches to cover the entire end of the key with smoky residue. He took the key back and inserted it once again into the lock. He withdrew it slowly and examined the end. There were scratches in the blackened surface, marking the places where the key had been prevented from turning. Hutch used the pointed end of the file to scratch the surface of the metal.

'That's brilliant,' said Joshua.

'Thanks,' said Hutch, and went back to sit on his mat. The Nigerian went with him.

'Will it open all the cell doors?' asked Joshua as Hutch began filing.

'Yeah, they use the same key for all the cells,' said Hutch. 'Otherwise the guards would have to carry dozens of keys.'

It took almost an hour of careful filing before Hutch tried again. This time the key turned slightly before meeting an obstruction. He used another five matches to blacken the key. There were only two places where the key had been blocked. He spent another hour filing. On the third attempt the lock turned.

Joshua slapped Hutch on the back, hard enough to rattle his teeth. 'You've done it!' he hissed.

Hutch gestured for the Nigerian to keep quiet. He slipped

off his training shoes. 'If the guards come upstairs, whistle.'
Joshua nodded. Hutch pulled the door open and stepped
on to the catwalk. He moved on tiptoe, keeping close to
the cells. All the cells ringing the catwalk had blankets
or sheets fixed to the lower half of the bars, high enough
to give them a little privacy but low enough so that the
guards could still look in on their rounds. Hutch kept
low so that the prisoners wouldn't see him. He took a
quick look down into the courtyard. It was deserted. The
Nigerian gave him a thumbs-up and Hutch continued along
the catwalk.

Harrigan's cell was on the far side of the block, close
to the corner. Hutch crept up and peered over the sheet.
It was the first time that Hutch had seen inside one of
the private cells, and he was amazed. The walls had been
painted a light blue colour and had a light fitting with a
low wattage bulb and a dark blue lampshade. There were
curtains over the window and several items of furniture:
a sofa, an easy chair and a wooden bookcase. It looked
more like a cheap hotel room than a prison cell. There was
a camp bed on either side of the cell. Harrigan was sitting
on his bed, his head down as if in prayer. The Canadian
was curled up on his bed, asleep.

Hutch ducked down and inserted his key into the
door lock. It turned and clicked. Hutch relocked it and
straightened up. Harrigan was still sitting up. He was doing
something with his right hand, something that seemed to
require a great deal of concentration. From somewhere
behind him, Hutch heard a low whistle. It was Joshua.
Harrigan took his right hand away from his left arm.
He was holding a syringe. As Hutch watched, Harrigan
loosened a tourniquet on his arm and sat back on his

bed, his eyes closed. Joshua whistled again, more urgently this time. Harrigan opened his eyes and stared at Hutch. His mouth dropped open in surprise. There was a third whistle, followed by a fourth, louder and more insistent. Hutch bent double and ran along the catwalk back to his cell. Down below he could hear boots on the metal stairway.

Joshua had the cell door open and Hutch slipped inside, breathing heavily. A guard appeared at the top of the stairs and began to walk slowly along the catwalk. Joshua closed the cell door. Hutch put the key in the lock and turned. It wouldn't move.

Joshua frowned. 'What's wrong?' he whispered.

'It won't budge,' said Hutch. He tried again, but something inside the lock was stopping the key from turning. The footsteps got closer.

Joshua clapped Hutch on the shoulder and dragged him away from the cell door. They rushed to their sleeping mats and lay down. Hutch's heart was pounding and he was soaked with sweat. He rolled on his side, turning his face away from the bars. He strained to hear the guard's footsteps. Each step was painfully slow and Hutch had to fight the urge to look over his shoulder. He closed his eyes tight and willed the guard to keep on walking. The footsteps stopped and Hutch imagined the guard putting his hand on the door, pushing it. He imagined the door opening and the guard looking inside. Then the footsteps started again and the guard moved on. Hutch breathed out.

'Close,' whispered Joshua from the other side of the cell. 'That was close.'

'Tell me about it,' said Hutch, his voice shaking.

'What was wrong with the key?'

Hutch picked up the file. 'It just needs a bit more work. It'll be fine.'

JAKE GREGORY STUDIED THE proffered tray of canapés, looking for anything with a calorie count of fewer than three figures. He searched in vain through smoked salmon whirls with cream cheese, hollowed-out boiled egg halves filled with caviar, and circles of toast piled high with foie gras. Gregory shook his head and the waitress looked at him sympathetically as if she understood what he was going through. A waiter hovered with a tray of fluted glasses but Gregory didn't care for champagne. 'Could you get me a Diet Coke, please?' he asked. The waiter nodded and disappeared.

Gregory surveyed the room with uninterested amusement: men in expensive tailored shirts and handmade suits, women in evening dresses and jewellery, just a standard midweek Washington cocktail party. In his off-the-peg blazer he felt like a grizzly bear that had wandered into a prayer meeting. John Mallen was at the far side of the room, holding court among a group of overweight movers-and-shakers who appeared to be hanging on his every word. Gregory caught Mallen's eye and the Vice President nodded. Gregory went over to stand by the window. He watched the Vice President's reflection. He was smiling and appeared relaxed, but there was a tiredness about his eyes and he seemed to have lost weight.

'So what do you do?' asked a woman who appeared at his elbow.

Gregory turned to face her. She was in her mid-thirties, a slightly heavy brunette with large hazel eyes and a mocking smile as if she was well used to working a room.

'Commodities,' he said.

She smiled and sipped her champagne. 'And is business good?'

'Oh yes,' said Gregory. 'Business is always good.'

'Angela Spackman,' she said, offering her hand.

Gregory shook it. 'Jake Gregory.'

'And what brings you to this gathering, Jake?' she asked.

'A gold embossed invitation,' he said. 'You?'

'Oh, I work for a public relations company This is pure business.' She stood with her back to the window and surveyed the room. 'They did well to get Mallen here. He doesn't get out much these days. Not since his son died. He's practically a recluse.'

The waiter returned with Gregory's Diet Coke.

'You're not the champagne type, are you, Jake?' asked Angela.

'You can tell, huh?' Mallen was making moves to extract himself from the group, patting one of the middle-aged men on the arm and nodding at another. 'You're going to have to excuse me, Angela. Duty calls.'

He left the woman and met Mallen in the middle of the room. They shook hands. 'Coke, Jake?' said the Vice President, nodding at his glass.

'Diet Coke,' said Gregory.

'Never could stand the aftertaste,' said Mallen. 'From the artificial sweetener.'

'You get used to it,' said Gregory. He sipped his drink and grimaced.

'It kills rats.'

Gregory held up his glass and stared at it. 'Diet Coke kills rats?'

'Not the drink, the sweetener. Gives them cancer. If they eat enough of it. I always reckon that you're safer with the sugar.' The Vice President was holding a glass of champagne but Gregory had yet to see him raise it to his lips. 'So, you have something to tell me?' said Mallen.

'We have a line to Zhou,' said Gregory. 'We hope to have his whereabouts identified shortly.'

'That's great news, Jake. I knew you'd come through. Everything else is in place?'

'It will be by the end of the week. I'm off to Myanmar tonight.' The Vice President frowned. Geography wasn't one of his strong points, Gregory knew. 'Burma,' he added, 'They call it Myanmar now.'

'Of course,' said Mallen.

'Did the request for assistance come through?'

Mallen nodded. 'A letter to the President, a personal plea that we help them in their fight against the drug lords of the Golden Triangle. The President will be sending an innocuous reply, a few platitudes, noting that the Burmese . . . do they still call them Burmese or are they Myanmarians now?'

Gregory shook his head. He had no idea.

'Anyway, the letter stays on file, so your back . . . I mean our backs, of course . . . are well covered. What about the helicopters?'

'They're on their way from South Korea, courtesy of the 4th Battalion, 501st Aviation Regiment.'

Mallen lifted his glass and toasted the DEA executive. 'I'm going to owe you one after this, Jake. You'll have a

marker you'll be able to call in at any time. I mean that.'
He gave Gregory the frank, open smile that gazed down
from posters at election time, but there was something
uneasy about the man's stare, something almost manic
in its intensity. Mallen gripped Gregory's shoulder and
squeezed it tightly. 'Let me know how it goes,' he said.
'Let me know as soon as that bastard is dead.'

'I will,' said Gregory.

The Vice President held Gregory's look for several
seconds, then his gaze softened and he released his grip
on his shoulder. Mallen walked away stiffly, his back
ramrod straight as if he was having to carefully control
his movements.

'Now I remember who you are,' said a voice at Gregory's
shoulder. He turned to find Angela Spackman standing
beside him. 'I wondered why the Vice President was so
interested in a commodities dealer. You're that Jake
Gregory, aren't you?'

Gregory shrugged. 'I'm a Jake Gregory,' he said.

'Of the DEA. I should have recognised you.'

'I try to keep a low profile,' said Gregory. A waitress
stopped in front of them with yet another tray of canapés
but Gregory waved her away.

'Still, I'm supposed to know everybody in this town.
That's what I'm paid for.' She put her head on one side
and looked at him with amused eyes. 'So, what does John
Mallen want with the DEA?'

Gregory swirled his Diet Coke around its glass. 'Chit-
chat,' he said. 'Nothing more.'

Angela smiled. She had full, generous lips and they
parted to reveal perfect teeth. 'Don't try to kid a kidder,
Jake. What are you doing after this?'

'What did you have in mind?'

She lowered her eyes in a gesture that was almost coquettish. 'Oh, I don't know. Dinner. Whatever.'

Gregory looked at his wristwatch and ran the numbers through his head. 'I'm sorry,' he said. 'I've got a plane to catch.'

She clinked her glass against his. 'Maybe next time,' she said.

Gregory ran the numbers through his head again. There was no way he could spare the time without missing his plane. 'You can bank on it, Angela,' he said.

HUTCH WALKED ACROSS THE courtyard, wiping his dusty hands on his shorts. Harrigan and the Canadian were sitting in their usual spot, their backs against the wall of the cell block and their legs stretched out in front of them. The Canadian was eating an orange. Before Hutch got close, Harrigan said something to the Canadian, who stood up and walked away. Harrigan squinted up at Hutch and scratched his left arm. Hutch knew that what he had thought were mosquito bites were in fact needle marks. There were more than a dozen on the arm.

'Are you ready to talk now?' asked Hutch.

Harrigan patted the ground next to him and Hutch sat down. 'How did you get the chains off so quickly?' asked the Irishman.

'Friends in high places.'

'Did they give you the key?'

'No. How long have you been using heroin?'

Harrigan shrugged. He stopped scratching his arm. 'Can you really get me out?'

'I can try.'

'And Billy Winter sent you in to get me?'

'Yeah. Sort of.'

Two trustys walked by, laughing. One of them was carrying a Frisbee. 'I thought they'd forgotten about me,' said the Irishman. 'I thought I was going to be in here for ever.'

'Is that why you started using?'

Harrigan ran his hands through his hair. 'It's been a year,' he said. 'You've no idea what it's like.'

Hutch thought about Harrigan's cell with its beds and curtains and bookcase. It wasn't exactly luxurious but it was a far cry from the rest of the cells in the block. Harrigan had it easy. 'Are you addicted? How long have you been injecting?'

'Not long,' said Harrigan.

'Can you stop?'

'I think so.' Harrigan's voice was hesitant, unsure.

'You're going to need a clear head, Ray.'

'Okay, okay. What's the plan? What are you going to do?'

'Come off the heroin first. Then I'll tell you.'

Harrigan looked across at Hutch. 'At least tell me when. Give me something to hold on to.'

Hutch got to his feet. 'Soon,' he said.

On his way back to the furniture factory, Hutch was intercepted by Pipop. 'Visitor,' said the trusty.

'Who?' asked Hutch. Pipop didn't reply, but started towards the administration block and Hutch followed him.

It was Bey. He nodded a greeting to Hutch and slid a pack of cigarettes across the table. Hutch sat down and slipped the pack into his pocket. The lawyer loosened his tie and unbuttoned the top two buttons of his shirt. There were three thick gold chains around his neck. He took them off and gave them to Hutch. They were heavy, each must have weighed at least two ounces.

'Is there anything else you require?' asked Bey.

Hutch shook his head as he fastened the chains around his neck. 'Give me the phone,' he said.

The lawyer took the mobile phone out of his briefcase, tapped in a number, and handed it to Hutch.

Winter answered after half a dozen rings. 'Hutch, old lad, how's it going?'

'Why don't you come and see for yourself?' asked Hutch.

Winter laughed throatily. 'You won't mind if I don't take you up on that offer, will you?' he said. 'You've met the boy?'

'He's a wreck, Billy. He's a sodding mess.'

'What do you mean?'

'He's injecting heroin.'

There was a silence lasting several seconds before Winter spoke again. 'How bad is he?'

'Like I said, he's a mess. Did you know?'

Winter ignored the question. 'Can you sort him out?'

'Oh sure, Billy, I'll just enrol him in the Betty Ford Clinic. How the hell do you expect me to get him off heroin?' There was another silence. Hutch had a sudden urge to yell at Winter, to curse him for his stupidity, but he knew that shouting wouldn't get him anywhere.

'You can get him out, right?'

'He can walk and he can talk, but he'll just be along for the ride. He's going to need his hand held all the way.'

'Okay, that's the way it'll have to be, then. When?'

'Three days.'

'How?'

'Have you got a pen?'

HUTCH SAT CROSS-LEGGED ON his sleeping mat and took out the packet of cigarettes that Bey had given him. The seal was already broken. Hutch tapped out one of the cigarettes and examined it. There was a small piece of metal sticking out of the end and Hutch picked at it. He slid a metal pick out, about two inches long, with a tapered tip. It looked as if it had been made from a hairpin and whoever had made it had done a good job. Hutch put the pick on his mat and took out another cigarette. It contained a slightly shorter pick with a more pronounced bend at the end. It was just as professionally made – Hutch doubted that he'd be able to do much better himself. A third cigarette contained a slightly longer piece of metal, a shim rather than a pick, which looked as if it had been made from piano wire.

By the time he'd checked the whole pack, he had a dozen picks, each one different, two improvised torsion wrenches, and two shims, lying in front of him. He put the cigarettes back in the pack as he stared down at the picks. It was a good selection, more than enough to open the handcuffs and leg-irons that the Thais used. In fact there probably wasn't a lock in the prison that Hutch couldn't crack using the picks, given enough time. They were good quality, too, handmade by someone who knew what they were doing. Hutch was capable of making the picks himself from materials available in the prison workshop, but it would have taken him several weeks.

He took off his right training shoe and one by one slid them under the insole.

THE LARGE MERCEDES SWEPT through the gates and stopped in front of the house. A big Chinese man wearing a black leather jacket and sunglasses stepped out and looked around, his right hand close to his chest. Only when he was satisfied that the area was clear did he open the rear passenger door. Tsang Chai-hin eased himself along the back seat and stepped gingerly on to the driveway as if he feared he would sink into it. He sniffed the air like a mole emerging into the daylight for the first time. He wrinkled his nose in distaste: the light breeze was blowing the smell of the kennels in his direction. He walked towards the front door, the man in the leather jacket following two steps behind and slightly to his left. It had been many, many years since Tsang Chai-hin had gone anywhere without an escort. He had many enemies in Hong Kong, enemies who would dearly love to see him dead.

The door opened before he reached it. Chau-ling seemed surprised to see him, worried even. 'Father?' she said.

'Is there something wrong?' Tsang asked with a slight shrug. 'Can I not even visit my own daughter now?'

'Of course you can,' she said 'I just wasn't expecting you, that's all.'

She walked to meet him, but there was no physical contact. Tsang was not a man who chose to display affection in public. In private, behind closed doors, he would hold his daughter, but he had never done so in front of others, as if it were a sign of weakness. He had always been that way, even when she was a child, and Chau-ling no longer resented it. She knew that her father loved her and she didn't need a kiss or a hug to prove it. Ricky Lim appeared at the door and Tsang noted his presence with a curt nod. Tsang would have preferred that it had been Lim who had opened the door and not his daughter, but he would not admonish the bodyguard until they were alone. In Tsang's mind, rebukes and affection were both best handled in private.

'I must speak to you, daughter,' said Tsang.

'It's about the ticket, isn't it?' she said.

'Inside,' said Tsang. 'I am an old man and must sit down.'

Chau-ling snorted softly. 'You will outlive us all, Father,' she said, and led him into the house. The man in the leather jacket did not cross the threshold but stood with his back to the door, his arms swinging freely by his sides.

Chau-ling took Tsang into the living room. He looked around and nodded slowly. 'An unusual mix of Chinese and gweilo taste,' he said. 'Neither one nor the other.' There were several wooden statues, mainly Buddhas, that Tsang thought must be at least a hundred years old, and there was a jade dragon on a bookshelf that he would have liked to have taken a closer look at if his daughter hadn't been standing there assessing his every move.

'Warren likes Chinese things,' said Chau-ling, ignoring the implied criticism.

Tsang looked around for somewhere to sit. The chairs and sofas all had huge cushions, bigger than pillows, and they looked as if they could swallow a person whole. Tsang shuddered. As if sensing his thoughts, his daughter pulled a wooden straight-backed chair away from the dining table and brought it over to the sofa. Tsang visibly relaxed. He sat down, his back as rigid as that of the chair. Warren's Filipino maid appeared from the kitchen and looked at Chau-ling expectantly.

'Can I offer you tea, Father?' Chau-ling asked.

'Tea would be nice. Thank you.'

Chau-ling asked the maid to prepare a pot of jasmine tea and the girl disappeared back into the kitchen. Ricky Lim stayed in the hallway, just out of earshot.

'It does well, this business?' Tsang asked.

'It gets better every year,' said Chau-ling. 'Dogs are status symbols, but people here are too busy to train them so Warren does it for them. And he sorts out their psychological problems, too.'

'Dogs have psychological problems?' said Tsang in disbelief.

'Of course. They get jealous, they feel rejection, they hate being cooped up in tower blocks. They're just like people.'

'Dogs are nothing like people,' said Tsang dismissively. 'Dogs are dogs. People are people. They should be treated as such. I could never understand why gweilos have such love for dogs.'

'It isn't the gweilos, Father. Most of our customers are Chinese. Most of our boarders come from Chinese homes.'

'Boarders?' said Tsang, confused.

'When their owners go away, they leave their dogs here,' Chau-ling explained patiently. 'Like a hotel.'

Tsang raised his eyebrows in amazement. 'A hotel for dogs?' He shook his head, almost sadly.

'Anyway, you haven't come all the way out here to talk about Warren's business, have you?'

Tsang didn't reply. He looked around the large room and suddenly realised that there were two large dogs sitting under a table, watching him intently. 'They won't bite, will they?' he asked.

'Only if I tell them to,' said his daughter mischievously. 'I wasn't going to go without telling you first.'

'Telling me?' said Tsang coldly. 'So, now you tell me, do you? I am no longer consulted, I am merely a servant to be told how things are?'

Chau-ling sighed in exasperation. 'That's not what I meant at all,' she said. 'I meant that I wasn't going to go without talking to you first.'

'That is nothing more than you promised me,' said Tsang.

The maid returned, carrying a tray on which stood a blue and white teapot and two cups. She put the tray down on a small table by Chau-ling's side, poured tea into both cups, then left them alone once more.

'Father, it is an open ticket. I bought it to save time. I wasn't going back on my promise. Anyway, I doubt that Ricky would let me get on a plane, would he?'

'Not if he wanted to continue working for me,' said Tsang.

'There you are, then,' she said with a dismissive wave of her hand as if she'd proved a complicated mathematical equation.

364

She handed him a cup of jasmine tea. He sniffed it cautiously and then sipped it.

'Is it okay?' she asked.

'It is drinkable,' he said, begrudgingly. 'Filipinos cannot make tea.'

Chau-ling drank from her own cup and then put it back down on the tray. 'I would have spoken to you first, Father.'

'I know,' said Tsang. He sipped his tea again, more enthusiastically this time, then put his cup down next to Chau-ling's, so close that they were touching. 'I have a problem,' he said. Chau-ling waited for him to continue. Tsang looked around the room again, but eventually his eyes settled on his daughter. 'I promised you I would make inquiries, and I have done. But I am loath to tell you what I have found.'

'But you promised that you would.'

'I know.'

'We had a deal.'

Tsang sighed mournfully. 'Why else do you think I am here, wilful daughter?' He clasped his hands together in his lap and looked at her with sad eyes. 'I want you to promise me that you won't go back to Thailand.'

Chau-ling leaned forward, her eyes wide. 'What did you find out?' she asked.

Tsang shook his head. 'Promise me,' he said.

Chau-ling closed her eyes and shuddered as if there were a draught. 'I can't,' she said, her eyes still closed.

'You must.'

'I love him, Father.' She opened her eyes. Tsang expected to see tears but there were none. 'I love him,' she repeated.

Tsang stared at her, his face like stone. He knew there was nothing he could say to convince her of her folly, nothing he could do to change her mind. Under other circumstances he would admire her stubbornness. 'Thailand is a dangerous place,' he said. 'More dangerous even than China. If you go, you go with protection.'

Chau-ling nodded eagerly. 'Agreed,' she said.

Tsang took a deep breath and let it out slowly through pursed lips. 'The man Bird, the man who hired the men who came to kill you, is working for another man. A gweilo. His name is Billy Winter. Do you know of this man?'

Chau-ling shook her head.

'He is from London originally. He is also in the drug trade. He is a dangerous man.'

'And he wants to hurt Warren?'

'No, it was you he wanted to hurt. He is going to get your friend out of the prison.'

Chau-ling sat stunned, her mouth open in amazement.

'This man Bird is recruiting a number of men in Bangkok. Soon, within the next few weeks, they intend to rescue your friend.'

'That doesn't make sense,' said Chau-ling. 'That doesn't make any sense at all.'

'It is true,' said Tsang. Lee had returned to his office just two days after their initial meeting, bringing information with him like a cat offering a dead mouse to its owner. Lee had sweated as he'd talked, sweated like a man in a sauna. Tsang had listened, then thanked him and shown him to the door. Lee had barely left the building before Tsang had given the order for him to be killed. There could be no forgiveness, not for one who had helped the men who had come so close to killing Tsang's only child.

'But why would Warren refuse to let me help him? Why wouldn't he take Khun Kriengsak's advice? Surely he'd try the legal channels before trying to escape?'

'I do not know how this gweilo's mind works,' said Tsang dismissively.

'Father, there's something wrong. I know that Warren wouldn't get involved with drug smugglers.'

'Nevertheless, this Winter and Bird are planning to rescue him. Of that there is no doubt. And they wanted to kill you. Do not forget that, daughter.' Chau-ling slumped back in the sofa. 'You can see why I am troubled,' said Tsang.

'I have to go back to Bangkok,' said Chau-ling.

Tsang nodded slowly, his lips set into a narrow line. 'I know,' he said.

BREAKFAST ARRIVED SHORTLY AFTER the cries of 'kao, kao' echoed up from downstairs. Each prisoner was given a piece of smoked fish a couple of inches long and a bowl of rice soup. There was a mosquito floating in Hutch's bowl. He handed it to the Hong Kong Chinese sitting next to him, along with the foul-smelling fish. Hutch had several pieces of chicken and some fruit in his locker and was expecting another delivery of food later in the day. It had been more than a week since he'd eaten the prison food and his stomach was all the better for it.

Hutch went over to sit down next to Matt. The American was chewing his fish and he grimaced at Hutch. His face was red and blotchy in places and the skin on his legs was dry and flaking. Hutch figured the American was suffering from some sort of fungal infection and he'd asked the trustys to bring in some medicine to treat it but they had yet to deliver.

'Matt, I need your help,' said Hutch.

'What's up?'

Hutch put his head closer to the American's. He didn't want to be overheard by the other prisoners who were collecting their washing gear and waiting for the cell door to be unlocked. 'I want you to swop cells with a friend of mine.'

The American grinned. 'What, is my body odour getting too much for you?'

'I'm serious, Matt.'

'Where's the other cell?'

'It's one of the private ones on the other side of the block.'

'And you'll fix it with the guards?'

Hutch pulled a face. 'Not exactly.'

Matt swallowed the remainder of his dried fish. 'What are you up to?' he asked.

Hutch took a deep breath. Matt's co-operation was essential if his plan was to work. 'I want my friend to go to court instead of you. I want him to take your place.'

Matt's eyes widened with disbelief. 'You're crazy.'

'It's only a formality. Every twelve days you have to appear before a judge so that the cops can keep you here.'

'I don't know, Warren . . .'

'I'll make it worth your while.'

'You've done enough for me already.' He pointed at his legs. 'You got the chains off for me and I don't know what I'd have done without the money

you put through. But I don't want to get into
trouble.'

Hutch fought the urge to laugh. The American had been
caught with five kilos of heroin in his luggage and was
facing a minimum fifty-year sentence.

Matt guessed what he was thinking. 'I know, I know,
I'm in a shitful of trouble already.'

'Your lawyer's not up to much, is he?' asked Hutch.

The American snorted dismissively. 'He's worse than
useless.'

'Okay, so here's what I'll do. I'll get more money paid
into your account and I'll get you a lawyer. The guy who
got our chains off seems to know what he's doing. I'll fix
it so that he takes your case.'

Matt looked at Hutch for several seconds, his eyes
narrowed. 'What are you up to? This isn't just about
getting your friend out of prison for a few hours, is it?
You're going to escape, aren't you?'

'You know I can't tell you anything, Matt.'

'But if I help you escape and they find out . . .'

'What? What can they do to you?'

'They could beat the shit out of me for a start.'

'I doubt it. Besides, you can tell them I forced you to
do it. Tell them I threatened you, tell them I pulled a knife
on you. Tell them anything.'

The American frowned as he considered Hutch's offer.
'Okay,' he said eventually. 'Okay, I'll do it. When?'

'Soon,' said Hutch. He patted the American on the
shoulder. 'Thanks.'

'Just make sure you put plenty of money in my account,'
said Matt.

Pipop appeared at their cell door with a uniformed guard.

The guard opened it and the prisoners spilled out, rushing to the bathing area. Joshua fell into step beside Hutch as they headed down the stairs to the courtyard. 'Everything okay?' the Nigerian asked.

'So far,' said Hutch.

PETER BURDEN AND BART Lucarelli were already seated with clipboards on their knees when Hal Austin walked into the tent. 'The early worms . . .' said Austin with a grin as he dropped down on to a metal and canvas stool. His shirt was soaked with sweat and his black skin was glistening. 'This heat is something, isn't it?'

'Reminds me of home,' said Burden.

'Home?' repeated Austin, fanning himself with his metal clipboard.

'Baltimore,' said Burden. 'This is nothing compared with a Baltimore summer, I tell you. Where's Roger?'

'Here,' said Roger Warner, stooping so as not to bang his head on the metal spar that ran across the top of the entrance to the tent.

Austin looked around the tent. Apart from the four stools and a large blackboard, it was empty. He looked at his wristwatch. It was just after nine a.m. 'Who's taking the briefing?' he asked.

Burden shrugged. 'Guy's name is Gregory. Jake Gregory.'

'No rank?' frowned Austin.

'No rank, no job description,' replied Burden, 'but when he says jump, we ask how high.'

'So what is he, a spook?' asked Warner, clicking a stainless-steel ballpoint pen.

'No, son, I'm not a spook,' said a clipped voice from the entrance to the tent. A squat, heavy-set man in green fatigues was standing there, watching them with amused eyes. He was in his mid-fifties, his hair greying and close cropped, his face almost square, with fleshy jowls that glistened with sweat as if he wasn't used to the humidity. Under his right arm he carried a long cardboard tube; in his left he had a can of Diet Coke. Gregory stepped into the tent and pulled the green canvas flap closed behind him. 'You got the name right, though.' He walked over to the blackboard and took a map from the tube. 'Though I'd as soon as you didn't remember who I am, just what I'm about to tell you.' He used large bulldog clips to attach the map to the blackboard, revealing large damp patches under his arms as he stretched upwards. He had to stand on tiptoe to reach the top of the blackboard. Warner grinned across at Austin. The newcomer definitely wasn't army: even the deskbound warriors of the Pentagon would never have allowed themselves to get so out of condition.

Gregory turned to face them and put his hands on his hips. His head swivelled on his thick neck as he spoke in a deep, gravelly voice. 'This is a DEA operation, sanctioned at the highest level. And that, gentlemen, means the office of the President of the United States.' He looked at their faces one by one as if stressing the importance of what he was saying. 'Having said that, you won't be wearing any medals as a result of what we're doing here. You go in, you do the job, and then you go home. If you do your job right, no one will even know you were here.

The details of the mission won't be appearing on your record, but you will not be forgotten, I can assure you of that. Do what's expected of you, and you'll be winning Brownie points that'll do more for you than medals ever can. Are we communicating, gentlemen?'

Austin and the rest nodded.

Gregory tapped the map with the back of his right hand. 'The Golden Triangle,' he said. 'Some seventy per cent of all the heroin sold in the West comes from here. Your target is the headquarters of a drug baron located somewhere in this area.' He tapped the map again. Austin frowned as he studied the map. The area covered by Gregory's hand was where Burma, Thailand and Laos met, and appeared to be nothing but rainforest. 'This particular drug baron controls thousands of acres of poppy plants in the Triangle. The Thais and the Burmese have been trying for years to apprehend him, but with no success. The DEA has lost half a dozen operatives trying to infiltrate the organisation and we're not prepared to throw away any more good men. That, gentlemen, is where you come in. We have obtained the consent of the Burmese authorities to launch a military offensive against the target, a surgical strike, if you like.' Gregory took a swig from his can of Diet Coke. 'The information we have so far leads us to believe that the target is in an area of rainforest in Burma some fifty miles over the Thai border,' Gregory continued. 'Unfortunately that information could well be out of date already. The drug baron is constantly on the move, rarely maintaining the same headquarters for more than a couple of weeks. That's why he's been impossible to pin down in the past.' He grinned. 'But within the next few days, that's all going to change. We're going to know exactly where he is. And I mean exactly.' He wiped his forehead with his sleeve before continuing.

'A beacon is about to be activated at the target, transmitting on a frequency which we will be monitoring through a surveillance satellite by the National Imagery Office. Once activated, we will have the co-ordinates of the target to within ten feet.'

Burden looked across at Austin again and smiled tightly. Austin nodded. With a beacon at the target they could fly blindfolded.

'Each of your machines will be equipped with eight Hellfire anti-armour missiles,' said Gregory. 'Six will be standard lock-on after launch guidance-coded to laser designators, but two will be modified to home in on the transmitter beacon.'

Austin raised his eyebrows, surprised by Gregory's technical knowledge. The operation of the Hellfire missiles wasn't classified, but it wasn't common knowledge either, and it was clear that the DEA man knew what he was talking about.

'Your target acquisition and designation sights will guide you to the beacon once it's in line of sight, and once you're within range you'll be able to release the modified Hellfires. Just fire and forget, gentlemen. Fire and forget. You can use the remaining laser-guided Hellfires to clean up the surrounding area. You'll be carrying a full load of twelve hundred rounds of ammunition for the chain gun to take care of any ground resistance.'

Lucarelli sniffed and lifted his arm. 'What's the range of the transmitter?' he asked.

'We'll be picking it up from orbiting satellites, but so far as the Hellfires are concerned, you'll want to be no further than two miles from the objective. Obviously the closer you are, the better.'

Warner raised a finger. Gregory nodded for him to speak. 'Is collateral damage a problem?' Warner asked.

Gregory shook his head emphatically. 'There won't be any good guys in the vicinity,' he said. 'Anyone out there is a legitimate target.'

'Opposition?' asked Burden.

'Nothing to worry a low-flying Apache,' said Gregory. 'Mainly automatic weapons, AK-47s and M16s, but they won't be expecting you. They're there to guard the poppy fields and protect the warlord; they're not geared up for air attacks. They're jungle fighters, nothing more. You'll be in and out before they know what's happening. It'll be a milk run.' Burden scribbled on his clipboard.

Austin studied the map. 'Fifty miles, you say?'

'That was then,' said Gregory. 'They could be up to a hundred and twenty miles inside the border now. We won't know until we get the fix.'

Austin nodded. Two hundred and forty miles wouldn't require long-range tanks and if that was the maximum distance they'd have to cover they would be there and back within ninety minutes. Not exactly a milk run, but like Gregory said, they'd have the element of surprise on their side.

'The technicians will be modifying the Hellfires over the next couple of days, but as of now I want you guys on permanent standby. We don't know when the beacon is going to be activated, but the moment it goes off you'll be away. Night or day. Austin and Warner will fly lead, Burden and Lucarelli, you'll be flying wing. Any problems?'

The Apache crews shook their heads.

Gregory nodded. 'Facilities here are basic, I'm afraid, as you've probably already discovered. The mosquitoes are lethal so use the nets and keep taking the tablets. I don't want you getting sick.' He put down his can of Diet Coke and unclipped the map from the blackboard.

The four men stood up and went outside together. About three hundred feet from the cluster of tents stood the two AH-64D Longbow Apaches, squatting like huge drab olive beetles on the grass, their main rotor blades drooping as if they were melting in the heat. The large sensors on the noses of the helicopters looked like the eyes of a giant fly, adding to the impression that they were giant insects and not machines. Technicians in camouflage overalls were gathered around the nearest helicopter, fitting missile installations to the undersides of the Apache's stubby wings.

'What do you think, Hal?' ask Warner.

'Piece of cake,' said Austin, taking a stick of gum from his chest pocket. He unwrapped it and popped it into his mouth. 'They won't know what's hit them.'

HUTCH WORKED ON AUTOPILOT as he ran through a mental checklist of everything he had to do. Matt had agreed to swop cells with Harrigan, the cell door key was now as perfect as he could make it, and Billy Winter had been briefed. Hutch figured that once Harrigan was wearing the brown uniform that prisoners had to put on for court appearances, the guards were unlikely to realise that he wasn't the American. The guards appeared to be interested only in the number of bodies and rarely seemed to look at faces. The other occupants of Hutch's cell would realise that something was up but there would be no reason for them to say anything. If anyone did make a move to alert the guards, Joshua had promised to intervene with Baz. Baz was by far the biggest man in the cell and was treated with wary respect by the rest of the prisoners. The Canadian would also be aware of the swop, but again Hutch assumed that he would keep his mouth shut. The biggest worry was Pipop. He was one of the few trustys who knew the prisoners by name and he would be sure to notice that Harrigan was in the wrong cell.

Hutch felt a light touch on his shoulder. It was Thep. The old man examined the bookcase that Hutch was working on and nodded his approval. He pointed over to the varnishing area. Hutch picked up the bookcase and carried it over to the varnishers. On the way back he was confronted by one of the carpenters. It was the big man with the ponytail who'd given him the file. Hutch tried to walk around the man but the carpenter stepped to the side with him. Hutch took a step back, but as he did so he realised that there was another man behind him. Both men were holding screwdrivers. Hutch looked around. Another carpenter was standing by one of the lathes, and moved forward. There was no sign of any guards or trustys. '*A-rai?*' said Hutch. What?

The carpenter directly in front of him held the screwdriver at Hutch's stomach, the handle tight in his fist. 'We want the file,' he said.

'I paid for it,' Hutch protested.

'Not pay. You rent.'

Hutch put his hands up. The screwdriver was only inches from his stomach. 'No one said anything about rent. I bought it.'

The carpenter shook his head. He jabbed the screwdriver at Hutch and Hutch jumped back. 'Ten thousand baht,' he said. 'I want ten thousand baht.'

It was a shakedown, Hutch realised. It wasn't about the file at all. They'd obviously heard that he had access to money from the outside and decided that they wanted some of it. 'I can give you the file back,' said Hutch. It was in the cell, hidden in the cement wall that cordoned off the toilet.

'Ten thousand baht,' repeated the carpenter.

The carpenter to Hutch's right stepped forward. Hutch moved away. They were forcing him up against a wall. There was no point in shouting for help: the noise of the lathes and wood-turning machines would drown out his cries. Two of the Thais in the varnishing team had seen what was going on, but they had turned their backs and were concentrating on their work.

'I don't have any money,' said Hutch. He knew they wouldn't believe him but he had to say something to buy time. There was only one way he was going to survive the confrontation and that was to show them that he was tougher and harder than they were. It had happened in every prison he'd ever been in. The easy way out would be to give them the money, but they'd take that as a sign of weakness and keep coming back for more.

The carpenter with the ponytail grabbed Hutch by the shirt collar. He noticed the gold chains that he was wearing and his eyes widened. Before he could react further, Hutch grabbed the screwdriver and brought his knee up into the man's groin. The carpenter gasped. Hutch held on to the screwdriver for all he was worth and stamped down on the man's foot. He twisted the man's arm and threw him against one of the other carpenters.

The carpenter to his left stabbed at his arm and drew blood. Hutch yelled out loud. He headbutted the ponytailed carpenter and felt his forehead smash down on the Thai's nose. Blood spurted over the man's mouth and chin. Hutch kept a tight grip on the man's arm as he turned, throwing the Thai off balance. Hutch kicked him in the stomach, hard, then kicked one of his knees. Not until the Thai went down did Hutch let go of the man's screwdriver. He punched him in the face, putting all his weight behind the blow. He felt a stabbing pain in his side but Hutch ignored it. His attention was totally focused on the man on his knees. He kicked him under the chin and the carpenter's neck snapped up. The man pitched backwards and lay on the ground, unmoving. The carpenter curled up into a ball, moaning like a sick child. Only then did Hutch turn to face the other two men. Less than five seconds had passed since the ponytailed carpenter had reached for Hutch's gold chains, but Hutch had inflicted enough damage to make the other two men think twice. They jabbed their screwdrivers at Hutch but their hearts weren't in it; they'd seen what he'd done to the leader of their group and they were reluctant to meet the same fate. The Thais backed away. Hutch took a step towards them, his hands up. They turned and ran. Hutch began to tremble. The strength drained from his legs and he leaned against the wall, gasping for breath.

A large figure loomed by his side. It was Joshua. 'What the hell was that about?' asked the Nigerian.

'Just establishing the pecking order,' said Hutch.

Joshua nodded at the carpenter on the ground, who was now struggling to his knees. 'Where did you learn to fight?'

'Self-taught,' said Hutch.

Joshua took Hutch's left arm and examined the scratch. 'You were lucky,' he said.

Hutch pulled his arm away. 'Yeah, wasn't I just.'

TSANG CHAU-LING HANDED HER passport to the immigration officer. He scrutinised the landing card she'd filled in on the plane. 'Why are you coming to Thailand?' he asked.

'I'm sorry?'

He gave her back the form and tapped it with his pen. 'Your reason for your trip. Business or holiday?'

Chau-ling looked at the form. She hadn't ticked either box. She took his pen and put a line through the box marked 'Business'. The immigration officer stamped her passport and waved her through.

Chau-ling waited for Ricky Lim. He hadn't said a word to her during the two-and-a-half hour flight from Hong Kong. He wasn't happy about accompanying her to Thailand, but he knew better than to express his reservations to her father. She smiled up at Lim as he joined her, but he refused to be mollified. 'Come on, Ricky, give me a smile,' she said.

Lim bared his teeth.

'You can do better than that,' she teased.

'Not right now I can't, Miss Tsang,' he said. He pointed towards the exit. 'Your car should be waiting outside.'

Chau-ling followed her bodyguard out of the terminal.

HUTCH SMEARED SHAVING FOAM over his stomach, rubbing it in with the palm of his hand. 'How do you know that I won't just keep on running?' he asked.

'I don't,' said Carver, lighting a Marlboro. He leaned back in his chair and watched Hutch shave his stomach with slow, careful strokes.

'That doesn't make any sense,' said Hutch, wiping the disposable plastic razor on a piece of towelling. 'What are you saying, that you trust me?'

'Something like that.' Carver flicked up the top of his Zippo with his thumb, then snapped it shut. 'How did you get the scratch on your arm?'

'Power struggle. Nothing major.' Hutch stopped shaving and looked at the DEA agent. 'Hypothetically speaking, Tim, suppose I get across the border and make it to Zhou's camp . . .'

'I'm assuming you will,' said Carver, continuing to flick the top of his lighter.

'. . . and what if I just don't press the button on your gizmo? What if I disappear into the jungle?'

Carver shrugged carelessly. 'It won't be like last time. There won't be any faked death, no nice, neat way out. The DEA will come looking for you, and they will get you. No matter how well you hide, they'll find you.'

'And then what?'

'There are some pretty heavy people in the DEA. People you wouldn't want to meet, believe me.'

Hutch pointed the plastic razor at Carver. 'Why is it that everyone I meet threatens me these days? I never get to hear the carrot without having the stick waved in my face.'

'Sorry,' said Carver.

'That thing isn't a bomb, is it?' Hutch said, nodding at the brushed metal box, about the size of a slim cigarette case, lying on the table next to Carver's hand. 'It's not going to explode when I press the button, is it? This isn't some sort of devious set-up?'

Carver smiled. 'No, it won't explode. It's a transmitter, not a bomb.'

'How do I know?'

Carver's smile widened. 'I guess you'll just have to take my word on that, won't you?' He leaned forward and brushed his fringe out of his eyes. 'You don't owe these people anything. Billy Winter is threatening your son, he set you up, he doesn't care if you live or die. He's destroyed your life and he did it without a second thought. You owe Zhou Yuanyi even less.'

Hutch started shaving again.

'I'm with the good guys, Hutch. I've no reason to betray you. I meant what I said. You help the DEA and the DEA will stand by you. A new identity, a new life, a life that will stand up to inspection, American citizenship. If you don't press that button, you'll be putting your life in Billy Winter's hands. Do you want to do that again?'

'I think I can trust Winter, despite what he's done.' Hutch finished shaving and put the razor on the table. He used the towel to wipe his stomach clean of the remaining foam. 'I want half a million dollars.'

Carver's eyebrows shot skyward. 'Say what?'

'Five hundred thousand dollars. This Zhou's got to be worth that much to you.'

'Why this sudden concern about money?'

'Think of it as an incentive. If I know I'm going to get half a million dollars, I'm more likely to press the button, right?'

'I guess so.'

'Is that a problem?'

Carver exhaled through his nose and stared at Hutch through the smoke. 'Not for me, Hutch.'

'And for your boss?'

Carver rubbed his chin thoughtfully. It was a relatively small amount to lose in the DEA's budget. And Hutch was right, it was a small amount to pay if it led to the trial and conviction of one of the biggest heroin suppliers in the world. 'I don't think it'll be a problem.'

'I have your word?'

Carver nodded. 'Yeah, you have my word.'

'In that case, I'll press the button. How long will it take the choppers to get there?'

'Half an hour, give or take.'

'There'll be shooting, right?'

'They're not going to go in with guns blazing, don't worry. It'll be a Ranger unit, they're trained for operations like this. In and out, a snatch squad.'

'And they'll take me with them?'

'Damn right.'

'What about Winter?'

Carver handed the metal case to Hutch. Hutch held it against his stomach while the DEA agent tore off a piece of flesh-coloured sticking plaster from a roll. 'Why are you so worried about him?' Carver asked.

'You wouldn't understand.'

'Try me.' Carver stuck the sticking plaster across the transmitter and spread it across Hutch's stomach.

'We were banged up together for a couple of years, that's all. You get close to a person when you're in prison, especially the sort of prisons I was in. There were times when he was the only man I spoke to for weeks on end.'

'How come?' Carver ripped off another piece of tape.

'We did time in the punishment block together, in Parkhurst. They called it the choky. You're banged up in your cell for twenty-three hours a day with just an hour for exercise. You eat on your own, you slop out on your own, you exercise on your own. The only humans you see are the guards, and they barely count as human. They call it solitary, but if you're lucky you can talk to the guy in the next cell. If you stand on your chair and stick your head out of the window, you can talk, just about. Billy Winter's voice kept me sane. He got me through it, he stopped me from going crazy. I did a full month in the choky in Parkhurst, and for three weeks of it Billy was in the cell next to me, talking, making me laugh, keeping me alive.'

Carver stripped the second piece of tape across Hutch's stomach. 'The Rangers will take him out, too. Just keep your heads down. They'll have your photograph, you won't be in any danger.'

'Glad to hear it.' He put his shirt back on and buttoned it up. 'How does that look?' He turned side on to give Carver a better look.

'Can't see a thing. Just be careful when you change into your uniform tomorrow.'

'I'll do it tonight when everyone else is asleep.'

'And what about Harrigan?'

'I'll take care of that tonight, too. What happens if I get the transmitter wet? Say I get caught in the rain?'

'It's sealed. Completely waterproof.'

Hutch patted the shirt. 'Five hundred thousand dollars, right?'

'You'll take a cheque?'

Hutch smiled thinly. 'You're sure you can get it?'

Carver put the Zippo back in his breast pocket. 'I'm sure. Providing that you activate the tranomitter. Is money that important to you, Hutch?'

Hutch rolled his shirt sleeves up. 'It's not the money. It's the principle.'

TSANG CHAU-LING AND RICKY Lim arrived at the prison gates just after one o'clock in the afternoon. Khun Kriengsak had sent a clerk from his office to help her arrange the visit and he took her along to the canteen where a uniformed guard was sitting at a desk. The clerk gave the guard a piece of paper with Warren Hastings' name on it, and then asked Chau-ling to produce her passport. The guard added the details to a list that already contained several dozen names.

'They will call him to the visiting area,' said the clerk, who spoke passable Cantonese. He took them through the arched entrance towards the visiting area. It was an L-shaped enclosure to the left of the main gate, with benches on the visitors' side. More than fifty visitors were already there, standing around and looking expectantly at a door on the prisoners' side. Several men in blue T-shirts and shorts were lounging around the door, laughing and smoking cigarettes.

'This is it?' said Chau-ling. 'Can't we have any privacy?'

'I'm afraid not,' said the clerk.

Chau-ling looked at the enclosure in disgust. On the visitors' side there were bars overlaid with wire mesh. She walked over and peered through. There was a gap of almost ten feet separating the mesh from another set of bars. The set-up was probably to prevent anything being passed to the prisoners, but it meant that she'd have to shout to make herself heard. Khun Kriengsak had said that Warren could only have visitors on a Thursday. She couldn't believe that that was the only contact he'd have with the outside world: shouted conversations once a week. She shuddered.

Several prisoners came through the door and headed down the barred walkway. Most were Thais. Their visitors rushed to the bars on their side. It was bedlam. Everyone began shouting at once. One woman was holding up her baby and crying, and an older woman was pressing photographs against the bars so that her son could see them. The shouts echoed off the walls and Chau-ling shuddered at the noise. More prisoners entered the walkway, several black men and a few Westerners. A middle-aged Australian woman burst into tears and put a hand up to her mouth at the sight of a pale, thin young man with an earring in his left ear. She staggered against her husband who put a comforting arm around her. Together they walked along the wire mesh, parallel to their son, seeking a place where they could talk. More Thais were funnelling through the door and the noise was getting louder by the minute. Chau-ling's heart jumped as she saw Warren.

'Warren!' she shouted.

He looked at her, confused. He shouted something at her but she couldn't hear him. She pointed to the far end of the visiting area and he nodded. Chau-ling told Lim and the clerk to wait. She kept looking at Warren as she walked behind the seated visitors. He seemed to have lost weight and he kept running his hands through his hair. She'd never seen him look so worried. He seemed to be in an even worse state than when he'd been arrested.

He found a space on his side of the bars and stopped. Chau-ling stood between a Thai housewife with a crying toddler, and a Nigerian man who was screaming at a black prisoner and waving a brick-sized wad of money.

'I'm sorry, Chau-ling,' Warren shouted.

She seemed surprised by his apology. 'Sorry for what?'

He gestured with his chin. 'This. This place, the trouble I've caused you.'

Chau-ling had to strain to hear him. 'You haven't caused me any trouble,' she shouted. Her face fell. 'Actually, that's not true,' she said.

'What do you mean?'

'You know a man called Billy Winter?'

He nodded hesitantly.

'And a man called Bird?'

Warren's mouth opened in surprise. She could see that he was lost for words.

'Warren, you do know them, don't you?'

'What is it, Chau-ling? What happened?'

'They sent two men to kill me, Warren.'

'What?'

386

'Two hired killers came to Hong Kong. They tried to kill me.' She looked around. She had to shout to make herself heard and was worried about being overheard. No one appeared to be paying her any attention.

'Chau-ling!' Warren shouted. She looked back at him. 'How do you know it was Winter?' he yelled.

The Nigerian man was shouting in his own language and his deep, booming voice was a constant distraction. Chau-ling tried to block it out. 'My father found out. He says that this man Winter is going to get you out of prison. Warren, what's happening?'

He shook his head as if trying to clear his thoughts.

'Warren, you have to tell me what's going on!' Chau-ling shouted. 'Who are these men? What hold do they have over you? Tell me and I'll be able to help you. Khun Kriengsak has got some very influential friends in Thailand. Between him and my father, there isn't any problem we can't deal with.' Her voice was becoming hoarse from all the shouting.

He leaned forward and pressed his face against the bars. The blood had drained from his face. 'Chau-ling, you have to listen to me,' he yelled. 'You can't help me, do you understand? Go back to Hong Kong. Go back to Hong Kong and forget about me.'

She looked at him in horror. 'Haven't you heard a word I've said? They tried to kill me, Warren. Two men with guns came to the kennels. If it hadn't been for . . .' She fell silent.

'What is it?' he asked.

Chau-ling took a handkerchief from her pocket and dabbed at her eyes. 'Mickey's dead,' she said. She blew her nose. 'He saved my life and they shot him.'

'Jesus,' he said. 'I'm sorry.'

'So am I,' said Chau-ling. She blew her nose again. 'He was a good dog.'

'I meant I was sorry about what happened to you. I had no idea . . .'

'What's going on, Warren? Who is this man Billy Winter?'

'An old friend.'

'An old friend? A friend of yours tried to kill me? Why?'

He glared at her with such intensity that she flinched. 'I don't know. I really don't know. Look, you're going to have to trust me, Chau-ling. Please go back to Hong Kong. Right now. Go straight to the airport and get on the first plane out of here. Go and stay with your father, he can protect you until this is over.'

'Warren . . .'

He pointed his finger at her face as if he was aiming a gun. 'Go!' he shouted. Before she could reply he turned his back on her and walked away.

'Warren!' she called, but he didn't look back.

TIM CARVER STIRRED HIS coffee with a pencil, then wiped it on his copy of the *Bangkok Post*. 'And then what happened?' he asked Nikom.

'She went back to her hotel with a Chinese guy. A big man. His name's Ricky Lim. I think he's her bodyguard.'

'Tell me again what they said.' Carver settled back in his chair and made notes as Nikom described the meeting between Hutch and the girl. Nikom had managed to get a place at the mesh close to Chau-ling, but hadn't been able to hear everything. There were gaps where the Nigerian man had been screaming at his friend, but Nikom had managed to follow the conversation fairly closely.

When Nikom had finished, Carver looked up from his notes. 'And she definitely said that Billy Winter tried to kill her?'

Nikom nodded. 'Definitely.'

'And what's her name?'

'Tsang Chau-ling,' said Nikom. 'According to the visitor's form she filled in, she works for Hastings in Hong Kong.'

'She mentioned her father. Do you know who he is?'

Nikom shook his head. 'I can find out.'

'Where's she staying?'

'The Shangri-La.'

Carver stood up and took his jacket off the back of his chair.

'Do you want me to come with you?' asked Nikom.

Carver shook his head. 'Nah, I'll handle it. See what you can find out about her father. Like how the hell he found out what Winter is up to.'

Carver took the lift to the ground floor and went outside. It was the start of the rush hour and the street outside was gridlocked. The DEA agent walked along the road, stepping to one side to allow a group of monks go by, and found himself a motorcycle taxi rider. The rider handed him a battered white crash helmet with a broken strap. Carver climbed on to the pillion. They skirted the worst of the traffic and in less than ten minutes the rider dropped Carver off in front of the

Shangri-La. By car, the journey would have taken more than an hour.

The receptionist wouldn't tell Carver what room Tsang Chau-ling was in and insisted on calling up to her room. Carver would have preferred to have gone up unannounced but even his DEA credentials didn't cut him any slack in the five-star hotel. The receptionist nodded, put down the telephone and told Carver that Miss Tsang was in room 1104 and that he could go up.

Carver tidied his windswept hair with his hands while he rode up in the lift. Motorcycle taxis were all well and good, but they did play havoc with personal grooming. He checked his face in the mirrored wall of the lift and dabbed away flecks of soot until he reckoned he was presentable. He knocked on the door of 1104 and stepped back. A man opened it, a broad-shouldered Oriental with close-cropped spiky hair and a dimple in his chin. He was a big man, at least two inches taller than Carver, and Carver wasn't a weakling. This was obviously the bodyguard whom Nikom had seen with the girl at Klong Prem.

'Is this Miss Tsang's room?' Carver asked.

'Who are you?' said the man. There was no menace in his voice but his sheer bulk was enough to intimidate Carver.

'The name's Tim Carver. I'm with the DEA.' Carver reached into his jacket to get his ID but the man grabbed him by the wrist and twisted him around. 'What the . . . ?' said Carver, as the man slammed him into the wall. Something pricked against his neck. He stiffened as he realised it was some sort of knife.

'Ricky, put him down,' said a female voice.

'He was—'

'Leave him alone,' said the girl, with a harder edge to her voice this time.

The point moved away from Carver's neck. As he turned, he could see it was an ice-pick in the man's hand. 'I was only getting my wallet out,' said Carver.

'You'll have to forgive Ricky. He's not housetrained yet. I'm Tsang Chau-ling.' She was pretty, with glossy black hair that she'd tied back in a ponytail, and razor-sharp cheekbones, but she looked tired as if she hadn't had much sleep over the past few days.

'I need to speak with you, Miss Tsang.'

'What about?'

Carver looked up and down the corridor. 'Could we do this inside, please?'

Lim moved to block the door but Chau-ling shook her head and he stepped back into the room. 'What's it about?' she pressed.

Carver took his wallet from his jacket pocket and showed his ID to her.

'I didn't doubt that you were with the DEA,' she said. 'I want to know what this is about.'

Carver put his wallet away. 'You were at Klong Prem prison today.'

Chau-ling put her head on one side. 'Yes,' she said hesitantly.

'And you spoke to Warren Hastings?'

Chau-ling looked at him for several seconds without speaking, then turned and went back into the room. Carver followed her and closed the door. It wasn't a room, he realised, it was a suite. A very large suite, with views over the Chao Phraya River. One night would probably cost as much as Carver earned in a week, he thought with a twinge of envy. Whoever her father was, there was definitely money in the family. Serious money.

Chau-ling went over to a sofa by the window and sat down, curling her legs underneath her. 'Do you want a drink or something?' she asked. Carver shook his head. Chau-ling spoke to her bodyguard in Chinese and he replied, his voice deep and guttural. He was clearly arguing with her but she looked at him coldly and even though he couldn't speak Chinese, Carver could tell that she was telling him to do as he was told. He bowed meekly and left by one of the three doors that led off the sitting room.

'Sit down, please, you're making me nervous,' she said to Carver.

Carver perched on the edge of a chair the back of which was shaped like an oyster shell. 'What's your relationship with Warren Hastings?' he asked.

'I help him run his kennels.'

'Do you mind telling me why you went to the prison today?' Carver already knew, but he wanted to see what her reaction would be, whether she'd tell the truth or lie.

Chau-ling narrowed her eyes. 'How did you know I'd been there?'

'We are automatically notified when drug-smuggling suspects have visitors,' lied Carver.

Chau-ling looked at him as if deciding whether or not to believe him, then she gave a small shrug. 'I just wanted to see how he was getting on,' she said. 'We're all very worried about him. How is the DEA involved?'

'It's a drug case. We investigate all drug seizures.'

'You know he's innocent, don't you?'

'That's for the court to decide.'

'He was framed.'

'Maybe he was.'

'So what has your investigation turned up so far?'

The question took Carver by surprise. He hadn't realised how easily she'd turned the tables and that it was now she who was interrogating him.

'You are investigating the case, aren't you? Or is there some other reason you came to see me?'

She looked like a teenager, curled up on the sofa, but her eyes bored relentlessly into his as she scrutinised his face for any reaction. Carver took out his pack of Marlboro. 'Do you mind if I . . . ?' he said and held up the pack.

Her eyes never left his face. 'I'd rather you didn't,' she said. 'Ricky has asthma and I don't want him wheezing all night.'

Carver couldn't tell if she was joking or not but he put the cigarettes away. 'Do you play poker, Miss Tsang?'

'Sometimes. Why?'

'Because if I was holding three queens and you were showing a pair of kings, I think I'd fold.'

'That's a compliment, is it? Or a subtle change of subject?'

Carver winced inwardly. She might well work as a kennel maid in Hong Kong but she was as sharp as any criminal lawyer he'd ever met. He wondered what Hutch had done to earn the love of such a beautiful, smart, self-assured woman. 'How about we both put our cards on the table?' he said.

'You first,' she said flatly.

Carver wanted a cigarette, badly. He looked around the room. The door that the bodyguard had gone through was ajar. Carver smiled as best he could. 'Warren Hastings is working for the DEA,' he said.

Chau-ling's face broke into a relieved smile. 'I knew it,' she said.

Carver immediately felt a flush of guilt. He hadn't actually lied, but he was being more than a little economical with the truth.

'I knew he wasn't guilty,' she said. 'I knew there was something more to it.'

'That's why you have to do what he said. You have to go back to Hong Kong.'

Chau-ling's smile was immediately replaced by a suspicious frown. 'How do you know what Warren said to me?'

'I spoke to him after your visit,' he said. That was a definite lie and he fought to keep his voice and gaze steady, certain that she'd pounce on any sign that he wasn't telling the truth. Chau-ling nodded but Carver could see that she wasn't convinced. 'He said you'd been attacked,' he added.

Chau-ling drew her legs tighter underneath herself as if trying to make herself smaller. 'Two men tried to kill me. Thais.'

'Do you know who they were?' Chau-ling shook her head. 'What happened to them? Did the police get them?'

'No. They're dead, I think. The dogs got one of them. I . . .'

She was interrupted by the reappearance of the bodyguard. He spoke to her in guttural Cantonese, obviously worried. She answered, her tone conciliatory. He said something else and she nodded. The bodyguard went to stand by the door. She'd obviously given him permission to stay.

'You were saying?' said Carver.

'I don't know what happened to them,' she said.

'But you know who hired them?'

Chau-ling nodded.

'So they must have been able to talk at some point,' said Carver. 'Did they give you any other information?'

'They didn't give me any information,' said Chau-ling coldly. 'They broke into my house, they tried to shoot me, and I defended myself. End of story.'

'The names you gave Warren. Billy Winter and Bird. What do you know about them?'

'Nothing. Do you know who they are?'

Carver fought to keep his voice steady. 'No,' he lied.

'I got the feeling that Warren did,' said Chau-ling. 'But we did agree that you'd show me yours first. What is Warren doing for the DEA?'

'He's involved in an undercover operation,' said Carver. It was practically the first true statement he'd made since sitting down.

'Yes . . .' said Chau-ling, encouraging him to go on.

'There isn't much more I can tell without putting him at risk,' he said.

'Don't give me that,' said Chau-ling contemptuously. 'I'm not a threat to him. And I'm hardly likely to go around telling anyone what I know.'

'Nevertheless . . .'

'Nevertheless my Aunt Fanny. Two men tried to kill me and I deserve to know why.'

Carver looked away. Down below on the dirty brown river, two long-tailed boats sped by filled with tourists. A water taxi was picking up passengers at a pier behind the Oriental Hotel.

'Well?' pressed Chau-ling.

'These men, Billy Winter and Bird, they're involved in a drug-smuggling ring. They recruit expats as couriers: they're less likely to be stopped than Asians. Warren was approached by Winter in Hong Kong, and he came to us. We decided the best thing would be for him to play along, to agree to help them.'

'But that doesn't explain why he's in prison.'

'We couldn't connect the drugs to Winter. At the moment we don't have a case.'

'So you're going to wait until Winter tries to get Warren out?'

'That's right. How did you know that they were planning an escape, Miss Tsang?'

The bodyguard said something in Chinese but Chau-ling didn't look at him. 'I'll pass on that one,' she said.

'We said we'd share information.'

'That we did, Mr Carver, but I have the feeling that you're not sharing everything with me, so you're going to have to allow a girl to keep a few secrets.' She stood up. 'So what happens next?'

'I'll keep you informed. But I think I can safely say that it'll all be over in a few days.'

'And Warren can come back to Hong Kong?'

'Yes.' Carver looked straight into her eyes, and he was as sure as night follows day that she knew he was lying. 'Now, will you promise me that you'll go back to Hong Kong where you'll be safe?' He corrected himself quickly. 'Safer.'

'Of course,' she said, and looked directly into his eyes. Carver was equally certain that she was lying.

The bodyguard showed him out, and it was clear from the look on his face that he'd have preferred to have another go with the ice-pick instead. Carver lit a cigarette in the lift and wondered just what he was going to do with Tsang Chau-ling.

HUTCH SAT WITH HIS back to the wall, listening to his sleeping cellmates. One of the Hong Kong Chinese was coughing, curled up in a ball on the blanket he slept on. Most of the prisoners had strips of cloth across their eyes to blot out the ever-present fluorescent lights. Over on the far side of the cell, Matt lay facing Hutch, his eyes open. He gave Hutch a weak smile and Hutch nodded. Hutch got up and went over to the lockers. He took out the brown T-shirt and shorts that he'd have to wear in court and changed into them, turning his back on the American so that he wouldn't see the transmitter taped to his stomach. Hutch had bought the uniform from the trustys and had made sure that the shirt was several sizes too big so that it hung loosely around his chest. He retrieved the key from its hiding place at the base of the concrete wall around the toilet and rinsed it in the water trough, then went over to Matt.

'Ready?' he asked.

The American nodded. He was sweating and kept swallowing nervously. Hutch bent over Joshua and touched him lightly on the shoulder. The Nigerian removed the piece of cloth that he'd tied around his eyes and sat up.

'Ready?' asked Hutch. Joshua gave him a thumbs-up.

Hutch unlocked the cell door and ushered Matt on to the catwalk. Joshua closed the door quietly and kept watch through the bars. Hutch and the American crept along the walkway, bent double so that they couldn't be seen from the cells they passed. When they reached Harrigan's cell, the Irishman was already waiting for them. Hutch inserted the key and turned it. The lock clicked and he pushed the door open. Harrigan was wearing his brown T-shirt and shorts and he gave Matt his ordinary clothes: a white T-shirt with Garfield on the front and a pair of denim shorts.

The Canadian was sitting on his bed, and waved for Hutch to come closer. 'I'm not happy about this,' he whispered.

'You don't have to be happy,' hissed Hutch. 'It's nothing to do with you.'

'Yeah, well, when the shit hits the fan, it's going to go everywhere.'

'Just say you were asleep. Say you were tripping. It's me and Ray they'll be after, not you. Besides, you've already been paid.' Hutch had given the Canadian one of the gold chains and some of Bey's money to buy his co-operation. And his silence.

'Well, now I'm not sure that it's a good idea.'

Hutch stared at the Canadian. 'What are you saying?' he asked. Harrigan and Matt were standing at the cell door, unsure of what was happening.

'I don't think you should go through with it.'

Hutch looked at the Canadian's eyes. The pupils were dilated and the whites were bloodshot. There was a smear of blood on his left forearm. Hutch grabbed him by the shirt collar. 'We're going through with it,' he whispered into the Canadian's ear. 'And you're going to keep your mouth shut. Do you understand?' The Canadian didn't reply. He turned his head away and grimaced. Hutch dragged him to his feet and marched him over to the bars. Matt and Harrigan moved out of the way and stood watching apprehensively. 'Do you see that guy over there? The big black guy?'

The Canadian stared across the catwalk at Hutch's cell. Joshua stood there looking out, his powerful arms folded through the cell door.

'You see him?' pressed Hutch. The Canadian nodded. 'That's Joshua,' Hutch continued, whispering into the Canadian's ear. 'Joshua's a very good friend of mine. A very good friend. If you screw this up for me, if you say one word to the guards, Joshua's going to get very angry with you. Do you understand?'

Joshua grinned and waved.

'If I were you, I wouldn't want Joshua angry with me. He's a big lad. Now why don't you go and shoot some more of that crap into your veins and get a good night's sleep?' Hutch let go of the Canadian's collar. The Canadian scurried over to his bed and sat with his back to them.

Hutch turned to Harrigan. 'Ready, Ray?'

Harrigan nodded. Hutch reached forward and held the Irishman's left wrist. He examined his arms, looking for fresh needle marks. He saw none.

'I'm clean,' said Harrigan resentfully.

Hutch knelt down. Harrigan took a step back but Hutch grabbed his leg. There was a small drop of blood on the Irishman's ankle. 'You stupid bastard,' said Hutch.

'I needed something,' whined Harrigan.

'You could ruin it for everyone,' said Hutch. 'Are you carrying anything?' Harrigan shook his head but Hutch patted him down to be sure. 'Okay, now stay close to me, and keep your head down.' Hutch looked over at Joshua. The Nigerian gave him another thumbs-up.

Hutch turned to Matt. 'Are you going to be okay?' he asked.

'Sure,' said the American. He seemed more confident now that he was in Harrigan's cell. He stuck out his hand. 'Good luck.' The two men shook hands.

Hutch and Harrigan stepped out of the cell and Hutch relocked the door. The two men crept back to Hutch's cell. Joshua opened the door and they slipped inside. Hutch locked the door and gave the key to Joshua. 'You might as well have this,' he said.

Joshua weighed it in his hand. 'Great, now all I have to do is to find a way out of the compound, cross two walls and a moat and I'm home free.'

'Don't get bitter and twisted,' grinned Hutch. 'And make sure you keep it well hidden.' The prisoners were searched on a regular basis by the trustys, but while the searches were generally perfunctory at best, they did occasionally turn over the cells looking for drugs and contraband.

'Don't worry, I'll take good care of it. You might need it when they bring you back.'

'Don't even joke about that,' said Hutch. He showed Harrigan where the American's sleeping space was. The Irishman wrinkled his nose in disgust. 'Next to the toilet?' he said.

'It's only for a few hours,' said Hutch.

'Yeah, we can't all afford private cells,' said Joshua. 'But if it upsets you that much, you can have my spot.'

'No,' said Hutch. 'He has to be at the far end of the cell. I don't want Pipop seeing him when he opens the door. And Ray, keep your face down until we're on the coach.'

Harrigan waved his hand, indicating the sleeping prisoners. 'What about these guys? Won't they say anything?'

Joshua grinned. 'Not if they know what's good for them,' he said.

'They've no reason to grass us,' said Hutch.

All three men turned to the door as they heard footsteps on the stairs. Joshua took a quick peek through the bars and motioned for Hutch and Harrigan to go to their places. By the time the guard walked by their cell, they were all lying down with their backs to the door.

TSANG CHAU-LING WOKE WITH a start. She sat up, her heart pounding. The room was in almost total darkness and she walked to the window with her arms outstretched, feeling her way. She pulled back the curtains and looked down at the river far below.

Her plane ticket was on the coffee table. She'd decided to do as the DEA agent had said and go back to Hong Kong. There was nothing more she could do in Thailand. She hoped that Warren would be all right, though she wished with all her heart that there was something she could do to help. There was so much she wanted to ask him, so much she wanted to tell him, but she would just have to wait until he returned to Hong Kong.

HARRIGAN REMAINED CURLED UP on his sleeping mat while the rest of the prisoners ate their morning meal. Hutch was so tense that he couldn't bring himself to eat.

Joshua didn't appear to have any problems and he ate Hutch's egg and soup with relish. The prisoners who were due to go to court changed into their brown uniforms as the dirty bowls were collected and passed back through the bars.

Joshua, now dressed in brown ready for his court appearance, stood by the bars, looking at the stairway. 'Here they come,' he said.

The prisoners in Hutch's cell gathered their washing gear from the lockers and waited impatiently for the guard to open their door.

The guard appeared at the bars. He slotted the key into the lock and turned it. Joshua looked across at Hutch and nodded. Hutch's heart was racing. The prisoners began to file out. Harrigan got to his feet but kept his back to the guard and the trustys. The Hong Kong Chinese prisoners dashed through, and Hutch followed them. He paused on the catwalk. Joshua stepped through the door and spoke to Pipop in Thai. Pipop replied and Joshua held out his hand and showed him one of the gold chains, Pipop's eyes widened and he took the chain from the Nigerian. The guard and the other trusty stared at the gold as Joshua explained that he'd found it in the cell. The guard reached for it but Pipop took a step backwards, reluctant to give up possession. Harrigan walked out of the cell, his face turned away from the men at the door. Hutch went with him down the stairs, leaving Joshua talking to the guard and trustys.

The prisoners who were due to go to court assembled outside the block. Harrigan stood next to the wall with his head down. Hutch stood next to him. 'Okay?' he asked.

Harrigan didn't look up. 'Sure.' He sounded distant, as if his mind was elsewhere.

Hutch grabbed him by the shoulders and shook him. 'Don't let me down, Ray.'

'I'm okay,' said Harrigan. He began to shiver despite the heat.

Hutch lifted the Irishman's chin. His pupils were dilated. 'Are you still high?' he asked.

'No,' said Harrigan. 'But I wish I was.'

More prisoners began to gather. A guard read a list of names off a clipboard while another guard did a head count. As their names were called, the prisoners stepped forward. There were nineteen names in all. Hutch stood next to Harrigan, their shoulders touching. Behind them were Joshua and Julian, talking in their own language.

Two more guards arrived, each carrying a large canvas bag. They emptied the contents on to the ground. One bag contained leg-irons, the other handcuffs. Leg-irons were locked on to those prisoners who weren't already chained, then they were all handcuffed. Once they were all chained they were marched in single file out of the compound and through into the courtyard where the coach was waiting with its engine running. It was one of the coaches that Hutch had seen on his first visit to the prison, white with wire mesh over the windows. The driver was slumped over the wheel, his forehead resting on his arms. Two armed guards climbed aboard.

Four guards with shotguns stood in a line behind the coach, one with a clipboard. Their fingers were off the triggers but they kept a close eye on the prisoners as one by one they were waved through the rear door of the coach.

One of the guards tapped on the windscreen and the driver sat up, blinking. He rubbed his eyes with the back of his hands and then smiled and nodded at the guard. He pulled a handle by his side and the rear door hissed open.

Sweat was pouring off Harrigan's face as he climbed on to the coach. His foot slipped on the metal step and his head slammed into the side of the coach but he recovered quickly, mumbling to himself. Hutch waited for the guard with the clipboard to wave him on, then he hurried after Harrigan. The Irishman slid on to a seat midway along the coach. Hutch joined him. Harrigan was sitting with his eyes closed, his hands clenched into fists on his lap. He was breathing fast and Hutch feared he'd soon hyperventilate if he didn't calm down.

'Take it easy,' Hutch whispered. 'Breathe slowly. Try to relax.'

Harrigan opened his eyes. He swallowed nervously. 'I'm okay.'

The last of the prisoners climbed on to the coach and shuffled to his seat. Another armed guard climbed into the back of the coach. He locked the cage in which the prisoners were sitting, then sat down in the guards' area with his colleagues, their shotguns on their laps. The remaining armed guard got into the front and sat next to the driver. The guard with the clipboard joined them and the door hissed shut. Hutch looked over his shoulder. The guards at the back of the coach were deep in conversation.

Hutch looked down at his leg-irons. They were old but in good condition, and glistened with a sheen of oil as if they'd recently been lubricated. That would work in his favour. The handcuffs were newer.

He lifted his right foot slowly and rested it on the shin

of his left leg. He slowly dropped his hands and loosened the laces of his right training shoe. He slipped his fingers inside and pulled out one of the shims.

Hutch set to work on the leg-irons. He fed the shim along the end edge of the swinging shackle and jiggled it in and out. He kept his back straight and looked out of the window, doing it all by feel so as not to attract any attention to himself. Suddenly the shim went in a full half an inch. Hutch eased the shackle free from the locking mechanism and said a silent prayer of thanks. He started work on the second leg, keeping his movements to a minimum.

The coach stopped. Hutch looked out of the window. The driver was waiting for the main gates to be opened. By the time the coach eased forward through the prison gates, the second shackle was open. Hutch exhaled, he hadn't realised that he'd been holding his breath. He pushed the leg-irons along the floor with his feet, slowly so they wouldn't rattle on the metal floor of the coach.

Hutch banged his knee against Harrigan's leg. Harrigan frowned. Hutch pointed at Harrigan's right leg and gestured for him to lift it. Harrigan did as he was told.

The coach accelerated down the road away from the prison. Hutch didn't know how much time he had, that would all depend on how bad the traffic was. He realised Harrigan was staring and he gestured with his chin for him to keep looking out of the window. Hutch's fingers were damp with sweat and the shim kept slipping in his grip. He pulled his hand away and wiped it on his trousers. He tried again, but no matter how much he wiggled the shim about, it just wouldn't go.

He lifted his hands and slipped the shim under his thigh,

then groped in his training shoe. He pulled out four picks before his probing fingers found the second shim. Hutch had a quick look over his shoulder, then he wiped his fingers again and inserted the shim along the edge of the swinging shackle.

The coach braked sharply and the prisoners lurched forward. Several cursed the driver. Hutch looked up. The coach had stopped at the level crossing. In the distance was an approaching train. A red and white motorcycle pulled up next to the coach. The driver was a big man wearing a full face helmet with the visor down. The motorcycle was big, too: a 750cc Kawasaki. The driver flicked up his visor. It was Bird. He looked straight at Hutch and smiled. Bird pushed his visor down and gunned the engine of his bike. Eventually the train rolled by, heading for Bangkok.

Hutch started on the leg-iron again. It took only a few minutes before the shim slid in between the two sets of teeth and he was able to slip out the shackle arm. He breathed a sigh of relief and tapped Harrigan on the leg to let him know that he'd finished. Harrigan put his leg down. Hutch wasn't going to bother with Harrigan's other leg: he'd be able to run well enough and the time would be better spent working on the handcuffs.

Hutch tried the shim on the handcuff around his left wrist, but he could tell after a couple of attempts that it wasn't going to work. The two sets of teeth fitted together too well and the shim wouldn't fit between them. The only way he was going to get the handcuff off was actually to pick the lock.

The coach rattled over the crossing and drove to the intersection with the main highway leading to Bangkok. Hutch was relieved to see how heavy the traffic was:

all the lanes were jammed and the cars and buses were moving at a little over walking pace. Bird was waiting at the side of the road. He'd parked his motorcycle and was crouched down by the side of it as if examining the engine.

Hutch slid the rest of the picks and the two torsion wrenches from out of his training shoe and put them under his thigh. He selected a pick with a turned end of about a millimetre and one of the torsion wrenches. Hutch had never tried to pick a lock one-handed before, but he'd spent hours practising at night in his cell, holding the two pieces of metal and imagining the cuffs were on his wrist, going through the motions until his fingers ached.

The coach edged into the southbound traffic, the driver over-revving the engine. Hutch inserted the pick and turned it slowly, feeling for the lever in the locking mechanism. When he'd located the tumbler by feel, he withdrew the pick. He wiped his fingers on his trousers and took a quick look around to assure himself that the guards weren't looking at him.

The coach moved into the central lane, forcing its way in front of a green and white taxi. Hutch swallowed. His mouth was bone dry. Suddenly he felt the final tumbler shift and the torsion wrench turned. He wiggled his left hand and the shackle arm slipped out several centimetres. Another shake and it popped completely out. He took the left cuff and fastened it around his right wrist. It seemed crazy to be handcuffing himself, but it was the only way to keep the cuff from flapping around. He transferred the pick and the torsion lever to his left hand then took another quick look around. The guards at the front and the back of the coach were relaxing.

The coach driver grated his gears as he accelerated. The traffic was moving faster; Hutch figured they were now probably moving at thirty miles an hour. He didn't have much time. He beckoned with his finger for Harrigan to move his right hand closer. Harrigan had to twist his wrist so that Hutch could reach the lock. He manipulated the pick with his right hand while he eased in the torsion wrench with his left. Harrigan continued to look out of the window. His hands were trembling, either from excitement or fear. Sweat ran into Hutch's eyes and he blinked, trying to clear them. He clicked the first tumbler back and twisted the torsion wrench. Suddenly the wrench snapped and Hutch's left hand jerked. He cursed soundlessly. He looked at the broken piece of metal in his hand. At least half an inch was still in the lock. Hutch pointed at the handcuff and made a shaking motion with his finger. Harrigan got the message and shook his right hand. Hutch watched intently but there was no sign of the missing piece. If it was jammed in the lock, he'd never be able to pick it.

He put the broken torsion wrench under his thigh and picked up the other one. He pointed at Harrigan's left wrist. Harrigan slid his left arm across his body so that Hutch could reach the handcuff. Hutch looked at his watch. It had been twenty minutes since they had left the prison. He was running out of time.

BILLY WINTER STRETCHED OUT on his sunlounger and adjusted his towel over his legs, the only part of his body not shielded from the sun by the fringed umbrella.

Even at nine o'clock in the morning, the sun was still strong enough to burn. He looked at his watch. Assuming everything went to plan, within minutes Hutch and Harrigan would no longer be prisoners. The trouble with Thailand, Winter knew, was that practically nothing went to plan. That was why he'd decided to spend the morning by the pool in full view of the rest of the sunbathing guests, just in case something went wrong. Winter knew the importance of a good alibi, and he figured it would be hard to do better than to be seen at the pool of the Oriental Hotel. He waved a poolboy over and ordered eggs and bacon, with wholewheat toast, orange juice and a pot of coffee. Breakfast was the most important meal of the day, his mother had always said, and Winter believed her.

'CAN'T YOU DO IT?' whispered Harrigan. His left arm was shaking even though he was supporting it with his right hand.

'Do you want to try?' hissed Hutch.

Harrigan looked away and muttered something to himself. Hutch looked out of the window. The Kawasaki was back, drawing level with the window. Bird had the helmet visor up. He nodded at Hutch.

'Shit,' said Hutch.

'Is he one of them?' asked Harrigan.

'When I give the word, put your head down and protect your face,' whispered Hutch.

'What about the cuffs?'

'You'll have to manage,' said Hutch. He gathered the

picks and shims together and stuffed them back into his training shoe.

Bird was looking over his left shoulder, then he straightened up. He took his left hand off the handlebars and held it up, fingers splayed. 'Five seconds,' said Hutch. Bird dropped his left hand and accelerated away.

THE TAXI DIDN'T INDICATE before changing lanes and the coach driver hit the horn. The taxi picked up speed so the driver didn't have to brake. The coach driver reached up with one hand and ran his fingers along the red cord from which hung a small Buddha, sitting cross-legged inside a clear plastic tube. Two small motorcycles zipped by his offside mirror. The sun glinted off the back window of the taxi and the driver pulled down his sun visor and squinted into the irritating brightness. The taxi slowed a little and the coach driver narrowed the gap between them. A minibus with tinted windows overtook him on his left, a tourist bus judging by the signs painted on the side. The minibus overtook the taxi. Another motorcycle went by. And another. The driver suddenly realised that all four of the motorcyclists were wearing identical lime-green vests. That was when the taxi slammed on its brakes.

THE COACH BRAKES SHRIEKED a second before the impact, giving Hutch just enough time to put his arms over his face and brace himself. The coach hit hard, its momentum carrying it forward, crushing the back of the taxi. One of the guards at the back of the coach went sprawling, his gun clattering on the metal floor. Several of the prisoners were thrown out of their seats and there were screams and shouts of pain. When the coach stopped moving, Hutch looked up. Traffic all around them had ground to a halt. He looked over his shoulder. The guard who'd fallen was on his knees, picking up his weapon. Hutch kept his hands low, hiding the fact that his hands were no longer cuffed together. He looked across at Joshua. Blood was streaming from the Nigerian's nose.

'Thanks a bunch, man,' said Joshua. 'You could have warned me.'

'Stay down,' said Hutch. 'It's not over yet.'

Harrigan lifted his head but Hutch put a hand on his neck and forced him back down.

THE COACH DRIVER PUSHED himself up off the steering wheel. He groaned and felt his forehead. He took his hand away. It was smeared with blood. He reached up and touched the Buddha hanging from the rearview mirror. He was lucky to be alive, and thanks were due to the talisman that had saved his life. The two guards with him in the cab had been wearing their seatbelts and were shaken but not hurt.

Down below, the taxi driver climbed out of his vehicle. The back of the taxi was crushed but the driver seemed to be unhurt. He examined the damage, shaking his head in disgust. He was a young man with the dark skin of an easterner and he had long, greasy hair that fell around his shoulders. He was wearing a baggy sweatshirt and faded blue jeans and looked as if he hadn't washed in a week. The coach driver pulled a handkerchief from the pocket of his uniform and dabbed at his forehead.

The taxi driver glared up at the cab of the coach and pointed at his taxi. The coach driver shrugged and smiled. It wasn't his fault. The taxi driver had braked for no reason. Anyone would have crashed into the back of him; it wasn't as if the coach driver had been speeding. He stroked the hanging Buddha again. The taxi driver walked around to the side of the coach and stood by the door, his hands on his hips. The minibus had stopped and the driver had put on its hazard warning lights.

The coach driver opened the door to his cab and looked down at the taxi driver. 'Are you hurt?' he said.

The taxi driver put his right hand behind his back as if scratching an itch. When it reappeared it was holding a large handgun. He motioned for the armed guard to drop his shotgun. A man climbed out of the back of the taxi. He had a gun in either hand.

THE DRIVER'S CAB WAS blocked off from the rest of the coach and the guards at the rear were unable to see what was going on in front of the vehicle. The three guards at the back of the coach peered out of the windows, anxious frowns on their faces. They talked among themselves and seemed more concerned about their own welfare than the injured prisoners. The rear door hissed open. The guards whirled around, caught by surprise. Two of the motorcycle riders were standing there, wearing full-face visors. Before the guards could speak, the motorcyclists tossed small steel canisters in through the open door and then ducked out of the way. White smoke belched from the cylinders and within seconds the guards were coughing and spluttering.

Joshua struggled to his feet. Hutch put his arm out across the aisle and grabbed his arm. 'Stay where you are,' he said.

BIRD RAN FROM WHERE he'd parked the big Kawasaki, towards the coach. Ahead of him, half a dozen men piled out of the minibus, their faces covered with scarves, large guns in their hands. They fanned out towards the coach. All around them cars were stopping, but the men were totally concentrated on the job at hand. In his left hand Bird had a length of chain, at the end of which were four stainless-steel hooks. He bent down as he ran, just in case one of the guards managed to get off a shot.

The men from the minibus ran to their prearranged positions around the coach, covering the windows with their guns. The coach had already half-filled with choking smoke. One of the guards staggered out of the rear door. A masked man pistol-whipped him and he slumped to the ground.

Bird reached the window where Harrigan and Hutch were sitting. He straightened up and attached the hooks to the four corners of the metal mesh covering the glass, then ran back to his motorcycle, playing out the chain between his gloved hands. At the other end of the chain was a carabiner which he clipped to the back of the machine's chassis. He stood astride the bike, clicked it into gear and gunned the accelerator.

TEARS STREAMED DOWN HUTCH'S cheeks. The rear of the coach was obscured by thick, white smoke but he could just about make out the figures of the guards. Harrigan was choking so Hutch told him to put his shirt over his mouth and to breathe through the material. Hutch looked out of the window. As he did he heard the wrenching of metal as the mesh screen was ripped from its mountings. Through the glass Hutch saw a man with a red silk scarf wrapped around the bottom of his face. He was holding a gun with both hands. Hutch ducked instinctively. When he looked up again he saw one of the motorcycle riders running up holding a sledgehammer. Hutch grabbed Harrigan by the collar and pulled him into the aisle. Harrigan fell to his knees, still coughing. Hutch dropped down on top of him as the sledgehammer slammed into the window. Glass showered over Hutch's back. He straightened up.

'Okay!' Hutch shouted. 'We're out of here!'

Harrigan didn't appear to have heard so Hutch picked him up by the arms and pushed him across the seat. Two men in motorcycle helmets and green vests held up their arms and reached for Harrigan. Harrigan flopped out of the window head first as if he were unconscious and the two men pulled him through. Hutch heard shouts from the back of the coach. He looked around. One of the guards was unlocking the door to the cage.

Harrigan's feet disappeared through the window. The door to the cage opened and a guard stepped through it, bringing his shotgun to bear on Hutch. Hutch raised his hands in surrender. The guard, coughing and squinting through the stinging smoke, looked in astonishment at Hutch's unchained hands.

The guard got to within six feet of Hutch, the barrel of his shotgun pointing steadily at Hutch's chest. He motioned with the gun for Hutch to lie on the floor. With a sagging heart, Hutch began to do as he was told. He dropped to his knees. Suddenly Joshua leaped to his feet and shoulder-charged the guard. The guard fell sideways, across two of the prisoners. His gun went off and lead shot smacked into the roof. The noise was deafening in the confines of the coach.

'Go, man!' screamed Joshua.

Hutch got to his feet as the guard pulled himself up. One of the prisoners he was lying on grabbed the gun and the two men wrestled for possession. Hutch bent down and took the lock-picking tools from his training shoe. He thrust them into Joshua's hand. 'Thanks,' he said.

'Just go, man,' Joshua yelled. The guard's shotgun went off again and the prisoner in the window seat jerked and fell into the aisle. Blood spurted from between his teeth. The guard pulled the shotgun from the prisoner's lifeless hands and tried to stand up. Joshua threw himself on the guard and began hitting him with both clenched fists.

Hutch hesitated for a second, then ran for the broken window.

BIRD FLINCHED AS THE shotgun went off for the second time. He unhooked the chain from the chassis of the bike and threw it to one side. He turned to look at the coach just in time to see Hutch throw himself through the window. He was caught by two of the helmeted riders and they half-carried, half-dragged him over to the motorcycles. Harrigan was already sitting astride one of the machines, his handcuffed hands in his lap. A guard stumbled out of the coach, his eyes closed. He was hit on the head with the butt of a gun and slumped forward, unconscious before he hit the ground. Bird climbed on to his Kawasaki. Traffic had now come to a complete stop in both directions. A coach full of Japanese tourists in one of the northbound lanes were clicking away with their cameras.

Suddenly a window in the prison coach exploded as a guard fired his shotgun. One of the masked men was hit, and he fell back, blood spraying from his chest. The man's companions started firing back with their handguns, pouring bullets into the coach. A large black man hurtled through the window and fell awkwardly on to the road. Bird's men emptied their guns into the coach, firing until the hammers of their weapons clicked on empty chambers.

Bird ran over to the man who'd been shot. Froth-flecked blood was bubbling from his chest wounds but he was still alive. Bird took a pistol from the waistband of his jeans and shot the man in the face.

There were screams and moans from inside the coach. Most of the windows had been shattered by the gunfire and there was broken glass all over the road. Bird ran back to his Kawasaki, threw his leg over it and turned the ignition switch. The masked men ran over to the parked motorcycles with the helmeted riders, tucking their weapons into their belts. Bird waited until he saw Hutch getting on to the passenger seat of one of the motorcycles before driving off.

HUTCH PUT HIS HANDS around the waist of the rider as he kicked the motorcycle into life. Hutch blinked his eyes rapidly, trying to clear them, and looked over his shoulder. The men with masks were all climbing on to motorcycles. Bird was already roaring away, his body bent low over the tank of his machine. Hutch looked around for Harrigan, then saw him on the back of one of the bikes.

'You okay?' Hutch shouted.

Harrigan didn't appear to hear him. The motorcycle he was sitting on jerked forward and for a heart-stopping second Hutch feared the Irishman would tumble backwards. Harrigan recovered his balance and sat straight, holding on to the rider's vest with both hands. The handcuffs stopped him from putting his arms around the man. Harrigan's motorcycle sped away northwards, driving in between the lanes of parked traffic. Several of the car drivers had got out to see what was going on and they had to leap out of the way.

Hutch's bike lurched forward and he gripped his rider tighter. All around him was the buzzing of 125cc motor-cycles, weaving in and out of the traffic. He took a last look over his shoulder. Joshua was half-jumping, half-shuffling away from the coach, laughing like a madman and making quite good progress considering that his legs and hands were still chained.

TIM CARVER SAT BACK in his chair and flipped the top of his Zippo with his left hand as he listened to the police scanner on his desk. It had turned into a bloodbath, according to the frantic transmissions coming from the scene. Two guards dead, two prisoners killed, and half a dozen wounded. Ambulances were on the way but the traffic was locked solid for miles in both directions. The police had tried calling in their helicopter but it had engine trouble and wouldn't be available for at least two hours.

Half a dozen motorcycle policemen had managed to get to the coach and they were doing what they could to keep the injured alive with the assistance of a doctor who'd been trapped in his car nearby. From the sound of it, at least one more of the prisoners wasn't going to make it.

It wasn't supposed to have happened that way, Carver knew. Hutch had said that no one would be hurt. He tapped his cigarette into the ashtray and considered his options. The Thai police didn't know of the DEA involvement, and by the sound of it Hutch, Harrigan and the perpetrators had got clean away. Carver's best course of action appeared to be keeping his mouth shut and letting Hutch get on with his run. He looked at his wristwatch. It was time to contact Jake Gregory.

THE SOLITARY MAN

THE TRAFFIC HAD STARTED to thin out and the motorcycle picked up speed. Hutch looked over the driver's shoulder. They were travelling at almost fifty miles an hour, against the traffic flow. Cars were sounding their horns and headlights were flashing but the eight motorcycle taxis paid them no heed. Hutch could see why they were using small machines and not the 750cc monster that Bird had been riding: the small bikes were highly manoeuvrable and able to squeeze between tight gaps. They zipped past a police car; the three uniformed officers inside climbed out and watched them go, scratching their heads. Driving against the traffic seemed suicidal, but it certainly cut down on the odds of them being pursued.

Ahead of him, Hutch saw the motorcycles turn off the main highway and into a narrow road which was blocked solid with traffic. The motorcycles bumped up on to the pavement and roared along it in single file, scattering pedestrians. Hutch was the fifth in the convoy, and Harrigan was on the bike behind him.

Two monks carrying black bowls jumped into the road to get out of the way. Each of the riders nodded an apology as they went by. A makeshift restaurant had been set up on the pavement, where an old man and an even older woman were serving pork and noodles. The bike at the head of the convoy smashed through the tables and stools, knocking over the charcoal burner and a huge stainless-steel pot of water. The boiling liquid splashed over one of the workmen who'd been spooning noodles into his mouth and he fell backwards, screaming in agony. As Hutch rode by, so close that the tyres were only inches away from the man's head, he could see that the water had gone over most of his chest.

At the end of the road was a hump-backed bridge over a canal and the motorcycle convoy raced across it. Below, a water-taxi flashed by, black smoke belching from its engine. The traffic tailed off and soon the motorcycles were racing along at more than sixty miles an hour, the wind whipping through Hutch's hair and tugging at his shirt. They turned sharply to the left and roared alongside the canal, past wooden homes on stilts and groups of children splashing and playing in the filthy water. Hutch looked to his left, back across the bridge. No one was following them, but he was unable to relax. It could all still go wrong.

They left the canalside after half a mile and turned down another road, little more than a dirt track that ran between ramshackle homes. Bare-chested men, and women in threadbare T-shirts and cotton dresses, watched them go, and naked children waved and jumped up and down as if they were a parade passing. Ahead of them was a corrugated-iron fence, flecked with rust as if it had been there for several years. Truck tyre tracks led to a gap several yards wide halfway along it. The motorcycles went through, one at a time. Inside was a building site. Work seemed to have stopped, because there were no workmen around and the site had an air of neglect.

Bird was already there, standing by the side of his Kawasaki and removing his full-face helmet. He waved at Hutch. 'Perfect, huh?' he said, dropping his helmet on the ground next to the bike and pulling off his gloves.

'Nobody was supposed to get hurt,' said Hutch, climbing

off his bike. The driver dismounted, too, and pushed the motorcycle over to Bird's Kawasaki. He let it fall sideways and it crashed to the ground. The rest of the motorcyclists were dumping their machines all around Bird's bike, and stripping off their helmets, gloves and vests. The men with masks were already piling into four nondescript saloon cars.

'It wasn't our fault,' said Bird. 'He fired first. You saw what he did. He killed one of our men.'

'It looked to me like you killed him, Bird.'

Bird walked over to Hutch, his shoulders hunched and his arms at his side like a gunfighter preparing to draw. He stood so close that Hutch could smell his garlic-tainted breath. 'He was dying. He'd have died if we'd tried to move him. If we'd left him, the police might have got to him.' He glared at Hutch as if daring him to argue. Hutch nodded slowly, but he wasn't admitting defeat, only that Bird had a point. Bird stared at him for several seconds, then he went over to a battered red Nissan pick-up truck and took a petrol can out of the back. Next to the truck were two wooden pallets and crates of leafy green vegetables.

Bird unscrewed the top off the can and began pouring it over the motorcycles. 'Anyway, it's too late to argue about it now,' he said dismissively. 'We got you out, that's all that matters.'

Hutch took a deep breath. Bird was right. There was nothing he could say that would change what had happened.

Harrigan came over, holding his handcuffed arms out to Hutch. 'Can you get these things off me?' he whined.

'I'll have to do it later,' said Hutch. 'I gave the picks to Joshua.'

'What the fuck for?' asked Harrigan.

'Because he saved my life, that's why,' said Hutch. 'What do we do now, Bird?'

Bird had emptied the can over the bikes. He tossed it on to the pile and looked around to check that he hadn't forgotten anything. 'The truck,' he said. Hutch looked at the Nissan and frowned. Anticipating his objections, Bird waved at the crates. 'The two of you lie down and we'll cover you up.'

'For how long?' asked Hutch.

'An hour. We've got a safe house fixed up about forty miles outside Bangkok. That's where we'll meet Billy.'

Hutch nodded. 'Come on,' he said to Harrigan. The two of them walked over to the pick-up truck and lay face down in the back. Two of the men placed the pallets over them. The bases had been cut away so that the slats of wood were an inch or so above their backs. The men began stacking the crates on the pallets. It was soon dark and claustrophobic. Bits of soil fell down on them. It was like being buried alive, Hutch realised. He fought back the feelings of panic. He forced himself to breathe slowly and kept telling himself it would only be for an hour or so. There was a loud whooshing sound followed by a series of explosions as the motorcycle tanks ignited. Bird climbed into the cab of the pick-up truck and started the engine.

TIM CARVER TAPPED OUT the number of Jake Gregory's satellite phone. Carver was in the DEA's Secure Communications Room and he was alone. One of the analysts had been on the line to the agency's Fort Lauderdale office in Florida and Carver had had to wait until he'd finished. There was a series of clicks, then a long pause followed by more clicks. Eventually there was a ringing tone. It rang out for a full minute before the phone was answered. It wasn't Gregory. Carver explained who he was and where he was calling from.

'He's briefing the helicopter crews,' said the voice at the other end of the line. The line broke up and Carver couldn't hear what else the man said.

'I didn't catch that,' said Carver.

'He's briefing the Apache crews, he'll be back in about half an hour.'

Carver sat bolt upright as if he'd been electrocuted. 'Can you get him to call me?' he said. 'As soon as he's finished.'

'Affirmative,' said the voice. The line went dead. Carver sat staring at the communications console. Something didn't make sense.

IT WAS STIFLINGLY HOT lying under the crates, the metal of the pick-up truck as hot as a griddle against Hutch's chest and the front of his legs. Something small with lots of legs fell on to his hair and he shook his head to the side to throw it off. He felt as if he'd been lying in the truck for hours but it was too dark to see his watch so he had no idea how much time had truly passed.

They'd driven over rough ground for several miles, dirt tracks probably, and then they'd driven fast and straight for a long time, which Hutch reckoned was probably the expressway, heading north. They'd been stuck in a traffic jam for a long time, and at one point he'd heard Thai voices, brusque with authority, and Bird's muffled voice replying. The traffic had picked up speed after that and the air around them had become progressively hotter and less breathable.

'I don't know how much longer I'm going to be able to stand this,' said Harrigan. 'My throat's burning up.'

'It can't be much longer,' said Hutch.

For a while the only sound was the growl of the Nissan's diesel engine and the ragged breathing of the two men. 'I'm sorry about what I said, about the picks,' said Harrigan.

'No problem,' said Hutch.

'I was scared.'

'So was I. Forget it.'

'It was messy back there, wasn't it?'

Hutch turned his head towards Harrigan. He could just about make out the shape of the man's head. 'You've seen people die before, haven't you? You were in the IRA, right?'

There was a soft laugh, then a sniff. 'The IRA isn't just about killing people, Hutch. It's an entire organisation. There are active service units that carry out the dirty jobs, but they're the minority. I never saw anyone hurt, much less killed.'

Hutch slid his arms up so that he could rest his head on them. 'Yeah, it was messy. It wasn't supposed to be, but it was.'

'Where did you learn to pick locks?'

Hutch smiled in the darkness. 'I was a locksmith in another life. I was one of the guys you'd call if you forgot your keys.'

'And how did you get involved in this?'

'It's a long story. A very long, very sad story.'

'They're paying you?'

'Maybe. But that's not why I'm doing it.'

'What then?'

'You really want to know?'

'Sure.'

'Billy Winter's blackmailing me. If I don't get you out, I go back to prison in the UK.'

'You were in prison?' said Harrigan, surprised.

'I did four years,' said Hutch. 'And I had another twenty-one to do before I got out.'

'You escaped?'

'Three times. But I only got clean away the last time.'

'From where?'

'Parkhurst. On the Isle of Wight. Some of your mob were there.'

'What did you do, Hutch?'

'I didn't do anything.'

'You got twenty-five years in Parkhurst for nothing?'

Hutch snorted. 'Life's a bitch, isn't it?'

The truck turned to the left, braked hard, then bumped over some rough ground and came to a halt. 'Sounds like we've arrived,' said Hutch. There was a grating, metallic noise and the truck edged forward a few feet. The grating noise was repeated, though this time it had a hollower ring to it. Hutch guessed they had driven inside a building. He heard the truck doors open and then the crates were bundled off. Fluorescent light streamed in and the two men covered their eyes.

Hutch rolled over and sat up. Bird was standing next to

the truck, grinning. 'Did you hear them at the checkpoint?' he said.

'The police?' asked Hutch.

'Yeah. They were searching all the vehicles on the expressway. They didn't even think of checking the back.'

Harrigan sat up, grunting with the effort. 'Where's Billy?' he asked.

Bird held up a mobile phone. 'I'll call him now. He wanted to stay out of the way until we were sure you're safe.'

'Yeah, that's Billy all right,' said Hutch. 'He was only ever caught with the goods once, and he swore it would be the last time.' He gestured at Harrigan's handcuffs. 'Have you got a file or something I can use to cut the cuffs?'

Bird pointed at a workbench and a rack of tools. 'Help yourself,' he said.

BILLY WINTER PUSHED HIS sunglasses up on the top of his head and sat up. He reached for the ringing mobile phone on the table by his lounger and looked at his wristwatch. Bang on time. 'Yeah?' he said.

'We're here,' said Bird.

'Any problems?' asked Winter.

'Nothing major. We lost one man.'

'Not one of mine?'

Bird's voice was cold. 'No, Billy. One of mine.'

Winter pulled a face as he realised he'd said the wrong thing. 'Sorry, Bird. I wasn't thinking. I'll be there in an hour. What's the traffic like?'

'Locked solid both ways. You won't get here in an hour, Billy. It'll take at least two. Three maybe.'

'How are the guys?'

'They're okay. Harrigan doesn't look too good, but we'll clean him up before you get here.'

'Good man. Thanks, Bird. And well done.'

Winter cut the connection and put the phone back on the table. A young poolboy in a gleaming white uniform with gold buttons came over with a brandy and Coke on a tray. Winter beamed up at him. It was early, they were still serving breakfast in the coffee shop, but Winter felt that he'd earned a celebratory drink. The poolboy put the condensation-beaded glass down on the table and handed the bill to Winter. Winter signed it with a flourish. 'It don't get much better than this, do it?' he said, handing it back.

THEY WERE IN A two-storey house with rough wooden floors and whitewashed walls. There was a bare minimum of furniture and nothing of a personal nature, except for a poster of the King of Thailand pinned to one of the living-room walls. Hutch sat on a cheap plastic sofa and rested his feet on a square coffee table while Harrigan slumped into an armchair. The blinds were drawn and the lights were on, and an air-conditioner set into the wall buzzed and whirred.

Bird came in and threw Hutch a can of lager. 'Thanks,' said Hutch. Bird said nothing and turned away. Hutch realised something was wrong. He suddenly knew what it was: Thais didn't like feet on furniture, or feet being used to point. He slid the offending limbs off the table and popped open the can of lager, draining half of it in several thirsty gulps.

'There's a bathroom upstairs if you want to shower,' said Bird.

'I'm okay,' said Hutch.

'It'll be your last chance for a while,' said Bird. 'There aren't many bathrooms where we're going.'

Hutch shrugged and began to work away with the hacksaw at the handcuffs on his right wrist. It would take time, but he'd get through them eventually.

Harrigan held up his chained hands. 'How about taking these off for me?' he asked.

Bird pulled his gun from out of his belt and pointed it at Harrigan. 'I could try shooting them off,' he said, sighting along the barrel.

Harrigan jumped out of his chair. 'Jesus Christ, Bird, stop fucking around!' he yelled. He kept moving, skipping around the room like a startled rabbit.

Bird laughed throatily. 'English humour,' he said, and put the gun away.

Harrigan stopped moving and glared at Bird. 'I'm Irish,' he hissed. 'And either way, it's not fucking well funny.'

Bird pulled a face. He took a pair of bolt-cutters from his back pocket. 'I'll use these instead,' he said. 'Unless you don't think they're funny enough.'

Harrigan held his arms out. 'Ha, ha, bloody ha,' he said.

Bird cut one of the links and then gave him a metal file.

Harrigan went over to Hutch and watched him sawing

through the metal shackle. 'Can't you pick them?' Harrigan asked.

Hutch didn't look up. 'If I had the picks, maybe. But this'll be quicker. The sooner you start, the sooner you'll finish.'

Harrigan sighed and sat down on the table. He began to file the handcuff on his left wrist.

THE RECEPTIONIST BUZZED THROUGH and told Tim Carver he had a visitor: Tsang Chau-ling. Carver ran his hand through his hair and groaned. He walked down two flights of stairs rather than taking the elevator to give himself time to think. Chau-ling was waiting for him in the reception area. Ricky Lim was also there but he didn't acknowledge the DEA agent.

'Have you seen the TV?' she said, jabbing at him with an accusing finger. He looked at her blankly. 'Why didn't you tell me he was escaping?' she said.

'Not here,' he said. He turned and walked to the elevator. Chau-ling followed him but Ricky Lim stayed where he was. They rode up together in silence. Carver waited until Chau-ling was seated and the door was closed before speaking. 'I can't tell you everything, Miss Tsang,' he said, sitting down and switching off his desktop computer.

'Everything? You haven't told me anything.'

'You have no right—'

'I have a right to know,' she interrupted. 'Did you know that people were going to die?'

'That wasn't the plan,' said Carver.

'Where is he now?'

'I don't know,' said Carver. Chau-ling glared at him. 'Honest to God, I have no idea where he is.'

'Did the authorities know about the escape in advance?'

Carver shook his head. 'Do you want a coffee or something?'

Chau-ling ignored his offer. 'So I guess if they were to find out that the DEA was involved, they'd be pretty upset, right?'

Carver tapped a cigarette out of his Marlboro pack and slid it between his lips. He reached for his Zippo.

'I'd rather you didn't smoke,' said Chau-ling. She smiled without warmth.

Carver studied her for several seconds before putting the cigarette back into the red and white pack. 'What is it you want?' he asked.

'I want to know what it is that Warren's involved in.'

Carver rubbed his chin thoughtfully. 'It's better you don't know,' he said.

'You sound like my father.'

Carver smiled and leaned back in his chair. 'Maybe your father's right.'

Chau-ling folded her arms across her chest. She tapped the fingers of her right hand against her forearm impatiently. 'I want to know what Warren's got himself into,' she said quietly. 'And if you don't tell me, Mr Carver, then I'm going to go to the Thai police and tell them what I do know.'

'What good do you think that'll do?' asked Carver.

'For a start, I think it'll make your life very difficult. Innocent people died, and you're responsible. Perhaps you'd like to go through what Warren went through and spend some time behind bars yourself. You know how the

Thais work – you'd stay in prison until you can prove that you're not guilty. Not a particularly pleasant experience. And probably the end of your career.' She smiled brightly. 'So, do you tell me what's going on, or do I go and talk to the police?'

'I'd rather you didn't do that, Miss Tsang.'

'There's a very easy way for you to stop me. Just tell me what I want to know.'

'You won't like it.'

'Try me.'

Carver began to flick the lid of his Zippo, but he kept his eyes on Chau-ling. 'For a start, his name's not Warren Hastings.'

THE SHACKLE FELL APART and dropped to the floor. Harrigan looked up. 'How did you manage to do that so quickly?' he asked.

'You've just got to keep at it,' said Hutch, picking up the pieces of the handcuffs and putting them on the coffee table. Harrigan had been working his file back and forth at a snail's pace and Hutch could tell that he'd be at it all day, so he'd taken over and finished the job for him. Harrigan massaged his wrists. 'How are you feeling?' asked Hutch.

Harrigan shrugged dismissively. 'I just want to get home, then I'll be okay.'

'It's going to be a while yet,' said Hutch.

'I know, I know.'

They heard a car pull up outside. Hutch looked across at Bird who was cleaning his handgun. 'It'll be Billy,' said

Bird, reassembling the gun and slotting in the magazine. He stood up and went out into the hall and opened the front door.

Hutch heard voices, then Billy Winter burst into the room, a cigar in one hand, a large wicker basket in the other. He was wearing a cream-coloured linen suit and brown shoes with spats. 'You did it!' he said. 'You deserve a bloody medal, Hutch!' Winter handed the basket to Bird and went over to Harrigan. 'Ray, it's good to see you again. I told you we'd get you out, didn't I?' He reached out his hand and the two men shook, though there was a definite lack of enthusiasm on Harrigan's part. Hutch went back to the sofa and sat down. 'A week at most and you'll be back in Grafton Street, drinking Guinness and patting some young Irish wench on the arse,' continued Winter, unfazed by Harrigan's silence. He turned to face Hutch and nodded appreciatively. 'It worked like a dream, didn't it? A bloody dream.'

'People died, Billy,' said Hutch coldly.

'Right, they did, that's right,' said Winter. 'But you got out and frankly that's all that matters to me.' He grinned at Hutch. 'You know what I wanted when I got out? The first thing I wanted?'

'A hooker?' asked Hutch.

Winter's grin widened. 'Okay, the second thing I wanted?' He did a soft-shoe shuffle over to the basket which Bird had put on the coffee table. It was tied up with a big red bow which Winter undid with a flourish. 'A good feed,' he said, and lifted the lid. It was a hamper, packed with food. 'From the Oriental Hotel,' he said. 'Nothing but the best for my boys.' He took out a whole roast chicken wrapped in plastic, a loaf of French bread, and an earthenware pot.

'Fresh bread, chicken, foie gras. There's smoked salmon in there somewhere.' He put them on the table and pulled out a bottle. 'And bubbly. Dom Perignon. Vintage. Have you any idea how much this stuff costs in Thailand?'

'Billy, I'm not one of your boys,' said Hutch, refusing to be drawn into the celebration.

Winter jabbed the lit cigar at him. 'Don't rain on my parade, Hutch.' He was smiling but there was nothing jocular about his tone. Hutch shrugged and looked away. It wasn't the time to pick a fight. Winter ripped off the gold foil and eased the cork out with a casual twist. 'That's the mark of an expert,' said Winter. 'No loud noise, no spillage: that's for amateurs.' He took four fluted glasses from the hamper and deftly filled them. He gave them each a glass, then raised his in the air. 'To crime,' he said, laughing.

Bird clinked glasses with him. 'To crime,' Bird echoed.

Winter walked over to Harrigan and touched glasses, then did the same with Hutch. 'Drink up, boys,' he said. Hutch and Harrigan did as they were told. Winter watched them both raise their glasses to their lips and drink. 'That's better,' he said.

CHAU-LING SAT IN STUNNED silence. Tim Carver leaned back in his chair and toyed with his lighter. 'Look,' he said, 'I really could do with a cigarette. Do you mind?' He held up his pack of Marlboro. Chau-ling made a small waving motion with her right hand. Everything she knew about Warren was based on a lie. Everything. Carver lit a cigarette and blew a cloud of smoke up to the ceiling. He tried to blow a smoke ring. It was a dismal failure, more oval than circular, and it dissipated within seconds.

'What did you say his name was?' asked Chau-ling.

'Chris Hutchison. His friends call him Hutch.'

'His friends?' hissed Chau-ling. 'His friends!' What am I? I thought I was his friend, yet I didn't even know his real name.'

'You have to look at it from his point of view,' said Carver. 'He'd left his old life behind. Hong Kong was a new start for him.'

Chau-ling shook her head violently. 'I was part of a cover story, that's all. The kennels, his friends, me – we were all a lie. He was living a lie and he made us all part of it.'

Carver said nothing. He blew another smoke ring towards the ceiling. It, too, fell apart quickly.

'I think I will have that coffee,' said Chau-ling.

'Cream and sugar?'

'Black. One sugar. Thank you.'

Carver left the room. Chau-ling put her head in her hands. She felt as if the floor had disappeared from underneath her, as if she were standing over an abyss and about to fall into it. She'd known Warren Hastings for almost three years, she'd worked alongside him, she'd fallen in love with him, and yet everything she knew about him was a lie. Chris Hutchison? Hutch? The names sounded strange; they certainly didn't belong to the man whom she knew. He'd been in prison, Carver had said. He'd been sent to prison because he'd killed a man and then he'd escaped and he'd run away to Hong Kong and from the day that he'd arrived he'd lied. It explained so much. It explained why he'd never talked about his past; why he was so vague about his life in Britain; why he seemed to have no friends outside Hong Kong.

Carver returned with her coffee and one for himself. Chau-ling composed herself. She didn't want the DEA agent to see how upset she was. 'Thank you,' she said. She sipped it. It was a machine coffee, bland to the point of being tasteless. 'You said before that he was helping you. What exactly is he doing?'

'It's a classified DEA operation. And I've told you enough already.'

There was a knock on the door to Carver's office and it opened before Carver could say anything. It was Ed Harris. He mimed putting a telephone against his face. 'Secure Communications Room,' he said. 'That call you were waiting for.'

Carver apologised to Chau-ling and told her that he had to take the call. 'I'll be right here waiting for you, Mr Carver,' she said.

HUTCH CLIMBED INTO THE back of the truck. Winter threw in the cushions from the sofa and three pillows that he'd taken from the bedrooms. 'These'll help,' he said.

'How long will we be in here?' asked Hutch. He had changed out of his prison uniform and into a baggy sweatshirt and jeans, doing so in the bathroom with the door locked so that there was no chance of the hidden transmitter being spotted.

Harrigan scrambled up with a grunt and Winter climbed in after him. Harrigan was wearing a black polo shirt and chinos. Hutch had claimed the sweatshirt because the polo shirt was fairly small and wouldn't have concealed the transmitter.

'It's twelve hours to Fang,' said Winter, straightening the creases of his trousers. 'We should be able to get across the border early tomorrow morning.' Winter turned to Bird who with another heavily built Thai was lifting cardboard boxes into the truck.

'It's going to be hot in here,' said Hutch. The vehicle was a big diesel truck with wooden sides painted in reds, greens and yellows, with the name of a haulage company on the side, and a tarpaulin roof. The heavily built Thai had arrived with it just as they had been finishing the contents of Winter's hamper. The back of the ten-wheeler had been filled with boxes and they'd all pitched in to unload them. They contained sanitary towels, which according to Bird were much in demand in Burma and were regularly smuggled across the border.

Winter handed Hutch a small battery-powered fan and a flashlight. 'Don't I think of everything?'

'If you'd thought of everything, I wouldn't have spent almost a year in that hellhole,' snapped Harrigan. It was the first time he'd spoken in almost an hour. Winter didn't reply. 'Bird, pass up the water, will you?'

Bird pushed a carrier bag containing half a dozen plastic bottles of mineral water along the floor of the truck.

Winter looked around to check that he hadn't forgotten anything. He nodded, satisfied. 'Okay, Bird, we're set. You can pack them in.'

Bird and the truck driver began loading the boxes into the truck. They left a space about four feet wide so the three men could sit in relative comfort. As the first boxes were put in place, Winter strung strips of webbing across the truck so that they wouldn't topple when the truck was moving, then he sat down next to Hutch. 'We can use the flashlight during the day, but not at night, just in case any of the light leaks out,' he said.

'Whatever,' said Hutch, leaning back against the wall of the cab. He folded his arms across his stomach and felt the hardness of the transmitter. He still hadn't decided whether or not he was going to activate it.

CARVER MADE HIS WAY to the Secure Communications Room. He went through the first door and pressed the button to switch on the 'Do Not Enter' red light then keyed in his security code to open the second door. A green button was flashing on one of the consoles. He picked up the receiver and pressed the button.

'Tim Carver,' he said. There was an echo of his own voice and then a full second's delay.

'Tim. This is Jake Gregory. Sorry about the delay in getting back to you but I had a few kinks to iron out here. You have something for me?'

'Affirmative,' said Carver. The satellite delay and the echo of his voice were distracting but he forced himself to concentrate on the director's voice. 'Our man is off and running.'

'That's good to hear, Tim. Were there any complications?'

'Two guards killed, and two prisoners,' said Carver.

The delay was longer this time. 'Sorry to hear that,' he said. 'Has it caused any problems?'

Only the presence of a very angry Tsang Chau-ling in his office down the corridor, thought Carver. 'Not so far,' he said.

'Okay, if there is any flack, let me know and I'll get you some help on damage control. Our man has the beacon?'

'That's affirmative.'

'Well done, Tim. Good job.'

'There is one thing . . .' said Carver. The words tumbled out before he was even aware of phrasing the question. 'The helicopters. Are they Apaches?'

The pause was even longer this time, and there was a suspicious edge to Gregory's voice. 'Why do you ask, Tim?'

Carver knew immediately that there had been no mistake. 'Because Apaches are attack helicopters. They're not the sort of helicopters that would be used to ferry Rangers. They're two-seaters. And they're tank-killers.'

'You know your choppers, son.'

'I nearly joined the army as a pilot. My eyesight wasn't up to it. But that's not the point.'

'I know what the point is,' said Gregory. His voice was harder, his words clipped short. There was a delay of several seconds. 'What is it you want me to say?' Gregory asked eventually.

'You're not going to bring out Zhou Yuanyi, are you?'

'No, son. We're not.'

'You're going to blow him away, aren't you? You're sending in Apaches to destroy his headquarters and everybody there. Including Hutch.'

'Hutch? Did I hear you right? What's Hutch?'

'Hutch is the man I persuaded to carry in the beacon,' snapped Carver. 'Hutch is the man who's going to be standing there when the Apaches arrive. Hutch is the man I've sent to his death.'

'You told me he was a convicted murderer,' said Gregory. 'He's hardly an innocent bystander.'

'You lied to me,' said Carver.

'I'd watch your tongue if I were you, son.'

'Why? I don't understand why you had to lie to me.'

Gregory's reply was garbled and Carver had to ask him to repeat himself. 'If *you* knew, *he'd* know,' said Gregory. 'You had to be able to look him in the eye and give nothing away. Look at it this way: how would you have felt knowing that you were sending him into a war zone?'

Carver didn't say anything.

'Did you hear me, son?'

'I heard you.'

'Well, think about it. If it helps, think of it as me protecting you from yourself. Now you've done your job, and you've done it well. Let me get on with mine.'

The line went dead. Carver couldn't tell whether Gregory had hung up or if they'd just lost the satellite connection. Either way, it didn't matter. He put down the receiver. He sat staring at the console for several minutes before going back to his office.

Chau-ling looked up. 'Is there something wrong?' she asked.

'What makes you think there's something wrong?' His Zippo and cigarettes were on the desk where he'd left them and he picked them up.

'You look terrible, that's why.'

Carver paced up and down. He lit a cigarette. 'I think you should go,' he said.

'I don't agree,' she replied. 'It's something to do with Warren, isn't it?'

Carver drew cigarette smoke deeply into his lungs. Hutch was on a suicide mission, and Carver had sent him on it. A war zone, Gregory had said. Apaches. Tank-killers.

'Tell me,' said Chau-ling, her voice soft and persuasive.

'Miss Tsang, I can't tell you anything. You're going to have to go now.'

'I'm not going anywhere,' she said determinedly.

'I'll have you escorted from the building,' he said.

'Why don't you do that,' she said. 'In fact, why don't you have them escort me to the office of the chief of police? I don't have an appointment, but I'm sure he'll want to hear what I've got to say.'

Carver rubbed his jaw. He was still trying to come to terms with what Gregory had done. The last thing he needed was to be blackmailed by Tsang Chau-ling, but it was clear that she intended to carry out her threat and Carver was under no illusions as to what would happen if the police did find out that he had been behind the attack on the prison bus. Relations between the DEA and the local police were strained and they would relish the opportunity of putting him through the third degree. At best it would be the end of his career, at worst he could spend the rest of his life behind bars.

Carver threw up his hands in surrender. 'Look, your friend Hutch and I have both been lied to. I've been used as much as he has.'

'Where is he?'

The DEA agent went over to the map behind his desk. He pointed at the area on the map where Burma, Laos and Thailand met. 'The Golden Triangle,' he said. 'Somewhere in here is a Chinese warlord called Zhou Yuanyi, a major heroin producer. We don't know where his base is, but Hutch is going to find out for us. The men who broke him out of jail are going to try to get him out of Thailand, him and another guy called Ray Harrigan. We're pretty sure they'll be taken to the warlord's base.' He lit another cigarette. 'Hutch is carrying a transmitter. When he gets to the base, he'll activate it.'

'And then what happens?'

Carver took a long pull on his cigarette. He held the smoke deep in his lungs for several seconds before exhaling. 'They lied to me,' he said.

Chau-ling looked at him anxiously. 'You have to tell me,' she pressed.

Carver leaned back against the map and folded his arms. 'Because if I don't, you'll go to the cops?'

'Because you owe it to Warren,' she said. 'To Hutch. Because if he's in trouble, I want to help.'

Carver laughed harshly. 'Oh, he's in trouble, all right.' He took another drag on his cigarette and spoke to her through the smoke. 'They told me they'd be sending in a team of Rangers to bring Zhou out. Hutch was supposed to be brought out with them, that's what I was told.'

Chau-ling sat back in her chair. 'But?'

'But they're not sending in Rangers. They're sending in Apache helicopters.'

'So?'

'Apaches don't rescue people, they blow things up, big time. Missiles, high explosives, bullets, they're attack helicopters. They're going to destroy Zhou's camps. And everybody there.'

'But Warren's going to be in the centre of it all,' gasped Chau-ling. 'He's going to be holding the transmitter.'

Carver blew a thin plume of smoke through clenched teeth. He didn't respond.

'You have to warn him,' she pressed.

'I can't.'

Chau-ling stood up, her fists clenched defiantly at her sides. 'You don't have any choice,' she said. 'You can't let them kill him.'

'It's too late, he's on his way.'

'It's never too late.' She wrapped her arms around herself. 'He trusted you, didn't he? You asked him for his help and he trusted you.'

Carver sat down and toyed with his Zippo. 'I promised him a new life. I told him that the DEA would get him a passport, a new identity. And money.'

'And instead you're going to kill him?'

'Not me,' said Carver defensively. 'It's not me.'

Chau-ling glared at him. 'Oh yes it is, Tim Carver. If Warren dies, it'll be on your conscience. Can you live with that?'

Carver stared at her but didn't reply.

HUTCH HELD THE FLASHLIGHT down so that the light pooled on the floor of the truck. They were rattling along a rough road and the cardboard boxes pushed against the webbing straps with each jolt and lurch. Billy Winter saw Hutch looking up at the boxes. 'That'd be a laugh, wouldn't it?' he said. 'Crushed to death by sanitary towels.'

'They can't get them in Burma, you say?'

'The country's in a shambles,' said Winter. 'Sanitary towels, detergent, batteries, all the basic stuff that we take for granted, they can't get. The Thai smugglers send them in, and in return they get heroin and teak. That's about the only thing of value they produce.'

'When did you get to be such an expert on South-east Asia?' asked Hutch.

'Picked it up along the way. I've been out here a few times over the past few years.'

Harrigan took one of the plastic bottles of water out of the carrier bag and screwed the top off. He drank deeply and then splashed some over his face. He offered the bottle to Hutch and Winter but the two men shook their heads.

'So what do you think of the E-man?' Winter asked Harrigan.

The Irishman frowned. 'E-man?'

Winter gestured at Hutch. 'That's what Hutch was in Parkhurst. An E-man. He was on the escape list. Not that that did the screws any good, he still got out. There isn't a prison can hold him; isn't that right, Hutch?'

Hutch shrugged. 'Leave it out, Billy.'

Winter wouldn't be deviated from his train of thought. 'How many prisons did you break out of? Three, wasn't it? Parkhurst, Whitemoor and . . .' He shook his head. 'What was the other one? Wasn't the Scrubs, was it?'

'Frankland,' said Hutch.

'Oh yeah, that's right. Frankland was the first one. Slipped out in a delivery van, right?'

'Sort of. There was a bit more to it than that.'

'But they caught him and threw him in solitary. Then they started moving him around from prison to prison, figuring that he wouldn't have time to work out a way of escaping before being moved on. Then he goes and breaks out of Whitemoor. That really pissed them off, didn't it, Hutch?'

Hutch couldn't help smiling, though at the time he hadn't thought it was funny. After his second recapture he'd received half a dozen beatings and spent several weeks in solitary. The prison officers didn't like to be made fools of and they were experts at administering punishment without leaving marks.

'That was when they sent him to Parkhurst on the Isle of Wight,' continued Billy. 'Couldn't take a leak without someone watching him. They reckon that someone on the E-list stands as much chance of escaping as winning the lottery. But Hutch here proved them wrong. Got out and got clean away this time.'

'How?' asked Harrigan.

'Hutch slipped out of the gymnasium during a weight-training session one evening. The screws were lazy, they spent most of the time in an observation box. They could see the gym, but there was a blind spot and they couldn't see a door at the back. Hutch had made a key.'

'Same as you did in Klong Prem?' Harrigan asked Hutch.

Hutch nodded. 'Took a bit longer, and I had to take a bit more care hiding it because of the strip searches.'

'Hutch got to the training workshop where they teach welding and metalwork and stuff. The same key opened all the locks. It makes life easier for the screws, you see. Once inside the workshop, Hutch had everything he needed, right?'

'Yeah,' said Hutch. 'Ladders, pliers, wire cutters, even a hosepipe. It was all in a storeroom.'

'How come it was so easy?' asked Harrigan.

Hutch snorted. 'If it was easy, everyone would have done it,' he said. 'It's finding the weakness in the system that counts, the flaw that the staff can't see. You have to be able to work out where the blind spots are, where the cameras can see and where they can't. There were fifty-three security cameras in operation the night I broke out.'

'And they didn't see you?'

'Nah,' said Winter. 'He was out two hours before they discovered he was missing.'

'How come?' asked Harrigan. 'How come you got through the wire and over the wall without anyone seeing you?'

'Because the screws have faith in the system, that's why. They don't see the gaps. All they see are the wire fences and the walls and the cameras and the dogs. They think like guards, they don't think like prisoners. They didn't think anyone could get to the storeroom because the prisoners are always in their cells or under supervision, so they didn't bother fitting double locks. A prisoner would never be in the storeroom on his own, so there was no need to have the tools securely locked away. The cameras watch the wire, so they cut down on the dog patrols. But there are never more than two guards monitoring fifty-three cameras. Do you think they spend all the time staring at the screens? Of course they don't. They drink coffee. They gossip. They read dirty magazines. They're human.'

'That's debatable,' joked Winter. 'But Hutch hasn't told you the best bit. How he got off the island.'

'How?' asked Harrigan. He had the wide-eyed look of a small boy being told a ghost story around a campfire.

'I flew,' said Hutch. 'I stole a small plane and flew away.'

Winter guffawed and Harrigan looked at him, wondering what was so amusing. 'He's being too modest,' said Winter. 'What he neglects to mention is that he'd never flown a fucking plane in his life before that night!'

'What?' Harrigan turned to look at Hutch in amazement. 'How come?'

Hutch shrugged, his palms spread upward. 'I was lucky, I guess.'

'Crap,' said Winter. 'He spent three months practising.'

'They let you take flying lessons in prison?' asked Harrigan.

Hutch and Winter looked at each other and burst out laughing. Hutch shook his head. 'One of the guys inside had worked as a commercial pilot. He taught me. We used to sit on my bunk and he'd go through all the controls, explaining what everything did and how it felt.'

'But you'd never taken off before?'

'Taking off was the easy part, it was the landing that was difficult.'

'Er, actually old lad, the way I heard it, it was more of a crash than a landing,' interrupted Winter.

'Yeah, well, it didn't quite go to plan,' admitted Hutch.

Harrigan shook his head in disbelief. 'You're winding me up,' he said.

Hutch reached for one of the bottles of water and drank before continuing. 'The way Ronnie told it, they land and take off at about sixty-five miles an hour, so it's no more dangerous than driving a VW. He said you just fly them parallel to the ground at sixty-five miles an hour, cut the engine, and keep the nose up. It'll land itself. Then it's just like driving a car. Providing I picked a big enough field to land in, the plane would come to a stop itself. But I never got to see if it worked. I hit bad weather, couldn't see a thing. I ended up ditching in the sea, and even a VW wouldn't have done me any good.' He touched the side of his head. 'The plane was smashed up pretty bad. I hit my head but the seat belt held. I went under but one of the doors had busted open so I managed to get out.'

'You were lucky,' said Winter.

'Yeah, well, how lucky can I be to end up sitting in the back of a truck full of tampons with two characters like you?' said Hutch.

Winter and Harrigan laughed and before long Hutch was laughing along with them.

'IF YOU LIGHT ANOTHER cigarette, I swear to God I'm going to make you eat it,' said Chau-ling.

Carver's hand hovered over his pack of Marlboro.

'Can't you open a window?' she asked.

'They're sealed so that the air-conditioning works,' said Carver.

'Yeah? Well, it's failing abysmally,' she said. She brushed her hair away from her face with both hands, tucking it behind her ears. 'You said Warren was working for you.'

'That's true. Sort of.'

'But you made it sound like you'd set the whole thing up from the start. That was a lie, wasn't it?'

Carver hesitated, but he realised immediately that his hesitation had given him away. 'Yes,' he said. 'They framed Hutch. They sent him inside so that he'd have to escape.'

'And you can prove that?'

Carver nodded. 'I've got them on tape.'

'So Warren is in the clear. You can prove he's innocent.' She studied him with unblinking eyes. 'What are you going to do?'

Carver swallowed nervously. 'There's nothing I can do.'

'You can warn Warren. Hutch, I mean. You can get to him before he activates the transmitter.' Carver shook his head. 'If you can't, I'm sure the police can.' When Carver didn't react, she stood up and headed for the door.

Carver didn't know if she was bluffing or not, but he couldn't take the risk. 'Wait!' he said.

She turned and looked at him, her hands on her hips. 'I'm waiting,' she said.

'Please, sit down.' Chau-ling did as he asked and looked at him expectantly. Carver pointed at the map on the wall behind him. 'This is jungle, Miss Tsang. Miles and miles of it. Most of it hasn't even been mapped. Why do you think the Burmese and the Thais haven't been able to do anything about the drug warlords who live there? Finding a needle in a haystack doesn't even come close.'

Chau-ling shook her head. 'He isn't across the border yet, is he? He's probably still in Bangkok.'

'So?'

'So first he has to get to the border, and he can't go

through the airport. He'll have to go by road, which means that we can get there before him.'

'We?' said Carver. 'When did this become we?'

'You've set him up to be killed, you and your damn organisation. And I'm not going to stand by and do nothing. We're going to get Warren back, you and I. Or I'll see to it that you and everyone else involved pays the price.' She looked at him with narrowed eyes. 'I can do it, Tim Carver. Believe me.'

'What can we do?' asked Carver. 'We're talking about hundreds of miles of border.' He traced his finger along the river that separated Thailand from Burma and Laos.

Chau-ling stood up and went over to the map. She stared at the area that the DEA agent had been pointing at. He was right.

'And you've no idea where he's going to cross?'

Carver rubbed the bridge of his nose. 'I know he's going to a town called Fang.' He tapped the map with his forefinger. Fang was a small dot several inches from the border.

'So we go to Fang,' she said.

'And then what? He's not going to be walking down the main street, is he? As soon as it gets dark, they'll be over the border.'

Chau-ling stared at the map. 'Look, if you're sure that he's going to be in Fang, then it seems obvious to me that they'll cross the border fairly close to the town. It wouldn't make any sense for them to go all that way and then travel miles and miles along the border before crossing. Would it?'

Carver looked at the map. He slowly ran his finger up from Fang until it reached the river that separated the two countries. 'But it's still too large an area. We'd need God knows how many men to keep watch. And the DEA doesn't have that sort of manpower in the whole country.'

Chau-ling smiled thinly. 'No, but I know someone who might do,' she said.

RAY HARRIGAN LAY CURLED up, clutching a pillow to his chest and snoring softly. Hutch played the light along the man's sleeping body. 'He looks like shit,' said Hutch.

'He'll be okay once we get him back to Ireland,' said Winter. 'Hell, I could do with a cigar right now.'

'Yeah, well, you should have booked a seat in the smoking section.' Hutch switched the flashlight off. There was no point in wasting the batteries.

'Takes you back, doesn't it?' said Winter. 'Just like the choky.'

'Not quite,' said Hutch. 'At least there's no screws rushing in for a spot of rough and tumble.'

Winter chuckled. 'Yeah, fair point. How much time did you do in solitary, Hutch?'

'Four months, six days,' Hutch answered without hesitation. 'Not all at once, though. You?'

'I forget.'

'I never really thanked you, did I?'

'For what?'

'For getting me through it. I'd been in solitary for fourteen days when they put you in the next cell, and I was going out of my head.'

'That's why they do it, old lad. It's not meant to be a pat on the back. I thought you coped okay.'

Hutch tapped his forehead. 'Not in here, Billy. They knew exactly what they were doing. They were trying to break me, and they would have done, too.'

'You want to know something funny, Hutch?'

'Sure.'

'I always feel safer in small spaces. I've a house in Wicklow with seven bedrooms, a snooker room, a living room you could ride a horse around, enough space for ten people. You know where I spend most of the day?'

Hutch shook his head. 'Where?'

'There's a small alcove off the kitchen, a sort of breakfast area. Just enough room for a small table and four chairs. That's where I sit. It's the only damn place in the whole house where I feel comfortable.'

'You don't have to be a psychologist to work that one out, Billy.'

Winter chuckled. 'Yeah. You and I are the same, Hutch. Jailbirds of a feather.'

'Not me. I couldn't stand prison, I can't bear to be locked up.'

Winter chuckled again, a dry, hollow laugh like pebbles being crushed underfoot. 'You don't see it, do you? You really don't see it.'

'See what?' snapped Hutch. He had the feeling that Winter was making fun of him.

'Why did you go into the kennel business, Hutch?'

'Because I like dogs. I've always liked dogs.'

Winter said nothing.

'What? What are you getting at?'

Winter shook his head. 'If you have to ask, old lad, then I'm not going to tell you.'

Hutch tried to contain his impatience. 'It's not like you

to be so enigmatic. Now what the fuck are you talking about?'

'Forget it. I'm just winding you up. Christ, I could do with a cigar.' He sighed deeply. 'You should get some sleep.' The truck bounced over a rough section of road and the driver braked sharply.

'I always knew you better than you knew yourself, Hutch,' said Winter smugly. Hutch didn't reply.

TSANG CHAU-LING ASKED TIM Carver to wait outside in the corridor while she made the telephone call. He picked up his packet of cigarettes and his lighter before going. Chau-ling closed the door to the office and dialled Khun Kriengsak's number. She told his secretary who she was and he was on the line within seconds. Chau-ling explained what she wanted, and why. She heard the lawyer exhale slowly. 'Can you do that for me, Khun Kriengsak?' she asked.

'I can,' he said slowly, drawing out each syllable as if seeing how far he could stretch them.

'It is very important,' she said.

'I am sure it is,' he replied.

'And you would be doing me a great service.'

'Your father has asked me to do everything within my power to assist you, Miss Tsang. I am more than happy to comply with his instructions. But may I ask if he is aware of what you're doing?'

'Not exactly, no.'

'Ah,' said the lawyer. 'That does put me in a quandary,

you see. It is your father who is my client, after all.'

'I understand, Khun Kriengsak,' said Chau-ling. 'But I would rather not tell my father.'

The lawyer exhaled again. 'Perhaps we could leave it this way, Miss Tsang. I shall do as you ask, and I shall not refer the matter to your father . . .'

'Thank you,' gushed Chau-ling with relief. 'Thank you so much.'

'I had not finished, Miss Tsang,' said the lawyer smoothly. 'I must tell you, however, that if your father raises the matter with me, I shall have to be honest with him.'

'That's all I can ask, Khun Kriengsak. Thank you.'

'Where will you be?' he asked.

'Chiang Mai,' she said. 'Then a town called Fang. I'll call you from there.'

'I know Fang,' said the lawyer. 'Be careful.'

'I will be.'

'And Miss Tsang, please do not even think about crossing the border. The Golden Triangle is a very dangerous place.'

'The thought hadn't even entered my mind,' said Chau-ling.

TIM CARVER WASN'T QUITE sure at what point he'd decided that he was going to help Tsang Chau-ling, even though to do so was likely to end his career with the DEA. The agency had gone to a great deal of time and trouble to set the trap for Zhou Yuanyi, and if Carver warned Hutch it would have all been for nothing. He'd never seen Jake Gregory angry but he had no doubt that it would be on a par with a raging thunderstorm. Against that, Carver knew that he wouldn't be able to live with himself if he knowingly sent a man to his death. He had at least to try to warn Hutch. If he was too late, or if Hutch and Harrigan still managed to get over the border and disappear into Burma, then Carver could at least tell himself that he'd done his best. That he'd tried.

He lit a cigarette and inhaled gratefully. She was a strong-willed girl, all right. There was an intensity about her that broached no argument, and he was sure that she was used to getting her own way. He could imagine her twisting her father around her little finger. Carver leaned back against the wall. Hutch was a lucky man to have earned the adoration of such a girl. That she loved him was transparently obvious. He wondered who she was calling. Who could she know in Thailand who would have the power to have the border watched? He went over to the water cooler and filled a paper cup. Ed Harris came out of his office.

'Hey, Ed, did you ever come across a girl called Tsang Chau-ling while you were in Hong Kong?' asked Carver. Harris had spent two years working out of the DEA's Hong Kong office.

Harris bent down and helped himself to water. 'Doesn't ring a bell,' said Harris. 'I'm on line to Washington. Why don't you run her name through the computer?'

Carver screwed up his empty paper cup and tossed it into the trash can. He looked at his office door. It was still shut. 'Yeah, why not?' he said. He followed Harris through to his office, closed the door and sat down on the edge of the desk as Harris tapped on the keyboard.

'You think she's bad?' asked Harris, his eyes on his VDU.

'No way,' said Carver. 'But she knows people.'

'Yeah. What makes you think that?'

Carver gave a half-shrug. He looked around for an ashtray. There wasn't one and he remembered that Harris was a non-smoker. 'Just a hunch,' he said. He held the cigarette vertically so that the ash wouldn't break off.

Harris sniffed and continued to tap away. He stopped and stared at the screen. His eyebrows went up and he clicked his tongue. 'Well, well, well.'

'What, what, what?'

Harris turned the VDU so that Carver could read the details on the screen. 'Your Miss Tsang is clean, but her father is a different kettle of drug dealer.'

'Her father?' Carver's eyes flicked across the screen.

'Tsang Chai-hin. Civic leader, one of the richest of the rich, chairman of half a dozen worthy causes, major shareholder in two of the biggest listed companies in Hong Kong, well connected in Beijing, and responsible for shipping something like two hundred tonnes of marijuana to the United States every year.'

Carver pulled a face as he scanned the file. 'Hearsay,' he said. 'He's never been indicted.'

'And whenever we search his ships, we find nothing. But you know as well as I do, that means nothing. The guy's so rich he can buy all the protection he needs. He's being watched, though. And you've got little Miss Tsang in your office? How about pumping her for information?'

'I don't think so,' said Carver.

'Is she pretty?'

'Definitely. A stunner.'

'How about just pumping her?' Harris laughed but Carver didn't think it was funny. He stood up and cupped his hand under the cigarette.

There was a knock on the door. Carver jumped and ash spilled on to the carpet. Harris got up and opened the door. It was Chau-ling. Carver could feel his cheeks redden, even though he was sure she couldn't have heard what Harris had said.

'I've finished,' she said. 'My friend can help.'

'Friend?' asked Harris.

'It's personal,' lied Carver. The fewer people who knew what he and Chau-ling were up to, the safer his career would be.

HUTCH STRETCHED OUT HIS legs, taking care not to disturb Harrigan. He wiped his shirt sleeve across his forehead. He was dripping with sweat. 'What is this Ireland thing all about, anyway?' asked Hutch.

'It's a long story,' said Winter.

'How long to Fang did you say?' Twelve hours? We've got time.'

Winter snorted softly. He said nothing for a few seconds, then sighed mournfully. 'Things have changed a lot since you were in Parkhurst. It's all drugs now.'

'You were never into drugs. Straightforward armed robbery, I seem to remember.'

'No future in it. There's less cash around, and there were

too many amateurs. Addicts trying to get the money for their next fix, holding up filling stations and pubs with knives and syringes and God knows what. It's not like it used to be.'

'But drugs, Billy? I never thought you'd get involved in drugs.'

'You wouldn't believe the money that's there to be made. I was bringing in marijuana from Holland, shipping it to Liverpool in containers. Three out of four shipments got through and each successful shipment was a ten-fold increase in our investment.'

'*Our* investment?'

'A few like-minded individuals, Hutch. No one that you'd know. We didn't even have to touch the stuff. We'd plan it, finance it, subcontract out the work and have buyers lined up in the UK. Jesus, the money poured in. It was almost embarrassing. Do you have any idea how much I'm worth these days, Hutch? Any idea at all?'

Hutch shrugged, but then realised that Winter wouldn't be able to see the gesture in the darkness. 'No,' he said.

'Twelve million,' said Winter, proudly. 'Twelve million quid. Not bad for a boy from Newcastle who failed his eleven-plus, huh?'

Hutch raised his eyebrows in surprise. Winter was right. Hutch had had no idea that he was so wealthy. If nothing else, it explained where the money had come from to pay for getting Harrigan out of prison.

'We were living in Spain, like gods. Anything we wanted we could have. The best food, the best booze, women – anything and everything. Five years we had, five great years, and then the authorities started getting heavy and we heard a whisper that they were

457

going to start extradition proceedings, so we bailed
out.'

'To Ireland?'

'We'd never done anything wrong there, and so long as
we didn't break any of their laws, we were dead safe. We
bought big houses, mine even had stables and a pool, and
we held court in all the best clubs. The women were a bit
rough but we could fly in all the girls we wanted.'

'Sounds perfect.'

Winter didn't appear to notice the sarcasm. 'It was Until
we had a visit from the Boys.'

'The Boys?'

'The Provos. The IRA. This was just before the ceasefire,
remember, when they and the Unionists were still knocking
each other off. I got dragged out of my bed by guys in ski
masks and taken off to some shed where a Paddy with
a big gun said that if I wanted to continue to live in
Ireland, I'd have to pay a tax. Quarter of a million a
year, they wanted. I paid it with a smile, Hutch. Small
change. Peanuts. Bloody Paddys had no idea how much
we were making. We all got visits, and we all paid up.
Everything was hunky dory until the ceasefire and all the
big boys had to find something else to do. Idle hands and
all that. Some of them looked at my business and wanted
a piece of it.'

Hutch frowned. 'I thought the IRA were anti-drugs?
Don't they execute drug dealers?'

'The Organisation is, sure. But there are bad apples
who are only in it for what they can get for themselves.
They know better than to bring drugs into Ireland, but
anywhere else is fair game. Besides, they took a sadistic
pleasure in shipping drugs into England. They started with

marijuana and ecstasy, and then they decided they wanted to get into the hard stuff. I had some connections, so I fixed up some meetings in Thailand. Ray here was up in Chiang Rai checking the first consignment when the shit hit the fan. Someone must have grassed. Anyway, Ray keeps his mouth shut and goes down for a fifty stretch. I get picked up by the men in ski masks again and told in no uncertain terms that it's down to me to get him out. His uncle's a big wheel in the Organisation.'

'So they threatened you and you threatened me.'

'You don't say no to the Provos, Hutch.'

They rode in silence for a while. It was stiflingly hot in the back of the truck and the battery-powered fan made little impression on the stale air. 'I would have helped anyway, you know,' said Hutch.

'I couldn't take the chance that you'd turn me down.'

'You didn't even try. We were mates, Billy. I owed you.'

'Hutch, the moment I told you what I wanted you started to scream blue murder.'

'Yeah, well, you were a bit of a shock after all these years. But you could have talked me into it. You didn't have to threaten my kid.'

'I'm sorry, old lad,' said Winter.

'Forget it,' said Hutch.

'I'll make it up to you, I promise,' said Winter. 'You won't lose out, you'll be able to start a new life when this is over, and you'll have all the money you could want.'

'What if this guy Zhou doesn't come through? Are you sure he can get us passports, stuff like that?'

Winter didn't say anything for a few seconds and Hutch wondered if he hadn't heard the question. When he did speak, Winter's voice was colder than it had been before. 'Remind me again, Hutch, when exactly did I tell you about Zhou?'

Hutch's heart pounded. He thanked his lucky stars that they were sitting in the dark because otherwise Winter would have seen the confusion written all over his face. 'Before I went into the prison. You said Zhou was going to get you and Ray out of the Golden Triangle.'

The silence was even longer this time, and if anything Winter's voice was several degrees colder. 'The thing of it is, old lad, I don't remember ever telling you Zhou's name.'

'Didn't you?' said Hutch, trying to keep his voice steady.

'It's not the sort of name I'd bandy about, if the truth be told.'

'So it must have been Ray. Yeah, I think it was when I told him you were going to get him out through Burma. For Christ's sake, Billy, what do you think? You roped me into this, remember? I'm the innocent bystander. What do you think, I'm some sort of grass? You think the cops are using me to get at you? You came to me, Billy. You fucked up my life. Who do I grass you to, Billy? Who can I talk to who won't put me behind bars for twenty years?'

Hutch flicked the flashlight on. Winter's face looked ghostly in the white light. His slicked-back hair glistened as if it had been oiled and his eyes were narrowed accusingly. He squinted into the light as he considered what Hutch had said. Suddenly he relaxed. He smiled and nodded. 'Yeah, you're right,' he said. 'You've got even more to lose than me.'

TIM CARVER WATCHED CHAU-LING hand over her gold American Express card. 'Is that her father's?' he asked Ricky Lim. Lim said nothing. 'Do you work for him, or for her?' said Carver. Again Lim didn't answer. 'I suppose being the strong, silent type is an advantage in your line of work.'

Lim turned to stare at Carver. His eyes were cold and hard and seemed to bore right through the DEA agent's head. Lim's thin, bloodless lips remained sealed as if they'd been glued together.

'Are you still carrying that toothpick?' Carver asked.

'It is an ice-pick,' said Lim.

Carver smiled innocently. 'Because if you were, it'd probably set off the metal detectors when we go to board the plane.' Lim's face fell.

Before he could react further, Chau-ling walked over brandishing three Thai Airways tickets. 'You're sure we can get a car in Chiang Mai?' she asked Carver.

Carver nodded. He took his ticket from her and examined it. It was in business class. 'Sure. And we can drive to Fang from there in about three hours.' He looked at his wristwatch. 'We should be there before dark.'

'Miss Tsang, I must speak with you,' said Lim in Chinese.

She looked at him, then nodded slowly. 'Mr Carver, could you leave us alone, please?'

As Carver walked away, Lim said, 'I am not happy about this, Miss Tsang.'

'If there was any other way, Ricky, believe me, I wouldn't be here, either.'

'Your father said—'

'My father said that you were to look after me,' Chau-ling interrupted. 'And you're doing that.'

'It could be dangerous. Your father would not approve.'

'First, I'm not doing anything dangerous, and you'll be with me, so what can happen? Secondly, we're not going to be there for more than twenty-four hours. One day, Ricky. You can take care of me for one day, can't you?' Lim chewed on his lip, unconvinced. Chau-ling smiled sympathetically. Lim's heart was in the right place, but she knew that he was no match for her intellectually and she felt almost sorry for him. She leaned forward conspiratorially. 'Look, Ricky, I could have given you the slip, you know? I could have just gone without telling you. Then what would my father have said?'

Lim sighed despondently. 'Very well, Miss Tsang. But please promise me that it will just be the one day.'

'I promise,' she said solemnly, looking at him straight in the eye the way she always did when she promised her father something. 'Now come on. Let's go or we'll miss our plane.'

Lim ran his hand over his jacket. He could feel the hardness of the ice-pick in its specially tailored pocket. 'I have to go to the bathroom first,' he said.

'Why, Ricky?' said Chau-ling. 'You're not afraid of flying, are you?'

Lim sighed mournfully. He didn't appreciate being teased.

BIRD WAS JOLTED OUT of a dreamless doze by the driver pounding his horn. To their left was a white-painted spirit house, bedecked with garlands of flowers, and the driver was using the horn to pay his respects to benefit from any good fortune that was to be had from the friendly spirits who lived there. Bird squinted at the milometer. They were almost halfway to Fang and were making good time. Bird looked across at the driver. He was staring ahead with wide eyes and his hands gripped the steering wheel so tightly that the knuckles had whitened. An hour earlier they'd stopped so that the driver could go to the toilet at the roadside and Bird had seen him swallow a couple of tablets. Amphetamines probably. Bird hadn't said anything: it wasn't unusual for long-distance drivers to use amphetamines to keep going, and at least he wouldn't fall asleep at the wheel.

They drove by vibrant-green rice fields, tended by farmers in straw hats, up to their knees in brackish water. Bird had come from a farming family, and he knew just how back-breaking the work was. His three brothers and four sisters had worked the small rice farm close to the border, trapped in the neverending cycle of planting and reaping with only the occasional bottle of Thai whisky to break the monotony. Bird still had calves that were scarred from countless mosquito bites that had gone septic because he had spent so much time standing in water. He had escaped to the city when he was twenty, following the two sisters who had become prostitutes in the tourist bars of Pat Pong.

It had been six years before Bird went back to the family farm, and when he did it was with a gold Rolex on his wrist and enough money to replace his father's four water buffaloes with a new tractor. His family still worked the farm, but the old wooden house had been torn down and replaced with a two-storey concrete building that had an inside toilet and a colour television.

The driver cursed and stamped on the brake pedal. Ahead of them a brown-uniformed policeman with a white belt and holstered gun was waving them to stop.

Bird banged on the wall of the cab, three hard slaps to let the men hidden in the back know that they were to keep quiet. 'Were you speeding?' Bird asked the driver.

The driver looked at him blankly. 'I don't know,' he said. 'How fast were we going?'

The policeman held a walkie-talkie to his mouth. As the truck slowed to a stop, Bird saw a white police car parked off the road. Another policeman, this one with three stripes on his sleeve, was leaning against the bonnet, his arms folded across his chest and his legs crossed at the ankles. At least it wasn't a roadblock, thought Bird. The policeman with the walkie-talkie walked slowly over to the driver's side of the cab and waited for the driver to wind down the window.

'Let me do the talking,' said Bird. He opened his door and climbed down.

The policeman was already taking out his notebook. 'You were speeding,' he said.

Bird apologised deferentially. He earned more in one day than the cop earned in a year, but they still had a long way to go and unless the policeman was treated with due respect he could hold them up.

'A fine has to be paid,' said the policeman, his pen poised

over the notebook. There were two levels of fine, Bird knew: one official, one unofficial. The unofficial fine was twice the official rate, but it did away with the paperwork. Nothing was written down, and the money went straight into the cop's pocket. It was a typical Thai compromise, one in which both parties prospered. Bird took out his wallet, handed over two thousand baht, and thanked the policeman for his consideration. Thirty seconds later they were back on the road, hurtling northwards at exactly the same speed as before.

CHAU-LING WALKED INTO THE arrivals area with Tim Carver and Ricky Lim following close behind her. A soldier in khaki fatigues was holding a sheet of paper with her name written on it in capital letters. He took them outside to where a large black saloon was waiting, its engine running. The soldier scurried ahead and opened the door for them. They sat in the back and the soldier joined the driver in the front.

'Who exactly do you know in the military?' Carver asked.

'A friend of my father's,' said Chau-ling.

'Your father has a friend in the Thai army?' Carver felt Lim stiffen in the seat next to him.

'My father uses a lawyer in Bangkok, the lawyer has family connections in the army, blah, blah, blah. Thailand is all about who you know, just like Hong Kong.'

'Your father must be a very important man,' said Carver. Chau-ling said nothing. Carver spoke to the soldier in Thai.

The soldier told him they were going to an army camp close to the border, about four hours away. Carver gave Chau-ling a sideways glance. He wanted to ask her more about her father, but he doubted that she would be naive enough to tell him anything. She was a smart girl, this Tsang Chau-ling; within a few short hours she had virtually taken control of the situation and given him the distinct impression that he was only along for the ride. He settled back in his seat. If he was just along for the ride, he might as well try to get some sleep.

THE TRUCK SWERVED FROM side to side, jolting Hutch awake. 'Are you okay, old lad?' asked Winter.

'Yeah. How much longer?'

'Not long now.' Harrigan snored loudly, and shifted his position. 'Sleeps a lot, doesn't he?' said Winter.

'It's the tension. I need to take a leak.'

Winter pushed an empty water bottle across the floor. 'Be my guest.'

'I'll wait,' said Hutch.

'It's pitch dark in here, nobody's going to see. Besides, it's not as if you haven't done it in front of me before.'

'I'll wait,' repeated Hutch.

The truck turned to the left and the cardboard boxes rubbed against each other. 'This might be it,' said Winter.

They made another couple of turns and awkward gear changes and bumped over something in the road. The truck stopped and they heard voices outside, then it lurched forward. Two minutes later the truck came to a stop again. This time both cab doors opened and closed and someone banged on the side of the truck. Harrigan woke up and began to cough. The coughs turned to retching and he threw up. The smell was nauseating in the confined space and Hutch put his hand over his mouth.

'Bloody hell,' said Winter. 'This is a linen suit.'

'Sorry,' said Harrigan, and retched again.

The back of the truck rattled down and they heard boxes being pulled out and stacked on the ground. Winter stood up and unhooked the webbing straps. The last of the boxes was removed and soft moonlight illuminated the back of the truck. Bird stood there, grinning. Harrigan was on his hands and knees, shaking his head. Hutch helped him to his feet.

Winter jumped down from the truck and examined his trousers, lifting each leg in turn. 'You were bloody lucky, Ray,' he said. He took a cigar case from his jacket pocket, extracted a large Cuban cigar and lit it with a match as Hutch helped Harrigan out of the truck.

They were parked at the rear of a multi-storey concrete building. To their right was the hum of large air-conditioners and the clanging of metal pans being knocked together. 'It's a hotel,' explained Bird.

Hutch looked at Winter in amazement. 'We break out of prison, we sit in the back of a truck for twelve hours, we're about to cross a border illegally and you check us into a hotel? What's the game?'

Winter chuckled softly. 'It's okay, old lad. Zhou owns it. We're safe here.'

The driver got back into the cab and lay down on the seat, his feet sticking out of the open window. Bird went around to the front of the hotel while Winter led Hutch and Harrigan through a door and up three flights of stairs to a deserted corridor. 'This floor is empty and the lift won't stop here. No one will see us,' said Winter.

'How long do we have to wait here?' asked Hutch.

Winter looked at his watch. 'A couple of hours at most. There's a guy coming who'll take us over the river into Burma. Once he's here we can go.'

Bird appeared with a key on a large acrylic key ring. He unlocked a door and they went inside. It was a large room with a double bed and basic furniture. A framed print of an ocean scene hung above the bed, slightly off centre. Winter nodded at a door to the left. 'There's a bathroom there. It'll be some time before we see another one, so make use of it. I'm going to have a shower.'

Winter strode into the bathroom with his cigar. 'Bird, we're going to need more towels,' he called.

Bird threw the door a mock salute and left the room.

Harrigan lay on the bed and stared at the ceiling.

'Are you okay?' asked Hutch.

'No,' said Harrigan flatly. 'I need a hit.'

'It'll pass.'

'You don't know what you're talking about,' said Harrigan, his voice loaded with bitterness. He rolled over and curled up into a fetal ball.

Hutch dropped into an armchair. He felt the transmitter press against his stomach. He wondered what would happen to Harrigan if he pressed the button and summoned the helicopters. Would the DEA allow Harrigan to keep his freedom or would they send him back to prison? And if they did send him back behind bars, how would Hutch feel? He still hadn't decided whether or not he was going to activate the beacon. A lot would depend on what happened once they crossed the border. In the bathroom, the shower kicked into life.

'DO YOU MIND?' ASKED Carver, showing the cigarette packet to Chau-ling. She shook her head and Carver lit one. They were sitting on camp stools in a green canvas tent illuminated by an electric bulb hanging from a metal pole. Ricky Lim stood at the entrance to the tent like a sentry on guard. There was a metal desk in the far corner of the tent, and a rusting grey filing cabinet next to it. On the filing cabinet stood a half-empty bottle of Johnnie Walker Red Label and several glasses.

'What do you know about this colonel?' he asked.

'Absolutely nothing,' she said.

Carver blew a smoke ring and then tried to blow a second ring through the first. He almost succeeded. 'Could you do me a favour?' he asked.

'What?' she said.

It was typical of her, thought Carver. Most people would have said 'sure' before knowing what favour was being asked, out of politeness if nothing else. 'Don't tell anyone that I'm with the DEA.'

'Why not?'

'Because we're not always on the best of terms with the military, that's why not.'

'You mean, you can't trust them?'

'This is Thailand, Miss Tsang. You can't trust anybody.'

Chau-ling raised an eyebrow. 'Why Mr Carver, are you including yourself in that generalisation?'

Carver didn't reply. He didn't enjoy crossing swords with Tsang Chau-ling. She always seemed to draw blood.

'Don't worry, your secret's safe with me,' she said. 'And I think it's about time we were on first-name terms, don't you?'

'I'm not sure,' said Carver. He smiled and tried another smoke ring.

Lim spoke in Cantonese, and stepped backwards into the tent.

'Somebody's coming,' said Chau-ling, standing up.

A stocky Thai in a colonel's uniform appeared at the entrance to the tent. He had close-cropped, jet-black hair and a broad jaw with skin as smooth as a child's. He smiled and offered his hand to Chau-ling, Western style, and when she held out hers he took it and kissed it softly. 'Enchanted to meet you, Miss Tsang,' he said. His accent was vaguely French. 'I am Colonel Suphat. I have been told to offer you every assistance.'

Chau-ling introduced the Colonel to Carver and Lim, using only their first names. The Colonel didn't ask why they were involved, much to Carver's relief. He was in enough trouble already without having to lie to the Thai military.

'Please sit down,' said the Colonel, motioning them to the camp stools. He went over to the filing cabinet. 'Can I offer you a drink?'

Carver was about to refuse when Chau-ling accepted the offer. The DEA agent figured that she was only being tactful so he nodded. The Colonel poured large measures of whisky and handed them to his three visitors, neat. He toasted them and drained his glass. Carver looked across at Chau-ling. Without flinching, she drank her whisky to the last drop. Lim did the same. Carver shrugged and followed suit.

'Now, you have no idea where the attempt will be made to cross the border?' asked the Colonel. He spoke directly to Chau-ling, as if the men were of no interest to him at all.

'We know they will be passing through Fang,' said Chau-ling.

The Colonel nodded. 'We will be watching the roads from Fang, but there are many. We think our best chance of catching them is at the river. We have increased our patrols, and we have men posted at regular intervals along the bank.'

'Colonel Suphat, your men won't shoot, will they?' asked Chau-ling anxiously.

'It has been made clear to me that they must be captured alive,' said the Colonel.

'Not just alive,' Chau-ling said quickly. 'Warren mustn't be hurt.'

'I understand,' said the Colonel. 'But they will be held in custody. They will have committed an offence by trying to cross the border illegally.' He collected their empty glasses. 'Now, can I suggest you make yourselves as comfortable as possible? I shall keep you informed of developments.'

Chau-ling thanked him, and the Colonel turned on his heels and left the tent.

Carver turned to Chau-ling. 'I don't believe this,' he said. 'You've got the Thai army eating out of your hand. I wouldn't get this kind of co-operation in a million years.'

'You don't have my father,' said Chau-ling.

For the first time, Carver realised that she almost certainly did know what her father was and what he did. But she did have a point. Without her father's influence, they didn't stand a snowball's chance in hell of preventing Hutch from committing suicide.

HUTCH LEANED OVER THE sink and stared at himself in the mirror. He looked terrible. His eyes were bloodshot, his skin was ingrained with dirt and his hair was lank and greasy. He'd lost weight, too. There was a set of scales in the corner of the bathroom and he stood on them and peered down at the dial. He was a full stone lighter than when he'd left Hong Kong. He stripped off his sweatshirt and jeans and washed himself with a wet towel, taking care not to get water on the sticking plaster. Carver had said that the transmitter was sealed and water wouldn't harm it, but Hutch wasn't sure how well the plaster would stick to his skin if it got wet. There was a sudden knock on the bathroom door and Hutch jumped.

'Hutch, the guide's here,' said Winter. 'Time to go.'

'Give me a minute,' said Hutch. He dried himself and swilled his mouth out with water from the tap, then stood for a few seconds looking at the sticking plaster and the bulge where the beacon was. There was another knock at the door.

'Come on, Hutch. There are people waiting for us on the other side.'

Hutch pulled on his clothes, checked himself in the mirror again and went out to join the others. The guide was a Thai in his late twenties, light skinned with narrow shoulders and a girl's waist. He was wearing a faded grey T-shirt and blue jeans and he kept looking at his watch as if they were already late. Winter had dumped his linen suit in a wastebin and changed into a green long-sleeved shirt with epaulettes, and brown corduroy trousers.

'Have you got stomach problems?' Winter asked Hutch.

'No, why?'

'You were in there a long time.'

Hutch shrugged. 'Yeah, well, I'm here now. What's the plan?'

'Back in the truck and up to the river. Nung here will take us across and into the Triangle. Then we're home free. Okay, let's hit the road.'

They went downstairs to the truck. Winter, Hutch and Harrigan got into the back while Bird woke up the driver. The boxes were stacked around the three men again and they settled down on the pillows.

The drive up to the river took the best part of an hour, most of the journey involving abrupt changes of direction and gear grinding. Several mosquitoes had joined them in the back of the truck and Hutch had acquired two bites on his neck by the time they juddered to a halt.

Hutch, Winter and Harrigan helped push the boxes out of the truck and then stood at the roadside.

'No problems?' Winter asked Bird.

'No, but we took a bit of a detour because Nung reckoned there were roadblocks.'

'Is that normal?'

'They were probably just looking for bribes. They don't get paid for a couple of weeks.' Nung spoke to Bird in

Thai and Bird nodded. 'Okay, the boat's already here. We should go.'

Nung led the way, taking them along the edge of a rice field to a line of palm trees. They disturbed a large grey water buffalo and it grunted a warning for them not to get too close. Harrigan slipped off the path and into the water.

'For fuck's sake, Ray, watch where you're going,' said Winter as Hutch helped pull Harrigan out.

'Come on,' hissed Bird.

The ground began to slope down and the field gave way to shrubs and bushes. Hutch heard the river before he saw it, its fast-flowing waters lapping against the muddy banks. Nung waved for them to stop. The water glinted in the moonlight, rippling and twisting like a million serpents. Hutch found it impossible to judge how wide the river was; the far side merged into the landscape so perfectly that there was no way of knowing where the water ended and the land began.

'That's Burma over there?' Hutch asked Winter.

'Myanmar,' said Winter. 'It's called Myanmar now.'

Nung disappeared down to the water's edge.

'You've crossed here before?'

'Twice. Don't worry, Hutch. This guy knows what he's doing. He goes back and forth every other day. Most of his family still live over there. The border means nothing to these people.'

Nung reappeared and started whispering to Bird. Bird shook his head. He waved Winter over. Hutch and Harrigan went with him. 'We might have a problem,' said Bird. 'The boatman says there have been several army patrols by here tonight, and there are army boats on the river.'

'That's unusual?' asked Winter.

'This much activity is, he says. Is it possible they know that we're going to cross?'

'I don't see how,' said Winter.

'Well, the boatman reckons it's too risky to go tonight. He says we should wait.'

'Fuck that. Who died and left him in charge?' Winter spat. 'Tell him to do as he's fucking told.'

Bird flinched at the intensity of Winter's outburst. 'It's you he's worried about, not himself.'

Winter calmed down. 'Okay, okay. Sorry. Look, offer him a few thousand baht, whatever it takes. But we go tonight. We're expected over on the other side.'

Bird and Nung went down to the water again. 'You handled that well, Billy,' said Hutch. 'A master of tact and diplomacy.'

'Ha bloody ha. Come on, let's go.'

Winter, Hutch and Harrigan went carefully down the bank. The wet clay was slippery and they moved slowly. 'There they are,' said Winter, pointing.

Ahead of them Hutch could make out a small wooden jetty sticking some twenty feet out into the river. At the end of the jetty stood Bird and Nung, talking to a man at the rear of a long, thin boat. There were eight planking seats along the length of the vessel, each big enough for two people. The boat was barely two feet above the waterline, with a large diesel engine fixed to the back. Connected to the engine was a long prop, raised out of the water, with a small propeller at the end. Hutch had seen similar boats operating along the river in Bangkok. The propeller could be dipped in and out of the water by the boatman, giving them a high degree of mobility and allowing them to speed through shallow water if necessary.

As they approached, Bird took out his wallet and gave the boatman a handful of banknotes, then turned and gave Winter a thumbs-up.

'Typical Thailand,' said Winter. 'There isn't a problem that money can't solve.'

'Maybe he's got a point,' said Hutch. 'Maybe we should wait.'

'Don't you start,' said Winter. He patted Hutch on the back. 'Trust me, old lad. We'll be a hell of a lot safer over there.'

They walked along the bank to the pier. Nung and Bird helped them down into the boat one by one. The boatman steadied them as they took their places. He was in his sixties with leathery skin and gnarled hands and a baseball cap pulled down low on his head. Harrigan and Winter sat together in the middle of the boat, and Hutch took the seat directly behind them. Bird took his place at the back. The boatman started the engine and revved it. Grey smoke belched out of the exhaust.

Nung untied the boat and scrambled to the front as the boatman lowered the propeller into the water and they surged forward. The engine roared as they picked up speed. Spray blew up across Hutch's face and the wind whipped through his hair. The sound of the engine was deafening and Hutch was sure it would be heard for miles. He tapped Winter on the shoulder. 'Isn't this a bit noisy?' he shouted.

'Ten minutes, max,' said Winter. 'There are plenty of these long-tailed boats on the river, even at night. Just settle back and enjoy the ride.'

Flecks of water blurred Hutch's vision and he took off his glasses and wiped them with the sleeve of his sweatshirt.

He put them back on and looked at the receding shoreline. Three figures were standing watching them. One of them was pointing, another was holding something up to his face. Hutch realised with a jolt that they were soldiers. He grabbed Winter's shoulder and shook it.

'Billy, we've been spotted!' he yelled.

Winter looked across at the three soldiers. 'Shit,' he said. He twisted around in his seat to check that the boatman had seen them, but the old man had already wound the engine up to its maximum. 'Keep down!' Winter shouted. They all ducked, but to Hutch's surprise there were no shots. He looked over his shoulder again. The soldiers hadn't moved, though they had been joined by two more men. The boat bucked and tossed as it cut across the troughs of the river, then it settled into a steady rhythm again as it powered through the water.

'They're probably not after us,' said Winter. 'It's drugs coming over from the other side that they're worried about. Trust me.'

Hutch didn't reply. He was sure it wasn't a coincidence that the army patrol had been on the spot.

When they were about halfway across the river, the boatman turned on to a course parallel to the banks. Nung was kneeling at the prow, peering forward. Occasionally he would wave his left or right hand, indicating that there were obstacles in the water ahead, usually drifting branches, and the boatman would make swift corrections with his prop. Ahead of them the river bent around to the right and the boatman took them closer to the Burmese shore. The vegetation seemed more dense on the Burmese side, with trees and bushes almost right up to the water's edge.

Suddenly Nung began to wave frantically. Hutch peered

around Winter's shoulder to see what was wrong. He and Winter saw the launch at the same time and they cursed in unison. It was painted grey, about a hundred feet long with a large naval gun mounted at the front. The red, white and blue Thai flag flew from atop the superstructure and in front of it was a massive searchlight, the beam of which swept across the water towards them. The boatman took immediate evasive action, steering hard towards port, away from the Burmese bank. Hutch's stomach lurched and he gripped the side of the boat. Bird reached into his jacket and drew his gun but Winter slapped him on the arm.

'Don't be stupid!' Winter shouted. 'You'd be wasting your bullets.'

The searchlight beam caught them and the boatman turned again but whoever was operating the searchlight knew what they were doing and the boat remained fixed in its brilliant glare. Thai commands were shouted at them through a loudspeaker, like the voice of some vengeful god, so loud that Hutch could feel the vibrations against his skin.

'What are they saying?' asked Harrigan, his voice trembling.

'They're wishing us a pleasant voyage, you stupid bastard!' screamed Winter. 'What the fuck do you think they're saying?' Winter gripped Bird's arm. 'Tell the boatman not to stop. Whatever he does, he's not to stop.'

Bird translated Winter's orders and the boatman nodded stiffly.

'Can we outrun them?' Hutch yelled.

'Not for long,' replied Winter. 'Besides, look at the size of that gun.'

The long-tailed boat veered back to starboard. For a

moment they escaped the searchlight but it quickly caught up with them, its glare blinding Hutch. He put a hand across his face to protect his eyes. The boat swerved yet again, skidding sideways across the water before the propeller bit and pushed them forward. Hutch slipped off his seat and fell backwards, banging his head. Winter reached back and helped him up.

More Thai commands were shouted at them through the loudspeaker. The boat was heading directly towards the Burmese shore, cutting across the flow of the river. They were still several hundred yards from the shore, and the army launch was rapidly gaining on them.

Nung had given up navigating and was lying face down in the prow. The boatman stood up so that he could get a better view of the water in front of them, gripping the handle of the prop with both hands.

Water splashed up over Hutch, drenching him and obscuring the lenses of his glasses again. It dripped down his face and into his open mouth and he spat over the side. The boat kicked and bucked and for a second it was out of the water and then it crashed down, knocking the wind out of him. He wondered how much punishment the small craft could take. One thing was certain: it wouldn't survive a collision with the army launch.

The boatman slammed his body against the prop handle and the boat turned almost immediately. Hutch realised what the man was trying to do: the long-tailed boat could turn on a sixpence and while it couldn't beat the launch for speed it had the edge when it came to manoeuvrability. The sudden change of direction was taking them behind the launch. Suddenly the air was split by the sound of gunfire, miniature explosions a fraction of a second apart, and bullets whizzed overhead. The boatman sat down heavily, holding on to his baseball cap with one hand.

'Jesus Christ!' shouted Harrigan. He was staring white faced at the launch. Two men were standing at the stern firing assault rifles from the hip.

'Keep your head down!' yelled Winter. There was another rattle of gunfire and more bullets shrieked overhead. The launch began to turn and the searchlight lost them. They raced through the darkness, the bottom of the boat juddering on the rough water. The boatman turned them towards the shore once more. The engine was screaming at full throttle, its pistons rattling and shaking as if trying to break free from their cylinders.

The searchlight beam flashed across the water ahead of them. The boat veered left, away from the murky brown oval of light and into the darkness. There were more bullets and shouts from the launch. Hutch looked over his shoulder. The army vessel had almost turned. There was no one manning the large gun on deck but the soldiers with the assault rifles had moved to the prow and put their weapons to their shoulders. Their aim didn't appear to have improved, though: the bullets were still going high. Suddenly he was blinded by the searching glare of the searchlight as it came to bear on their boat. He turned away, blinking to clear his eyes. Bird and Winter were silhouetted in the brilliant white light.

All three of them saw the floating log at the same time, but only Bird had time to shout a warning before the long-tailed boat slammed into it. Hutch grabbed at his seat but the shock of the impact tore his fingers from the wood and he felt himself start to fall. The boat toppled to the right as it soared through the air. Hutch pitched into the air, his arms flailing, and something banged into his leg, hard. He saw Winter fall backwards, his arms going up to protect his head, and then Hutch hit the water and went under. He managed to hold his breath at the last minute but water still forced its way into his nose and he felt a searing pain in his forehead. He kept his eyes closed and tried to stay under water because the propeller would be flailing somewhere overhead but he felt his lungs start to burn and so he kicked for the surface.

He coughed and spat and started to tread water. The long-tailed boat was on its side, its prop sticking out of the water and the propeller screaming like a tortured animal. The boatman clung to the side of the boat, his legs in the river. The boat remained fixed in the centre of the searchlight beam and harsh Thai commands were screamed over the loudspeaker. Hutch's stomach began to cramp with the effort of keeping his legs moving. His training shoes had filled with water and his wet clothes were starting to drag him down. He looked around frantically, kicking hard to try to raise himself out of the water. He saw two dark shapes off to his left. Winter and Bird. Then another shape, coughing and spluttering. Harrigan. Hutch began to swim towards them. He tried the crawl but his wet shirt was too much of a drag so he switched to breast stroke.

The shore was only fifty yards away and Hutch was a good swimmer, so he was confident that even in the fast-flowing river he'd have no problems making it to the bank. His main worry was the army launch. The soldiers must surely have realised that there was only one man with the capsized boat.

Hutch caught up with Winter and the rest. Winter was panting and Bird was helping to keep Harrigan afloat.

Winter forced a grin when he saw Hutch. 'Good job I wasn't wearing the suit, hey?' he said. A wave sloshed over his face and he shook his wet hair out of his eyes.

'Can you make it?' asked Hutch.

'Yeah,' said Winter, 'I think so.' His breast stroke was passable, Hutch could see, and he didn't appear to be panicking. So long as Winter kept his head he'd be okay.

'Where's Nung?'

'On his way to shore. Swims like a fucking fish.'

'Okay. You go ahead, I'll help Bird with Ray.' Winter nodded and concentrated on swimming. Hutch swam over to the two men. Harrigan was on his back, making no attempt to swim, while Bird dragged him by the collar. Harrigan had his eyes closed and was breathing through his nose, snorting like a frightened horse. There was blood on his forehead and a gash on his cheek.

Hutch got on the other side of Harrigan. He grabbed him around the neck and started scissor-kicking. Together they made their way towards the bank, fighting the current all the way. Hutch had to stay low in the water to support Harrigan, so he couldn't see where the launch was, but he could hear the dull throb of its engines. Water splashed over Harrigan's face and he began to choke. Hutch tightened his grip on the man's neck and kicked harder. Hutch's kicks were more efficient than Bird's and he realised he'd make better progress on his own.

'Bird, you look after yourself,' Hutch said. 'I can handle him.'

Bird immediately let go of the Irishman and began to breast stroke towards the bank, which was now only fifty

482

feet away. Hutch took a quick backwards look. Winter was already clambering out of the water.

'Soon be there, Ray,' Hutch said encouragingly. 'Try to relax.' To Hutch's surprise, Harrigan did as he was told and lay limply in the water. The searchlight beam flashed across them but it didn't return and when Hutch finally felt the slippery riverbed under his feet the bank was in darkness.

Hutch struggled to his feet, supporting Harrigan under his arms. Bird slithered across the mud and together they pulled the Irishman into the undergrowth. All three men lay on their backs, gasping for breath. In the distance they heard the rattle of gunfire but no bullets came their way. Harrigan rolled on to his front and began to vomit. Hutch patted him on the back. He heard the rustle of bushes being pushed apart and a figure stumbled towards them. Hutch lifted his foot defensively, ready to lash out, but he realised it was Winter.

'Well done, old lad,' Winter whispered. He touched Bird lightly on the shoulder. 'You okay, Bird?'

Bird opened his eyes. 'Right as rain,' he said. He grinned. 'English humour, right?'

'Almost,' said Winter. He knelt down beside Harrigan, who was still spewing up yellowish liquid. 'That's it, Ray. Better out than in.'

'How did they miss us?' asked Bird. 'They had us right in their sights.'

'Just be thankful they did,' said Winter.

Hutch got to his feet, his wet clothes sticking like a second skin. 'Is Nung here?'

Winter gestured with his thumb. 'This way. He's not a happy bunny. We're about half a mile away from where we're supposed to be and we're going to have to hurry.'

CHAU-LING WAS SITTING WITH her head in her hands when Colonel Suphat appeared at the entrance to the tent. He seemed agitated and went over to the filing cabinet and poured himself a large measure of whisky without asking if anyone else wanted a drink. Tim Carver stood up. He dropped the butt of his cigarette on to the floor and ground it out with his foot as he waited for the soldier to speak.

'I am afraid it is a case of good news and bad news, Miss Tsang,' he said slowly, his French accent less pronounced than before.

Chau-ling said nothing. She remained seated and looked up at the Colonel, expectantly. Ricky Lim stood behind her, his arms folded and his face impassive. He had barely moved during the five hours that they'd been in the tent.

'There was an attempt made to cross the river tonight,' said the Colonel. 'So your information was correct. We have apprehended the boatman and the vessel they used.' He paused, swirling the whisky around his glass and staring at it as if hoping to find some relief from the embarrassment he was clearly feeling. 'Unfortunately, the men on board managed to elude our launch. They have crossed into Myanmar.' He drank from the glass, a swift movement that was almost robotic, but didn't swallow immediately. He rolled the liquid around his tongue several times, then tilted his head back as he swallowed.

'Thank you for trying, Colonel Suphat,' said Chau-ling. She turned to Lim and spoke to him in Cantonese, then she asked Carver to wait outside for a few minutes.

Carver nodded and the two men left the tent.

Chau-ling smiled at the Colonel. 'Suppose that someone wished to follow the men, Colonel Suphat. How would such a person do that?'

'That would be difficult, Miss Tsang. Not to say illegal.' For the first time he met her glance.

'Of course, but hypothetically speaking?'

'One would need a guide. Someone familiar with the area. And a boat. But neither would be a problem in Fang. You . . . I mean such a person . . . would have to hire someone. I, of course, could not allow one of my men . . .'

'Of course,' said Chau-ling. 'But suppose such a person were to attempt a crossing tonight?'

'Ah,' said the Colonel, as if only just getting the point. 'That would not be a problem. I have already ordered my men to withdraw from the area. And the launch is needed elsewhere.' He drained his glass and went over to the filing cabinet to pour another. 'May I offer you a drink?' he asked.

'Thank you,' she said.

He refilled his glass and poured her a large measure of Red Label. He smiled benignly as he handed her the whisky. 'I would warn you, Miss Tsang, and I mean you as opposed to the hypothetical person to whom we were referring, that the Golden Triangle is a very dangerous place. Be careful.'

She took the glass and toasted him. 'Don't worry, Colonel Suphat,' she said. 'I will.'

HUTCH SHIFTED UNCOMFORTABLY IN his saddle. The horse he was sitting on wasn't much bigger than a donkey and it had a jerky walk that meant he could never relax. He looked over at Winter and grimaced. 'How come you get the big horse, Billy?'

'Rank has its privileges. Anyway, you're a dog man, right?'

'Yeah, I should just be grateful that you didn't give me a St Bernard.' Hutch looked over his shoulder. Harrigan was sitting slumped in the saddle. His horse wasn't much bigger than Hutch's. Harrigan gave Hutch a half-wave. Bird was bringing up the rear and seemed to be having a hard time keeping up.

They were winding their way along a trail through thick jungle. Dawn was just about to break and the tree canopy was full of bird song. Something small settled on Hutch's neck and he slapped it. They had been riding for the best part of six hours, stopping only to allow the horses to rest. Nung, the Thai who'd taken them across the river, had handed them over to a Burmese guide, a short, bow-legged man in his early sixties who was wearing camouflage fatigues and had a rifle slung over his shoulders. He hadn't said a word to the Westerners; he'd simply pointed to the horses and grunted. By the time Hutch, Winter, Harrigan and Bird had mounted, the Burmese guide was already riding off down the trail.

'How much longer to the camp?' asked Hutch.

'A day. Depends.' Winter ducked as a huge dragonfly

sped by, its shiny purple body as long as a man's hand.

'Depends? On what?'

'Zhou has got several camps, he moves between them. I don't even know which one we're going to.'

'What's he like, this Zhou?'

Winter grinned. 'He's difficult to describe. He's what you might call a character.' Winter's horse stumbled and he pulled back on the reins to steady it. 'But make no mistake about it, Hutch, he's a vicious bastard. Be careful what you say around him.'

TSANG CHAU-LING STEPPED OFF the boat and slipped on the bank, falling on to her hands and knees. 'Careful,' said Carver behind her.

'I didn't do it deliberately, Tim,' she said coolly. She clambered up the bank and wiped her hands on her trousers. The clothes she was wearing were too large, but they were all that Carver's guide had managed to find late at night. The boots she had on were several sizes too big but she'd put on three pairs of socks and they didn't rub too much.

Ricky Lim followed her up the bank, a look of disgust on his face. He and Chau-ling had had a furious argument earlier that evening, and the bodyguard was still bristling. Lim had at first refused to go with her and had threatened to call her father but Chau-ling had told him that if he did that then she would leave him behind. Lim had been furious, but eventually he'd had to admit defeat.

Tim and the guide he'd picked up in Fang climbed out of the long-tailed boat and it sped away back to the Thai side of the river. The guide was a thin man with gaunt features, called Home. The DEA agent said he was one of the best guides in northern Thailand and that most of his family still lived in Myanmar. Colonel Suphat had given them a map showing where Hutch had crossed the border and Carver and Home studied it in the moonlight.

Lim loomed over Chau-ling. 'It's not too late to change your mind,' he said.

'I can't,' she said.

'I don't understand why you're doing this,' he said.

Chau-ling bit her lower lip. She hadn't told the bodyguard why she and Carver were so desperate to reach Hutch, and she thought it best not to enlighten him. 'I'm sorry, Ricky. I really am. But I have to go after him. If you want, you can go back. You can wait for me in Fang.'

Lim barely managed to suppress a sneer. 'Do you have any idea what your father would do if I let you go in alone?' he said.

Chau-ling looked away. She knew. Lim stood glaring at her until Carver came over. 'Ready?' he asked.

Chau-ling nodded. Lim grunted.

'Home can get us horses from a village about a mile away. He reckons he knows which trail they've taken and he's a good tracker. They won't know they're being followed so they probably won't be hurrying.'

'You think we can catch them before they get to Zhou's camp?' asked Chau-ling.

'I hope so,' said Carver. 'Come on, Home is getting nervous.'

JAKE GREGORY STRETCHED OUT his legs and rubbed the back of his neck, kneading the tense muscles with his knuckles. He hadn't slept for more than twenty-four hours and he didn't intend to rest until the operation was over. He drained his can of Diet Coke and tossed it into the metal wastepaper basket. It was the sixth can he'd drunk during the night, for the caffeine rather than the taste.

Gregory was sitting at a field desk, on which were a radio transmitter and a map of the Golden Triangle in a clear plastic case. He stood up and did a few stretching exercises, then went to the tent flap and stared at the reddening sky. There were still a few stars visible directly overhead but the moon had disappeared. Gregory gazed up into the heavens. Somewhere up there was the satellite that was keeping a watch over the Golden Triangle, scanning for the frequency of the beacon carried by Tim Carver's mule. The satellite was being monitored by the National Imagery Office in the Pentagon, acting under instructions from the Vice President, and as soon as the beacon was located a man in the Pentagon would radio Gregory, who would send the Apaches on their way. Gregory looked at his watch, then turned to stare at the transmitter on his desk, willing it to burst into life.

There was a pattering sound on the roof of the tent as if someone was throwing small stones at the canvas. The noise became louder and more insistent and soon the rain was a solid sheet of water beating down on the tent. Gregory closed the flap and went back to his desk.

THE RAIN CAME DOWN in an incessant stream so that it felt to Hutch as if he were riding underwater. His horse kept its head down and its ears back and tested the trail with each step as if it feared that the path would be washed away in the downpour. Hutch couldn't see for more than fifty feet ahead of him and he followed the horse's example and kept his head down.

They left the jungle and rode across a field of burned vegetation, the soil turned into a liquid black mess by the rain. The field sloped sharply to the right and the rainwater cascaded down to the valley below. The guide took them up to the crest of the hill and they followed the ridge towards another thickly wooded area.

Hutch stood in his stirrups to take the weight off his aching backside, then sat down again. The horse grunted its disapproval. He could feel the transmitter against his stomach. He still hadn't decided whether or not he was going to activate it. He didn't believe that Tim Carver would come up with the half a million dollars; he had only brought money into the equation to convince the DEA agent that he was co-operating. Hutch couldn't care less about the money, all he wanted was to get out of his present predicament in one piece and to be allowed to start a new life. Whether that new start came from Tim Carver or Billy Winter made no difference to him.

The rain stopped as quickly as it had begun. Hutch's horse shook its head and snorted. Hutch patted it on the neck. The guide spurred his horse on now that visibility had improved.

Eventually the trees began to thin out and the vegetation on the ground became less dense, then they emerged on to a hillside which had been planted with crops. The fields were dotted with tree stumps, and women in black jackets and wide-brimmed straw hats tended whatever vegetables it was that they were growing. The women paid them no attention as they rode up to the brow of the hill.

In the distance, Hutch saw a village: a scattering of wooden and straw huts on stilts at the edge of the tree line. A group of naked children were chasing a chicken through a patch of mud, laughing and shrieking in their excitement. They stopped when they saw the men on horses. For a few seconds they froze, then they turned and ran into one of the huts.

The guide took them through a rectangular archway built of wooden posts covered with carvings. It was about nine feet high and nine feet wide.

'Don't touch it,' said Bird from behind Hutch. 'It's a spirit gate.'

Hutch looked at the carvings. There were birds, animals, fruit, and, incongruously, two AK-47s. On one end of the crossbar was a carved man's face, with a woman's face at the other end. At the base of the gate were baskets and earthenware pots and rough wooden statues of a man and a woman with grotesquely exaggerated sexual organs.

'The Akha people believe that the gate keeps out everything bad,' said Bird. 'It's sacred.'

They rode through the gate and by a fenced-off area containing half a dozen sickly pigs. They dismounted in front of one of the huts, tethered their horses and went inside.

An old woman in a black skirt and a brightly embroidered

jacket was sitting on a bed which was little more than a layer of logs with a thin mattress over it. Spread out on a low table in front of her was a meal: a wooden bowl of sticky rice, roasted ears of corn, smoked fish and bananas. The guide motioned with his hand that the men were to eat. They sat down around the table and helped themselves.

As they devoured the meal, the old woman took a three-foot-long bamboo tube from a hook on the wall. She opened a small metal tin and took out a ball of a sticky, black substance. It was opium, Hutch realised. As he swallowed handfuls of rice he watched the old woman prepare her opium and put her mouth over the open end of the pipe. The sickly-sweet smell filled the hut and she exhaled with a dreamy look on her face.

Harrigan watched her, enthralled. 'Hey, Billy . . .' he began.

'No,' said Winter.

'You don't know . . .'

'Don't even think about it,' said Winter. 'I've got to deliver you back home in good condition, Ray. And that means no dope.'

'It's only smoke,' protested Harrigan.

'It's opium,' said Winter. 'And opium is just one step away from heroin.'

'When did you join the anti-drug squad?' sneered Harrigan.

'Selling is one thing; using is another. Only dickheads use it, Ray. You should remember that.'

Harrigan said nothing. He continued to eat but kept his eyes on the old woman as she smoked.

SMOKE FROM CARVER'S CIGARETTE blew across Chau-ling's face and she coughed pointedly. 'Sorry,' said the DEA agent. He flicked the half-smoked Marlboro into a muddy puddle. It had stopped raining two hours earlier but they still wore the green plastic ponchos that Home had given them. The jungle was steaming around them and water still dripped from the tree canopy overhead. Home had dismounted and was talking to a group of hilltribe women in black jackets and wide trousers with baskets filled with firewood on their backs. One of the women pointed off to the west, smiling broadly.

'Do you think we'll find them?' asked Chau-ling.

'Having second thoughts?' said Carver.

'Absolutely not.'

'Home knows what he's doing. He's over here every week or so.'

'He's a smuggler?'

'He's a businessman who does occasional favours for the DEA.'

Chau-ling looked at him, her eyes narrowed almost to slits. 'You don't care who you use, do you?'

Carver looked stung by her remark. 'Hey, I'm here with you, aren't I? I'm trying to put this right.'

'Okay, but your organisation uses people, doesn't it?'

'They do what they have to do to get the job done.'

Home left the women and climbed back on to his horse. He rode over to Carver and they spoke in Thai. 'They're about three hours ahead of us,' Carver told Chau-ling.

'They must have stopped for a while. If we keep up the pace, we should catch them by this evening.'

Home moved off down the trail and Carver, Chau-ling and Lim followed him. Chau-ling drew up next to Carver and they rode side by side. 'You're not getting away that easily, Mr DEA Agent. You didn't answer my question. What gives you the right to use men like Hutch?'

'We have to fight fire with fire.'

'That's a cliché, and it's not even an appropriate one. Hutch isn't part of the problem, it's nothing to do with him. This man Winter was using him, and now you're doing the same. It's not fair.'

Carver smiled and shook his head in wonder. 'How old are you, Chau-ling?'

'Why?' she asked, defensively.

'Because you're old enough to know better, that's why. Life isn't fair. If it was, the warlords of the Golden Triangle and the cocaine cartels of South America wouldn't be flooding America with drugs. You don't beat these people by playing by the rules.'

Chau-ling opened her mouth to reply, but before she could speak a shot rang out and the guide pitched backwards off his horse. Chau-ling's mount reared and she toppled from her saddle. She hit the ground hard and the fall knocked the breath out of her. Her frightened horse galloped off through the trees. There were more shots in the distance, louder than the first one.

Ricky Lim jumped off his horse and ran over to her. He knelt by her side and looked down at her. 'Are you hurt?' he asked.

'Just winded,' she gasped. 'What . . . ?'

A large chunk of Lim's head exploded in a shower of

red and he fell across her chest. Warm blood trickled over Chau-Ling's face and she screamed. Lim's body trembled and then went still. Chau-ling pushed him off her and rolled away, still screaming. She scrambled to her feet and looked frantically around.

Tim Carver was still on his horse but he'd dropped the reins and was sitting with his hands up in surrender. Three men in jungle fatigues had surrounded him. They jabbed at him with the barrels of their rifles as they shouted at him in a language she didn't recognise. The horse was scared, its ears were back and its eyes were wide and staring.

Chau-ling backed away, then turned and began to run, panting in terror. She looked over her shoulder. One of the men fired, shooting Carver's horse at point-blank range. The horse dropped where it stood and Carver fell to the side, one of his legs trapped under the dead animal.

Chau-ling tripped and staggered against a tree. The men were kicking Carver, screaming at him with every blow. He curled up to protect himself, his arms up around his head. Chau-ling knew there was nothing she could do to help him; all she could do was to try to save herself and to go for help. She pushed herself away from the tree, then froze. There were two men standing behind her, wearing the same sort of fatigues as the ones who were kicking Carver. One of them pointed his rifle at her face and said something to her. She raised her hands slowly. The other man grinned and stepped forward. He raised the butt of his weapon and slammed it against the side of her head. She fell without a sound.

THE SKY WAS DARKENING when Hutch saw the compound for the first time. They'd been accompanied by Zhou's men for the previous hour, hard-faced men in camouflage fatigues carrying M16s. The men had appeared from out of the jungle without a word and had kept their distance. They joined the convoy in ones and twos until there were a dozen of them, walking with almost no sound through the undergrowth.

'Don't look at them,' said Winter out of the corner of his mouth. 'Pretend they're not there.'

Hutch followed Winter's instructions, but it was difficult to ignore the men. Most of them had their fingers on the triggers of their weapons and Hutch doubted that they had their safety catches on. He fixed his eyes on the compound gates. Around the compound was a fence of sharpened bamboo stakes. Its entrance was guarded by two men wearing sarong-style trousers and camouflage jackets. To the right of the main gate were three wooden stakes, and Hutch saw with horror that there were bodies impaled on two of them, decomposed bodies that had been ravaged by birds and insects until they were virtually unrecognisable as human. The third stake was topped by a gleaming white skull.

He twisted around in his saddle. Harrigan was staring open mouthed at the grisly remains.

'Don't stare,' hissed Winter.

'Billy, what the hell have you got us into?' said Hutch.

'Relax. He's on our side,' replied Winter.

They passed through the gate and by a group of huts made from wooden planks with thatched roofs. Men in camouflage uniforms were lounging on small stools in front of the huts. Several were stripping down and oiling guns. They all looked up to watch the riders go by.

The largest building was in the centre of the compound. It was built on thick wooden stilts and had the relative luxury of a corrugated-iron roof. Nung led them behind the building to a corral where they dismounted and tied up their horses. Two small boys rushed forward with buckets of water which they poured into a wooden trough. Hutch stopped to admire a huge white horse.

'That's Zhou's,' said Winter. 'Watch it, it's mean.'

Hutch walked slowly towards the animal. It snorted menacingly and stamped its hoofs, but Hutch spoke to it softly and reached out his hand. The horse eyed him warily but allowed Hutch to pat it gently on the flanks. 'He's a softie,' whispered Hutch. 'A big softie.'

'Yeah, well, let's see how you get on with its owner,' said Winter.

Nung went off to one of the thatched huts while Winter led Hutch, Harrigan and Bird to the front of the large building. Two men with rifles were standing guard at the bottom of the steps leading up to the entrance, and barred their way.

'Bird, tell them to be nice,' said Winter.

Before Bird could speak, music blared from inside the building. It was several bars before Hutch recognised the tune. It was Billy Ray Cyrus singing 'Achy Breaky Heart'. Hutch looked across at Winter in amazement.

'He's a country and western fan,' said Winter. 'Don't ask me why.'

The music suddenly increased in volume, so much so that the metal roof began to vibrate. Zhou Yuanyi appeared at the top of the steps. For a moment he didn't see the three visitors, and stared out over the compound, his hands on his hips. He was wearing black jodhpurs, riding boots and a white silk shirt and his eyes were hidden behind Ray-Ban sunglasses. His right foot was tapping to the music, but it stopped dead when he noticed the four men staring up at him. He disappeared back into the building and seconds later the stereo was switched off. Zhou reappeared and shouted down at the guards, who stepped aside, and Winter led Bird, Harrigan and Hutch up the steps.

'Billy, my friend,' said Zhou. 'You had a safe journey, I hope?'

'Uneventful,' said Winter. He made no move to shake hands. Instead he put his hands together and gave him a wai. Bird and Harrigan did the same. Zhou returned the gesture, Hutch stood with his arms folded. Zhou wasn't a big man; he was slightly overweight with a chubby face and soft, baby-like skin. He reminded Hutch of a boy he'd known at school, a boy who was always eating sweets and always had a note from his mother to excuse him from gym class. It was hard to believe that this was one of the most powerful warlords in the Golden Triangle.

If Zhou was offended by Hutch's reluctance to wai him, he didn't show it. He gave him a beaming smile. 'You must be Hutch. Billy has told me a lot about you.'

'Not too much, I hope.'

'That you were the only man who could get Ray out of Klong Prem. And he was right.'

'I did have an incentive,' said Hutch.

'Sit, sit,' said Zhou, waving them inside to cushions

scattered around the teak floor. Zhou sat on a teak bench so that they all had to look up at him. He had a large handgun in a holster in the small of his back, an ornate weapon with carving on the barrel and strips of mother-of-pearl on the handle. An elderly servant in white jacket and black pants brought in a bottle of whisky and five glasses and they toasted each other. The servant switched on two standard lamps at either end of the room then left them alone.

'First we shall drink, then you can shower, and then we shall eat,' said Zhou. 'Then I have planned a little entertainment.'

'Entertainment?' asked Winter.

'Not girls, Billy. Not girls.' Zhou roared with laughter. 'I have never met a man with such an appetite for girls,' he said to Hutch. 'He is a terrible man.'

'Terrible,' agreed Hutch.

Zhou waved his tumbler of whisky at Winter. 'Two of my men were caught stealing from me. I have been waiting for your arrival so that I can deal with them.' He laughed again. Winter laughed too, but he gave Hutch a quick sidelong glance and Hutch could see that the laughter was forced.

'So, Hutch, do you like country music?' asked Zhou.

Hutch shrugged.

'Billy Ray Cyrus is a great favourite of mine. Do you like Billy Ray Cyrus?'

Hutch shrugged again. He couldn't think of anything to say. 'How long will we stay here?' he asked.

'A few days,' said Zhou. 'A week at most. A man is coming from Yangon with the paperwork. He will take photographs for your new passports, then he will go to Bangkok to process them.'

'What sort of passports?' asked Hutch.

'British. American. Whatever you wish.'

'It's that simple?'

'We have contacts in most embassies in Bangkok. It will not be a problem. My man will then get you the requisite visa in Yangon, and you can leave on a scheduled flight to anywhere in the world.'

'I told you it wouldn't be a problem,' said Winter. He patted Harrigan on the back. 'You'll be back in Ireland before you know it, Ray.'

Hutch got to his feet and put his untouched whisky on a side table. 'Is there a toilet I can use?' he asked.

Zhou clapped his hands and the old servant appeared. 'He will show you where it is,' said Zhou. 'It is primitive, I'm afraid.'

Hutch followed the old man down the steps and around the side of the building. They walked by a water tower from which several hosepipes ran to various parts of the compound. The latrine building was a wooden hut with a bamboo door at one end. The old man pointed to it and shuffled back to the main building.

The smell assailed Hutch's nostrils as he opened the door. The toilet was even more basic than the facilities he'd had to use in Klong Prem. There was a large hole in the ground, a pit about three feet wide and twelve feet long, over which had been placed a number of roughly hewn planks, and a tin bath filled with water.

Hutch stood on two of the planks and urinated into the pit. The smell was nauseating and Hutch held his breath. He zipped up his fly, lifted his sweatshirt and peeled the sticking plaster off his stomach. He held the transmitter in his hands for a second or two, wondering if he was doing the right thing. He didn't owe Tim Carver any favours, and the DEA agent had been as ruthless as Billy Winter in forcing Hutch to do what he wanted. But whereas Hutch and Billy had a history, he knew nothing about Carver.

'Better the devil I know,' Hutch said to himself. He dropped the transmitter into the hole. It floated on the brown, crusty surface, then slowly dipped sideways and disappeared into the foul-smelling mess. The surface bubbled and plopped and then went still.

Hutch washed his hands in the tin bath and then went back outside and began to walk around the compound. The sun had almost gone down and oil lamps were being lit and hung from the roofs of the huts. The electricity supplied by the generator was confined to Zhou's building, to power his lights, fans, refrigerator and stereo.

At the far end of the compound was a wooden hut with a barred door. There were two men standing inside, with their hands in the air. Hutch frowned, wondering what they were doing. He walked towards the bars. As he got closer he could see that their hands were chained to a rafter and that they were having to stand on tiptoe to take the weight off their arms. They looked up anxiously as Hutch approached, then seemed relieved when they saw that he wasn't one of their captors. Hutch realised that they must be the entertainment promised by Zhou. He shuddered as he remembered the impaled bodies at the entrance to the compound. The men began to shout in their own language, obviously imploring him to help. He backed away. No matter what fate Zhou had in store for them, there was nothing he could do.

Zhou's stereo started up again, Billy Ray Cyrus at full volume. By the time Hutch got to the front of Zhou's building, Zhou, Winter, Harrigan and Bird were standing at the entrance. Zhou had his gun in his hand and he raised it skywards. He pulled the trigger and the shot echoed around the compound. To Hutch's amazement fifty of Zhou's men rushed forward and formed into ranks as if they were on parade, but almost immediately they began to line-dance to the record, clapping their hands and stamping their feet in time with the music. Hutch watched open mouthed. Zhou stood with his hands on his hips, grinning at the display and nodding his appreciation. Despite the gathering gloom, he was still wearing his Ray-Bans.

SHE WAS LYING FACE down and something was banging against her stomach. There was a strong smell, a smell she remembered from her childhood. Her pony, the pony her father had bought her for her tenth birthday. Robbie, it was called. It had died when she was fifteen and she'd cried for a month. Tsang Chau-ling opened her eyes. Her hands had been tied with rough rope and she couldn't move her legs. She had a throbbing headache. She looked to her right, past the rear of the mule they'd tied her to. Three men were walking in single file, their rifles held close to their chests, and behind them was another mule. All she could see was a vague shape slung across the mule's back but she knew it must be Tim Carver. She turned her head the other way, wincing from the pain. Ahead of her were another five men, one of them with a radio strapped to his back and a short antenna wobbling above his head.

'Water,' she said. She repeated the request in Cantonese,

louder this time. She wracked her brains for the Thai word
for water but then remembered that she was in Burma and
they probably wouldn't understand anyway. One of the
men walked up to her. All she could see was his boots
and camouflage trousers so she twisted her neck to look
up at him. 'Water,' she gasped. The man smiled showing
several broken teeth. He lifted his rifle and smacked the
butt against the back of her head.

THE OLD MAN BEGAN clearing away the plates while
Zhou poured himself a large measure of brandy and
handed the bottle to Winter. Hutch sat back in his chair
and looked across the table at Harrigan. The Irishman
seemed as perplexed as Hutch at their surroundings. They
were sitting at a long table which had been covered with
a red cloth on which were three silver candelabras with
burning candles. The meal they had eaten – several
varieties of meat curry, rice and slices of roast pig
– had been served on fine china that wouldn't have
been out of place in a five-star hotel; the wine was an
excellent claret which they drank from crystal goblets,
and the cutlery was solid silver. It was hard to believe
that they were in the jungle hundreds of miles from the
nearest city.

Winter passed the brandy to Hutch but he shook his
head. 'Take it,' hissed Winter.

Hutch did as he was told. Even though Winter was
smiling and laughing throughout the meal, Hutch could
see that he was tense and taking care not to offend their

host. Hutch poured brandy into his glass and then gave the bottle to Harrigan.

'So, Ray, how does it feel to be a free man?' asked Zhou.

Harrigan shrugged. He seemed to be having trouble speaking and had said only a few words throughout the meal. 'Okay. I guess.'

Zhou turned his attention to Hutch. The flickering candles were reflected in the lenses of his Ray-Bans. 'So tell me, Hutch, how did you escape from Klong Prem?'

Hutch explained how he'd switched the two prisoners and how Bird and his men had attacked the coach on the drive to the courthouse. Zhou seemed fascinated by Hutch's ability to pick locks and he asked for a demonstration. He ordered a padlock to be brought to the table and asked Hutch what else he needed.

'Paperclips,' said Hutch. 'Or any piece of wire if it's thin enough.'

'I have paperclips,' said Zhou. He went over to an ornate desk in the corner of the room and returned with a handful. He stood over Hutch and watched as he picked the lock. It took Hutch thirty seconds of careful probing before he handed the open padlock to Zhou. Zhou held up the lock for everyone to see. 'Incredible,' he said. 'And you can pick any lock?'

'Most. Given enough time.'

Zhou went back to his seat. 'And how did you learn such a skill?' he asked, pouring himself another large measure of brandy.

'I was a locksmith. A long time ago.'

Zhou sniffed his brandy appreciatively, then gulped it down like a ravenous dog, draining his glass in two swallows. He licked his lips. 'And how did a locksmith end up in a British prison?'

'It's a part of my past that I don't like to think about,' said Hutch.

Winter stiffened and he flashed Hutch a warning look.

'But I'd like you to tell me anyway,' said Zhou, his voice cold and flat. He bared his teeth in a semblance of a smile. 'If you would be so kind.'

Hutch stared at Zhou for several seconds, then he nodded. 'I had a partner. He let me down.'

'How?'

'We installed a security system at a stately home in Sussex, real state-of-the-art stuff. Six months later they were robbed, and whoever did it knew their way around the system. They knew where the sensors were, where the cameras were, everything. It had to have been an inside job. Then the police searched our warehouse and found a painting. My partner fingered me.'

'Fingered?' repeated Zhou.

'Blamed,' explained Hutch. 'He said I did it.'

'And they believed him?'

Hutch shrugged. 'He was very persuasive.'

'But surely they would have discovered the truth eventually?'

'Maybe. But by then it was too late.' Hutch took a deep breath. He didn't want to continue but Zhou was leaning forward, eager for details. 'They put me in a prison on remand, until the trial. Three guys attacked me in the showers. For my phonecards.' He saw Zhou frown. 'Plastic cards that allow you to make phone calls. They're a sort of currency in prison.'

'And what happened?'

'They attacked me with a knife. I defended myself. One of them died. The other two guys lied, they said I'd attacked them.'

'And the authorities believed them?'

'It was two against one. I got twenty-five years. For something I didn't do.'

Winter chuckled. 'Parkhurst was full of innocent men,' he said.

'What do you mean?' asked Zhou.

'It's a saying we had. No one ever admits to being guilty in prison. Unless they're up for parole.'

'It was an accident, Billy,' said Hutch. 'He came at me with a knife. I didn't mean to kill him.'

'I'm not talking about that,' said Winter. 'I'm talking about the robbery. The stately home. The robbery you always said you weren't involved in.'

'It wasn't me. It was my partner.'

Winter helped himself to another brandy. 'Let me ask you something, Hutch. Something I've always wanted to know.' He paused and sipped his brandy before continuing. 'When you escaped from Parkhurst, after everyone thought you were dead, how did you pay for your passport? Where did you get the money from to start again?'

'I had money.'

Winter shook his head. The old servant appeared with a box of cigars and offered one to Zhou. He took one and used a silver cigar cutter to snip off the end as he listened intently to the conversation.

'But you couldn't use your bank accounts, could you? That would have proved that you were still alive. The cops would have been all over you.' The servant offered the box of cigars to Winter and he took his time selecting one. He rolled it between his fingers, then bit off the end savagely, like a cat killing a mouse. 'So where did you get the money from, old lad?'

'I forget.'

Winter screwed up his face as if he'd smelled something bad. 'I know you inside out, Hutch. I know you better than you know yourself.'

'So you keep saying. Can we change the subject?'

'You did the robbery, Hutch. We both know you did. And instead of admitting it you've been punishing yourself ever since.'

'You're full of shit.'

'Am I? Look at the new life you made for yourself. Dogs in cages. With exercise runs. A security gate. Closed-circuit television. Don't you see it, Hutch? You built your own prison. Just like I did. I bought my big house and I sit in one tiny room. You escaped and ran straight into a prison of your own making.'

'No,' said Hutch quickly. 'We're not the same.' Winter laughed dryly. The sound annoyed Hutch more than the man's words. 'Fuck you, Billy.'

They were interrupted by the sound of clapping. It was Zhou, standing at the head of the table and applauding the two of them. 'Excellent entertainment, gentlemen,' he said. 'Excellent. But I think I can do better. Come with me, outside.'

The men got up from the table and followed Zhou to the door. Zhou shouted commands and half a dozen men ran off. They reappeared with the two prisoners whom Hutch had seen earlier. They were shaking with fright. One of them had wet himself.

'Billy, do we have to watch this?' asked Hutch.

'We do exactly what he wants,' whispered Winter.

'He's going to kill them.'

'Eventually, yes.'

Zhou marched down the steps, his riding boots clicking on the hard wood. His men grabbed the prisoners and half-dragged, half-carried them to the entrance to the compound.

Winter, Hutch, Harrigan and Bird followed apprehensively. More of Zhou's men emerged from their huts carrying blazing torches. Soon there were more than a hundred men following Zhou as he strode out of the compound.

Two wooden poles had been prepared, each more than twenty feet long and sharpened to a point at one end. The two prisoners knew what was going to happen and they began to scream for mercy. Hutch and Harrigan stayed at the back of the crowd.

Harrigan was shaking. 'What's he going to do?' he asked.

'Impale them,' said Hutch.

'Jesus Christ.'

They looked on in horror as the pointed stakes were pressed against the men's stomachs. Ropes were used to bind the men to the poles, then, when Zhou raised his arm, the poles were swung upwards. Both men screamed in pain as their own bodyweight forced them down on the spikes. Their legs kicked, but the more they wriggled the more they impaled themselves. Harrigan put his hands over his ears trying to blot out the noise.

The poles were slotted into holes in the ground and earth shovelled in. Blood dripped down the stakes as the men's cries began to fade. After a few minutes they were both still, their hands and feet pointing towards the ground.

'Are they dead?' asked Harrigan, taking his hands away from his ears.

'I don't think so,' said Hutch. 'I think it's going to take a while.'

Harrigan shuddered and turned away. 'He's crazy, isn't he?'

'I'd say that was a pretty accurate assessment, Ray.'

One of Zhou's men pointed down the hillside and shouted something. A convoy of uniformed men and mules was approaching. 'Now what?' asked Winter.

The new arrivals came along the trail and up to the compound. The leader was a stocky soldier with a leather jacket and a brand-new M16 slung over his shoulder. He went up to Zhou and began talking earnestly to him. Zhou slapped him on the back and walked over to one of the mules. His men gathered around him.

There was something tied across the back of the mule. Hutch moved forward to get a better look. It was a body, the hands and feet tied with ropes.

'What is it?' asked Harrigan.

'Another victim, I reckon,' replied Hutch.

Zhou reached down and grabbed the hair of whoever was tied to the mule. He pulled the head up, grinning cruelly. Hutch caught his breath as he saw who it was. Chau-ling. He took a step backwards as if he'd been struck in the chest.

JAKE GREGORY TAPPED HIS fingers on the field desk. He looked at his wristwatch for the thousandth time. There was a quiet cough at the entrance to his tent. Gregory looked up. It was Peter Burden. The pilot nodded at the radio receiver on Gregory's desk.

'What's it they say, a watched pot never boils?' he said.

'That's crap. Any pot will boil eventually.' Gregory gestured at the radio. 'But I'm starting to wonder if I'll ever hear from my man in the NIO.'

'Me and the boys were planning a poker game. Do you wanna make up a five?'

Gregory cracked his knuckles. 'Nothing I'd like better, but I've got to stay close to this baby. Once the transmitter goes off, I've no idea how long it'll stay on.'

'Because of the battery?'

Gregory shook his head. 'Because I don't know how long it'll be before Zhou Yuanyi discovers what's happening. If he finds the transmitter . . .' He left the sentence unfinished.

'We were wondering,' said Burden. 'The guy that activates the beacon. Does he know what's going to happen when he presses the button?'

Gregory looked at the pilot with unblinking eyes. 'Enjoy your game, son.'

Burden turned and went back outside. Gregory began tapping his fingers on the desk again.

HUTCH CLOSED THE LATRINE door. An oil lamp was hanging from the rafters in the centre of the room and it cast a flickering shadow against the wooden walls as Hutch walked towards the foul-smelling pit. His mind was filled with visions of Chau-ling meeting the same fate as the two men Hutch had seen killed: impaled on a stake, screaming for her life. Hutch knew that he had to do something. He had to get help, and there was only one way he could do it. He had to summon the DEA's helicopters and hope that they would get to the camp in time to rescue them.

He knelt down beside the pit and stripped off his sweatshirt. He turned his head to the side as he plunged his arm into the brown, treacly mess. His stomach heaved and he tried to think of something else as he groped around in the faeces. His arm went in all the way up to his shoulder and he still hadn't touched the bottom. The smell was a hundred times worse now that he'd disturbed the surface and as he slowly withdrew his arm the liquid sucked at his flesh with a loud slurping noise. Hutch stood up. He held his arm to the side as he went over to the tin bath where he washed his arm and then stripped off the rest of his clothes.

He went back to the pit and took a deep breath before lowering himself in. It clung to him, wet and cold and lumpy, and he tried to distance himself from what he was doing because if he thought about it he knew he'd be sick. He held on to one of the planks and felt around with his feet, his toes squelching on the solid matter at the bottom. The smell was worse than anything he'd ever smelled before, worse than anything he'd ever had to deal with in the kennels. He'd shovelled up more than his fair share of dog shit, but this was something else; this was human waste and his mind reeled with the awfulness of it. His right foot nudged against something and he screwed his toes around it and lifted. It slipped and he tried again, pushing the metal box against the side of the pit until he got it up to knee-height, then he reached down with his hand. It was the transmitter. He stripped off the shit-smeared plaster and pressed the button as Tim Carver had demonstrated. There was no click, no buzz, no sound or flashing light to let him know that the beacon had been activated, no way of knowing if it was working or not. He tossed the transmitter on to the ground and pulled himself out of the pit, gasping for breath.

HAL AUSTIN WAS HOLDING three queens and had just thrown ten dollars into the pot when Jake Gregory rushed into the tent. Austin and his three colleagues jumped to their feet, the poker game forgotten.

'It's on,' said Gregory.

Austin smiled tightly and nodded at the others. 'Rock and roll,' he said.

Gregory handed slips of paper to Warner and Lucarelli. 'These are the co-ordinates. I'll confirm over the radio once you're airborne.'

The four men headed outside. 'Good luck,' Gregory called after them.

It was a clear night with a quarter moon and myriad stars overhead. Austin jogged towards his Apache, Warner at his shoulder. 'Okay, Roger?' said Austin.

'Fine and dandy,' replied Warner. 'Nice night for it.'

They climbed over the Apache's starboard wing and into the cockpit, Austin taking the rear seat and Warner dropping into the co-pilot/gunner position. Warner's seat was some nineteen inches lower than the pilot's, giving Austin an unrestricted view, though the two cockpits were separated by a transparent acrylic blast barrier. Austin shut the cockpit windows and settled into his seat between lightweight boron armour shields. He flicked on his avionics switch. Green and orange lights illuminated the Apache's instruments. He slipped on his helmet and swung the radio mike up close to his lips. 'Check, check, check,' he said.

'Loud and clear,' said Warner.

They quickly ran through their pre-flight check list, then Warner used the data entry keypad to programme the internal navigation system and enter the laser codes that would help send the laser-guided Hellfire missiles to their target. As the gunner initiated the Apache's weapons systems, Austin looked over to his right, where the main rotor blades of Burden and Lucarelli's Apache had already started to spin. Austin started his own turbines.

Gregory's voice came over his headset. 'You're cleared for take-off,' he said.

Austin clicked his microphone switch. 'Cleared for take-off,' he acknowledged. He rotated the handgrip on his collective-pitch lever with his left hand. Above his head the rotors whirled faster and faster. He pulled the collective up, altering the pitch of the main rotors, and the Apache began to lift off the ground. Austin kept the helicopter within ground effect as he pushed the cyclic-pitch stick forward. The Apache's nose dipped down as it accelerated over the grass, towards the tree line. He pulled on the collective and increased the power and the helicopter leaped into the air like a thoroughbred eager for the off.

HUTCH COULDN'T GET THE smell of the pit off his skin no matter how many times he rinsed himself. He shuddered to think what diseases he could have picked up by immersing himself in human faeces. He used a plastic bowl to splash the last of the water in the tin bath over his legs and then shook himself dry as best he could before putting his clothes back on.

He slipped out of the latrine and headed for Zhou's building. No one saw him: almost all of Zhou's men had congregated at the front of the compound. He threw the transmitter under the building, close to one of the massive stilts. Carver had said that the satellite would pick up the signal to within ten feet, so he wanted it to be as close to Zhou as possible.

Hutch peered around the stilts. Half a dozen men were carrying Chau-ling's body towards the hut where he'd seen the two prisoners earlier in the evening. He ducked out of sight and watched from underneath the building as the men took Chau-ling inside the hut. A few minutes later they reappeared. He waited until they'd gone before dashing over to the hut and looking through the barred door. Chau-ling was hanging from the roof by her arms, unconscious.

'Chau-ling,' he hissed. There was no reaction. Her head was slumped down on her chest, her eyes closed. 'Chau-ling!' he said, louder this time. He looked around, but there was no one within earshot. 'Chau-ling!' There was still no reaction. Hutch examined the lock on the door. It was an old brass padlock, similar to the one that Zhou had given him to pick. Hutch checked his pockets but he had nothing he could use. He cursed and slapped the bars in frustration.

THE OLD WOMAN WOKE with a start. 'Grandmother, Grandmother,' said an urgent, frightened voice by her side. 'Wake up.'

The old woman licked her chapped lips. Her eyes felt gritty and her throat was sore and she could tell from the ache in her bones that she'd only been asleep for a few hours. 'Go to sleep, child,' she said.

'Ghosts,' said the little girl. 'Ghosts are coming.'

The old woman rolled over and blinked her eyes. 'What? What did you say?'

'Ghosts. Can't you hear them?'

'Child, what are you talking about?' The old woman strained to see her grand-daughter in the light of the flickering oil lamp that hung from the rafters of their hut.

The little girl knelt down beside the old woman. She was shaking. 'Can I sleep with you, Grandmother? Please.' Her voice trembled as much as her body.

Before the old woman could answer, the little girl threw herself on to the sleeping mat and slipped her arms around her grandmother's waist. The old woman raised her head. She could hear nothing out of the ordinary, just the wind rippling through the trees and the night-time insects buzzing and clicking. The little girl buried her face in the old woman's neck.

'I heard them,' she whispered. 'They flew through the air, like . . . like . . . like dragons.'

The old woman smoothed her hair and settled back on the sleeping mat. She was eighty years old but could remember when she too was frightened of ghosts.

WINTER LOOKED AT HUTCH as he walked into the room. 'Where've you been, old lad?' he asked.

Hutch patted his stomach. 'Tummy trouble,' he said.

Winter grinned wolfishly. 'That impaling business got to you, didn't it?'

'Something like that.'

Zhou and Bird were standing together with their backs to him. He walked over to the table. The plates had been taken away but the candles still burned in their candelabras and the wine and brandy glasses were still there. He stopped dead when he saw what Zhou and Bird were looking at. A man was sitting on the floor, his hands tied behind his back. It was Tim Carver. His hair was matted with blood and his left eye was swollen. Carver showed no recognition as he looked at Hutch. Zhou drew back his arm and slapped Carver, then backhanded him. The two slaps echoed like pistol shots. Hutch's mind whirled. What on earth were Carver and Chau-ling doing together, and what had prompted them to cross over into Burma? It made no sense, no sense at all. She was supposed to be back in Hong Kong. And Carver was supposed to be in Bangkok, waiting for Hutch to operate the beacon. How had the two of them got together, and what had possessed them to cross the border?

516

Winter waved a blue passport at Hutch. 'He's an American,' said Winter. 'And in this part of the world, a Yank means only one thing.'

'DEA?'

Winter made a gun with his hand and mimed shooting Hutch in the chest. 'Right first time, old lad.'

Zhou hit Carver again.

'What's the story?' asked Hutch.

'That's what we're trying to find out.'

Zhou took his gun from the holster in the small of his back and jammed it up against Carver's neck. 'Tell me why you are here,' he said, enunciating each word slowly and precisely.

Carver started coughing. He turned his head away. There was a gash on his right cheek, and scratches on his neck. Zhou turned the gun around and brought the butt down on the top of Carver's head with a sickening crunch. Carver slumped to the floor, unconscious. Zhou glared down at him, then slowly put his gun back in its holster. He strutted back to the table and sat down. 'Sit with me!' he boomed.

Winter, Hutch, Harrigan and Bird took their places around the table. Zhou passed the brandy bottle and one by one they refilled their glasses. Harrigan's hands were shaking and he spilled brandy on the tablecloth as he poured.

'I hate the Americans,' said Zhou. 'I hate their hypocrisy.' He looked around the table at his guests as if daring them to argue with him. 'They need me. They need me but they pretend that I'm public enemy number one.' The sunglasses came to bear on Hutch. Hutch could see himself reflected in the lenses of the impenetrable Ray-Bans. He smiled and nodded, wanting the man to keep on talking, even though he could make no sense of what he was saying.

'Last year the murder rate in New York City was half what it was in 1990,' Zhou said. 'Year on year there has been a twenty per cent fall in violent crime right across America. I read that in the *International Herald Tribune*. Do you read the *Tribune*, Hutch?'

Hutch shook his head. There were two paperclips on the table, close to the base of one of the candelabras.

'You should. You really should. It lets you know how America thinks.'

'I'll read it,' said Hutch. He rested his right arm on the table. The paperclips were only inches from his fingertips.

'Do you know why the crime rate is falling in America?' asked Zhou. They all shook their heads. He tapped his own chest. 'It's because of me. Because of the heroin that I send to America. Ten years ago it was crack cocaine that Americans used. Crack cocaine is a dangerous drug: it causes mood swings, it boosts aggression. A crack cocaine addict is a dangerous animal, Hutch, as dangerous as an injured tiger. But heroin, ah, heroin is different. Heroin is calming; a man on heroin doesn't go out and steal a car or mug a tourist: he sits and dreams. Heroin addicts still steal but they tend to do so without violence. And because I have kept the price down, fewer crimes are committed. I have done the United States a great service, yet they treat me as if I was a gangster. The Colombians, they are the real villains, they are the butchers.'

Zhou looked around the table again. His audience was transfixed. Hutch edged his hand forward and put it over the paperclips.

'Who here has ever taken heroin?' Zhou asked.

Harrigan raised his hand uncertainly. So did Bird.

'It is a harmless release, nothing more,' Zhou continued. 'It has been used as a medicine for centuries. You could use heroin for fifty years and suffer no ill effects. Hundreds of thousands die every year in America from lung cancer caused by smoking cigarettes. Smoking causes heart disease, and half a million die from that every year. Who dies from heroin? Only fools who use too much, who overdose because they are careless. Heroin is safer than tobacco, safer than alcohol.'

Hutch slipped the paperclips into his pocket.

Zhou got up from the table and went to stand at the entrance to the building. He looked out over his compound, his hands clasped behind his back. 'Nobody forces anyone to take heroin. I supply a need, nothing more. We don't advertise like the tobacco companies, we don't push our product down people's throats. We don't sponsor sports events, we don't run special offers to get them to try our product.' He turned around and put his hands on his hips. 'People take heroin because they want to. Because they like it. I give people what they want, and they call me a criminal.'

'Doesn't seem fair, does it?' said Winter.

BART LUCARELLI PUNCHED IN the co-ordinates of the transmitter's location into the data entry keypad with his left hand and cross-checked the numbers on the video monitor. A single digit wrong and they could be tens of miles adrift, and the jungle at night was as featureless as an ocean. He slipped the piece of paper that the DEA executive had given him on to the clipboard fastened to his right thigh.

'Okay, Bart?' asked Peter Burden through the headset.

'Data's in,' said Lucarelli. 'We should be within range of the transmitter within twenty-five minutes.' He scanned the VDU which was showing an infrared display from the acquisition/designation sight in the nose of the Apache. The sky was clear ahead, just as Gregory had said it would be.

ZHOU GRABBED CARVER'S HEAD and put his face close to the DEA agent's ear. 'You will tell me why you're here,' he shouted. 'You will tell me and then you will die.'

Winter looked at Hutch and raised an eyebrow. Zhou's interrogation technique left a lot to be desired.

Zhou slapped Carver, splitting his lip. Zhou looked at his hand in disgust, then took a napkin from the table and wiped it.

Winter waved the old servant over and selected another cigar. As he lit it, Hutch stood up and rubbed his stomach. 'I'm going to have to use the latrine again,' he said.

'Yeah? Sure you're not just wimping out?' Winter gestured at the bound DEA agent. 'Bit much for you, is it?'

'I don't get a kick out of seeing people being hurt,' said Hutch. 'And I didn't think you did, either.'

Winter leaned closer to Hutch. 'You can't show any

weakness here, Hutch,' he whispered out of the corner of
his mouth. He looked around theatrically. 'It's a jungle.'
He laughed uproariously as Hutch went outside.

THE FARMER SAT IN the doorway of his house, listening
to its timbers creaking in the wind. His wife was upstairs,
asleep, their four children curled up on mats behind him.
He leaned back against the door jamb and closed his eyes.
It had been a good harvest; he'd been right about the quality
of the land. The poppies had been tall and healthy with an
average of five flowers per plant. Zhou Yuanyi had been
well pleased with the crop. Not pleased enough to pay
the farmer a bonus, but pleased enough to ride down to
the house to thank the farmer personally. The farmer had
seen Zhou coming on his white horse and had ushered his
daughters inside before going out to meet him. Zhou's taste
for young girls was well known in the area and the farmer's
eldest daughter was rapidly approaching puberty.

There was a half-empty bottle of Thai whisky by the
farmer's side and he reached for it with his eyes closed.
His fingers grasped the neck and he raised it to his lips and
drank deeply. He deserved a drink: he'd chosen the land,
he'd supervised the planting of the poppy seeds, and he'd
been in charge of the harvesting of the crop. He was sure
he'd get two more decent harvests from the land, maybe
three, before the soil was exhausted and it was time to
move on.

In the distance he heard a rumbling growl, like a tractor
running at full throttle. The farmer opened his eyes. There

wasn't a tractor within fifty miles: the hills were too steep for machinery to do the ploughing and the work was done by sure-footed buffaloes. The growl deepened and he took another drink from the bottle. It was coming from the west and getting louder by the second.

The farmer stood up and stretched. He peered at the night sky, studded with a million stars. He'd seen planes pass overhead before, but they'd never been as loud as this. And planes made a more regular sound, a constant drone. This was a clattering roar with a high pitched whistle. He'd never heard a sound like it before.

Something moved at the periphery of his vision and he turned his head. He was fifty years old but he had perfect eyesight. Far off in the distance, following the ridge of a line of hills, two objects moved across the sky. He could barely make out the shape of the silhouettes, but they obliterated the stars as they passed. The farmer took another drink from the bottle. He knew what they were: helicopters. He'd seen helicopters before: the Burmese army used them to search for the poppy fields, and to ferry troops around. But there was something different about the sound these helicopters made. They sounded bigger, and, somehow, more menacing.

HUTCH LOOKED OVER HIS shoulder but there was no one close by. 'Chau-ling!' he whispered. She murmured incoherently. Hutch straightened the paperclip and inserted it into the padlock. He felt for the tumblers. It had been so easy at the dining table, but now he was trembling and there seemed to be no feeling in his fingers. He shook his hand to restore the circulation and tried again. The paperclip slipped from his fumbling fingers and fell to the ground.

THE JUNGLE FLASHED BELOW the Apache, as dark and seamless as the sea. The cyclic between Bart Lucarelli's legs moved as if it had a life of its own, following the movements made by Peter Burden in the pilot's seat behind him. Lucarelli was staring straight through the armoured windscreen panel but he was taking in information through the monocle sight of the Honeywell Integrated Helmet and Display System which effectively superimposed the Apache's key flight data on an infra-red picture of whatever he was looking at. Lucarelli's ears were sweating under the headset, but he ignored the discomfort. 'Thirty-five klicks,' he said.

'Thirty-five,' repeated Burden.

Lucarelli looked over his right shoulder. The other Apache was just behind them. He gave a thumbs-up to Warner but the other navigator didn't return the gesture. He was probably too engrossed in his own instruments.

Lucarelli turned back to his cockpit display and let his eyes play over the instruments, most of which duplicated those on the pilot's panel. The co-pilot's cockpit was equipped with the controls and instrumentation to be able to fly the Apache, and Lucarelli was as capable a pilot as Burden, but on this mission he had only two tasks: to get them to the beacon, and to fire the Hellfire missiles. Like the DEA executive had said at the briefing, it would be a milk run.

ZHOU PICKED UP A fruit knife off the dining table and tested its sharpness on his thumb. He went over to Carver and pressed the tip of the blade against the DEA agent's throat. A dribble of blood ran down the stainless steel. 'Did you see the men I impaled?' Zhou asked through clenched teeth. 'That's what I'm going to do to you. Do you know how long it takes to die that way?'

Carver twisted away from the knife, but Zhou pushed it deeper into his throat. For a moment it looked as if Zhou was going to kill him there and then, but he had a sudden change of heart and withdrew the blade. Blood poured from the cut. Zhou sneered at Carver 'Look at you. Bleeding like a pig.'

The contents of Carver's pockets were on a side table. Zhou flicked through the DEA agent's passport. 'I see you've visited our country before. Thailand, Laos, Hong Kong, Vietnam; you've been to a lot of places, Mr Carver. So what brings you to my domain?' He threw the passport into Carver's lap. 'And why no visa this time? How did you get into the country? You're with the DEA, aren't you?'

'I'm not with the DEA,' said Carver. 'I'm a tourist. I—'

Zhou stepped forward and sliced the knife across Carver's

mouth. Blood spurted in a crimson fountain and Carver's head jerked backwards.

'Don't lie to me!' Zhou barked. 'I am not stupid! When you lie to me, you're saying that I am not an intelligent man, that I can be fooled by simple words.' He picked up the second passport, the one he'd taken from the girl. There was blood on Zhou's fingers and he smeared it over the pages as he went through it. 'This girl, who is she? Is she also with the DEA?'

Carver shook his head. 'No,' he said.

'Hong Kong Chinese. I killed a man from Hong Kong last month.' He looked at the photograph in the front of the passport. 'It's the first time the DEA has used a girl.'

'She's not with the DEA,' said Carver. He had difficulty forming words, every movement of his lips causing him agonising pain.

'Tsang Chau-ling,' said Zhou. 'I'm going to have some fun with this Tsang Chau-ling.'

Bird looked up as if he'd been stung. 'What?' he said. 'What did you say her name was?'

THE BUFFALO BOY WALKED between his animals, talking to them in a low, hushed voice. Normally they lay down to sleep as soon as the sun went down, but something was upsetting them. When they were lazy or disobedient, the only way to make them behave was to hit them with his stick, but the Buffalo Boy knew that they had to be calmed with soft words. One of them, the biggest, with huge backswept horns as thick as the boy's thigh, stamped a hoof on the ground and grunted.

The Buffalo Boy tucked his stick under his arm and patted the animal's flank. He'd never seen them like this before. Even snakes didn't scare them this much. Two of the females were edging away from the herd and the Buffalo Boy ran over to bring them back. He heard the noise then, far off in the distance. It sounded like a truck being driven up a hill, its engine straining against the gradient. It wasn't a truck, though, the Buffalo Boy knew, because there were no roads near by, just fields and tracks and jungle. He held his stick in both hands as if preparing to beat off an attacker.

The noise became louder and louder until it was a roaring growl that he could feel vibrating through his chest. Still he could see nothing, just the trees and stars and the hills in the distance.

'It's not a dragon,' he whispered to himself. 'There aren't any dragons. Not here.'

The big bull buffalo lowered its horns and pawed at the ground as if he too was preparing to meet an attacker. Together they waited for the source of the noise to reveal itself.

The roar reached a whistling crescendo and then two massive shapes swooped overhead and the Buffalo Boy ducked involuntarily. The herd scattered in panic and the Buffalo Boy turned around to stare after the helicopters as the slipstream tugged at his tattered T-shirt and shorts. The grass around him whirled and whispered as if it was being ruffled by unseen hands.

The Buffalo Boy stood stock still, staring after the helicopters. He wondered how much a helicopter would cost. One day, he promised himself, when he was as rich as Zhou Yuanyi, he'd have his own helicopter. And a Mercedes. And a gold wristwatch studded with diamonds.

The helicopters disappeared from view but the Buffalo Boy didn't move until the noise of their turbines had faded away.

THE PADLOCK CLICKED OPEN and Hutch pulled it free. He threw it to the side and yanked open the barred door. He rushed to Chau-ling and lifted her head. Her eyelids flickered and Hutch felt a wave of relief wash over him. She hadn't moved all the time he'd been working on the padlock and while he knew they wouldn't have bothered locking up a corpse, he had still feared the worst.

'Chau-ling,' he said, stroking the side of her face.

She opened her eyes and looked at him in disbelief. 'Warren?' she said.

'What the hell are you doing here?' he asked.

She put her head back and looked up at her bound hands. She forced a smile. 'Just hanging around,' she said.

Hutch hugged her and she grunted. 'Maybe you should get me down first,' she said, then suddenly stiffened. 'Did you activate the transmitter?' she asked.

Hutch was stunned. 'How did you know—?' he began, but she cut him off mid-sentence.

'Did you press the button?' she asked.

'Yes, it's all right. Help's on the way.'

'No, you don't understand,' she gasped. 'They're not coming to help. They're coming to kill Zhou Yuanyi. They're going to kill everybody.'

Hutch took a step back, surprised by her ferocity. 'What the hell are you talking about?'

'Just get me down. Quickly.'

'I think you should just leave her where she is,' said a voice. Hutch whirled around. It was Bird. In one hand he was holding Chau-ling's passport, in the other, a large automatic.

Hutch raised his hands. Bird stepped into the cell. He dropped the passport at Hutch's feet. 'I know about the girl,' he said, 'but what's your connection to the DEA agent?'

'Bird, I just want to get out of here, that's all. I've done what Winter wanted, I helped you get Harrigan out.'

'You're working with Carver, aren't you? That's why they didn't shoot us at the river.' He pointed the gun at Hutch's face. 'I should kill you right now.' His face broke into a malicious grin. 'But I think Zhou will be more than generous if I let him do it. He loves to torture traitors.'

Hutch took another step back. 'I'm not a traitor, Bird. I don't know what Carver's doing here, or why he brought Chau-ling with him. But I'm . . .' He lunged at the gun but Bird easily evaded the attack. Hutch raised his hands again. 'Okay, okay. Take it easy.'

Bird gestured with the gun. 'Come on, we'll go and see what Billy has to say.'

'We don't have time for this,' said Chau-ling.

Bird ignored her. He motioned for Hutch to leave.

'The helicopters are coming, they're going to kill us all,'

Chau-ling cried. 'Why won't you listen to me?' Tears ran down her face.

Bird turned his head and looked at her as if seeing her for the first time. 'What do you mean?' he asked. 'Who's coming?'

Chau-ling spat at Bird's face and he flinched reflexively. Hutch lashed out with his foot and kicked Bird's wrist. The gun flew through the air and thudded against the wall of the hut. Bird grabbed for Hutch's throat. Hutch ducked and punched him in the solar plexus, putting all of his weight behind the blow. Bird staggered back, winded. Hutch kept up the offensive, hitting him twice more in the stomach and then kicking him between the legs, the attack so fast and furious that Bird had no chance to defend himself. Bird bent over, his arms around his stomach. Hutch dived for the gun but Bird kicked out and sent Hutch sprawling. Hutch managed to get to the gun but as his fingers gripped the butt, Bird grabbed him by the hair. Hutch twisted around and smashed the gun into Bird's face. Bird fell to his knees and then pitched forward, hitting the ground like a felled tree. He managed to push himself up on to his knees but Hutch hit him with the gun a second time, crashing it down on the back of the man's neck. Bird fell to the ground again. This time he didn't get up.

'Hurry,' implored Chau-ling. 'We don't have much time.'

BART LUCARELLI FLIPPED HIS monocle sight to the side and leaned forward to press both eyes against the eyepieces of the TADS/PNVS display. 'There she is,' he said.

'Got it,' said Burden. 'Do you wanna check that Hal and Roger have picked it up?'

Before Lucarelli could click his microphone switch, Roger Warner's voice came over the headset.

'Contact at three miles. Do you have it?'

'Affirmative. Three miles.' Lucarelli switched his VDU display from the navigation phase to the attack phase and changed the map scale to 1:50,000 to get a close-up view of his target. He flicked the switches that armed the Hellfire missiles. 'Missiles armed.'

The cyclic between Lucarelli's legs moved towards his groin as Burden put the Apache into a gentle climb. Altitude would help the missile guidance systems lock on to the distant transmitter. Two miles was the optimum range; close enough so that the missile would be sure to lock on to the signal, but far enough away to ensure that the Apaches wouldn't be fired upon. According to Jake Gregory, the men on the ground had nothing more powerful than assault rifles, which would be useless against the heavily armoured helicopters, but there was no point in taking unnecessary risks.

Lucarelli used his left thumb to orientate the Apache's radar to the target area and scanned it. He swallowed as he scrutinised the visual display. Less than half a mile to go. There were two pistol grips either side of the TADS/PNVS system which controlled the forward-looking infra-red sensor and fired the Apache's weapons. Warner slid his hands around them in a soft caress. One pull of the trigger with his left hand and a one-hundred-pound Hellfire missile would be launched. It was an awesome weapon, its seventeen-pound warhead was more than capable of taking out an armoured tank. Warner could only imagine what havoc it would wreak on the jungle camp.

HUTCH AND CHAU-LING WALKED purposefully across the compound as if they had every right to be there. Chau-ling kept her face down. Three of Zhou's men passed them without a second glance. Hutch had Bird's gun tucked into the waistband of his jeans, covered by his sweatshirt.

'How long before they get here?' he whispered.

'I don't know,' she said. 'Tim just said that they'd pick up the transmitter and home in on it.'

'But where are they coming from? From Thailand?'

'I don't know.'

Another group of soldiers walked by, smoking cheroots and talking among themselves. One of them looked at Hutch. Hutch smiled and the soldier smiled back.

The two guards at the base of the steps to Zhou's quarters moved to block their way but Hutch said 'Zhou Yuanyi' and rushed by them. Chau-ling hurried after him, taking the steps two at a time. The guards turned and watched them go, unsure whether or not to go after them.

'Don't look back,' whispered Hutch. He stepped across the threshold and pulled out the gun.

Zhou was standing over Carver, pistol-whipping him about the face. Winter and Harrigan were watching. All three men had their backs to Hutch. The only person who saw him walk across the wooden floor was the old servant, who scurried away into a side room. Chau-ling stayed in the doorway. Hutch kept his arm outstretched with the gun pointing straight at Zhou's head.

Winter turned first. He took his cigar out of his mouth. 'What's up, old lad?' he asked. His voice was relaxed, but his eyes were hard.

Hutch didn't look at him. He walked right up to Zhou and put the gun against the back of his neck. Zhou stiffened and Harrigan's mouth fell open in surprise.

'Anyone moves and he's dead,' said Hutch.

'You've been watching too many movies,' said Winter. 'You're not going to pull the trigger, and you know you're not.'

Still Hutch didn't look at Winter. He took the gun from Zhou's hand and stepped back. 'Don't push me, Billy,' he said. 'I've nothing to lose any more. You've taken everything away. Chau-ling, take this gun.' He held Zhou's gun behind him and Chau-ling took it, gingerly, as if she was afraid it might go off accidentally.

'We can talk about this, Hutch,' said Winter.

'I'm through talking,' said Hutch. He grabbed the back of Zhou's collar and forced the gun against the back of his head. 'Now, we're going to walk very slowly out of here.'

'Walk where, old lad?' asked Winter, an amused smile on his face.

'Just out of here. And stay where I can see you. Ray, get a knife from the table and cut him free,' he said, gesturing towards Carver.

Harrigan did as he was told. Chau-ling kept him covered with Zhou's gun.

'Young lady, I'd take the safety catch off if I were you,' said Winter.

'Ignore him, Chau-ling.'

'I was just trying to help,' said Winter.

'Stay where I can see you, Billy. And put your hands in the air.'

Winter raised his arms. He looked longingly at his cigar. 'Can I put my cigar in my mouth?'

Hutch ignored him. 'Tim, are you okay?'

'Oh, it's Tim, is it?' said Winter. He put the cigar in his mouth then put his hand back in the air. 'Old friends, are you?'

Carver stood up unsteadily. 'I'm okay,' he said.

'Chau-ling, help him,' said Hutch. He pushed Zhou towards the entrance. He kept the barrel of the gun hard up against the back of the man's neck.

'I will kill you,' said Zhou savagely. 'I will kill you slowly.'

'Of course you will,' said Hutch, tightening his grip on Zhou's shirt collar. 'Ray, drop the knife and kick it over against the wall.' Hutch watched as Harrigan obeyed his instructions. 'Now go outside. Down the steps.'

When Harrigan reached the bottom of the steps, Hutch told Winter to follow him. 'Do I have to keep my hands in the air?' Winter asked.

'Billy, if you carry on like this, I'm going to shoot you in the leg. Now get down there with Ray.'

'You are a dead man walking,' said Zhou. 'Do you hear me? A dead man.'

'I died a long time ago,' said Hutch. 'Chau-ling, keep well away from Billy and keep the gun pointed at his chest.'

Winter tapped his breastbone with his finger. 'Right here, dear,' he said.

Hutch pulled Zhou away from the entrance to give Winter plenty of room. Winter shook his head sadly as he went outside. 'Big mistake, old lad. Big mistake.'

Hutch waited until Winter was standing next to Harrigan before he pushed Zhou to the entrance. The two guards had shouldered their rifles and were aiming up the steps. Hutch tapped the gun against Zhou's head. 'Tell them to back off,' he said.

'You tell them,' hissed Zhou.

'Tell them to back off or I'll blow your head off.'

'Blow my head off and you won't have a hostage.'

'Tell them!' Hutch shouted.

'No.'

Hutch's finger tightened on the trigger but he knew that Zhou was right. He pushed him forward, keeping a tight grip on his collar. 'Keep close behind me, Chau-ling,' he said as he started down the steps. She helped support Carver who was having trouble walking on his own. More of Zhou's men ran over, guns at the ready. A dozen. Twenty. Thirty.

'A dead man walking,' said Zhou.

'If I die, you die with me,' said Hutch.

'And the girl, too?'

'Shut up,' said Hutch.

'I'll make you a deal,' said Zhou, his voice suddenly silky smooth. 'Let me go and I'll allow the girl to live.'

They were halfway down the steps. More soldiers appeared to Hutch's left, shouting and pointing their M16s and AK-47s. 'Keep walking,' said Hutch.

Zhou shouted at his men. As one they aimed their guns at Chau-ling.

'What did you say?' asked Hutch, jamming the gun harder against Zhou's skull. 'What did you say to them?'

'I told them to shoot the girl when I give the word.'

Hutch looked over his shoulder. 'Behind me, Chau-ling, get close behind me.' Chau-ling was shaking with fear. She had one arm around Carver, and was waving the other from side to side, not sure where to point her gun. 'Come on, stand next to me,' Hutch urged.

'Drop your gun,' said Zhou. 'Drop your gun or she dies.'

HAL AUSTIN PULLED BACK on the cyclic and lowered the collective as he put the Apache into a hover, almost five hundred feet above the treetops. The second Apache was a hundred feet to his left and slightly behind him. Austin clicked his microphone switch. 'You okay over there, Pete?'

'Ready when you are,' said Burden.

'Okay,' said Austin. He dipped the Apache's nose slightly. 'Let her go, Roger.'

Austin's Apache rocked as the first missile streaked away from the right-hand stub wing. It arced upwards and then dipped down as the missile's radio frequency seeker kicked in and guided it towards the distant transmitter. Even through the helmet's night vision system, Austin couldn't see the target, though it was visible on the radar screen. Without the transmitter, they'd have spent weeks searching for the camp.

Burden's Apache fired the first of its missiles. It shot

away after the first Hellfire. Warner let his second Hellfire go, and it was followed almost immediately by another from Burden's Apache. Austin kept the helicopter in a steady hover, compensating for the buffeting caused by the firing. Austin followed the progress of the missiles through the monocle sight.

'Looking good, Roger,' he said. 'It's looking good.'

HUTCH PUSHED ZHOU DOWN the steps, keeping a tight grip on his shirt. All the soldiers were shouting and making stabbing motions with their guns. Hutch kept Zhou moving, forcing him away from the building and towards the compound gates.

'Give it up, Hutch,' said Winter. 'You don't stand a chance.'

Soldiers crowded around Hutch and Zhou, so close that he could smell their sweat. He began to drag Zhou around in a circle. Zhou had to put his hands out to the sides to keep his balance. 'I'll fire,' said Hutch. 'Tell them I'll fire.'

'A dead man walking,' said Zhou. He began to laugh, a sound like rattling stones.

The night air was suddenly split by a shrieking sound and something streaked over their heads. A second later the building exploded. The force of the blast threw Hutch to the side and he lost his grip on Zhou's shirt. He felt a blast of burning air that seared his exposed skin. He covered his face with his hands and staggered away from the building as bits of timber and metal ripped through the air around him.

A second explosion sent him sprawling again. A piece of timber clipped his shoulder and he felt the flesh rip open. He fell to his knees and started to crawl. The air around him seemed to have been sucked away, it was like breathing in a vacuum. He looked around for Chau-ling. She and Carver were lying face down in the dirt. He pushed himself up off the ground and headed towards her but a third explosion knocked him off his feet and he lay on his back, gasping for breath.

'THREE,' SAID LUCARELLI, HIS face pressed against the TADS/PNVS eyepieces. 'And four.' He sat up straight and flicked across the helmet's monocle sight. 'Four hits.'

'Nice shooting,' said Burden over his headset.

'Fire and forget,' said Lucarelli. 'The frequency seeker did the rest.'

'Ready to activate the laser guidance system?' asked Burden.

'Coming right up,' replied Lucarelli. He used the monocle sight to target the laser designator and pressed the laser trigger on the right-hand mission grip to lock the missile on to its target. The four frequency-guided Hellfires had all hit the same area of the warlord's camp and it was well ablaze, with tongues of red and yellow flames leaping into the night sky. Now that they knew exactly where the camp was, the remaining missiles could be independently targeted. Lucarelli picked out a group of huts which he figured were barracks for the troops or storage facilities, and aimed the laser at the largest. He pressed the missile trigger on the left-hand grip and the missile streaked away in the general direction of the camp, almost immediately reaching its maximum speed of Mach 1.17.

The missile soared upwards, and then it arced down towards the jungle as the laser receiver in its nose sent instructions to the fin control, guiding the missile towards the reflected laser light on the target. The Apache rocked from side to side but the cyclic moved between the co-pilot's legs as Burden swiftly compensated for the motion.

A laser-guided missile roared away from the other Apache.

Lucarelli waited until the Hellfire had exploded before sighting his laser on another area of the camp. He had plenty of time. It was like shooting fish in a barrel.

HUTCH KNELT DOWN BESIDE Chau-ling. She was unconscious but he felt for a pulse in her neck and it was strong and regular. He lifted her up, surprised at how light she was in his arms. The soldiers who had just minutes earlier been threatening to kill them were running for their lives, those who weren't lying dead on the ground. The floor was littered with corpses, discarded weapons and bits of burning debris.

'Hutch?' It was Carver, struggling to his feet.

'Can you walk?' asked Hutch.

Carver's hair was red and matted with blood and his mouth was badly gashed. He put his hand to the side of his head and then stared at his bloody palm.

Another missile shrieked overhead and hit the water

tower. Hutch ducked as bits of metal and concrete exploded around them.

Carver saw Zhou's gun in the dirt and he picked it up. He ejected the clip, checked that it contained bullets, then slotted it back. 'Come on,' he said, 'there'll be nothing left of this place by the time they've finished.'

They ran for the entrance to the compound.

ZHOU YUANYI OPENED HIS eyes. The night air was filled with screams and shouts from terrified men. Something burned his hand and he pulled it away. All around him were small pieces of burning wood, the remains of his headquarters. Something whistled through the air like a banshee and exploded into the latrine building as he stood up. There seemed to be fires everywhere, crackling and spitting. Two Chinese mercenaries ran past Zhou, AK-47s in their arms, their eyes wide and fearful. There was another whistling sound overhead and one of the barracks exploded. The impact blew Zhou backwards and he hit the ground hard. He lay stunned for a few seconds, the taste of blood in his mouth, then he rolled on to his front and got to his feet, his ears ringing.

He ran towards the armoury. He knew it was the most dangerous place to be, but he also knew that if the camp was being attacked from the air then it was his only chance of fighting back. AK-47s and M16s would be no use against helicopters or planes. There were two guards crouched outside the armoury, assault rifles clutched to their chests, frozen in fear.

'Open the door!' Zhou shouted.

Another missile screeched overhead. It arced downwards and ripped into the base of the transmitter tower. It exploded in a ball of orange flame and the tower toppled sideways.

One of the guards unclipped a key ring from his belt and tossed it to Zhou. 'Open it yourself,' he shouted. He grabbed his colleague by the shoulder. 'Come on, let's get out of here.'

Zhou held out his arms. 'Stay with me,' he shouted.

The guard who'd been carrying the keys shook his head vehemently. 'If we stay here, we're dead.'

Zhou stepped forward and pulled a pistol from the man's belt. He pointed it at the guard's face. 'If you run, I'll kill you here and now.' The two men stared at each other. The second guard slipped his finger inside the trigger guard of his AK-47. 'There are missiles inside,' said Zhou. 'I can shoot them down. If we don't do something they'll kill us all.'

The guard glared at Zhou, then he nodded slowly. He put down his assault rifle and held out his hand for the key ring. Zhou gave it to him. As the guard fumbled for the right key, two more missiles exploded inside the compound, so close that the ground shook under Zhou's feet. The door opened and Zhou pushed his way inside. He rushed through an anteroom lined with assault rifles and into the main storage area which was filled with boxes of ammunition and grenades. He pointed to the four metal cases containing the Grail missile systems.

'Take one each,' he said. 'And hurry.'

The armoury trembled as another missile exploded outside. Zhou grabbed one of the cases and ran for the door. The armoury was a potential death trap and he wanted to get as far away from it as possible.

Half a dozen soldiers in camouflage uniforms ran by, bent at the waist to keep their heads low. 'Can you see where they're coming from?' Zhou shouted.

One of the soldiers, an officer, pointed to the west. Zhou stared into the darkness but couldn't see anything.

SOLDIERS WERE POURING OUT of the compound, many of them burned and bleeding. 'Which way?' Hutch shouted at Carver

'The jungle,' said the DEA agent. 'We can take cover in the trees.'

Another missile ripped into the compound and blew one of the huts into a thousand flaming pieces. Hutch tripped on a discarded AK-47 and almost lost his footing. A soldier looked over in his direction. It was Home. Home screamed at them and took aim with his rifle. Hutch tried to run but with Chau-ling in his arms he could barely manage a jog. Home fired and the bullet whizzed over Hutch's head. Home shouted something else and put his rifle to his shoulder again. Hutch's heart was pounding and all the strength seemed to have drained from his legs. He was going to die, he realised. There was no way he could run, no way he could escape the next bullet.

Suddenly Carver stepped between him and Home. The DEA agent fired, three shots in quick succession, and Home fell backwards into the mud. Carver pushed Hutch between the shoulder blades in the direction of the compound gate.

ZHOU FLICKED THE CATCHES on the case and lifted the lid. The Grail launching unit and tracking unit nestled in their foam rubber compartments. The two armoury guards joined him and dropped the cases on the ground next to him.

'Be careful!' he screamed.

The guards said nothing.

Zhou assembled the missile system, exactly as the Ukrainian had showed him. The Ukrainian had been a good teacher, patient and encouraging. Zhou had been one of half a dozen men who had been trained in the use of the weapon, though he'd never actually fired one. It was simple, the Ukrainian had said. Arm, aim and fire. The infra-red homing system in the missile would do the rest, provided it was pointing in the general direction of the target. The most important thing to remember was to check that there was no one standing behind you when you launched the missile. Zhou turned his head to warn the guards to stand clear, but they had already run off.

Zhou hefted the launcher on to his shoulder. Another missile streaked across the night sky, heading for the inferno that was the compound. Zhou had lost count of how many explosions there had been. Eleven. Twelve. Thirteen. Maybe more. He pressed his eye to the sights and searched the sky in the direction the missiles had come from. He could just about make out two helicopters, hovering above the tree line about two miles away. As he watched, one of the helicopters launched another missile. They were cowards, thought Zhou. They didn't fight like men: they hid during the fight and fired their missiles from a distance, convinced that they were safe. They were wrong. Zhou smiled as he tightened his finger on the trigger. They would soon find out just how wrong they were: they were well within range of the Grail missile.

He settled the sights dead centre on the nearest helicopter. He tensed his shoulder in anticipation of the recoil and pulled the trigger.

HUTCH REACHED THE OUTSKIRTS of the jungle and slowed to a walk. Carver was already there, leaning against a tree and dabbing the knife wound on his face with the bottom of his shirt. Hutch put Chau-ling on the ground.

'How is she?' asked Carver.

'Unconscious,' said Hutch. He felt for a pulse again. It was strong and he could see her chest rise and fall as she breathed. There was a red welt across her left cheek as if she'd been slapped, and myriad cuts on her forehead. Hutch leaned forward and kissed her on the nose. 'I'm sorry,' he whispered.

She moaned, but her eyes remained closed.

Hutch looked up at Carver. 'Why? Why are they doing this?' he asked.

'They wanted Zhou Yuanyi dead.'

'And me? What about me?'

'I didn't know,' said Carver earnestly. 'I honestly didn't know. That's why we're here.'

Hutch raised his eyebrows. 'You came after me?'

'To warn you.' He winced as he dabbed his lip. 'Though if it hadn't been for your girlfriend there, I don't think I would have been so quick to leap into the lion's den.'

'Yeah, well, I'm glad you did,' he said as he gently stroked Chau-ling's cheek.

ROGER WARNER JUMPED AS the warning bleep went off in his headset. He scanned his VDU. 'Incoming,' he shouted.

Hal Austin's voice was unruffled as if they were doing nothing more stressful than discussing the weather. 'I have it.' The Apache was already banking to the right.

'It's tracking us,' said Warner. He scanned his panel display. The incoming missile would be using one of two systems, either chasing the heat from the two massive T700-GE-701C turbines or homing in using its own radar. The infra-red indicator was flashing, 'Infra-red,' he said. The two chaff and flare dispensers on each side of the tail boom some six feet from the tailplane contained countermeasures for both types of missiles. He fired an infra-red decoy flare. It shot away from its cartridge leaving behind a plume of grey smoke. 'Cart fired,' said Warner. The flare exploded to the left of the Apache. Warner stared at his VDU as the helicopter continued to dive to the right. In theory the heat generated by the pyrotechnics should be a bigger attraction than the helicopter's turbines. Warner fired a second cartridge, just to be on the safe side.

Austin had already activated the Apache's pulsed infra-red jammer. Sited above the mid-fuselage, it was putting out pulses of IR frequencies designed to confuse the missile's seeker head. 'There she goes,' said Austin. The missile began to move away from the Apache, towards the flare.

Warner exhaled. He'd been holding his breath from the moment that the missile warning had gone off. The missile's path was inexorably heading away from the Apache.

'Oh fuck,' said Austin.

Warner frowned and scanned his VDU and instruments. He suddenly realised what had upset the pilot. The missile was going away from them all right, but it was now heading directly for Burden and Lucarelli's Apache.

BART LUCARELLI STARED AT the VDU screen in horror as the missile warning beeped in his headset. He'd fired off two infra-red flares but it was clear that the missile wasn't fooled. The cyclic between his legs was pushed as far forward as it would go as Burden put the Apache into a dive. Lucarelli knew it was too late. The missile hadn't even been fired at their helicopter, and if it had been then the standard evasion techniques would have neutralised it within seconds. It was the other Apache's flare that had sent the missile heading in their direction, too close to be distracted. Burden banked the Apache to the left, so quickly that Lucarelli's stomach lurched. He couldn't take his eyes off the screen. In his headset he heard Burden start to speak, but before he could get a word out the missile struck and the Apache exploded.

HUTCH STARED UP THE slope at the burning compound.

Carver knelt over Chau-ling. 'She's coming around,' he said. Chau-ling coughed and tried to sit up. 'Easy, stay where you are,' said the DEA agent.

'Warren . . .' said Chau-ling.

'I'm here,' said Hutch. He crouched down beside her and brushed her bloody hair away from her face.

'You have a lot of explaining to do,' she said.

'I know.' He smiled despite himself. He patted Carver on the shoulder. 'Take care of her, Tim.'

'What do you mean?' said Carver.

Hutch stood up. He ran his hand through his hair as he stared at the inferno. 'I have to go back for Billy.'

'No!' Chau-ling shouted. She sat up and stared at him, her skin ghostly pale and streaked with glistening blood. 'You can't go back!'

Hutch shook his head. He didn't look at her.

'Don't be stupid, Hutch,' said Carver. 'It's suicide.'

'I can't leave him there.'

'He's dead already,' said Carver.

'You don't know that.'

'You don't owe Winter anything,' said Chau-ling.

'I do,' said Hutch.

'What?' asked Carver. 'What's he ever done for you?'

'You wouldn't understand.'

Hutch started up the slope.

'Wait!' shouted Carver. He tossed Hutch his gun.

Hutch caught it and nodded his thanks. He looked at Chau-ling. Tears were streaming down her face and she had her arms out towards him, a silent plea for him to stay. There was nothing he could say to her. He turned and headed back up the slope towards the flames.

HAL AUSTIN WATCHED IN despair as the wreckage of Burden and Lucarelli's Apache plummeted down towards the treetops. One by one the bright spots disappeared on his helmet's night vision display and within seconds all he could see was the jungle canopy.

'It was my fault, Hal,' said Warner, his voice crackling over the headset.

Austin held the Apache in a static hover, its nose pointing towards the compound which was now engulfed in smoky flames. 'Can it, Roger,' he said.

'If I hadn't fired the cart . . .'

'If you hadn't fired the cart the missile would have got us.'

'But . . .'

'Later, Roger. We've got work to do. Can you see where it came from?'

'To the right of the compound.'

'We're going in.' There was silence from Warner. 'We're going in, Roger. Activate the chain gun.'

The Apache's Hughes XM230 chain gun was mounted in a cradle below the helicopter's nose. While the missiles were being fired, the gun was inert and locked out of the way. Warner's left hand reached forward to the weapons console and he armed the gun. It was capable of firing up to 625 rounds a minute and Warner could aim it using the helmet's monocle sight, allowing him to shoot wherever he was looking, but for greater accuracy he'd use his head-down display. He slid his hands around the grips either side of the TADS/PNVS system, his right thumb resting on the chain gun fire button and he lowered his eyes to the display. 'Let's do it,' he said.

HUTCH SEARCHED AMONG THE bodies around the pile of burning wood that was all that was left of Zhou's headquarters. He found the old servant, a piece of smoking metal embedded in his back, still alive but fading fast. A soldier grabbed at Hutch's foot and Hutch jerked it away. The soldier's left leg was missing and he was lying in a pool of his own blood. It was a scene from hell.

He saw the lower half of a body wearing jeans sticking out from underneath a jagged chunk of concrete from the water tower. He pushed the concrete away. It was Harrigan. His eyes were wide and staring and his throat was a bloody mess. There was no need even to try feeling for a pulse.

'Hutch?' Winter's voice was a hoarse whisper.

Hutch looked around. 'Billy? Where are you?'

Winter raised his arm. He was about fifty feet away, lying under the body of one of Zhou's soldiers. Hutch pulled the corpse off him. Winter's shirt was soaked with blood.

'Oh Jesus, Billy,' said Hutch, sitting back on his heels. He touched Winter's chest, looking for the wound. Winter tried to sit up but Hutch put a restraining hand on his shoulder. 'Lie still, Billy. You've been hurt.'

'Bullshit,' said Winter. 'That's not my blood.'

'Are you sure?'

'Sure I'm sure. Help me up.'

Hutch gave him a hand and Winter pulled himself up. Almost immediately he keeled over. 'My leg,' he said. 'Christ, it hurts.'

'Is it broken?'

'I don't know. Maybe.' He looked down at his injured leg. A jagged piece of bone was sticking through the material of his trousers. 'Yeah,' said Winter, ashen-faced. 'It's broken.'

Winter looked around the compound. Every building had either been destroyed or was burning and the air was thick with choking smoke. 'Which way?' he said.

'Over there,' said Hutch, putting his arm around Winter, allowing him to take the weight off his injured limb.

ZHOU THREW THE LAUNCHER to the ground. His hands were shaking. He'd lost sight of the missile almost as soon as he'd fired it and he'd been amazed to see the helicopter burst into flames followed several seconds later by the sound of the explosion. Zhou was exhilarated. He'd done it. He'd actually done it. He'd shot down a helicopter. His heart pounded and he was breathing in short, ragged gasps. It had been so simple, just like the Ukrainian had said. Arm, aim and fire. It had been the first time Zhou had actually fired a Grail missile, and he'd brought down a helicopter. He looked around, wanting to share the excitement with someone, but he was alone.

Panic-stricken soldiers were running down the hillside away from the compound. The armoury was ablaze and there were periodic explosions as the grenades and ammunition exploded. There wasn't a single building still standing. The destruction had been absolute as if the attackers had been determined to raze the compound to the ground.

Zhou peered into the darkness. The dark shape that was the second helicopter was growing larger. It was heading his way. Zhou scrambled over the grass on his hands and knees towards the remaining metal cases. He grabbed the nearest and fumbled with the catches.

'BLOODY HELL, LOOK AT that,' said Winter. 'Look at the size of it.' The helicopter was huge, a black beetle-like monster that sped towards them, its nose down. Winter had stopped in his tracks and was staring at it, his mouth open in amazement.

'Billy, get down,' said Hutch, and shoulder-charged Winter out of the way. The two men crashed to the ground. Winter grabbed at his injured leg, gritting his teeth in pain. Hutch saw a section of the corrugated iron that had once been the roof of Zhou's building. He wasn't sure how much protection it would offer but he pulled it over them none the less.

WARNER COULD SEE THE men on the ground through
the night vision sensor as clearly as if it was daylight. He
smiled. The 30mm rounds would go through the sheet
of metal as if it was tinfoil. But he wasn't interested
in them, he wanted the man with the rocket launcher.
The man who'd killed his friends. He scanned the area,
then saw him, bending over something. Warner centred
the man in his sights as Austin put the helicopter into a
steep dive. Warner adjusted his aim accordingly. The man
lifted something up and put it on his shoulder. Warner
swallowed. It was a rocket launcher.

There were twelve hundred rounds of ammunition under
the rotor gearbox, as close to the Apache's centre of gravity
as possible so that firing the massive gun wouldn't disrupt
its trim. Warner had enough firepower to keep the massive
gun pouring out bullets for a full two minutes but he fired
only a short burst, his eyes glued to the VDU display. He
felt the Apache shake as Austin let go an infra-red cartridge
as a precautionary measure.

ZHOU SLIPPED HIS FINGER over the trigger of the Grail
launcher and squinted through the sight. The helicopter had
gone. He swung the launcher around, frantically trying to
locate it. Nothing. Just stars and clouds.

Suddenly he heard a whirring, roaring noise and a black

shape swooped towards him, so low that it seemed to be flying through the flames. Zhou put the launcher back on his shoulder. He heard screeching sounds above his head and something ripped through his chest, tearing and shredding like a million machetes. He fell backwards, his mouth filling with blood, the launcher falling from his lifeless hands.

THE HELICOPTER ROARED OVERHEAD, its gun clattering loudly. Hutch pushed the corrugated iron away and helped Winter to his feet.

'Who the hell are they?' asked Winter.

'DEA,' said Hutch.

'The DEA have helicopter gunships?'

'Looks like it.' He supported Winter around the waist and they ran towards the entrance like contestants in a three-legged race. Behind them the helicopter went into a noisy hover, its rotor wash kicking up dust and debris.

Something whacked the back of Hutch's leg and he stumbled, his gun flying from his grasp. Both men fell to the ground. Winter screamed in pain. Hutch examined the back of his own leg. There was a small black hole in his jeans and the material was stained with blood. The leg was numb, but as he peeled away the denim the pain hit him, lancing into his flesh like a hot iron. He'd been shot.

He looked up. A figure was striding towards him, cradling an AK-47. It was Bird, his face contorted with rage.

'You!' screamed Bird. 'You did this!'

'GOT HIM,' SAID WARNER, unable to keep the elation out of his voice. Generally he was like ice in combat, cold and hard, his emotions suppressed as he got on with his job, but the man with the missile launcher had killed two of his friends and Warner's adrenal glands had gone into overdrive.

'Nice shooting,' said Austin, putting the Apache into a climb that made Warner's stomach turn over. The helicopter banked to the left. Below, Warner could see the compound ablaze. There wasn't a single building untouched by the flames.

A group of half a dozen soldiers in camouflage uniforms fired assault rifles at the Apache, but the bullets had no effect on the armoured underside.

Another group of uniformed men raced out of the compound. One of them was on fire, and was slapping his burning shirt as he ran. He stumbled and fell, the flames engulfing his face, and then the helicopter banked to the right and Warner couldn't see him any more. Warner bit down on his lip, hard, and closed his eyes. He wondered how long it had taken Peter and Bart to die.

'One more pass and then we're out of here,' said Austin, putting the helicopter into a steep turn.

'DON'T,' SAID WINTER. 'DON'T kill him.'

Bird gestured with the barrel of the AK-47 at the carnage

around him. 'Look what he did, Billy. He brought the helicopters.'

Winter tried to stand up but the pain in his leg was too much and he fell back.

'Don't beg, Billy,' said Hutch. 'Don't beg for me.' He got to his feet. If he was going to die, he didn't want to die lying on the ground. He looked around for the gun that Carver had given him. It was lying next to the sheet of corrugated iron, well out of reach.

Bird put the stock of the AK 47 against his shoulder and took aim at Hutch's chest. Hutch stared coldly at Bird. He realised with a terrible certainty that he wasn't scared.

Bird's finger tightened on the trigger.

'Bird, no!' screamed Winter.

The helicopter seemed to come from nowhere, swooping down like a massive bird of prey, its gun rattling. Bird's upper body jerked as if he'd been electrocuted and blood spurted from a dozen wounds. He remained standing for a full second, then he fell backwards, the AK-47 still at his shoulder.

AUSTIN PULLED BACK ON the cyclic and the Apache climbed above the smoke. 'We're going home,' he said into his radio mike. 'There's nothing more to do here.'

Warner nodded but didn't say anything.

'Roger, you okay?'

Warner nodded again, but still didn't reply. His finger was

still pressing the chain gun trigger, but all the ammunition had been expended.

'CAN YOU SEE HIM?' asked Chau-ling.

'No,' said Carver.

Chau-ling leaned against a tree and slid to the ground. 'He's dead, isn't he?'

Carver said nothing. A section of the bamboo fence fell to the ground in a shower of sparks. There was a rattle of small explosions from inside the compound, the sound of ammunition detonating. Every building was ablaze and even from their hiding place in the jungle Carver could feel the heat of the flames. No one had emerged from the inferno for at least ten minutes, not since the helicopter had flown away. He couldn't imagine that anyone could be inside and still be alive. His legs began to shake and he fought to keep them steady.

Something moved inside the compound, just inside the entrance. A figure, staggering from side to side as it dodged burning debris. No, two figures. Two men.

'I see them,' said Carver.

IT WAS AN AWKWARD bounce and the boy did well to get the ball under control. He feinted to the right, tapped the ball to the left, and sent a defender completely the wrong way.

'He's good, isn't he?' asked Chau-ling.

The boy splashed through a muddy puddle. The goal-keeper was screaming at his defenders to get back.

Hutch nodded. The boy looked around but he was on his own; he'd run so quickly that he'd left the rest of his teammates behind. A small group of teenagers in raincoats and long scarves were jumping up and down along the sideline shouting for him to shoot. 'He's really good,' agreed Hutch.

She slipped her arm through his and shivered. 'Did you use to play?'

A defender almost a head taller than the boy rushed for the ball and slid into a fast low tackle, but the boy easily evaded the attack. The spectators began to scream with excitement.

'No,' said Hutch. 'I was never really good at team games.'

She pressed herself against him. She was wrapped up against the cold in a black cashmere overcoat, warm leather boots, a red scarf that she'd wound around her neck several times, and bright red ear-muffs.

On the pitch the boy slammed the ball into the net. The goalkeeper dropped to his knees as if seeking absolution, while the small boy was engulfed by his teammates.

The referee, a portly, balding schoolmaster with pink cheeks, blew hard on his whistle and picked up the mud-stained ball.

'Maybe some time in the future . . .' she said.

'Maybe,' he echoed, unenthusiastically. He exhaled and his breath immediately fogged in the cold spring air.

She tightened her grip on his arm. 'No,' she said. 'I mean it. When he's old enough to understand. You can tell him what happened, you can tell him why you had to go away.'

'He thinks I'm dead,' said Hutch despondently. 'It might be better if it stays that way.'

'Don't be stupid,' she said tersely. 'You're his father. Of course he'd want to know.'

The schoolboys ran back down the pitch to restart the match.

'Maybe,' said Hutch, this time with a little more conviction. 'His mother would go ballistic, though.'

'She needn't know,' said Chau-ling. 'When he's an adult, it'd be between you and him.'

The referee blew his whistle again and the ball was kicked sky high with a loud thud.

'He's a good-looking boy,' said Chau-ling, resting her head against his shoulder.

Hutch put his arm around her. 'Thanks,' he said.

She looked up at him quizzically. 'For what?'

'For suggesting that we come here.' He gave her a small squeeze. 'For making me come here.'

'It had been a long time since you'd seen him,' she said, watching the schoolboys' frantic efforts to get possession of the ball. 'I thought it was important.'

Hutch shivered. 'We should go,' he said.

They turned away from the football pitch and walked across the grass to the waiting Mercedes. A driver wearing a peaked cap waited patiently at the wheel with the engine running.

'Aren't you going to miss Hong Kong?' he asked.

She shrugged inside the overcoat. 'It's not the same as it used to be,' she said. 'And I can always visit.'

The driver rushed out of the car and opened the door for them. Chau-ling slid in first. Hutch followed her and the driver closed the door behind him.

'How was the game?' asked Tim Carver.

'Enthusiastic,' said Hutch.

'Your boy's okay?'

'He's fine.' Hutch settled back in the plush leather seat and ran his hands through his hair. The driver put the Mercedes in gear and drove off smoothly. It was hot in the car and Hutch took off his gloves and unbuttoned his coat.

Carver reached inside his jacket and took out two blue passports. He gave one to Hutch and one to Chau-ling. Chau-ling put hers in her coat pocket without looking at it, but Hutch opened his. It was his photograph, but a different name. Another change of identity. Hopefully this would be his last.

'We've arranged an apartment for you in Fort Lauderdale,' he said.

'At least it'll be warm,' said Hutch.

'There's a bank account with half a million dollars in it, and I'll be pressing for more,' said Carver. 'After the way they treated you, I don't think the DEA is going to object.'

Chau-ling sniffed huffily. 'Money isn't going to be a problem,' she said, looking out of the window.

Hutch reached across and held her hand. They drove away from the school in silence.

THE RED ROLLS-ROYCE CORNICHE glinted in the afternoon sun as it purred down the mountain road. Billy Winter took his cigar out of his mouth and jabbed it at the sea off to his right. 'Girls, it don't get much better than this, do it?'

The girls giggled appreciatively. The one in the front seat was a short, chunky blonde with close-cropped hair and a perpetual pout. She was wearing a low-cut top that showed off an indecent amount of tanned cleavage and she stroked the back of Winter's neck as he drove.

The girl sprawled across the back seat was a redhead, eighteen years old with long legs and a skirt that was little more than a bandage around her waist. 'It's a dream, Billy,' she said, raising her arms in the air. She stretched like a sleepy cat and purred with pleasure.

Winter grinned. Life couldn't be sweeter. A new country, a new life, a Corniche with the top down and two teenage girls who did it for love – almost. He took a long pull on the cigar and exhaled through his teeth. The smoke was whipped away in the wind. Winter looked out over the sea. 'What about a boat, girls?' he said cheerfully. 'What would you say to a bit of a cruise?'

'Lovely, Billy,' said the blonde.

Winter clamped the cigar between his teeth and reached over to caress her thigh. He stroked the soft skin, then slipped a finger inside her shorts. The girl leaned back and opened her legs invitingly. Winter's grin widened.

The siren jolted him out of his reverie and he jerked his hand back. He looked in his driving mirror. The motorcycle policeman behind him pointed to the side of the road with a gloved hand. 'Now what?' muttered Winter. He didn't think he'd been speeding, but then he didn't know what the speed limit was anyway. He braked and brought the Rolls to a gentle halt.

'What's wrong, Billy? asked the redhead. She twisted around in her seat and looked over the top of her sunglasses. The policeman parked his motorcycle about fifty feet behind the Rolls and dismounted.

'Nothing's wrong,' said Winter. He pulled his wallet out of his blazer pocket.

'Fucking cops,' snarled the blonde.

'Be nice,' said Winter. He slipped out his driving licence and folded a couple of banknotes around it. 'We'll soon be on our way.'

The policeman shrugged his shoulders and began to walk towards the Rolls. His leather jacket had a fluorescent yellow stripe running across it and there was a matching stripe running down both legs of his leather trousers. He made no move to take off his helmet and left the tinted visor down. There was a holstered gun on a thick belt around the man's waist and he put his right hand on it like a gunfighter about to draw. Winter was always nervous around armed policemen: they seemed to have less respect than villains when it came to firearms.

Winter took another banknote and added it to the others. It was probably more than the cop made in a week, but it was better to err on the generous side. He patted the blonde on the thigh.

The policeman walked up to Winter's door. Winter smiled and passed him the licence and money. The policeman took them without a word. Winter turned to the blonde and grinned. She blew him a kiss and Winter's smile widened.

The smile froze when he turned back to the policeman. The gun was now in the man's gloved hand. Winter looked up, his mouth open in shock. All he could see was his own reflection in the helmet's visor.

'This is for Ray Harrigan,' said the man, his voice muffled by the helmet. Before Winter could protest, the man pulled the trigger. The hammer clicked, but there was no explosion.

Winter bared his teeth and glared at the man. 'You stupid Irish wanker,' he spat. 'Can't you Paddys do anything right?'

The girls began to scream. The blonde scrambled over the back of her seat, trying desperately to get away from the gunman. Winter ignored her. He began to laugh, an ugly disjointed sound, the laugh of a man who knew he was already dead.

The gunman calmly ejected the dud cartridge, aimed and pulled the trigger again. This time it didn't misfire.

STEPHEN LEATHER

THE DOUBLE TAP

'Masterly plotting . . . rapid-fire prose'

Sunday Express

'A fine tale, brilliantly told'

Oxford Times

The assassin – the world's most successful contract killer – ice-cool, accurate and elusive. An anonymous professional with a unique calling card   one bullet in the head and one in the chest for each of his targets.

The Judas goat – an ex-member of the SAS, Mike Cramer is the perfect sacrificial bait. When the FBI discover the next name on the assassin's hitlist, Cramer is set up to take his place.

The wild card – Cramer's past has caught up with him. Ex-IRA extremist Dermott Lynch blames Cramer for his lover's death and he's out for revenge.

As Cramer trains for the most dangerous mission in his career, Lynch hunts down his sworn enemy. And the unknown assassin silently closes in on his target.

The players are in position for the final deadly game . . .

HODDER AND STOUGHTON PAPERBACKS

STEPHEN LEATHER

HUNGRY GHOST

Ex-SAS hired killing machine Geoff Howells is brought out of retirement and sent to Hong Kong, his brief to assassinate a Chinese mafia leader, Simon Ng. But Howells finds Ng is well guarded, and devises a complicated plan to reach his victim – only to find himself the next target . . .

Hong Kong policeman Patrick Dugan has been held back in his career because of his connections – his sister is married to Simon Ng. When the Ng's daughter Sophie is kidnapped, and Simon herself disappears, Dugan is caught up in a series of violent events and an international spying intrigue that has run out of control . . .

Tough writing, relentless storytelling and a searingly evocative background of Hong Kong in the aftermath of Tiananmen Square make *Hungry Ghost* a compulsive read.

'The sort of book that could easily take up a complete weekend – and be time really well spent . . . as topical as today's headlines'

Bolton Evening News

'Very complicated. Fun'

Daily Telegraph

HODDER AND STOUGHTON PAPERBACKS

STEPHEN LEATHER

THE CHINAMAN

The Chinaman understood death.

Jungle-skilled, silent and lethal, he had killed for the Viet Cong and then for the Americans. He had watched helpless when his two eldest daughters had been raped and killed by Thai pirates.

Now all that was behind him. Quiet, hard-working and unassuming, he was building up his South London take-away business.

Until the day his wife and youngest daughter were destroyed by an IRA bomb in a Knightsbridge department store.

Then, simply but persistently, he began to ask the authorities who were the men responsible, what was being done. And was turned away, fobbed off, treated as a nuisance.

Which was when the Chinaman, denied justice, decided on revenge. And went back to war.

'One cannot bear to put it down because one has to know what happens next'

Glasgow Herald

HODDER AND STOUGHTON PAPERBACKS

STEPHEN LEATHER

THE LONG SHOT

'In the top rank of thriller writers'

Jack Higgins

The plan is so complex, the target so well protected that the three snipers have to rehearse the killing in the seclusion of the Arizona desert.

Cole Howard of the FBI knows he has only days to prevent the audacious assassination. But he doesn't know who the target is. Or where the crack marksmen will strike.

Former SAS sergeant Mike Cramer is also on the trail, infiltrating the Irish community in New York as he tracks down Mary Hennessy, the ruthless killer who tore his life apart.

Unless Cramer and Howard agree to co-operate, the world will witness the most spectacular terrorist camp of all time . . .

'*The Long Shot* consolidates Leather's position in the top rank of thriller writers. An ingenious plot, plenty of action and solid, believable characters – wrapped up in taut snappy prose that grabs your attention by the throat . . . A top-notch thriller which whips the reader along at breakneck speed'

Yorkshire Post

HODDER AND STOUGHTON PAPERBACKS